Genesis

A Trilogy of James

LittleHawk

ISBN: 1-4515-1439-5
ISBN-13: 9781451514391

dedication:
To my little angel,
Samantha Littlehawk McLaughlin
My niece who was named for me

JAMES

"The baby." She mumbled in his ear. He made some indistinct response and thrust deeper making her throw her head back and moan lustfully. "James!" She was begging now. He smiled and kissed her neck.

"Come to me." He ordered huskily sitting up to lift her to meet him. "Just come to me!"

"The baby!" She was trying to squirm away. He had heard the distant calls of their son but had hoped she would have been more interested in him. No luck.

"Let Mum get him! I want you!" His thumbs dug into her hips as he held her. "For once let her get him!"

Maria fell back into the bed and gazed up at her husband. His dark blonde hair was a mess and his blue eyes blazed with need. He was a tall man on the verge of thirty, handsome, well built and endowed. She whimpered as he moved deeper. She was a woman of medium height and build with dark brown hair and eyes just as black as the night. In her own opinion, she had some filling out to do. She was only 19 and a little slow in the development part. Even after the baby, her breasts were small and her hips narrow. She always thought she was built like a boy. A young boy! Now as the baby cried in the other room the milk began to flow. James leaned in to suckle.

"James!" He kissed the little gold crucifix she wore around her neck. She was never without it. Maria called it her symbol of faith. James was a scientist. He had faith in books and science. God and religion was as real to him as Santa Claus and the Easter Bunny. He liked the crucifix because it looked wonderful hanging between her engorged breasts.

"Mum has him already changed and the expressed milk in his cup. By the time we roll out of here she'll have breakfast on the table and everything packed!" He replied with his mouth full of milk and her tit.

"Denying your son! What will my father say?" She teased relaxing and tugging at his wild hair.

"You had better not tell him!" He warned tickling her.

"Stop!" She squealed laughing. "Don't tickle me!"

"Then come to me!" He ordered moving into her again.

"James! Jimmy is crying!" She moaned at his industrious attempts for an orgasm from her. She fought him, but he would prevail.

"Mum would never hurt him! She'd die for that boy!"

"She'd die for this boy!" She thrust against him making him have to fight for control.

"And for Jimmy!" He moaned breathing deeply against her attempts of making him come before her. "I wish you could trust her."

"I do! But he is my son!"

"And mine!" He was moving faster now. "And I love him. And I love you and I want you to come to me!"

Her body seized up and the release was enough to make her almost scream with a fascinating mixture of pleasure and pain. Every time. It was more than she wanted and never less than she needed. Her whole body would shudder and she would lose her senses momentarily. Afterwards she would be exhausted and fuzzy headed. James Sinclair was a fabulous lover. He fell into the bed with her and lay watching her profile in the coming sunlight. Mum was humming and Jimmy was gurgling. No doubt chewing on the nipple of his bottle with his newest tooth.

Watching his son do that made him wince. The thought of him doing that on the lovely nipple of his little Maria revolted him. He knew that nursing was the best for a child. But he was jealous of his son's continuous use of her breasts. Yes, he was selfish, spoiled and extremely self-centered. However, he was getting better. He shared her with his son. She stretched her body and moved closer to lay her head on his shoulder. Jimmy had her nose. A little, button nose and her coloring. The deep dark tanned skin tone of her Hispanic heritage. However, he had his father's eyes, mouth and hair. His revenge on her family. He loved watching his son crawling among the other darker babies.

"The albino of the bunch!" Her father would declare as he lifted the boy up proudly. "The little Prince!"

Alejandro Vargas was bigger then life. And most men. Tall, wide shouldered with dark hair and eyes, with hands the size of dinner plates. He was a war hero. Overly decorated and underly compensated. A pillar in the small community he had created. James always felt very inadequate in his presence and the presence of any of his sons. Especially when they were talking of killing him. They knew he spoke Spanish fluently and understood it. The threats were never subtle.

He sometimes hated going to their home. The Stronghold frightened him at times with its primitive prophecy of dire survival of mankind. The people who lived there believed in the end. Long ago words from prophets and whispers among the religious sector. All had come to a vision that was being lived out by her family. Even its name was ominous. The Stronghold. And a stronghold was just what it was. It was a mountain range. A large mountain range that sat just on the outskirts of the New Reconfigured United States. In fact, half of it was in the New Reconfigured United States and the other half was in the Republic of the Americas. The huge granite mountain range was impenetrable. There were several entrances but they were hard to find and when found were very heavily guarded with large, well-armed men. Many hikers had been frightened to death as they were herded off the property at gunpoint. Many tales of the nomads had reached the cities over the years.

There were houses outside but only for show. A small settlement at first glance. Almost all lived within. Only the guards and their families lived outside. Because of its location, anyone coming within twenty miles of it were greeted by the hoards of children, dogs and goats running about while women did gardening and laundry, giving the appearance of a lightly populated settlement. But it gave off the feeling that the area was more than lightly populated. James estimated that well over three hundred people lived within. But that was only an estimate since he had never really been inside the Stronghold for more than a day or two at a time. Even after two years of marriage to Maria.

The first time he had been to the Stronghold he had gone wide eyed in awe of it all. He had volunteered when he learned of the opportunity to meet the great Alejandro Vargas. His daughter was being recruited to attend the university and they were asked to go and talk to him. The true apple of her father and brother's eye, she was the smartest. A damn prodigy. She finished high school by the age of fifteen and from her picture and application was more than suitable. When faculty had been asked to volunteer for the trip James had jumped at the chance. To meet and talk to the great Alejandro was something he could not pass up. He did not care if the man let the girl come. He just wanted to meet the reclusive hero. It didn't matter if they convinced Alejandro to let her leave the Stronghold. The only place she had ever known.

Mounted men with guns greeted them as the van turned off the main road. The horses rode along side the vehicle until it got closer to the houses. Then they were waved to a stop. They were asked to step out of the vehicle and searched. Dogs sniffed them as the van was searched. The other professors were shaking in their shoes in fear, but James was giddy with excitement. They drove into the settlement surrounded by the mounted men. More armed men directed them where to park. They were then led to a stand of trees and the house that was built half hidden in the trees. It looked ancient and mystical.

They house itself was very calm and warm. The smells of cooking food filled it. People were bustling about. The man himself sat at the table of the kitchen listening to them. His grey speckled black hair glistened in the sunlight and his black eyes glared at them in a cold amused way. His sons stood behind him looking just as menacing. Then there were the dozens of cousins, nephews and followers beyond the open doors that opened to the cobblestone patio. Alejandro was a man of few words. He listened. He nodded and listened. The other professors talked and James watched the man's huge weathered hands peel an orange and carefully section it. He held out the slices to the children that were running around. They took them in trade of kisses and ran about laughing. The talking was over. The offer was on the table.

He leaned on his elbows and gazed at James. The young professor had been sitting there smiling at him stupidly.

"What have you to say?" Alejandro asked in his deep voice.

"What was it like to stand alone against the rebellion?" James asked quickly as a wide-eyed child who was speaking to Santa Claus. The man smiled.

"Scary as hell!" He laughed a long loud boisterous laugh.

"Tell me?" James begged as if he were a schoolboy.

"Let's take a walk." Leaving his colleagues behind, James followed Alejandro through the settlement.

Alejandro had been six days past his eighteenth birthday when he had enlisted in the United States Army. It had taken him that long to sober up from the celebration of his birthday. He married Olivia, his sweetheart, four days later and little Alejandro Jr. was born ten months later. Senior was overseas fighting for his country for most of his career. He came home and then left again to fight different wars, and when he returned there was a new son waiting. Sometimes there were just headstones of friends and family. Their home was just outside the Stronghold. The small town of Mendoza. When the rebellion began, he moved his family into the Stronghold and others followed. But so did the rebellion.

The government was split and the Stronghold was dead in the middle. A no man's land. Nothing could live there so they were left alone. Because of the granite walls, computers and other electronics were useless. Son after son left to be educated and returned to raise a family and bring something to the community. Miguel brought the wind farm. Julio the solar panels. Roberto designed and built the homes they lived it. Ernesto farmed and cultivated what the people ate. Stephano developed the system of storing the food in the caves that were under the mountain range. Ricardo saw to the training of the men. Thomas educated the children. Manuel cared for the animals and stock. Juan and Antonio handled the legal matters, Alejandro Jr. and Joaquin dealt with the finances. But that was now. Then he had only ten sons.

The soldiers had come and Alejandro had stood in the middle of the road on his horse and announced that he was an independent citizen and not willing to fight for anything but a United States! He had retired from the military and although he was a soldier, he would only fight for his family. The general had ordered all the men to join them or die. Alejandro sat waiting. The guns were raised and fired on that hot day. The dust rose and through it all, he still sat astride his stallion. The horse snorted and Alejandro fired one shot. The general fell dead. Then men followed Alejandro and fought for their freedom. Jose, Trino, Alberto and Francis had died that day, but the Vargas men had not been defeated. They stood their ground for ten years.

The government was split. Alejandro petitioned the two countries and was granted the wasteland known as the Stronghold for his people. The exact amount of people that were there was never known. Orphans, widows, broken soldiers and the old went to the Stronghold and stayed. The Vargas army provided food, shelter and comfort to the minions. Their home became a refugee camp taking in all the subjects of the government that no one wanted to care for or deal with. The refugee camp grew to a kingdom. And Alejandro was their king. Strong, firm, calm, just and caring. His sons were the princes and the diamond in the crown was his one daughter. The Princess Maria.

Alejandro and James walked about the grounds. He would only allow James a peek into the entrance of the Stronghold. A lot of trees, some fruit groves and then wilderness. Why was he so secretive of this? There were miles beyond his view. A large building stood empty as if waiting. Alejandro nodded to him as an invitation. James walked to it. Peering in the windows, he saw the beds. Hospital beds. He looked at his host. The man smiled. A strange knowing smile that made James look away.

"Are you a doctor?" He asked herding him back to the entrance.

"Yes. I am a physician." James replied simply.

"You are famous."

"So are you."

"I saved my people. You saved the world." Alejandro had done some research on him.

"I found an anomaly." James replied simply. "It was an accident. I was looking for something else."

"But the cure was there?"

"Staring at me." James stopped to recall the moment he realized what he had done. Cancer. He had found the cure. Years too late to save his mother and millions upon millions of others, but there it was staring back at him in the microscope. He sat staring, wondering what in the hell he had just done. He was twenty-five and although a prodigy in his own right, a practicing doctor by age twenty-one, he was still shocked.

"So you make the millions, save the world and give it up to teach?"

"Teach and research." James sighed slightly. He liked the teaching but not the research. Too boring.

"But would you like to ever heal people again?" There was more to this question than James could imagine.

"Of course. I dream of one day having a clinic of my own."

"A free clinic?" The man was walking slowly with his hands behind his back. James sighed again. If only. But no one would leave him alone. He had tried the free clinic and it was not a good thing. While the poor waited outside dying, the senators, movie stars and rich pushed their way in. He had taken the teaching job to escape it all. Gave him time to do a bit of research on his father's work. Being a famous doctor was not what he wanted.

"Yes, a free clinic." The man nodded and led him out of the Stronghold.

"Mija!" He called and a horse raced up to them. The girl swung down and hugged her father. She was more beautiful then her photo. It did her no justice. Slim, slight and lovely. James felt his breath catch. He had seen her photo in the application file but overlooked it when he saw her father's name. Now he was taken aback by her beauty, grace and elegance. "This is Professor Sinclair."

"Pleased to meet you." Her eyes were captivating. He held her hand in his and smiled at her like a puppy. She was embarrassed and pulled her hand from his.

"Professor, I want my daughter to study medicine. Not a nurse! A doctor. That building is the clinic. I want her to run it in ten years. Can she do that?" James tore his eyes off the girl.

"Yes, medical school should be nothing to her. Residency and..."

"Good!" The man slapped him on the shoulder making him take a step forward to keep from falling over. "She wants to go to your school. She will work hard and come home to take care of the sick." Maria shrugged and looked over at her horse that was wandering away. Her long black hair fell over her shoulder like a satin curtain. "Until then, you will bring her home every other weekend and attend to the sick."

"What?" James looked around at all the children running about.

"Shots, medicine, a broken bone here or there. Nothing serious. We are very healthy here." Alejandro held out his arms as if to give him the kingdom. "Every other weekend."

"You want me to attend to these people?" James stood dumbfounded. "I can't!"

"Why not?" Alejandro waited to see the answer. Maria wondered also. Was the man prejudiced?

"I can't treat children." He turned to the man. James looked panicked. "I can't! The old and ill you expect to pass on but children...." He shook his head. A little girl limped by. Her leg turned painfully in. "That! That scares me. A simple operation as an infant and she would be running with the rest! This...this is an abomination! Society simply tossed the poor to the wind!" James walked over to sit beneath a tree.

"So fix it!" Alejandro ordered casually. "Can it be fixed?"

"Yes, but now it will be painful and she will need therapy and..." He looked so conflicted. "It will hurt her." He said it softly. "I can't justify hurting her to heal her."

"Doctor," Alejandro squatted down before him. "three universities have come for my Mija. Three. You are the only man who has spoken to me as if I were an equal."

"You are a hero!" James replied simply.

"I am a man. If you make that little girl walk, you will be the hero." James looked at the little girl as she limped past him again. So easy and so painful. She was a beautiful child. A beautiful, crippled child. The little girl laughed as she limped along. James sighed.

"Every other weekend?"

"Friday, come and sleep. Saturday attend the sick. Sunday, church, then take Maria back." Alejandro stood and held out his hand. "Deal?"

The little girl was laughing again. James was watching her walk and how her foot was bent. How she dragged it. It wouldn't be a bad surgery. They would need more than their little clinic had. He was sure of it. He would need Alise and Alfie. No one else would venture out here. There were rumors of what happened to those who went against the great king in his kingdom. He looked about. Just in the trees. Hidden from view were the men. He was almost certain a rifle was trained on him the entire time he was there. One mistake and he would simply vanish. The man was giving him his only daughter and he was to bring back a healer. He looked to Maria. She was studying him. She had such a serious passion in her eyes. Would he do it?

"You had better work you skinny ass off!" He warned taking the offered hand, standing and shaking it.

And so, Maria had come to the university. James was put in charge of her. She was just sixteen and needed guidance. So everyone thought. The dorms were fun and lively. She had no problems with her studies. In fact, she whizzed through them and past the other students. Her poison was Tequila, which she seemed to have been weaned on. The first two months he saw her every other day. She was always polite, happy and seemed to be adjusting well. He had been afraid she would be an oddball but no, she was just Maria.

To everyone she was different, but not disliked. She could use a computer but hardly ever did. She would pour through books in the library, copying by hand entire passages that she could easily have on her laptop. She wrote everything in a little calendar notebook she carried in her messenger bag. She didn't even have a cell phone. She would sit and write long letters home. It was mystifying to see the little girl lugging books around that could have easily been downloaded. James often counseled her. He bought her a PDA, which she used as a paperweight. If she didn't have it written down, she had it filed away in that brain of hers.

"Why do you do that?" He had asked sitting down at the table across from her in the student union. She was drinking coffee and writing away.

"Do what?" She asked only looking up to be polite. Her long lashes seemed to float over her eyes.

"Write it all down." He sipped his coffee and looked at the books she was reading.

"I remember it better." The head bowed back to write.

"It could all be downloaded."

"I don't use electronic devices." She shrugged.

"Why not?" He asked noticing the PDA holding down her homework.

"What if there is a black out?'

"There are safety lights everywhere. You aren't afraid of the dark are you?" He teased lightly. He was terrified of the dark.

"I mean a nuclear blackout." She set her pencil down to give him her full attention. Very respectful, yet there was something about her that made him feel like a lovesick schoolboy wanting to tease the girl he liked.

"Impossible." He laughed as if she were telling him about Santa Claus. Whom he believed to be real until he was almost nine. She had a way of making him feel foolish.

"Nothing is impossible. It is coming. We must be able to deal with whatever is handed to us." She looked around the large room filled with young people. "If there was one now, how many would be able to survive? They can't even open a door!" True. All the doors were motion activated. Eye scans allowed entrance. Maria had asked for a doorknob to be put on her door and had taken a bit of ribbing over it, but didn't falter. She looked away from eye scans and hit the manual button.

"Bullshit!" James laughed.

"My father says it will come to pass." She replied almost offended and returned to her writing. "He has seen it in his dreams."

Dreams? The great Alejandro refused to be called a prophet but his dreams were famous. A head injury from childhood had left him with horrifying nightmares of things to come. He said things would happen and they would. Ten, twenty years down the road, but they did come to pass. He had manipulated his followers with his dreams and the Stronghold had been built. Against all speculation, it had survived and thrived. He demanded respect from his children and those who followed gave it to him as if he were their new father. He was their king.

James enjoyed the little time he had with Maria around campus. There it had to be professional. Every other Friday at five she was waiting for him for their trip to the Stronghold. It was a long boring drive. Nothing but desert and wilderness. Once you left the city there was nothing. Just the long highway that was hardly used anymore. No one traveled outside the city. There was no need to. Alise and Alfie were interesting to Maria. The first ride home she stared at them most of the drive. Mostly Alfie. He looked curious to her. The whole artificial life thing was scary enough but when they looked like a large robot with a translucent body and all the working fixtures and wiring visible, it was unnerving. Only Alfie's round pleasant face was humanoid. He seemed not to notice her as he drove.

Alise was altogether different. She sat in the passenger seat. She would look back at the girl and smiled a sweet soft smile. Her long blonde hair was tied back simply and she was dressed casually. Her eyes were a soft blue. She was beautiful with a kind face. Maria stared at her and she only smiled. She looked at Alfie and he only stared straight ahead. He would smile now and again but nothing that showed any real emotion. He was capable of it. James told her so. He was just not ready to open up to her.

"A bit wary and shy of strangers." He had leaned close to whisper. She smelled lovely. Orchids?

"She looks like your mother." Maria noted upon the first meeting of the droids. There were pictures of James' parents in his office. While waiting to talk to him she would study them.

"My father built her after my mother died. She raised me." James looked over at the girl as she sat pondering the idea. "She is an Artificial Life Intelligence Surrogate-Experiment. Alise. She is my Mum. Alfie is a bit shy but he is a surgical assistant. In addition, he has a very wry sense of humor. He'll talk to you soon enough."

"Don't you have any real friends?" The girl asked seriously.

"I have a lot of friends. These are my family." Alise smiled wider. "We need people we trust to do what we are doing and we need them to keep a secret. Alfie and Alise will not tell anyone."

"They won't work in the Stronghold. Nothing electronic will."

"They will. Everything on them is internal. No signal needed." James reached over to grab her hand. She was shaking. "Don't be afraid. They won't hurt you." She held onto his hand. "My father had a vision of life years ahead of his time. He made provisions for them so that they would always be able to care for me."

"They take care of you?"

"Yes. I told you, they are my family." He laughed at the look she gave him.

"No one will trust them." Maria sighed.

"No one has to. Only me. I cannot do surgeries and the anesthesia and deal with the instruments. I need them. Unless there is someone there who can help me?"

"No, the old doctor died last year." She smiled slightly at the memory of the old man.

"There has been no doctor for a year?" James asked shocked by the concept.

"No. No one came with training. So I go to get it."

"Why don't people just go to the city?"

"They do not leave the Stronghold. Many have never been out. They are born there and have no desire to go. Some do. They go, but most seem to come back." She settled into the seat.

"And you? Will you return?"

"I have to."

"You don't have to. You could live out here and visit."

"No, I have to." She looked back at the droids. "I don't think I would be very good living on the outside. When it happens I would not be able to get back in."

"What happens?"

"The war with them." She nodded to the front seat.

"That is a myth!" James laughed.

"Is it?" She looked at him. "Ask my father."

"No, I don't think he likes me. He calls me Heinie." She laughed.

"Jaime. James in Spanish. The J is pronounced as and H."

"No, it's Heinie. I always feel like he's calling me an ass."

"Are you?" She asked laughing.

"No! At least I don't think so!"

"Ask him. He will tell you. Seriously James, my father, all of us know ,everything is run by droids. Everything. All they have to do is gain recognition and they will want us gone." She had a grave look on her face as she spoke.

"Why would you think that?"

"Because if they can do everything better than us, faster than us and never tire, then there is no need for us. We are nothing but useless. Taking up space. And we would be a threat to them." Somehow, it did make sense in an ominous way.

"There are no electronics in the Stronghold?"

"None. Because of the granite they don't work." She looked out the window in a frightened homesick way.

"How do you live like that?" It was impossible to imagine.

"Very well." She replied simply.

To be so sure of one's destiny at such a young age was mystifying to James. His father had made his millions by developing a droid to care for children. The latter day Alise. But none of them had compared to the original. Alise was more than a surrogate mother, she was his wife in every meaning of the word. Until the day he died, James McMillan Sinclair II had enjoyed sexual relations with his droid. James Jr. had not known she was a droid until he was in his teens. She had simply been Mum until then. Alfie had always been there. A droid for practical purposes. And Alfie had been around since his grandfather's day. He was practical and set in his ways. He was the surrogate favorite uncle. Always ready to play, talk, help with homework and ease the heartaches of young manhood.

James had grown up with them. They woke him in the morning, drove him to school, helped him with his schoolwork and everything else parents did. James Sr. was a busy man and had little time for his son until James was a teen. Then there was the university they shared and the life they lived around each other. Days could go by and not a word would pass between the two. James would stir his coffee and pass the butter to his father as the man was reaching for it. It was a boring life of sorts. They were both busy men.

James love life had been very limited. He was boring to teens his age and annoying to the college students he was around so he kept to himself. It wasn't until his residency that he found "love" in the arms of several nurses who taught him love, sex, several positions and levels of intimacy. Nothing serious, but wonderful experiences just the same. He had then thrown himself into his practice until the death of his father made him take a break and turn to research. There in the lab, he found solace, peace…and a cure for cancer.

From the first weekend visit to attend to the people, James and Maria clicked. She was easy to talk to and understood everything he said even when he said it wrong. He spoke Spanish but the people insisted on talking to Maria. He was famous, but they didn't trust him. The first weekend no children were seen. Only the old and one young man with a dislocated elbow. He checked blood and heart rates. Without an electronic microscope, he depended on Alfie for analyzing blood and urine samples. But the people were terrified of the tall humanoid machine. He was quickly moved into the back room and waited patiently for his services to be needed.

Alise was so human like that no one knew she wasn't. Well, not until she kept reaching into her pocket and pulling things out. Like a magician with his tall hat, she pulled everything from that pocket. Thermometers, urine cups, tongue depressors and even a stethoscope. Maria had closed her eyes as one patient ran from the clinic screaming in terror. Alise had simply smiled. Maria peered into the pocket. James had laughed at her and had the droid lift up her shirt and reveal an empty translucent belly. Well not empty. She had everything stored in it. She simply reached into her pocket that went into her belly and retrieved what she needed. Alejandro had laughed at her. The droid had smiled at him sweetly.

For months, they went every other weekend. Then it was Christmas and she was going home for a month. Driving there was fun but the trip back was miserable. James missed her terribly. The next week he fought not to jump in the car and go to the Stronghold. By now, the children were brought out and he had plenty of reasons to go and check on his patients but it wasn't that. Maria was just 17. For her birthday, he had bought her a calligraphy set. She had kissed his cheek and he had blushed for days. He was more than ten years older and he was terribly attracted to her. It was almost criminal!

The week of Christmas he went and he stayed. The back of the clinic was his apartment. He had books, a bed, a television with recorded movies and music. Nothing electronic. No radio, no computer, no cell phone. Nothing that needed a signal. He might have been lonely without Alfie and Alise but he had plenty of company. The men came to talk, the children came for candy. And Maria came. They would take walks alone into the groves and she would explain things to him. How they lived and he found it interesting. Not just the subject, but also the sound of her voice.

Christmas day, he went to Mass. A child was christened. James watched the ceremony and his eyes caught something. Something on the wall behind the baptismal. Words. After the service we walked over to read it. 'One will be born of a divided nation. One who bring men to their knees. One who will unite us all.' He ran his hand over the words. They were old. Probably there since the old mission had been built. He felt the presence and turned to find Alejandro standing there.

"What is it?" James asked.

"A prophecy." The man shrugged.

"For?" James stood to face the man.

"For us to survive." James nodded to the man. "We must go."

He was then escorted to the main house for the Christmas celebration. It was cold and wonderful. Children everywhere, food piled high and a large tree decorated brightly. Singing, laughter and Maria. He was so content it was hard to think of leaving. The New Year's party was just as wonderful. There was nothing but food, humor and real fellowship. He had stepped under the mistletoe and had to kiss one of the older single women. He had hoped to kiss Maria but she was obviously off limits to him. Her brothers made that clear. Alejandro was looking to set James up with a wife, but not his daughter. There were others, Stronghold men, that Alejandro wanted for her.

On the ride back Maria was bubbling with happiness and excitement. James drove her to her dorm and carried her bags to her room. Everyone was coming back and she was busy greeting and setting dates for coffee and study. As they stepped into her room, he kicked the door shut. She stood waiting with a slight smile on her flushed face. He dug the crushed mistletoe from his pocket and held it over her head. She stood waiting. He gathered her in his arms and kissed her. Her coat was pushed off. His fell to the floor and then he had her on the bed. She didn't fight. He didn't ask. As the sun set, he had her.

He woke to the coming dawn with her still in his arms and decided this was what he wanted. Yes, he could go to jail. He could lose his job. And for all that was holy, all of that was a better alternative should her father find out. Or her brothers! She looked so young sleeping in his arms.

They woke together and found the bed bloody. She was embarrassed. He was ashamed. She was a child and he had taken what was not his to take. If she had offered, it might have been different but slowly and painfully, she climbed from the bed. While she showered, he changed the sheets and dressed. She returned smelling fresh and clean. He tucked her into the bed and climbed in with her to hold her. Together they sat thinking on what they had just done. And accepted it.

From then on they were together nightly. He was her teacher in more ways than one. Not one to brag, he felt as if he had much to teach and she was a willing and beautiful student. There were times he could not wait and would summon her to his office where he would take her on his desk. It was dangerous and fulfilling. He adored her. She was what dreams were made of. He would watch her leave his office and cross the campus with her hair bouncing behind her as she hurried. He always kept her too long and she would be running to catch her class. By the end of January, she was pregnant.

"I'm sorry." She spoke softly through the tears. "I have to leave."

"Leave?" She had come to his office and stood before his desk teary eyed.

"I must go back to the Stronghold. Tonight."

"Why?" He stepped around the desk to hold her and she stepped away from him. "What is wrong?"

"I have to go!"

"Has something happened? Is someone ill?"

"No, not exactly." She would not look at him. He stood debating on what to do.

"You have to tell me. I can't just let you go." She shook her head. "For God's sake! Maria, I love you!"

"That is the first time you have said that." She whispered in a relieved voice.

"Is it?" He was confused and now afraid. He didn't like being afraid. "Will you tell me?" She shook her head. "I'll drive you." He offered afraid to let her go without him.

"You can't!" She sobbed, still stepping away from him.

"Why not, damn it?" He slammed his hand down on the desk. She jumped and he felt foolish. "Just tell me?"

"I'm pregnant." The world slowly stopped moving.

He had violated Alejandro's one and only daughter. The baby of his twenty-one children and not only had he violated her. He had gotten her pregnant. He stepped back behind the desk and sat down. What to do? She was 17. He was almost 28. He took in a deep breath and picked up the phone. He called Alise to tell her he would not be home for dinner.

Maria and he argued all the way to the car. He had a firm hold of her arm and he was not letting go. He set her in the front seat and drove. She begged, she cried and she pleaded, but he ignored it all as he drove and thought of what he had to do. Things had gone awry. He needed to face what he had done and he had to make amends, but he prayed that they let him live long enough to see his child born. Maria sat sobbing. He held her hand the entire way and felt each sob and shudder that raced through her body. He wanted to comfort her, but was afraid of where that would lead. They were in enough trouble as it was.

Alejandro had been sitting on a bench under a tree when they pulled up. He smiled and that smile faded as Maria stood before him with tear streaked face. Alejandro stood, like a giant rising from the earth. She didn't run to him. She stood crying. Instantly the others came, as if by instinct, and stood with their father. James thought of running.

Alejandro Jr., Miguel, Thomas, Julio, Roberto, Stephano, Ernesto, Manuel, Antonio, Ricardo, Juan and little Joaquin who was two years younger than James and a good thirty pounds heavier. The youngest could have torn him to shreds with one hand behind his back. If he put the machete down. The Disastrous Dozen as he had playfully called them. Of twenty sons, 12 survived. Two had died at birth, one before his fifth birthday, one in a car wreck and four in the rebellion. Then there was Maria, the baby.

Standing before the whole family he wondered about his sanity in coming. It wasn't just that there were huge, angry, heavily armed men, but Maria's her mother was there also. And that woman frightened him terribly! Although he didn't think the men would shoot him, or all jump him but the mother…Olivia she was terrifying. As Maria stood looking down and James explained Olivia shrieked, grabbed a knife from one of her sons and dove at James. Alejandro had stopped her, but she kicked, bit, cursed and hit him like a mad woman. Olivia screamed damnation at Alejandro, all of them…and James.

They were separated. Maria was dragged off deep into the Stronghold. James was roughly shoved to the clinic. The door was shut and several men stood waiting when he opened it. Many of them had been vying for the hand of the Princess. Many others had watched her grow up and were surrogate uncles. James shut the door and sat to wait his fate. The next day, patients came. Many were simply curious. Some gave him words of support. Several gave him religious artifacts, crosses, charms and medallions. They all said they would pray for him. He saw patients and waited. It was days before Alejandro came to see him. Alone. The large man walked into the clinic and sat down. He held out his hand. It was cut and festering. James sat down to tend to him. Why had Alejandro waited? Why? Was he afraid he might just kill James?

"She is my baby." Alejandro spoke calmly.

"I love her." James' hands were shaking as he cleaned the cut.

"So?" Alejandro asked as James took in a deep breath to steady his hands as he gave the man a shot.

"So I will marry her and I will see her through school then we will both come back here!" He tightly bandaged the hand. "If you will have me as the doctor?" He stood and walked over to the cabinet. "I want my children raised here. Once school is done, she and my child are coming here. Out there is not for them or for me. Not anymore." He was looking at pills. His hands shook as he counted and poured some into another bottle. He took deep breaths.

"And if I say no?"

"You will have to kill me to keep me from her. She is my life." He handed Alejandro a bottle. "Two a day for seven days. Take with milk."

"Cow or goat?" Alejandro looked at the pill bottle in his hand.

"What?"

"Milk? Cow or goat?"

"It doesn't matter." James sat down. "I'm doing this all wrong."

"What? Not milk?"

"No! Alejandro!" James ran a tired hand over his face. "I wish to marry your daughter. I love her. I took privileges with her. I should be beaten. Do that! Whip me!

But I ask that you allow me to marry your daughter! If I am not good enough...then just shoot me because I can't live without her! So I beg you! Let me marry Maria!" Alejandro sat looking at the pills.

"I will tell you the same thing I told Mija." Alejandro sat back and gazed at the man. "The sins you commit in this life, they follow you to the next. There, before your maker, you are judged and forgiven. But the sins of the fathers, and mothers haunt the children left behind."

"I love Maria and I love my child." James spoke firmly.

"You love what you have not seen?" A raised eyebrow from the man almost made James laugh. They were large and bushy and always reminded him of furry caterpillars.

"I love Maria. It is her. It is us. It is ours." Alejandro nodded understanding this.

"You have to ask her mother." The silence was deafening.

"Just kill me now!" James cried half jokingly.

"No, Olivia would kill me then!" Alejandro laughed rubbing his jaw. "She wants you dead and she wants to do it. And she wants you to suffer."

"What if we run away?" James was half-serious.

"Olivia will hunt you down. You have to make her agree. Maria can't. The girl has been trying, but Olivia will not budge."

"Is Maria alright?" James asked suddenly.

"She is fine. She cries a lot." Alejandro stood and walked to the door. "She is in the chapel praying that some horrible disease eats your hide off. My wife, that is." He left. James laid his head down on the table.

"James?" Alise stood waiting for her orders. "Are you not well?" The droids had followed after James had been gone two days. Their concern for him was overwhelming. Once they were ushered into the clinic, he had fallen in Alise's arms and cried like a baby. He felt small and helpless again.

"I am in trouble!" He blubbered.

"No one will hurt you." She calmly noted pushing his hair back from his face. "I am here." Alfie had stood calmly by the door waiting for orders.

"James?" Now Alise's concern was on the verge of anger.

"I'm fine." He rubbed his face.

"Why does the woman want you to have staph?"

"Mum, forgive me, but could you go to the back for a bit?" Without question the droid left him. He sat thinking. How to handle the large man had been relatively easy. The small woman was a different story all together. He took off his lab coat and reached for his jacket. He paused and gazed up. "Dad? If you are up there with mom, pray for me?"

He stepped outside to be greeted by two armed men. He ignored them and took the path through the orchard to the chapel. James knew this was the smaller one. But he knew she would be there. As he walked, he thought of what to say and how to say it. He ignored the men following him and the looks of the people as he walked past them. His mind was on one thing and one thing only: he had to see Maria. He could deal with everything if he could just see her again.

The chapel was dim. Not dark. Many candles were lit. The woman was sitting at the front kneeling. There before the large carving of Jesus on the cross. Olivia was small and fine boned. She looked very delicate. Very vulnerable. And very beautiful. Even after the birth of twenty-one children. She was kneeling with her folded hands holding the rosary. James sat down next to her. Several of her sons were sitting in the next pew. He felt the heat of their hate on his back. He crossed himself and knelt next to her waiting. A tear trickled down her cheek. With his handkerchief, he gently wiped the tear away. Was this what Maria would look like in years to come? He could live with that.

"How old are you?" James was tired and at first wasn't sure he had said it aloud. It seemed as if the hatred had gone from heated to icy cold. Olivia finished her prayer, crossed herself and sat back slowly. Her dark eyes searching his as he sat back with her.

"I am sixty nine years old." She answered simply.

"Remarkable." He handed her the handkerchief and sat gazing at her.

She was in better health than women half her age and she even looked years younger. The skin was still firm around her eyes. Her black eyes were fiery. The fire in them flashed as she glared at him. He had seen that same fire in Maria. He hoped his child had these eyes. The fiery eyes that were defiant and somehow sexual when angered. Not one grey hair! How was this possible?

"What is?" She asked dabbing at her glistening eyes.

"That I can look at you and see my wife in fifty years." He smiled slightly. A quick glance back at her sons and he sighed. "Though I don't think my sons will be as big as yours. My men are small boned."

"It is genetics, is it not? Our family breeds warriors." She sat taller with her chin out. He looked at her sons again and shook his head.

"Olivia, with the luck I have, my sons will be built like Maria and my daughters Amazons." The woman stared at him for a long moment before she laughed.

"If only that would be the worst. I pray that God gives you nothing but daughters!" James looked shocked then turned to his future brothers-in-law.

"Which one of you will stand for my daughters should I not survive through her teen years?" James asked of Maria's brothers. Twenty sons. Maria, the only girl. And she had been a handful. "One of you must. I am the last of my family." Repeated James. Still none said a word. "Look here mates, if history repeats itself and my daughter comes here pregnant and I am dead, one of you must stand for her because the other eleven will be keeping my darling Maria from killing the bastard!" The smiles started slowly. Olivia chuckled.

"She is my baby." She cried softly.

"She is my darling." He set his hand over hers. "My life. If I can't be with her, then I can't live. You must then promise to find someone who will love her and the child." He sat waiting.

"You wish to marry her?" The woman asked coldly.

"I think I always knew I would be her husband." He looked back at the sons. "Or die trying. I asked Himself and he said I had to ask you. I think even he is afraid to cross you."

"He is." She looked to the crucifix that hung on the wall. "He is a smart man." They sat for a long time. No one spoke. Her eyes were on the crucifix and her Savior.

"You cannot see her until the wedding." She spoke firmly. "You must talk to the priest and confess your sins. He must agree that you have done your penance to marry you." She handed him his handkerchief and stood. "Then you may see her again." She started to walk away. The row behind them stood in unison.

"Tell her…" James cried, the woman stopped but did not turn. "Tell her please that I suffer as she does. Tell her not to cry. That I will do what is needed and suffer for both of us but please, tell her not to cry." Olivia continued on. James looked down at the handkerchief and the rosary he now held. The sons filed out. One, he wasn't sure which, set a hand briefly on his shoulder as he passed. He stood and looked for the priest. "No time like the present," He thought.

It was a week before the wedding. He was nervous. He had no idea why. He had survived the worst. But standing at the front of the church with Alejandro Jr., he felt the sweat running down his back. He looked to the fully loaded pews and saw the smiling faces of Alise and Alfie sitting alone on the front pew. The only friendly and smiling faces. Some joker had put a bow tie on Alfie. He seemed to like it. He kept straightening it. The music began and once she stepped into view, his knees began to give.

"Whoa hombre!" Alejandro Jr. held him up. "You sick again?"

The brothers had taken him to a deserted corner of the Stronghold on horseback. He had been afraid they were going to kill him. He was pulled from the saddle and pushed into a cave. He was shaking in fear. He had done all the father had said. Olivia had even commented that he was worthy. He just knew he was going to die, but instead Alejandro was there with several others. The cave was large and dark but he could smell it and see it. Casks of it lined the walls. The still was perking away in a corner close to the entrance. His bachelor party had gone well after dawn and he had been sick all morning. Now he stood gazing at her.

"She's beautiful!" he replied dreamily. And she was. The white dress flowed behind her; the veil could not hide her sparkling black eyes or that lovely smile. It was all worth it. He would do it all again for her. Except maybe drink that clear poison that Joaquin had concocted.

Alejandro stopped short of the altar and looked to his wife. She sat gazing at James. He did not blink. It was all on her. She nodded and Alejandro brought his one and only daughter to the altar. He spoke loudly and clearly that he and his wife gave their daughter. Her hand was warm and steady in his. James was shaking like a leaf in the wind. It was Valentines Day and he was getting married to a young child bride carrying his child. He stepped with her up to the priest and bowed his head.

After the celebration that lasted well into the night, he and his wife were herded to a small cabin set far back in the woods from the clinic. It was small but cozy. James had thought they would simply stay in the clinic but that was unheard of. Alejandro's daughter had a home. Part of her dowry. He had taken her to bed that first night as man and wife as if it were their first time together. Tangled in the bed sheets he laid his head on her stomach and massaged the firm flat area where his son lay waiting. She tugged lightly at his hair. He kissed her stomach and moved to lie next to her, taking her into his arms.

"I love you." he mumbled sleepily. "I never really got a chance to tell you that." He hugged her to him.

"I knew," she replied simply.

"Thought so."

"We have to go." Her soft voice brought him back to the present. He sighed watching her rise from the bed.

In the past eighteen months, Maria had blossomed, from child to woman. Jimmy's birth had been uneventful. He had been born in the Stronghold. A little early, but healthy. It was to be the last visit to the Stronghold before she was confined to bed. He had a feeling she was in the early stages of labor but she had played it off. They drove to the warehouse, parked the car and loaded the truck. Maria paced and breathed deeply. But she kept shaking her head when he asked to examine her. She waved him off and looked around at the area.

The warehouse was just that, a big empty warehouse. To the eye of anyone. James had purchased it with help from Joaquin and Ernesto. The parking garage gate was still bolted shut. Alfie had made that almost impenetrable. There was graffiti on it but it was still locked. Alise got out and opened it. They drove down to the second then third level. Each level had a locked door that was impossible to open without a key. The third level held the supplies. It had been stocked floor to ceiling with non-perishable items, from medical supplies to military ready to eat meals. Enough for a small army. Which is what they had. James didn't agree with the visions of the king but went along with it. The only thing he would not purchase, store, or transport were weapons. His refusal was accepted.

He, Alise and Alfie, loaded farm supplies, feed, medical supplies and food into the large box truck. They climbed in for the drive to the Stronghold and he settled into the back seat to hold Maria. It was their time together. She had always wondered why it was Alfie who drove. James did not seem the kind to need a chauffer. She had asked and James had smiled at her.

"Once you leave the city there are no lights on the road." She had looked out the car window and saw nothing but darkness. She was used to it. "No one travels at night but marauders. Alfie and Alise can see in pitch-blackness. I'm afraid I might miss a turn and end up in a ravine." Maria had laughed at him.

That day she had been quiet, at least until it was too late to turn back. Many times, in the past, he had simply laid her down on the back seat and had his way with her on the long drive. Like two teens in the back seat, they had been sexually free after an order to Alise and Alfie to not look back. Many times, they arrived rosy cheeked and exhausted, only to fall into their bed in the cabin and go at it again. That day he set his hand on the bulge and felt the contraction. The on going argument was where the baby was to be born. He had put his foot down and booked a room at the hospital in the city. She had not agreed but had said nothing. Now it was too late.

"Damn you!" he had yelled and she had moaned loudly. For over two hours she had suffered in silence. Now the secret was out and she was not keeping quiet. Alfie didn't look back but pushed the gas pedal to the floor. At the Stronghold they barely stopped to be admitted. The truck was not checked but sped through to the clinic.

"Get Alejandro and Olivia! Now!" James ordered as he hurried to get things ready while Alfie carried Maria. She was taken from him by Stephano as Joaquin ran for the rest of the family.

There was little time. She was laid on the bed, stripped and within minutes of her parent's arrival little James McMillan Sinclair IV made his appearance into the word without a hitch. A whopping 8 lbs. of baby boy was held bloody and screaming by his grandfather with his grandmother looking on. Maria had simply closed her eyes and slept. James was too shaken to care for her, so Alise did what was necessary with the assistance of Alfie. He analyzed the placenta and umbilical cord and literally beamed as he declared the child perfect. Which got him a good smack on the back from Alejandro. The man yelped and danced about holding his aching hand afterward. Alfie had only smiled and took the hand rolled cigar offered.

Maria could not sit up alone. Alise set her up in the bed and sat behind her holding the girl up to help her suckle the child. Olivia was not happy with this situation. She did not want the droid anywhere near her grandchild. She was about to object, when the droid spoke. The voice was softer than usual, the face kinder, if at all possible. Maria leaned back against the woman and with urging held her son to her breast.

"I am here," Alise stated the fact softly. "If only to care for him and you. I am here." Maria nodded and moved the child to her breast. "He needs a lot and there are times you cannot give all to him. I can. I am here only to care for him and you."

"Breakfast!" Now Alise was calling to them. He heard her singing to Jimmy.

"Told you." He mumbled dragging himself from the bed. "She has everything under control." He grabbed his wife as she stepped past him. "She is capable." He kissed her softly.

"He is my son. It is for me to do." She gazed up at him.

"And I am your husband. Should I ask her to service me?" He teased and received a swift kick for it.

"OW! I was kidding!" He kissed her again.

"I find you plugged into the toaster oven and I will be at the Stronghold for good!"

Alejandro playfully called Alise the toaster oven and Alfie the microwave. Alfie kept to himself rarely leaving the clinic, but Alise followed the older man whenever possible. She said it was to make an accurate record of him for his grandson. But James thought she might be missing the attention of an older man. Olivia didn't like it at first and James had explained it to the droid. It was not unreasonable that the woman was possessive and jealous of her husband. Alise sat stone faced. He had hoped she would stop, but instead she went to Olivia and asked to follow her around for a visit. To record all she knew.

"Behind all great men, there is a woman," the droid noted.

Olivia was flattered and allowed the droid to accompany her on visits to homes on the outlying areas with her armed guards. They took food, medicine and other supplies. Since Alise did not look like a droid, she was simply introduced as Dr. James' mother, which pleased the droid to no end. Olivia also learned how to handle the ever ready to please Alise by keeping her hands too busy to reach into a pocket to retrieve whatever was needed.

Years before, Olivia and Maria had gone with only one bodyguard out of the Stronghold. A trusted man. They were set upon by several men in vehicles who knew Alejandro and believed him wealthy. The desperate men had snatched the young girl and carried her off into the desert. The guard had been killed. Olivia had been battered but she had followed them into the desert keeping good pace with them until her husband and sons caught up to her.. Alejandro looked at the tracks and smiled.

"They only took Mija. We had better catch them before your mother kills them." So they had raced after her on horseback.

She was still running when they stopped her. The camp was just ahead. They had to hurry. Olivia would not stop to rest but climbed up behind her husband. They descended on the men with their own kind of justice. Through the fighting, Olivia had slipped off the horse and run from truck to car to jeep and tent looking for her daughter. She found her beaten, stripped and tied in the back of a jeep with a man ready to mount her. Alejandro knew from that day on never to cross his wife. Since that day, Maria had not left the Stronghold and Olivia only went out with no less than four guards and a gun of her own.

Now Olivia and Alise walked along and talked. Alise listened and asked questions to clarify things and set it all to memory. Olivia ignored the puppy-eyed droid that now followed her husband about after that day. James wasn't sure why until he had asked Alise. She had sat thinking and replaying the conversation in her memory banks. She frowned and then shook her head. She was folding Jimmy's clothes. James sat next to her and took the small shirt from her hands. He held her hand.

"What is it, Mum?" he asked softly.

"I think I angered her." The droid replied.

"How?" James asked knowing that human response was hard for the droid to process at times.

"Did you know that Maria was kidnapped as a child?"

"Yes." He had heard of it. Part of the reason Olivia had wanted to kill him. "How did you know of it?"

"Olivia told me. She showed me where they had taken her and killed their friend." The robot sat.

"And?" Sometimes he felt a need to smack her on the back to get her going.

"I don't know how she could have let those men be killed." Alise sighed and the light in her eye blinked. It was a fluke. It always happened when she was confused or hurt. His father had not fixed it. He said it was her way of crying. "They killed all those men. Did you know that?" He frowned.

"Yes, I know. Mum…" How to explain the reason to hide murder?

"They were going to rape her. She was only 10 at the time." The droid's eye blinked again. "I just don't know how she was strong enough not to kill them herself!" James sat staring at the kind face of his Alise. The droid he trusted his son to. She was equipped with some programmed emotional responses but, she now having emotions.

"Mum…" He was in shock.

"I know. Don't tell anyone." She smiled slightly at him. "I am not real, but I am not stupid."

"So she was angry?" He asked wanting not to delve too deeply into the subject of her aptitude.

"Yes, at them for not letting her kill them." The droid began to fold the clothes again. "I would have been too.

It is a mother's duty to protect."

It was not just Olivia who trusted the droid. Alejandro would allow her sit with the children around the fire as he told stories. Some fiction and some of the past and the coming war. The children all sat in awe of the man. Even their parents leaned in to listen. Jimmy would sit quietly in Alise's lap and gaze at his grandfather with his bright eyes. All the stories were recorded in her. She would be able to replay them to the children when they got older. Miguel called her the walking video camera.

"When it happens, the Stronghold will close." The man looked at all the faces. His voice deep, ominous and frightening. "All inside will make it. Or die fighting. But if you leave the Stronghold, you must return quickly! We will only hold the door for you for a very short time. The outside will try to get in and we will have to hold our ground. For you and your children. You must get to the Stronghold!" His voice boomed. A hand settled on his knee. He looked into Alise's eyes.

"I will get James, Jimmy and Maria to the Stronghold." Alise spoke bravely. "If I have to carry them."

"I bet you will my little Tostador Más." He patted her cheek and it glowed a bright red as she gazed lovingly up at him.

"I will. You can disengage me if you want. Destroy me, but I will keep your family safe." The man's hand moved from her face in shock. "I know no one will trust me when it happens." She continued. "But I cannot care for them as well as you can." She sat waiting. Alejandro looked up at James who sat in shock.

"You bring them here safely to me," he patted her cheek again. "and you can heat up my coffee." A joke between them. Alejandro could never figure out why his coffee was always hot when Alise was around. Maria had laughed as she told him that when he wasn't looking, the droid would put her finger in it and heat it instantly. He had made a face as he gazed into his cup.

"She has a little crush on you." James explained.

"I'm married!" The king roared. "To a woman!" He looked into his cup again. "A woman who would cut it off if she caught me plugged in to the toaster oven!" They had all laughed. He sipped his coffee. "I hope she washes that finger!" After that, he would be reading or listening to someone talk and as Alise walked by he would hold out his cup for her to dip her finger in. Olivia rolled her eyes at him but never said anything. She did, however, freshen his cup more often herself the old-fashioned way. With a pot of fresh coffee.

"Mama!" James let go of his memories as his son called. He moaned and let his wife go. She rushed to her son and left James with a want in his loins. He was somewhat jealous of his son more and more, yet he wanted another child. With the breastfeeding he knew it was slim until the brat was weaned, but practice didn't hurt. He headed for the shower. "Mama!" yelled Jimmy again.

"I am here!" She announced to the boy sitting in the highchair with a bowl of cereal and fruit. "Mijo! Did you miss me?" He gave her a cereal encrusted kiss and was trying to climb from the chair. "Careful!" He was in her arms and rooting in her blouse for an opening. "You just ate!" She sat down with him in her lap.

Jimmy tugged at her blouse. He had simply tossed his sippy cup to the floor at the sight of her. The transition from bottle to cup had been easy, but he was not about ready to let go of the tit! Maria unfastened her blouse and slid her bra down. Jimmy practically lunged at her and clamped down making her yelp. She cradled the little curly blonde head against her as he got himself in a better position. The boy acted as if her were starving! He bit down again and Maria cried out.

"Little piranha." James noted stepping into the kitchen wet and naked. He reached for coffee and toast.

"James!" Maria glared at him and then nodded toward Alise.

"She changed my diapers!" He laughed leaning to kiss his son and then his wife. "There still some left in there mate?" He asked licking his lips. She pushed him away.

"Get dressed!" Her face was burning as he walked past her. "Alise? How much longer?"

"Most physicians agree that age two is a good time to stop." The droid smiled at the boy. "He is growing well. I would say to start preparing him to stop by August."

"I wonder how long James would have fed?" She mumbled softly.

"Until well after his second birthday." The droid replied simply. "He was like this one!"

"But his mother died when he was…" Maria stopped herself at the droid's face. Maria wasn't sure she wanted to ask the question. "Well, I have been cutting back." She looked up to find the droid still staring. Did she want Maria to ask the question?

"You are with child." The droid smiled tenderly. "Just now."

"What?" Maria jumped at the comment.

"You. You have just conceived. I can see it in your eyes!"

"How can you see it?" Maria felt her face burn red. The droid knew what they did in the bed. She was well educated in sexual relations, but it was still embarrassing.

"It is in your eyes. The change." The droid was still smiling. "You may need to stop feeding sooner to let your body recuperate from him." She reached and lifted the boy from his roost. He was asleep. Maria looked at the face of her sleeping son and laid her hands on her stomach. Just now?

"Don't tell James yet." Maria smiled. "I'll take a test at the clinic. Keep my secret?" The droid smiled at being included in a secret. "April 1st. A new year baby." She smiled. "He won't believe it anyway."

~

It took them an hour to get out of the city and to the warehouse. Another to gather and load the truck. Maria and Jimmy ran about playing with Waldo. The German Shepard barked and raced about, making Jimmy scream with laughter as they both chased the ball. The dog had been trained to sniff out droids by Ricardo. With the help of Alfie, who would run and hide, the training of dogs had become easier. Each dog was trained to bark and attack any droid at command. The word 'Alfie' spared the family droid from destruction. Dogs were helpful in guarding the Stronghold from intruders, including the armies that used droids now.

The dog had originally been named Bruno. He was a big dog and even Maria had been unsure of him. Jimmy renamed him Waldo after the strange little man in the picture puzzle books. He was forever wandering in the house asking where was

Waldo. So the dog had been renamed and become one of the family. He was a good watchdog and he was protective of the baby. Alise was forever ordering Waldo out of the kitchen because Jimmy had a habit of feeding him what he didn't want to eat. The dog loved broccoli. Steamed with butter.

James loaded three boxes from the car into the truck. Maria looked at them and smiled. Chocolate. He was infamous for having candy for the children of the Stronghold. He shrugged at her. He was getting bad about giving in to the children. Especially the one he had sired. The need for a dentist was getting stronger. One of Alejandro Jr.'s sons was in school for that. He needed to hurry and finish!

They all climbed in the truck for the ride. Jimmy was holding his book at the ready. Reading to him had become the new pastime for the long drive. Once he was asleep Maria and James either read or talked. It was a nice little family time before being set upon by the mobs of family.

"Where is my boy?" Alejandro roared as he walked to the truck. As soon as they pulled up to the Stronghold, the man was calling for his grandson. James handed his son down to his grandfather, squealing and kicking with delight. He was tossed high into the air, making James wince.

"Give him here!" Jimmy was snatched up by Olivia to be smothered with kisses.

"How was the drive?" Alejandro asked Alfie.

"Fine Sir. All clear. No incidents. The skies have been clear also." Maria and James both looked to her father. He had dark circles under his eyes. Sleep had been difficult for him. Dreams haunted him. He had once again been talking to Alise and she had been using her influence on Alfie to drag him into the conspiracy theory.

"Good! Good!" Alejandro smiled and the droid moved to help the men unload the supplies from the truck into horse drawn wagons to be taken off for storage.

"Waldo!" The dog took off into the brush after a rabbit. Jimmy squirmed to be put down to follow in the hunt.

James and Maria were needed in the clinic, so Alise took up her position of bodyguard to Jimmy and followed him and whoever was carrying him about. It was to be a short visit. It was almost summer break, so James and Maria had been preparing to come for the summer. Once there, they would not leave for the entire three months. Since there was too much back home to be done, this was a one-day trip. They made the most of it. Maria spent time talking to her mother about breastfeeding and James and Antonio dealt with the purchase and transport of more MREs. Black market purchasing was very expensive and dangerous at times.

"Is Papi okay?" Maria asked her mother as the woman continued to kiss her grandson.

"He is troubled but nothing to worry about. He does this. You know that!" The headed to the clinic. "His dreams. At times I wonder if he is not crazy." Olivia sighed. "But it will pass. Everything does. How is everything?" A quick change of the subject.

There was something on the air. The place was almost deserted. There were people still about, but the gardens were not well tended and there was no stock in sight.

"Fine. But I need to check something."

"What?" Her mother noticed right away.

"Come with me to the clinic?"

"Dinner will be ready soon. I should check on it." The woman looked back to the main house where the animal was roasting on the spit. It smelled wonderful.

"I think you want to check on this first." Maria smiled.

"Tell me!" The woman demanded as they hurried to the building.

Dinner was eaten and the fire built. They sat around it talking and laughing. Night came early in the Stronghold. And winter lasted longer. Maria yawned and snuggled closer to her husband. James pushed aside her hair and shirt then kissed her shoulder. She smiled off into the night. Her mother was watching her. They had both stood waiting as Alfie tested her blood. The droid smiled slowly at them and nodded. Olivia had screamed, causing James and Antonio to come running into the room. The older woman stood looking at the confused men.

"A mouse!" She yelled as she stormed out of the clinic. This had caused James, Alfie and the other assistants in training to sanitize it from top to bottom. Maria had slipped out to see her mother and her son. Now, she sat wondering how to tell James. It was a very early test. Not conclusive. Many pregnancies spontaneously ended before the first month. She wondered if she should wait. Now she yawned again.

"We should get on the road." James whispered kissing her temple. "Home and bed?" He nuzzled her neck. She nodded and curled up in his arms. Bed with him sounded wonderful.

The goodbyes were said. Hugs, kisses, tears and well wishes. Jimmy was passed around for hugs and kisses. Olivia and Alejandro had wanted them to leave the boy, but he went with his parents. They were escorted out of the Stronghold and the entrance blocked behind them. The huge iron gate moved across the opening as they drove off in the night. Maria always winced when she heard it. Jimmy was asleep and Alise set the carseat in the front with the droids. In the darkness, James took the opportunity to have a little time with his wife.

It was a moonless night. They fumbled with their clothing as they struggled to enjoy each other. Maria was breathing hard and moaning. James wanted her to be quiet and then again, he wanted her louder. She was more into it now and he liked that. The dangerous side of her excited him. Now that Jimmy was older, they had time to explore the sexual satisfaction of their marriage. Things that were put on hold until after his birth. Slowly they were growing into man and wife. No longer teacher and student lover.

For the extent of the ride to the warehouse they were naked and assaulting each other. He was relentless in trying to get her to be bolder and more adventurous. She still held back, forcing him to push her harder and ride her longer. Once exhausted, she was more apt to give in to his desires. The clothing was found as the gates were opened. Dressing in the dark and cramped quarters had them giggling like school kids. They fell out of the truck, holding onto each other, drunk on each other.

The truck was parked. Jimmy was loaded into the car and for once, James climbed in behind the wheel. Waldo jumped into the back and lay down. He was tired with all the rabbits he had chased. James pulled out onto the upper level and looked to the city. It was dark. Then Waldo made a deep noise in his throat. Not a whine but more like a soft growl. As Alfie locked the final gate, James got out and looked towards the city. He stood listening. There was a humming. Like machinery. The ground rumbled. Maria climbed out and stood next to him. They looked to the city and saw... nothing. The slamming of the final gate made them jump.

"James?" Maria moved closer to her husband. "Where are the lights?"

They were not there on the horizon. Whenever they got this close to the city they could see the glow of it on the horizon. The smog glowed. It was somewhat of a comfort to them. From one home to the other. Now it was pitch black. The rumbling continued. James looked to Alfie and he too stood looking to the city. His eyes glowed a deep blue as he scanned the horizon for what was not there. Alise now moved to them. She set a hand on each of their shoulders. James turned to face her.

"James, we must get out of here. Back to the Stronghold." James reached for Maria and looked to the car where Jimmy slept safely in his seat. "It is happening."

"What is happening?" Maria asked quickly.

"We must go now before nothing moves. It will be hard to walk the entire way." James looked back to the city and then at his wife. "Before it all stops."

"Get in the car. Alfie, drive as fast as you can." They hurried into the vehicle and sped off into the night. Back the way they had just come.

"What does it mean?" Maria asked as Alise turned on the radio. Nothing. No static, no elevator music, no sports...nothing.

"Your father was right." James was looking out the back window.

"What's happened?" Maria was checking her son. "A blackout?"

"No." Alfie finally spoke. "Annihilation." His voice hung on the night.

Maria realized that they were traveling at a dangerous speed. She put on her seat belt and looked over at Alise who sat on the other side of Jimmy.

"He will be all right." The droid reached forward and put her hand on James' shoulder. "I have told you this and you must believe me. He will be alright."

"If it comes to it..." He looked back the darkness. "Save my son." Maria felt her stomach turn. She held onto her son's little hand.

"It will be all right." She repeated herself. Her voice was firm.

"It will be all right." Alfie echoed her sentiment.

They drove on into the night. Maria began to pray softly. She wanted her father. She wanted the safety of his arms and the Stronghold. The little car sped on. Whatever was coming was coming on them fast. There was light behind them. Waldo began to bark and growl waking Jimmy. As the baby cried, Maria shushed him and looked at the glow. A dull greenish glow that should have been the city lights was definitely moving towards them. At a fast rate. Alise leaned close to the child as if to kiss him and a hiss came from her mouth. The baby fell into a gas-induced slumber. Suddenly the car stopped. It rolled to a stop. It was dead. James reached back and took Maria's hand in his.

"Mum? Give me my son." Jimmy was lifted out of the seat and handed to his father. In the dim light of Alfie's blue face, James gazed at the sleeping boy and kissed him. "I love you," he whispered and handed the boy to his wife. Maria held him close as she realized what was happening. "Mum, take him. Keep him safe." The child was taken and Maria sobbed. "Alfie? My wife?" The droid and the man stared at each other. The man held out his hand. The droid took it and shook it.

"It has been a pleasure, James." The droid climbed from the car, opened the back door and pulled the sobbing woman out. He handed her messenger bag to her and she slung it over her shoulder. Then he handed her the revolver. He had pulled it from somewhere and now pushed it into her hand.

"Where…?" She asked looking at it.

"Your father." The droid replied. She slipped it in the bag with the other things she might need.

"GO!" James ordered and Waldo shot out of the car and into the night. He would make it to the Stronghold. He had been trained to. Maria watched the night swallow him up.

"James?" James held her close, kissed her and touched her face tenderly.

"Maria? I love you." He looked past her as Alise disappeared into the darkness. He kissed her roughly. "Run!"

She had no choice. Alfie simply pulled her along. The green was upon them. Maria stumbled and the droid lifted her up and ran carrying her. They made it maybe two hundred yards before they found themselves cut off by four of them. Maria screamed. Alfie set her down and pushed her behind him.

They were frightening. Taller than Alfie. At least six feet tall. They were mostly translucent. A glowing green. The little green men urban legend had definitely grown up. Humanoid, with less characteristics than the average household droid.

"Do you relent?" one asked solidly. Maria felt Alfie's hand pushing her.

"Get to the desert." He ordered softly. "I will find you."

"Alfie!" She turned to find two more behind them.

"Do you relent?" one asked again in a very calm drone voice. As if asking if they took milk in their tea.

"Run!" Alfie moved quickly knocking three down with one massive blow while pushing her into the darkness.

Maria stumbled and fell into one's arms. She kicked and screamed. The green droid looked her over and held her out from him, her feet off the ground, kicking. He tilted his head from side to side. His eyes glowed a brighter, blinding green as he scanned her from head to toe. He looked over at the fighting to his left. He simply dropped Maria and went to help. She scrambled to her feet to run. The light was there. Green…glowing. James stood by the car. Arms extended waiting. There were several droids there. Her husband stood tall and alone.

"Do you relent?" A voice asked. James looked off into the darkness where his son had gone. Then back at Maria and Alfie. "Do you relent?" The voice asked again. James McMillan Sinclair III lowered his arms and stood taller. "Do you relent?" If anything his son would know he died defiant.

"FUCK OFF!"

There was a sudden burst of bright light, and James was thrown over the car. He landed on the pavement with a sickening crunch.

"James!" Maria ran to him. A set of translucent hands grabbed her and lifted her up. She fought to get loose.

"A woman of breeding age," the voice noted calmly.

"Bring her," the same voice ordered from behind her. They had the same voice. All of them!

She turned and saw what remained of Alfie lying in the road. He had been torn in half. His upper body was intact and lying by the road. His left arm was closer to her. His legs were flung about. She got her hand into her bag and pulled out the revolver. With it pointed right at the droid that held her, right at his head, she fired. He stepped back and dropped her. She scrambled to her feet and ran to Alfie. He wrapped his remaining arm tightly around her.

"Do not look in their eyes," he ordered softly. "They will kill you and the child if they know." She sat back to look at him. "Don't let them see into your soul." She was jerked from his arms and his blue face light dimmed to nothing. She looked up at the remaining half of the face of the droid she had shot. The gun blast had blown the rest away.

"Do you relent?" There was another burst of light from the direction of James, and then nothing.

"James!" Maria screamed into the darkness.

"Do you relent?" The question again. Maria fought to get away. The gun was taken from her hand easily. She stopped fighting and sobbed. The gun was pointed at her. Maria Olivia Octavia Vargas Sinclair closed her eyes and waited.

MARIA

"The baby." Maria mumbled holding her hands to her abdomen. She stood letting the water wash over her. She was shaking. The warmth had long ago left the shower. She sobbed into the corner where she stood. Her mind was spinning. She had just been raped repeatedly. When she was younger she had been stolen. A quick knock to the head and she woke with a man on top of her, and then he was gone, and her mother was wrapping a blanket around her. She had cried then in fear of what she didn't understand. For what had almost happened. This time it had happened and she had been awake, coherent and worst of all, she wasn't sure she had been raped by a human.

"Child bearing?" The voice was different from the rest. Soft and cold. "Is that her?" Was that the name they had given her? She blew half of a head off and now she was simply "Child Bearing"?

Maria sat up and looked about. Someone or something had hit her in the head and now she had a headache. Looking around, she found herself in the company of several women. All scared. They were standing against the wall as if trying to stay away from something. One woman was clutching her bright red purse to her chest as if to shield herself. She was holding a crucifix in her hands. Her bright red nails looked bloody. Maria touched the cross around her neck and looked over to see what they were avoiding. There were six of them walking among them with a human. He was the one talking. She tried to stand and couldn't. Her bag was still on her and she dug in and then remembered they had taken her gun. It had been dark a second before, but now that the man was there, the lights had come on.

"Her!" The words were spoken and two hands lifted her to her feet. A hand lifted her face. Alfie's words were in her ear. She closed her eyes. "Pretty!" The words swam in her head. "Look at me!" Alfie's warning made her think of the baby and go limp. "It is her?" The voice asked.

"Yes." The drone voice replied.

"Bring her, her, her, her, and her." The man ordered. She heard screams and felt herself being carried away. "Dispose of the rest." Was she being brought or being disposed of? Several women were screaming. Shrieks of terror. They were moving now. Pleadings went on and on. She simply kept her eyes closed and prayed.

"Put her in observation." The order was given.

The screams faded as she was carried away. She was set on the table and left. It was dark as she opened her eyes. She dug in her bag and pulled out the flashlight.

The room was bare. The walls were white as was the floor and ceiling. It was unlike anything she had ever seen. There was a mist floating about and sticking to the walls and floor, as if she were floating. But she wasn't. Was she? She moved off the table cautiously, tapping her toe on the solid floor. Each step was taken slowly to ensure there was still a floor there. What if it ended and she simply fell into nothing? She made her way to the door. There was no knob. She touched the wall and felt for anything. A scanner, a button, anything? Nothing. She hit the door with the flashlight.

"You are not permitted to leave." A voice noted calmly.

"Fuck you!" she yelled, remembering her husband's last words. There was silence. She stepped back from it. There was nothing but silence and the soft humming of machinery. She walked around the room and then back to the table. Her head was pounding. She leaned on it and sobbed for her husband and her child. Where were they? Had they escaped? Had Alise kept her promise? No. James was dead. She had seen it with her own eyes. He was gone and so was her child. Waldo had to make it. He had to let them know. They had to find Jimmy!

The door opened and she whirled, around almost falling over. There were four of them. She pulled back to swing the flashlight and her hand was caught and simply held. They stood waiting. The door was open. Maria tried to get loose and get to it but it was impossible. She wouldn't look them in the eye. Her eyes darted here and there as her heart raced. She had to get out. She had to get away. She had to find her son. She had to see if James was still alive. She had to do something!

"Will she do?" The drone voice asked.

He stepped into the room, wearing flowing robes. Before, she had not noticed what he was wearing. The robes were long and colorful. He stood tall. As tall as the droids. In fact, they were all the same. The droids and him. It was as if he were a model. They were all him. Just without skin. The profile was the same. Now Maria waited as her arm went to sleep. She tried again to pull loose but her hand and the flashlight were simply held.

"Are you positive?" The man asked looking her over.

"Confirmed." The drone voice replied.

"Yes." The man answered giving her a curious look. "She will do. Prepare her." He turned and left without another word. They were on her then.

Her clothes were stripped off and she was lifted up on the table and held there. It seemed as if it were hours before the door opened again. She was shivering and unable to move. The hands held her still. Cold iron hands. Gently, but firmly. He stepped into the room and was wearing nothing. She closed her eyes and remembered how James had done that just that same thing that morning. The human walked around the table as if inspecting her. Another one of those things was with him, but he was blue, not green. He seemed to be in charge, and he was different. Not so mechanical in his movements. He reminded her of Alfie.

"They are fragile?" The man asked gripping her chin in an iron grip making her scream out in pain.

"Very. Adam, you must be gentle." The new blue one pointed out.

"What is wrong with the skin?" He was bent over staring at her stomach. She was goosebumped and shivering from the cold.

"She is cold." Blue noted.

"Cold?" Adam stood up to look at Blue questioningly.

"They are fragile. Their climate must be controlled. Increase temperature," Blue ordered, and the room began to warm. Adam watched the goosebumps disappear in awe.

"She is considered pretty?"

"Yes. Very. And she is a child bearer." Blue moved to the head of the table.

"She is the one?" Adam asked as a small child would.

"Yes. Shall we proceed?" Maria looked away. Adam climbed on the table. The intense pain made her scream.

"What is it? I thought this was enjoyable?" Adam was kneeling between her spread legs.

"You must lubricate them." Blue noted moving to the man.

"I thought they were self lubricating?" Adam looked at her face. She was crying now.

"They need stimulation." Maria cursed as Blue inserted his finger and moved it about. It was ignored. The mind might declare something but the body acted on its own. "Now try." Blue stepped back and Adam was in her. He was large, thick, long and not at all enjoyable. He was thrusting in her hard and fast. It went on and on. He wasn't sweating. Maria was crying and begging now.

"How long?" Adam asked. He was not even winded.

"Until you feel satisfied." Blue explained calmly. Maria fought against the hands but she could barely move.

"I think I am." He thrust deeper and she felt the clenching of his balls against her as he ejaculated. He sat back looking down at her curiously. "Was it successful?" Blue was leaning down to look at her face. She would not look at his eyes. He tried and she shot her eyes away.

"I don't think so. Again Adam." And so, Adam did it again and again and again. Each time it was the same. He wanted to look at her eyes. She would not look. Adam sat patiently waiting. "Maybe another position?" Blue declared as he walked around the table.

"Position?" Adam asked looking down at her. "What is that?" His fingers traveled over her breast.

"Milk. She has had a child. She was feeding it. It will dry up in a few days."

"Dry up?" He squeezed the tender breast and the milk spilled forth.

"They only need it when a child is born. To sustain the child." Blue was walking around the room. "Adam. Come here." The man jumped off the table and walked over to the wall. It was as if the TV had been turned on. They stood watching whatever it was in fast forward. Maria tried again to move and couldn't. She was ready for them to just kill her rather than have that man on her again. If he was a man.

He was handsome. Tall and muscularly lean with dark hair and deep blue eyes. Again, he looked vaguely familiar and that frightened her. His skin was very soft but not warm. As if he was not alive. She noticed that his body was not sweating. After a workout like that, James would have been drenched. And breathing as if he were having a heart attack. It wasn't just how Adam felt but how he acted. As if he were a child just learning. He was childlike in ways, and in others he was dominating. They took orders from him. He took advice from Blue. Now Adam was walking back to her. She closed her eyes and readied herself.

"Get her up." He ordered softly. She was instantly standing. "Release her." They did and she had to hold onto the table to keep from falling over. He was gazing at her. "We need a bed. Clean her up." He spoke thoughtfully looking at her breast. "Attend to it. I will be waiting." He walked from the room with Blue behind him.

Now she was in the shower sobbing. This was a nightmare. Who was he? What was he? What were they? Were they computers who gained cognition? Were they from outer space? She looked behind her and they stood waiting. She couldn't stand it! Why had they not killed her? What had they done with the other women? Were they too being stimulated, lubricated and raped? She fell to her knees and prayed that God would keep her Jimmy safe. At least God could do that for her.

The water was getting cold. She looked about as she stood. There was no soap. She used her hand to rinse herself. The substance on her body was not like a real man's seed. It was slimy and the texture was wrong. It wasn't gritty but it wasn't smooth. The scientist in her told her to pay attention to it. To analyze it. The woman in her screamed to get it out of her. She stepped away from the showerhead and the water stopped.

They stood waiting. No towel. She didn't move. What did they want from her? Two stepped forward and took her by the arms. She was led out and into the room she had come from. But it was different. There was a bed, a dresser, a set of nightstands and lights. It was a dream. This could not have happened. How did they do this? How did they get that big bed through that little door? She was shivering when the door opened. She looked over her shoulder to see Adam enter with Blue. Adam looked different. Not so much curious, but determined.

"Pull her across the bed." Blue ordered. "Face down." Maria began to fight and was quickly subdued. She screamed into the bed as he "stimulated her", clumsily and roughly. She felt his other hand on her ass, digging his fingers into her flesh. Once lubricated, he took her from behind. Violently. There was no air to scream. He had her by the hips, thrusting and waiting.

"Do it." He ordered softly. What did he want her to do? She sobbed and fought but the hands held her. Then she was breathing and trying not to cry. "Do it,." He ordered again. What? Her body was exhausted but it was responding to him, even though she fought with her mind and spirit. She moaned then. And her body seized up. "Yes!" Adam was happy. He finished and stepped back. She was set in the bed. She and tried to slow her breathing.

Adam sat on the bed next to her and pushed her hair from her eyes. His hand followed the curve of her face. He kissed her gently and childlike. He was looking down at her. She tried to look away. He moved down to take her breast in his mouth. She bit her lip and winced as the painfully full tit was pinched and the milk shot forth. He gasped and swallowed, climbing in the bed with her to get in a better position to suckle. Once the tit was drained, he moved to the next. Her hands tried to push him away but they were quickly pushed into the bed.

"It will dry up?" He asked again as a child would.

"Yes." Blue replied.

"I want it. Daily. I want her." He looked at her face.

"Adam..."

"I want her." There was something in his voice.

She was angry. She could have killed him with her bare hands if she could get loose. Blue leaned down to gaze at her. Alfie's words were lost. She glared and Blue stood up. He walked around the bed and looked at her lying there exhausted and fully exposed. She was afraid for a second that he might want to mount her. She was sure she would go insane if he did. He nodded and her hands were released. She sat up slowly and pulled the bedding around her. Adam looked at her curiously and even helped her.

"Modesty. A human trait." Blue noted as if writing in a journal. "I believe it was a success."

"Was it?" Adam asked quickly. "It was the position?"

"I believe so." Blue was looking at her again. She closed her eyes to him. He quickly moved closer. "Look at me." She would not. "Either look at me or we will do it again to be sure." She couldn't bear it. Taking a deep breath Maria looked up into his eyes. He stepped back. "It was a success."

"Yes! The position?" Adam asked again.

"I think so." Maria looked away. How in the hell could there be spiteful aliens?

"Good." Adam reached to touch her face and she turned away.

"Shall we take her away?" Blue asked suddenly.

"No, I said I want her."

"Adam..."

"I want her!" He sounded like a spoiled child. Blue backed down.

"What is your name?" Adam asked quietly. She did not answer so he gripped her chin hard.

"Maria." She gasped.

"Mary, mother of Jesus!" Adam smiled brightly. "Perfect." Blue nodded.

"As you wish." The drone voice was almost bitter.

"Clean her, feed her and I'll be back." With that, he left and she was thrust into the shower again. As they stood watching, she kneeled in the water and prayed.

~

A woman brought her food. A human woman. She was older and terribly frightened. Her hands shook as she set the tray on the bed. Maria had wrapped the sheet around her and curled herself into a ball. She wanted to wake from whatever nightmare she was having. The woman looked at the things that stood guard and then at Maria. She hesitated at first then moved into the room. The guards did not move. The door shut and the woman moved forward. Maria sat up slowly.

"I brought you food." Maria looked at the tray. A can of soda, a bottle of water, some snack cakes, a sandwich and some cookies. "It was all I could find. It was either this or the shit they feed us."

"Who are you?" It was hard for Maria to speak. Her throat was dry.

"Linda." The woman opened the bottle of water and handed it to her. Maria nodded and took a long drink.

"Where am I?"

"In Adam's room." The woman looked around at the guards.

"Are they shut down?"

"No, resting. If you try and run they will wake." Linda's voice was low. Not a whisper, but low. "Their hearing is a bit off. They can hear for miles away but low tones are hard for them to pick up. Screaming and yelling they zone in on it."

"What is happening?"

"The end." Linda sighed gazing at the tray.

"Are you hungry?" Maria was starved but felt for the woman. She was dressed in jeans and a t-shirt. Blonde with blue eyes and she had a slight build. She looked like she had been through the wringer too. And she was human. Now Linda shook her head.

"It is for you."

"I share." Maria was trying to open the snack cakes but couldn't.

"Here." Linda took it from her and did it.

"Take the other." Maria handed her one. Linda was looking at Maria's arms. There were bruises up and down where she had been held down. Maria pushed the cake into Linda's hand. "Nuclear?" Maria asked softly.

"What?" Linda asked biting into the chocolate cake.

"Was it a nuclear war? Are they from some invading country?" She nodded to the guards.

"There was no war." Linda replied through a mouthful of cake. "We were invaded. Three days ago."

"Three? What day is it?"

"Tuesday. They came Sunday morning, well actually in the middle of the night. Everyone thought it was a meteor or some shit like that. A green light in the sky. Everyone was in the park or on rooftops with telescopes and then the green fog cleared and they saw the ship."

"Ship?"

"Spaceship I guess, or plane or whatever they came in. It happened all over the world I suppose. No news from anywhere. They just came, asked us to relent and took over. Nothing works. No TV, no radio, no phones, nothing. Total darkness!" Linda sighed. "We were told to go on with our lives."

"Go on with your lives?" Maria gulped down the water. "In the dark ages?"

"Well, as best we could. Some people ran and were brought back. Since we all live in cities I guess we're easy to contain. They just patrol the outskirts. None of us wants to go out into the wastelands. That's No Man's Land. I don't think them things have even ventured that far." Linda nodded to the green droids by the door.

"Why are they here?"

"No clue." She put the paper from the cake on the tray. "Some women were taken, the men subdued and here we are waiting."

"What about the rebellion?" Maria whispered.

"What rebellion?" Linda almost laughed. "Our troops were defeated in less than six hours. The government is at a standstill. Our president ran!" She chuckled. "His damn plane crashed, taking our government with it! Nothing works! The can't even set off a nuclear bomb if they wanted to!"

"No one will stand against these things?" Maria set the bottle down.

"A few stood." Linda took a very deep breath. "They were blown to bits." Maria leaned over the side of the bed and vomited. Now the guards were moving. Linda grabbed the tray and jumped out of the way. Maria was lifted out of the bed and set back in the shower. She held the sheet around her and did not step close to the showerhead. Linda stood holding the tray and watching as the room was cleaned. Maria was pushed back to the bed. "If only they were real." The woman mumbled. "I couldn't get my Mike to pick up his socks!"

"They aren't real?" Maria thought that maybe she was simply going insane.

"Not real men. The only real one is that Adam. The rest are just...hell, I don't know what they are. But I know one thing; no woman is in danger from them." She nodded to them. "No dicks. Unless they have them in their pockets and put them on." Maria felt ill again and sank into the bedding.

"Does anyone know what they want?" Maria asked shivering.

"Nope. They don't talk. Only give orders and ask if we relent!" Linda sat down on the bed and set the tray closer to Maria. "Look, I got three kids. I was told to feed you so could you eat." Maria bit into the sandwich. "If I feed you and you eat, then I might be able to feed my kids." Maria nodded.

"How did you end up here?"

"They gathered us and asked for someone to care for you. No one moved. My kids are hungry and scared."

"What about the others?"

"I said I'd do it." Linda shrugged.

"Are your children with your husband?" Maria asked, reaching for a cookie.

"No, with my mom. She's trying to put a kitchen together. These guys don't eat so there's not much to work with. She kind of followed me. Been living with us since my dad passed. I'm their only kid."

"I have twenty brothers." Maria wished they would come for her.

"Twenty?" Linda's voice rose and the guards turned to look at her. She suddenly looked frightened.

"Only twelve are still living. I'm the baby."

"Still, twelve? Wow! I thought I had my hand full with three."

"I keep hoping they will come for me."

"Don't." Linda warned.

"Why not?" Maria fought to open the soda. Linda opened it.

"You want your men dead?" No, she didn't. She took a sip and handed it to Linda. The woman smiled and sipped. "I need whiskey more." She chuckled.

"Tequila." Maria sighed longing to be good and drunk.

"What of the men?"

"Working. Gathering what they can and trying to keep their families going. They give us some stuff to 'sustain us' as they put it. Tastes like shit!" She looked at Maria. "You don't look so good."

"I feel like I've been through a meat grinder." Maria sat back against the pillows. "I could really use some tequila and salt." She laughed, wiping away a tear.

"What'd they do to you?" The woman asked softly. Maria shook her head. "Adam?" Maria nodded. "Him and old Blue Boy?" Linda snorted, opening another pack of snack cakes.

"Just Adam." Maria pulled the sheet around her tighter.

"He don't look so bad. Not real, but not ugly. He reminds me of the old Ken doll. Too perfect. But I guess he is equipped?" The woman waited for an answer that didn't come. "Having one of them on me might make me want to dive off this heap though."

"What are we in?"

"Like a floating building." The woman looked around. "Me bringing my kids and mom in here has people talking but I had to take a chance. It was getting crazy out there. It's big in here. We got our own room and we can go around a bit. Doors open and you can go but if the door don't open you got to get away from it."

"Your husband didn't come with you?"

"No." Linda looked down.

"How will he find you?"

"When I die, he'll be waiting." The woman smiled slightly. "My Mike stood against them." There was pride in her voice. Maria nodded as tears filled her eyes. Linda wiped a tear away. "My kids are mad that I came. But I won't have them starve. If there is to be a fight I figure the more you know about who you fight the better off you are." Maria set her hand on the woman's and nodded. The door opened. "I know who you are." The blood drained from Maria's face. She held onto the crucifix. "Don't let them." The woman spoke quickly.

"Leave us." Adam ordered. Linda gathered up the trash and hurried past him and Blue Boy. Adam sat on the bed facing Maria. "It is time." He reached to pull the sheet from her and she held it firmly. "Modesty." He smiled at her and pulled the sheet away exposing her breasts. She closed her eyes as he leaned in to suckle.

He came daily. He had not attempted sexual intercourse again. After the first time, she fought, and was quickly subdued. Now she just sat and let him drink to his fill as Blue Boy stood back watching. Each time he acted more human. He would kiss her check or pat her head. His hands held her gently now. Blue Boy kept telling him how fragile she was. The bruises had appeared quickly and upset Adam. He traced them with his fingertips. All of them. She had been held as he examined her body. The lower one made her cry out when pushed on.

"What are these?" He asked.

"Contusions. The blood vessels below the skin rupture." Blue Boy replied.

"Are they permanent?"

"No. They fade as the ruptures heal." Adam touched the one on her cheek. "They are fragile."

"And these?" Adam asked brushing a tear off her cheek and rubbing it between his fingers.

"Tears. Emitted when in pain or anguish." Adam turned to look at Blue Boy. "Other human attributes." Adam nodded and licked his finger. "They are salty."

"How do we stop the contusions and tears?" Blue Boy had no answer.

"Stop holding me down!" Maria answered angrily. Adam nodded. He waved his hand and magically the hands were gone from her body. She grabbed the sheet and pulled it up around her. He looked confused.

"Are you angered?"

"Yes! You want to look and taste, fine! I don't think I can stop you, but I don't want an audience!"

"What does that mean?" Adam tilted his head at her the way Jimmy did when she tried to talk to him. She looked away. Jimmy, her son. She looked at Adam and found her senses. Linda's words were just sinking in. To know an enemy was how to defeat one. Her father had told her that.

"That means tell them to leave us alone!" Her voice was stern. He sat back from her. At first she thought he might strike her and readied herself. He moved his hand. It waved slightly towards those behind her.

"Leave us." The guards exited, but Blue Boy remained.

"Him too." She ordered, holding the sheet tighter. He waved his hand again and Blue Boy exited. The hand floated in the air for a moment then slowly moved to grasp the sheet. She let it slide from her hands and closed her eyes as he suckled.

A child. Adam was a child. Adam was under the influence of Blue Boy, but he was the one in charge. He had not quite realized that. Like a spoiled child, he made his choices of his desires and needs. He needed a woman. He chose Maria. He wanted her. He wanted to feed from her. He wanted the comfort of her body and her conversation. She winced as he bit down and she felt his hand move along her hip and lift her to him. Linda was right. This was the best way to fight for now. She set her hand on his shoulder to steady herself and pushed his hair back with the other as she did with James.

His hair was strange. Thin. Soft. It was almost as if it were spun silk. The scientist kicked in and she ran her fingers through it. At the scalp it was knobby as if it had been inserted into his skull. She had seen that done once at the school theater. They were assembling a corpse for a play. A woman sat with a small buttonhook like tool and put the hair in. It was long and straight. No body to it. Not real. But Adam's skin felt real. Soft and viable. But then, no elasticity to it. She could feel the hard muscles beneath, the surface but the skin did not move over them. As if it were connected to the muscle directly.

He moved to suckle the other breast and she fought to remember what she had been praying to forget. His body was different. Not warm. Not cold. His fingers, soft and stiff at the same time. She ran her hand down the length of his arm and over his fingers that were holding her ass. There were no fingernails. She looked down at the hand resting on her breast. No, they were there but…it was something she had seen before at the hospital. In a premature baby. The nails were the last to develop. Adam was not complete!

He sat back licking his lips. He was never out of breath. He never sweat. What was he? He licked the dripping milk off her breast and stomach as a cat would. His tongue. It was rough. Not soft. And dry. Could he even taste? She gazed into his eyes and found them interesting. Green with gold and blue mixed in. The pupil moved as if to spin as a camera would to focus. It was amazing! An old Beatles song came to mind.

"The boy with kaleidoscope eyes," she mumbled.

"Lucy in the sky with diamonds." He noted casually. She couldn't help but look shocked. "I have been studying your culture. Your music, entertainment and history." That one got her. She hoped he hadn't gotten to the rebellion yet. "I am now studying your mating rituals."

"Whoa!" She reached for the sheet and he lifted it over her gently.

"Romance." He sat waiting. As if for her to explain.

"What are you?" She asked suddenly.

"I am Adam." He said it as if it should mean something to her. "I am the first. I am son of God."

"Jesus was the son of God."

"I am the first." He said it again. "I am created in his image." The Bible was flashing before her eyes. Early teachings in the religion classes.

"Why are you here?" She fought to file it all away, process it and move on before they could be interrupted.

"To populate the earth."

"It is populated. Are you attempting genocide?" He looked confused. She had to remember to talk to him as she would a child. "People live here already."

"Not like me. God made me. I am the first."

"So what's gonna happen to the ones that were here already?" He sat staring at her. "Are you planning on destroying them all?"

"No. I am a good God."

"God? There is only one God!" She fought the panic as he spoke of blasphemy.

"I am in his image."

"What is a God?" She asked slowly.

"Me." He looked around. "Did you eat? Are you satisfied?"

"Linda was nice. The food was good." She was trying to think of what to ask next. The door opened and Blue Boy stood waiting. Even with no facial expression he looked angry. Maria decided she needed more time with Adam. She quickly sat forward into his chest. "Hold me!" She begged into his chest. His arms clumsily encircled her. "Don't leave me with them." He looked back at Blue Boy.

"Comfort," the droid noted.

"Leave us." Adam ordered and the door shut.

"Are we being watched?" she asked.

"Watched?"

"Recorded? Like cameras or such?"

"For record. For history. The Archive watches all."

"Just like the toaster oven." Maria felt hope remembering Alise. Hope for Jimmy.

"What?" Adam sat looking confused.

"No!"

"No what?" He had that flustered look on his face that she had seen on small children.

"No, this is our bedroom. You do not record in here. This is private. This time in here is ours and ours alone." She sat back slightly. "Not all is to be shared." He nodded and looked up.

"Discontinue Archive." He looked at her again and she could see he was trying to please her. "I will hold you." She moved back into his arms. He held her and she tried to think. What to ask? What to imply? What to do? "Do you want sexual relations again?" She sat back from him quickly.

"NO!"

"Was it not enjoyable?" The urge to slap him was hard to keep at bay.

"No, it was not!" She replied through gritted teeth. He looked upset and confused. There was panic in his eyes. Like a boy caught doing something wrong. The embarrassed panic. "That is private. You did that to me without my consent in front of those things and..." she looked up at the ceiling, "...archived it! It was not sexual relations! It was rape! It was with out my consent and..." She began to cry, "...it hurt!"

"It did?" He touched her face to brush the tears away. "I stimulated you to lubricate you."

"Jesus Christ!" She moved away from his touch. "How fucking romantic!"

"Not yet." He noted looking at his wet fingers. "He is to come later." She blinked at him as if to clear the blurry figure and make sense of it. "I will hold you. I will comfort you." Now she had done it. The old helpless damsel in distress times ten. She sat up and let him hold her. She moved her head several times against his chest. "What is wrong?" He asked looking down at her.

"I can't hear your heart. Don't you have one?"

"Yes, I am a compassionate and gracious God, slow to anger, abounding in love and faithfulness, maintaining love to thousands, and forgiving wickedness, rebellion and sin. Yet I do not leave the guilty unpunished; I punish my children and their children for the sin of the fathers to the third and fourth generation. I am a kind God, strict, firm, loving, forgiving and I have a heart." With that, it began to beat. Maria fought not to scream. She began to tremble. "Are you cold?" She nodded. "Increase temperature."

"What am I?" she asked softly.

"Mine. You are as a queen. You are kind, beautiful, gracious, loving and obedient." The words washed over her and she wanted to run.

"Why me?" she asked fearfully.

"Because you are who I chose. Who was ordained."

"By whom?" She fought to process it all.

"By me. I will comfort you. I will hold you. I will not make you cry again. I will make the next sexual experience enjoyable for you." Maria moved from his arms, leaned over the side of the bed and was sick.

~

"I don't know what you did but thanks." Linda stepped into the room and set the tray on the small dinette table. "Alone?" She looked about and saw no guards.

"Just the ones outside the door and Adam says they are only there in case someone tries to hurt me." Maria was dressed in a pale blue jogging suit.

"I figured blue would look good on you." Linda sat down and lifted the lid off the dish.

"Thank you."

"Roast chicken. My mom is a flash in the kitchen. She says to say thanks. The kids really needed some toys and clothes. Especially toys. The were driving her nuts. How did you manage that?"

"I told him keeping his subjects happy would ensure their allegiance and devotion. He had to show them that he was a kind God. And that you were taking care of me so you had to be taken care of. And your children were an extension of you."

"Is that what he is?" Linda opened the soda and set the small bottle of tequila on the tray. "I snatched it from the liquor store. I was only able to get a few things. Blue Boy said it was not viable subsistence. Whatever the hell that means. I had to fight for the shampoo and conditioner. Now the toothpaste and brushes were interesting to explain. And the razors—Wow! They are just a lost cause! But Honey, you were getting funky."

"I appreciate you going against Blue Boy for me."

"No problem. He's all air. But a lot of it. I wonder if he floats under those robes. He got any feet? And why are he and Adam the only ones who wear clothes? They the only ones with schlongs? I mean Blueboy acts like a dick! He was even objecting to the bras. Said they would get in the way of Adam's feeding?" The look Linda gave her made Maria's skin crawl. It did sound bad.

"I'm lactating. I was breast feeding my son." She shrugged. Linda, like her, longed for companionship and talked a mile a minute. "He now feeds."

"EW!" Linda shook violently. "Well at least he dresses better."

"I noticed. That was you?" He had come dressed in jeans, a nice shirt and loafers.

"No, you! He said he wanted to dress as you would like." Linda made a face.

"What?" Maria laughed at the facial expression.

"I asked what size he wore. He just flopped open that robe and stood stark naked baring it all. I about shit! I just got a ton and let him pick what he liked." Linda shuddered again.

"Modesty is not a trait he has learned yet." Maria laughed lightly.

"So I noticed. They seem to just be studying us."

"I know. Do you have any idea what they are doing?" Maria asked softly.

"Procreating." Linda stood and walked over to look at the flowers that were on the dresser.

"He's practicing romance. I think I say a word and he goes and researches it. He tries to please me." Maria sat down to eat. "Have you eaten?"

"Yes, I am now the official food taster." Linda made a face. "As if my mom would poison anyone."

"They are a bit over the top."

"My mom makes plenty and the kids all eat with me. Then whatever is left over Adam gives to who is outside. There are a lot who don't like the subsistence we were given. It has all the vitamins and nutrients but tastes like cardboard and other foods are scarce and expensive. You know, the cockroaches climb out of the woodwork. Most of the groceries and markets were taken over by the mob. It costs to live now."

"So money is still in use?"

"Not really. And they want a lot more than money."

"Meaning?"

"There are some who follow Adam just to climb to the top." She gazed at Maria. "Over the bodies of those who are weak, old, dying or dead." There was disgust in the woman's voice.

"How old are your children? Your mother?" Maria cut into the chicken and sighed. "This is so good!"

"My mom is a great cook." Linda smiled. "She's in her late fifties. Won't tell me exactly. A bit vain and all. Looks forty. When I was younger she told people we were sisters." They laughed. "My boys are Mike, he's almost ten, Billy just turned eight and Joey is five. Why?" She would brag on her children but was wary of giving too much away. She was protective of them.

"I know of a safe place." Maria was whispering and chewing hoping it made the archive hard to pick up.

"Really? More salt?" Linda leaned closer.

"They cannot get us there." Maria looked up and gazed at Linda. Her eyes told the woman all of it. Maria was running. Did she want to go with? "My son is there. At least I hope. That is where he would have been taken." The final note. She was going to do it with or without help. "There is room for all."

"What do you need today? I was told to do the shopping for your needs." Linda moved the dessert closer. Her hand was shaking. Maria set her hand on it and the woman gripped it tightly. "I will do anything!" The tears welled up in her eyes.

"I need chocolate." The door opened then and Adam walked in. Blue Boy stood outside the door.

"How is it?" he asked, nodding at the plate.

"Delicious." He smiled at her. She noticed that Linda was looking down. She brushed the tears away and moved out of his way. He sat there, as close to Maria as possible.

"Delicious?" A different word for him. He was like a sponge soaking up all she said.

"Would you like a bite?" She cut the chicken and offered it to him on the end of the fork. He leaned closer to him. She knew that hungry look in his eyes. She wanted to thrust the fork into his kaleidoscope eye. "Open your mouth." He obeyed and she set it on his tongue. "Bite it." She ordered and he did. She pulled the fork out and her hand shook. She wanted to stab him! If not for her child, she would have. "Chew." He did all the while his eyes were on her.

"Leave us." He ordered and Linda scrambled for the door. Maria bit into the chicken even though she had lost her appetite.

"The food is good. The texture and flavor…" he removed the fork from her hand and stood pulling her towards the bed. She chewed and swallowed past the lump of fear in her throat.

For the better part of two weeks she had avoided having relations with him by basically treating him like a child. A student. But the child was maturing quickly. He was now a man and he had wants and needs. Yet, it was as if all he did was to please her. She commented that his skin was cold, now it was warm. She complained that he had no saliva and his tongue was like sandpaper on her breast and now his kisses where moist. She suggested things and he did them to please her. Now he was looking at her and wanting a pleasure she was not sure she was able to give. He lifted her effortlessly into his arms and set her on the bed.

"Talk to me?" He asked unzipping the jacket of the jogging suit. Her breasts were full and waiting. His fingertips lightly traveled over the bra. The intricate lace was fascinating to him. He pushed the strap off the shoulder and massaged it gently. The deep brown nipple hardened and he smiled. "Like a cherry. Tell me about your day or something?" His lips covered the nipple and she winced. Gentle or not, it was an intrusion.

"Who told you that?" She asked holding onto him as he moved her back on the bed.

"What?"

"That it was like a cherry?"

"Your entertainment." He began again. She would have to wait. Once he started he had to finish before he was ready to talk. He was getting better at touching. It was light and gentle. He massaged the breast and then would reach under her to rub her back. Her mind was screaming for him to get off of her, but her body ached for the contact that was as close to human as she was going to get. Now he was kissing her and moving to the other breast. Half way there.

"What entertainment?" She jumped at the nibble on her breast.

"Archived." He mumbled into her breast.

"Movies?" Good God! Was he watching porn?

"Shhh!" He sat up and held a finger to her lips. "I am a good student. Even you said so." He was pulling at her jogging pants.

"Whoa!" She grabbed his hands and held them. He did not resist when she pushed him away but would usually leave looking like a hurt puppy. Now his kaleidoscope eyes flashed. The white of it actually turned a funny glowing blue. "Slow down." She sat up from under him. "Tell me what you've been studying?" He sat back and gazed at her. The blue was like the eyes of Blue Boy.

"No, it is time for you to be obedient." He pulled her to him and kissed her passionately. "I give you too much freedom." The words of Blue Boy no doubt. "It is time for you to fulfill your duties."

"Duties?" She was wiggling out of his hold.

"To please me." He lifted her off the bed as if she were a feather and repositioned her. He was on her holding her down on the bed. "I want it to be enjoyable for you as well as me." He kissed her again. "Would you prefer the other position?"

"NO!" She tried to think of how to stop this and knew there was no way to. He wanted her to orgasm. To come to him. Even the damn robots had egos!

"Then what?" He sat up slightly.

"What do you mean?" She asked quickly.

"I have given you candy, flowers, food, clothes and everything you desire! I have provided for you!" He was getting flustered. She did this to him often and in the beginning he backed down, but now, he was becoming more human and worse, male. "It is time for you to please me!"

"Okay. Just don't go so fast. Slowly." She fell into the bed and gazed at him. A handsome young Adonis who wanted to please her sexually. Before this, if she could have cloned him she would have been wealthy. Cloned?

"Slowly?" He looked confused again.

"Adam, you are the first?"

"Yes. I am created in his image."

"Are the others clones?"

"Clones?" He cocked his head to the side as if thinking. He looked to the wall and the TV screen came on. The words flashed quickly across the screen. "A cell, group of cells, or organism that is descended from and genetically identical to a single common ancestor, such as a bacterial colony whose members arose from a single original cell. An organism descended asexually from a single ancestor, such as a plant produced by layering or a polyp produced by budding. A DNA sequence, such as a gene, that is transferred from one organism to another and replicated by genetic engineering techniques. One that copies or closely resembles another, as in appearance or function." He gazed at her. "They are what I was," he explained.

"Which is?"

"The beginning."

"Adam, how old are you?" He sat looking at her shaking his head. Confusion was hard for him to deal with.

"I do not know."

"Were you born?"

"I was created." She was confusing him, and although it was a good defense it was information she wanted. Information she was filing away. She needed it. She didn't know why, but she did.

"Adam, they are what you were. Does that mean those green things will be like you?"

"No. I am the first." His hand went to her stomach. "He is to be what I am." The baby. She took in a breath and waited. "This time it will happen."

"This time?"

"There were others." He sat back to look at her. "Are you jealous because you are not the first?" She bit at the offer. Anything to keep him off of her.

"Yes!" She pushed him away trying to look angry.

"Don't be. The last was a long time ago. After the last, it was decided I should come here. Not let them be brought to me. It is easier." Her mind was spinning.

"Easier?"

"They are fragile." She felt revolted.

"Brought to you? How?"

"Some would come and bring them back to me. One at a time. They were like you, fragile. They did not always survive the trip." He reached out to caress her cheek. The bruise had faded but he liked to touch her there. Right on her dimple.

"How many?"

"Many. It was decided that I would come here."

"Who decided?"

"Me." He leaned in and kissed her. "You are all I want." She closed her eyes to him. "Why do you do that?" He sat back suddenly.

"What?"

"Close your eyes when I kiss you?"

"Everyone does. I don't know why." He sat thinking.

"Eat. I will be back." He stood to leave her.

"Fasten your belt," she called. He stopped to look down at it.

"Why do you wear these?" he grumbled fumbling with the buckle.

"To hold your pants up," she teased.

"I meant pants!" He left her.

She climbed from the bed and returned to her meal. She had to eat. She had to keep her strength up. She was going to need it and her wits to get out of this. Plus the food was very good. He returned as she finished her pie. He lifted her into his arms and carried her back to the bed.

"You can't keep doing this," she mumbled, angry at herself for liking the attention he was bestowing on her.

"What?"

"Just pick me up!" She kicked her legs and he set her down. "What exactly is going on? You ask a question and then disappear. Where are you going?"

"To the Archive," he replied simply.

"What is the Archive?"

"This is Archive." He held out his hands and looked up. She shook her head. Then it happened. The walls became television screens. All over. All different images, music and sounds flooded the room. Maria had to put her hands over her ears. It was all too loud and too much. "Stop." She saw his mouth move and it stopped.

"You have been intercepting radio, TV, and everything else and storing it?" She looked at the now dark walls.

"Yes, to learn."

"Adam, are you plugged into Archive?"

"Plugged in?" Again with the tilt of the head.

"Are you part of Archive?"

"No. This is Archive. I am Adam." He cupped her chin in his hand and lifted her face to kiss. "I want you."

"Whoa. Let's slow down." She stepped back.

"Why?" The flash again. "You are to be obedient and loving!"

"But I am not a machine!" She glared and it was he who stepped back. "There is more to romance than sex!"

"What is there?" He stood waiting and not patiently. She knew there was no way out of this now. She looked up and around. "No Archive!" He looked down, ashamed that she had pegged him. "None! What goes on in here is between us. It's private!"

"Archive off!" He said it quietly.

"Come here." She pulled him to the bed. "Lie down. On your back." He obeyed. She sat down and moved him to where his arms were folded behind his head. A comfortable position to talk. At least this was how James would lie when they talked. Plus his hands would be busy and not pawing at her. She crawled into the bed next to him and lay on his chest with her hands folded under her chin. "We humans do more than have sex. We talk, get to know each other, fall in love, and then make love."

"Love?"

"Not the same as sex." She was looking down at his neck. He didn't have an Adam's apple. She thought that was ironic. "Love is something stronger."

"Who do you love?" He asked quickly. "Me?" Maria wondered what to say?

"My son." His eyes flashed again. "And I hope to love you."

"Where is your son?" The way he said it frightened her. As if he were going to fight a rival for her affection.

"I don't know. I think that is what hurts so much." She fought the urge to cry. "To not know."

"Your husband?" She wanted to scream that his green assholes had killed him. But she didn't.

"He's dead." Her voice was low.

"Would you like me to find your son?" She sat up slowly. "There are children being housed in several locations. He might be there. I could have it checked?" He took her hand in his and looked at it.

"How would you know he's my son?"

"Your blood. He will have your blood. We are cataloging them." Cataloging them? She was suddenly afraid. "Would you like me to have him brought here? Would it make you happy?" His finger flicked a tear away and she blinked. She hadn't realized she was crying.

"Alive? Healthy? To live?" She was hoping for the impossible.

"Of course." His soft voice and smile told her he was becoming more human and he sucked at lying. But she had to hope that if Jimmy was not among those being "catalogued", then he was in the Stronghold.

"Please?" He set his hand on her shoulder and rubbed tenderly.

"Make love to me?" He moved his hand to the back of her head and pulled her down to kiss. "Satisfy me and I will have him found." She closed her eyes. "Then we can discuss love."

"What do you want?" She asked halfheartedly.

"All of it. All that I have seen." His voice was like that of a child in a toy store on Christmas. "Archive!" The movie magically appeared on the wall. James had taken her to the theater to see this. Her heart sank. Dinner, a movie and lovemaking in the car.

"This?" She asked. He nodded. "Turn it off."

"Archive off!" He sat waiting as she searched in her heart for the strength to go on. "Seduce me." He ordered. "I want you to seduce me." Obedient and loving. She sat up and unzipped the jacket. "And I want you to mean it." His voice had a tone to it that told her he had been studying human nature along with romance. A warning tone full of arrogance and power.

"Men in power are the most dangerous," her father had once told her. "How they use it is the weapon. For good of the people is one way. To dominate and destroy is another. Unfortunately, history has shown that most men go the latter route."

She moved from the bed and got undressed. He watched her with the curiosity of a boy seeing his first naked woman. She walked to the dresser and pulled out the nightgown that Linda had brought her. Soft satin pink with a lace bodice. He liked lace. She pulled it on and turned to face him. He was scanning her from toe to head and back again. Her heart was racing and she was shaking. Jimmy. She had to do this for Jimmy and the one she carried. She touched the crucifix she wore around her neck and said a quick prayer.

"Dim the lights?" They dimmed.

"Would you like music?" he asked.

"No Archive," she ordered. He stood and walked to her.

"No Archive." He took her in his arms and kissed her. For Jimmy, she reached for the front of his pants and tugged them open. She kissed his neck, then taking a deep breath, she went to her knees.

~

"Cartoons!" Linda laughed as she entered with bags. "I actually miss those. Not at much as my kids do." She set the bags on the table. "How did you manage that?"

"It's the Archive." Maria replied breathlessly. She stopped the treadmill and walked over to see what Linda had brought her this time.

"A treadmill?" Linda looked at it.

"I said I wanted to go for a walk outside." Maria frowned. "I need exercise. This is what I got."

"So now you run?"

"Need to keep up. Need stamina." Maria opened a bottle of water and drank.

"Wow? They don't want you outside?"

"I guess not. The Archive has been intercepting radio, TV, internet and everything else and storing it for him. It's like a big computer. All you do is ask it and it has it filled away. This is how he is learning." She lifted out the halogen flashlight and set it on the table next to her bag.

"Where'd you get that?" Linda eyed the black leather bag.

"It's mine. They gave it back. After it was searched, scanned and decontaminated. They gave me back my clothes but they were cleaned." She frowned.

"You wanted them dirty?" Linda laughed.

"The shirt smelled of Jimmy. My son." She dug in the bag and pulled a picture from her notebook.

"He is adorable!" Linda gushed looking at the smiling face.

"He is." Is. She had to keep telling herself that he was still alive.

"When was the last time you saw him?"

"That night." Maria put the picture back. Adam said he did not want to look at the child. He was jealous of her love for him. At least he had let her keep the photos. The only thing missing from her purse had been the gun. Her notebook had been gone through. She looked it over to ensure that nothing was in it that would help them find the Stronghold. She had always been careful of that. Her father taught her that much. Never talk of the Stronghold.

"Almost two months? I don't know what I would do if I couldn't see my boys for two months. Although there are times I would have liked to have given them away." She chuckled at the bad joke.

"Maybe I can get him to let the kids come and watch some cartoons with me?" Maria offered.

"I don't know. They aren't allowed above the first level. They're my bargain basement babies."

"You are on the bottom of this thing?"

"Yep. You are penthouse." Linda smiled.

"And you've seen if from the outside?"

"Of course! Why?"

"What does it look like?"

"You ain't ever seen it?" Maria shook her head. "It's like a block!" Linda shrugged. "A big square block. No windows but you can see out. I mean, it's like them. Looks like you can see through it. It floats and stuff reflects off it like buildings and clouds. But it moves on its own. No motor I don't think. I ain't seen an engine room. It's quiet too. But if something comes close to it, it moves. Like a bird or such." Linda was thinking hard.

"How do you get out of it?" Maria asked suddenly.

"A door is open just past the kitchen. Stairs just appear when I step up. It's real close to the ground."

"How close does it hover?"

"Just over the top of buildings. Depends where we're at. In town, close to the tops of the buildings. When we step off? Seven feet? They don't have to duck to walk under it. There's always like four under it. One at each corner. They don't move or even ever look at me when I go. I guess 'cause one of them is with me."

"And the boys?"

"The boys can't leave. Only me and my mom." Hostages. "I guess to ensure we come back?"

"I think so." Now it occurred to her that she really did want Jimmy with her father. Then Adam couldn't use him to get to her. But what of the other? Her hand went to her abdomen.

"Still?" Linda asked softly.

"Nightly." She couldn't help but look ashamed. Adam had turned her into his concubine.

"Hang in there." The woman stood and looked at the cartoon. "It can't go on forever."

"Can't it? According to him. he is as old as time." There was disgust in her voice.

"Does he hurt you?"

"No, he is very gentle." That made it worse. He had actually become a very accomplished lover. Always wanting to please her as well as enjoy her. And as for being endowed, he was gifted. "Always."

"How long?" Linda asked softly. Maria looked up.

"I'm about two months? I guess another month and I will start showing." Linda nodded. Another month. Four weeks to prepare. The door opened and Adam stepped in. Maria pulled a top out of the bag and held it up to her.

"Leave us." Linda was already moving out the door. She wasn't even out before he had Maria in his arms. He was kissing her and pulling at her clothes.

"I need to shower." She laughed trying to pull away. "I'm all sweaty!"

"You taste so good sweaty." He was now on his knees to her. She was sorry that he had ever discovered porn! He was worked up! He dug his fingers into the tender skin of her hips. She stopped fighting and let him push her up against the wall. Taste? Now that he had developed his taste buds, she was at the top of the menu almost daily. He was a non-stop machine!

"Okay!" She set her hands on his shoulders to better get situated for his assault on her. For Jimmy, she kept reminding herself, as she let herself go to him. At least his tongue wasn't sandpaper anymore. Slowly Adam was becoming more and more human. As if each day he was absorbing more of humanity. She thought of this as he violated her. She had to keep her mind busy or it would drive her insane.

"Cartoons? Children like them?" He asked stretching in the bed.

"They were made for children." Maria explained. He smiled at her.

"I like it when you do that."

"What?" She sat up smiling.

"Smile. Really smile." He reached up and pushed her hair back from her face. "I like it when you sleep."

"When I sleep? Are you checking up on me?" She leaned in to kiss him.

"Yes, sometimes I come to watch you sleep."

"Why don't you just sleep in here with me?" She had been wondering about that.

"I do not sleep." He was massaging her breast again.

"Why not?" She bit her lip as he effortlessly lifted her above him and then lowered her so her breast slid into his mouth. She moaned in uncontrollable pleasure. He laid her next to him and rolled onto her, moving his hand between her legs. Discovering this special torture had amused him to no end.

"I don't," he shrugged, smiling at her sheepishly.

He was becoming more human with each day and she was becoming more dependant and attracted to him. After the initial feeling of rage and violation had dissipated, she had become used to his 'feedings' and looked forward to the time with him. James was dead. There was no betrayal in being attracted to Adam. Mainly because he was becoming everything she had ever wanted in a man. He was becoming James. At times she was unsure what her true feelings for Adam were.

With James, she had been both a child and a virgin. She had dated and kissed boys. She had even petted with some, but with a dozen brothers and her father's men watching her, it had been impossible to explore her sexual desires until she had gone off to college. There she had been busy and attracted to James, the older, sophisticated man who made her laugh and teased her like her brothers did but smiled at her as if she were a woman. In the clinic, he treated her as an equal and more. He looked to her for help with the people of the Stronghold. He was the teacher, she the student. With Adam, the roles were reversed. She the teacher and he the student. The fast learning student.

"So you don't sleep. You don't sweat. You don't..." She tickled him and he only gave her a curious look. "You aren't ticklish and you never laugh."

"Does that bother you?" She was afraid of this question. What if she said yes and he began to sweat profusely?

"I'm not sure. It just makes you so serious." She started to climb from the bed. He pulled her back to him.

"I wasn't finished." His hand moved back to her pelvic area. He moved her beneath him. "Would you like for me to sleep with you? Nightly?" He moved slowly into her.

"You don't sleep. What good would it do?" She drew in a breath. He was learning her body better than James ever had. Why was she always thinking of James?

"I could lie with you? Give you comfort?"

"No, I think you would try this all the time and I do need sleep." He looked down at her stomach and then laid his warm hand on it.

"For him? To care for him?" She nodded and his face clouded over. "And I am forgotten?" He stood and walked away from her and the bed.

"Why would I forget you?" She pulled the bedding around her.

"There is no mother. He is the Alpha and the Omega. I am the Alpha. You are my Omega, so what will I be when he arrives?" Again, he sounded like a child. A very spoiled child.

"You cannot be jealous of your own child!" He turned to glare at her. "This is what love is! You love him! You are his father! You would die for him! This is love in the purest form! The love of a child and a parent!" She started to climb from the bed.

"Stay!" He moved to sit next to her. His hand went to her stomach. "How will he look? Like me?"

"Maybe. He might be a she and she might look like me!" Maria laughed lightly.

"It must be a boy." Adam sounded cold. "I must have a son."

"Then it must be a boy and it must look like you." She lied and prayed he would not notice. There was a fear in her heart for the child she carried. It would look like James.

"Will he?" Adam was fascinated with her abdomen.

"Of course he will." She leaned forward to kiss him. The little gold crucifix sparkled.

"Why do you wear that?" He asked reaching to touch it. She wanted to say it was a symbol of her faith but knew better.

"It was a gift from a wise man. When I was a child and sick, he gave it to me." He nodded and watched it sparkle in the light. He wanted to rip it off her.

"Was James the name of your husband?" He asked suddenly.

"Yes." She sat back. "How did you..."

"You call out for him sometimes." The cold look and tone. "In your sleep." No not always in her sleep.

"I have nightmares. Of how he died." She looked away. He turned her face by placing his hand on her cheek and gazed at her.

"Tell me what you would like to do? Anything!"

"I want to go outside." His face darkened.

"To leave me?" He accused.

"To see the sky. The heavens. Where you came from." She kissed him.

"I will have the children sent for." He kissed her. "We will watch cartoons." Her request was tossed away.

"Can I take a shower first?" Maria asked trying to get away from him.

"No!" She thought he was playing.

"Come get me!" She got away and ran for the shower. He was right behind her. The water poured over her and he snarled as the water hit him. It sounded like an animal. Maria jumped and pushed herself into the corner. He was pacing and brushing the water off as if it burned. "Adam?"

"Get out of there!" He growled. She stepped away from the showerhead and the water stopped. She held out her hand to him. He kept pacing.

"Get it off you!" She dried herself quickly.

"What is it?"

"Nothing." Maria wasn't sure what to think. He looked scared. Something new. In all the time they had spent together, he had been mad, frustrated, sexually frustrated, confused and manipulative, but never frightened. A mental note she filed away. He still didn't move to her until she was dried. She pushed him down onto the sofa and climbed into his lap.

"What is it? What scares you? The water?" He blinked, his eyes spun and then settled on her face.

"I am a brave God. I am not scared." He was lying.

"Yes, you are. You are my brave Adam." She kissed him.

"Now we can watch cartoons?" She laughed at him.

~

"Are they safe with him?" Linda asked softly.

The three boys were brought to the room and Adam invited them to sit with him on the sofa. The cartoons began and the frightened boys moved from the sofa to sit on the floor with a large bowl of buttered popcorn and sodas. Adam was with them almost instantly. Soon Maria heard him laugh for the first time. It was as if he were observing the children's behavior. He tried it a couple of times cautiously and then just laughed. Mike, the oldest was very wary of him. Adam stared at the boy in confusion. Maria saw it. The wonder in Adam's eye. Was this boy to grow to a man? Would he be for him or against him? An ally or a danger.

"Mike!" Maria called to the boy. "Come help me?" The boy quickly moved from the man's glare.

"What is it?" Linda asked picking up on the tension.

"Mike is almost a man." Maria pointed out. Mike stood looking up at them. He was an average sized boy with blonde hair and brown eyes. Linda said he looked just like his father. And that he had been there when his father had died. "Mike, I need a favor from you."

"What?" The boy did not trust her.

"I need you to act like a little boy. Like your brothers. Laugh and act silly."

"Why?" Obviously, she annoyed the boy as much as Adam.

"He thinks he's the man now." Linda sighed.

"That's the problem," Maria mumbled. "Mike, if you act like a man, Adam may make you leave. I think your mother would like you to stay."

"I can go back to our room." The boy had the preteen attitude.

"I don't mean here. I mean the earth." Linda gasped.

"As a child, you are not a threat." Mike looked up at the woman. "We need you to be a man, but play at being a child. Just for now. We need you to take care of your brothers." The boy looked to his mother's frightened face.

"What do I got to do?" he asked.

"Smile. Laugh. Act silly and don't glare!" Maria hissed. "Be a child!" She handed him another bowl of popcorn.

"Okay." He walked over to the sofa and poured the popcorn onto Adam's head. Maria felt her heart stop. Adam jumped up with eyes of rage, shock and confusion. The other boys laughed and began throwing the puffed kernels at each other as they jumped around. Maria began to laugh. Then Adam scooped some up and threw it too. He was laughing. Mike looked over his shoulder at his mother and shrugged.

"I'm gonna beat that boy!" Linda chuckled. "After I hug him! He is just like his daddy! God! I miss that man!" The cartoon was over. "Time to go!" Linda announced.

"Another!" The boys all begged running to her.

"Another! Yes!" Adam begged too.

"One more, then off to bed!" Linda ordered.

"Another Archive!" Adam called and the next movie started. Maria had selected four cartoons for the boys to choose from. They all raced for the floor.

"We'll make some more popcorn!" Maria called. Linda followed her to the kitchen area.

"How is it?" Linda asked softly.

"Not sure." Maria hoped that Archive was busy keeping Adam happy so that their conversation was lost in the noise of the movie.

"What will we need?"

"Are we still in the city?"

"Yes." Linda got another bowl out of the makeshift kitchen that had been set up.

"Then just our wits and guts." Maria shot a look over at Adam.

"It is far. Getting there is the challenge."

"This thing moves around the city. Daily."

"Moves?" Maria looked over towards the males. They were all into the cartoon.

"Like a planet orbiting. On Tuesdays, I can get food and Wednesday clothes. It just moves. Except this last Tuesday. They don't go out in the rain." Maria gave her a confused look. "I guess they might rust?"

"Interesting." Maria thought of Adam's reaction to the water.

"We take our afternoon snack by the door. Let the kids get some fresh air and see the outside. It was raining out and the droids wouldn't even come near us. We could have just dove out. Glad one of them didn't fall out."

"The door is open?"

"Yeah, it lets the air in for the circulation."

"When is it over the university?"

"Which one?"

"New World?"

"Sundays." Linda said. "Yeah, usually Sundays."

"It will have to be a Sunday," Maria mumbled. "soon." They looked back to see the boys laughing. Joe and Billy were on either side of Adam but Mike was by himself. Adam was watching him. "Real soon."

The cartoon ended and the children were hustled off to bed by their mother. Adam and Maria cleaned up the popcorn. At first Adam had told her not to bother, but she was picking it up anyway. She didn't want droids in there with them. He helped and together they got the dwelling cleaned up. Maria settled down on the bed and sighed setting her hand on her stomach. What would happen if he were born here? She had to get him out. Away from Adam. Away from the floating block.

"What are you thinking?" Adam asked sitting next to her.

"If he is well," she smiled slightly.

"Would you like to see him?" She gazed at Adam and nodded. He pushed the entire bed across the room and close to a wall as if it were on wheels.

"What are you doing?" He pushed her shirt up and set his hand on her bare abdomen.

"Watch." He touched the wall and as if it were a sonogram, the baby was there. "There he is." Maria saw her son. He was no more than a blip on the screen but he was there.

"He's beautiful," she mumbled. Adam looked at her curiously.

"He does not look like me!"

"He is developing!" She laughed, setting her hand over his.

"He is small."

"He will grow." She wove her fingers into his. "Big and strong like his father." Adam smiled at her. She was thinking of James as she said it. He moved to sit on the bed and the image faded.

"Come with me." He pulled her hand and she followed.

In the hall, there was smoke. No, fog. Like the room the first time she saw it. It was dark but there was light were Adam walked. She held tightly to his hand, following closely. They walked and walked and then they were going up. She clung to him, afraid of what was to come. Then she smelled it. Fresh air! She looked up and saw stars! They stopped and they were on top of whatever they had been in. She stepped away from him and smiled looking up.

"Hello!" she laughed, looking up at the twinkling stars. She spun around with her hands out from her. The night air felt wonderful. She ran from him.

"Maria!" He was after her. She ran, letting the night air wash over her and through her hair. "Stop!" He grabbed her from behind and held her to him. "You could fall!" She saw that the darkness went on and on. Somewhere it had to end. She relaxed in his arms.

"And if I fell?" she teased.

"You would die," he replied simply.

"I mean would you miss me?" she asked, turning to look over her shoulder at him.

"I don't know." His face held confusion.

"Then I might have to push you off." He thought on the threat.

"Would you still be here when I came back up?"

"The fall would not kill you?"

"No. I am a God." His face was serious. She leaned back against him and stared out into the night. "Yes."

"Yes what?" She leaned forward to look over the edge. It was at least a hundred or more feet to the ground. It would kill her. Not the fall, the sudden stop at the end.

"I would miss you." He pulled her back to him.

"Thank you," she whispered, looking up at the sky. The sky she thought she would never see again.

"I have to go away." He spoke softly.

"What? You're leaving me?" She turned to face him.

"I have to go away."

"How long will you be gone?" He pushed her shirt up and leaned in to suckle.

"A while." She was dry but he yearned for more. He dropped to his knees and pulled her to him.

"Days? Weeks? Hours?"

"Days." He moved to the other breast. She ran her hand through his hair. It was the same. It did not grow. Adam now had fingernails, but no hair on his body. Anywhere. "I will return. But, I must go. I must see what my kingdom looks like."

"Any word on Jimmy?" She asked softly. It had been several weeks.

"No. The James' seem to haunt me." He sighed and sat back. She was getting good at killing the mood.

"What?" She wasn't sure she had heard him.

"Nothing. I will look while I am out." He stood and kissed her. "If I find him I will come back sooner."

"Promise?" She kissed him repeatedly on his face.

"I promise!" He liked it when she was playful, but it usually meant she wanted something.

"Can I go with you?" There it was.

"No. You are safer here. You will be looked after here." She nodded but looked away. "I worry." He kissed her as he spoke.

"I know. But I worry too!" She pouted.

"Let's go to bed?" He took her hand and then they were going down. Into the bowels of his home. Back in the room, she climbed into bed and sighed. She smiled to herself. She had seen the sky, the stars and the heavens.

"Thank you."

"Move over." He climbed in the bed with her and held her. The lights dimmed. "Go to sleep."

In the darkness she wondered why he was going. He had simply announced he would be gone. She relented without a fight and lay patiently waiting for him to finish. Then he fed. She wanted to go. To leave the confines of this prison. But then again his absence would give her time to plan. To get ready. She was running every day on the treadmill and was sure she could do it. But what of Linda? Linda's mother and the children? They had to get to the warehouse. Once there, she could leave them and make it to the Stronghold. It had been three months but she was sure it was still there. That Jimmy was there.

~

Two days. Adam was gone for two days. She had gotten Linda to find her a breast pump and expressed her milk to store for him. Each time she sat to perform the task, she missed him. The way his tongue licked at her and then his mouth covered the nipple. She held his head while he fed. Then he would move his hand to her pelvis and satisfy her while he fed. Afterwards, he would feed on her again and then make love to her.

The kids were running about with the new toys that Linda had gotten them. Her mother was watching an old movie in one corner and a cartoon on in the other. Dinner was on the table and Maria and Linda were filling glasses with beverages. It was the Fourth of July. A day to celebrate. Even though there were now two Americas, it was still celebrated. At least in the Stronghold. And they needed a reason to have fun anyway. Every time one of the kids passed by the door it opened. And there stood the guard. He was just standing there watching.

"You think this is appropriate?" Linda asked, laughing at the movie her mother was watching.

"Call it wishful thinking!" Mom replied bitterly.

Maria watched the images flash across the wall. A movie about an alien invasion on the Fourth of July and how the beings of Earth joined together to attack and defeat them. She knew how the woman felt. With Adam gone, she had been reviewing history through the Archive. It was a risk but she was feeling terrible. Morning sickness and homesickness were taking their toll on her.

Just that morning she had been bold. She knew that Archive was somehow connected to Adam and that he was in turn watching her while he was gone through Archive. She was careful. She had warned Linda. But she had tried to be sneaky. Archive, when asked to perform too many tasks too quickly sometimes stalled. Like a computer freezing. It took a few seconds for it to reboot, but there was that instance of total freedom when Maria was sure Adam could be fooled. She knew that Adam reviewed all she had watched. He could see it all at an amazing speed and take it all in.

"Archive: American History!" The revolution came on the wall, pages from an encyclopedia. She had soon learned that much of what she wanted to see was censored. "Civil war!" It was on the next wall. "Cuban Missile Crisis! Vietnam conflict! Korean War! WW I! WW II! Iran Contra!" Soon she had the room spinning with different information in print or on video. She stood in the middle staring at one. The Rebellion of 2055.

There was little information on this small conflict. It was lost in all the explanation of the dissolution of the United States of America and the forming of the New Reconfigured United States and the Republic of the Americas. But one face was there. Just for a moment or two. A face that made her heart soar. A younger Alejandro stood with his wife and fourteen children outside the small town of Mendoza. Then there was a close up of her father. He was so brave and handsome. She drew strength from this and then spun to focus on the Revolt Cuban. The fifty- second state in the union. The last before the dissolution. Tears fell as she stared at the island, famous for cigars and its large resorts.

"Any word?" Linda asked, carrying the glasses to the table.

"None. No one talks to me."

"Not even Blueboy?"

"No. Every once in a while the door opens and he is just standing there." As if on cue, the door opened and the guard stepped in. The door shut. He did not move farther into the room.

"What you need, hon?" Linda asked setting the glasses down and turning to receive a solid blow to her left arm sending her flying across the room. The boys screamed. Mom screamed and Maria screamed. The guard moved towards Maria and she backed away from him. He pointed at her and then down at her stomach.

"Abomination!" The droid noted calmly, pulling back to strike again. There was a loud 'clunk!' and he stopped to turn and face Mom. The skillet she wielded hit him again. He looked confused. The green was glowing brighter, then flickered! The guard pulled back to strike again. The older woman stood waiting.

"Come on you bastard!" she yelled, hitting him again! "Damn bastard!" the woman screamed.

"Mom!" Maria hit him over the back of the head with the pitcher of tea. The pitcher shattered and liquid poured all over it. The guard reacted by jumping about as if it were on fire and tried to get the liquid off of him

"Lights out! Run, Mom!" Maria ordered. There was total darkness. Mom banged into Maria, sending her to the floor. The woman fumbled and dragged her to her feet.

"Come on now! We have to get to the children!"

"Cartoons! Six of them!" The walls came alive and the noise was deafening. The droid stood in confusion as the women hurried over to the children.

"I seen a movie once about aliens that our water was poison to them!" Mom yelled over the noise.

"Grab her!" Maria, the boys and Mom half-carried, half dragged the unconscious Linda into the shower as the droid charged. The water came on and he stopped dead. The lights glowed, flickered on and on but he did not advance on them. "Lord! What in the hell?"

"They don't like water!" Maria announced.

"It makes them mad!" Mike noted. "Crazy mad!" The other boys were huddled behind the women. Mike stood glaring at the droid defiantly. "Maybe we can point the water at him?" The droid took a step back.

"Get over here!" Maria jerked the boy back under the water.

"Let go of me!" The boy yelled.

"What did I tell you? If they think you are a hazard to them, they will dispose of you! Your mother needs you! Live today! Fight tomorrow!" The boy turned his glare from the droid to her.

"I don't plan on fighting them! I plan on destroying them. Just like they did my dad." He moved to sit with his mother. Maria prayed that Archive had not heard that. She knelt down next to Linda.

"I think her arm is broke." Mom was using her body to shield her daughter from the now hot water.

"Archive! The water! Archive!" The water was getting hotter. Maria pulled the children from under it and the droid moved closer. "Adam! Help me!" She screamed and the door opened. Archive stopped the movies and the water. Maria was about to scream when Blue Boy stepped up behind the droid and tapped him on the back of the head and pushed. The green glow stopped.

"Slight disruption." Blueboy noted, looking at them curiously. Maria stood glaring at him.

Two droids came in and removed the defective one. They half carried, half-dragged Linda to the bed. Maria checked her friend over. Yes, her arm was broken and she had a concussion, but she was alive. The boys looked terrified. Well, two were. The other was flicking water in every direction. Blue Boy glared at the boy and Maria jerked him to her. She handed him some towels and sent him to dry and comfort his brothers.

"Is it broken?" Blue Boy asked looking over the woman.

"Her arm is." Maria was mopping the water off her face.

"We will dispose of her." The boys began to yell in protest.

"You will not!" Maria stepped up to the droid. He did not back down but she could tell he was nervous. "Is there a medical facility?" Blue Boy did not move or answer. "I will tell Adam!" She warned. "I will be angry and it will make Adam angry!" Blue Boy seemed to be unsure. "I will not let him feed! I will not let him touch me!"

"There is such a facility," he finally spoke.

"Help me get her there!" She ordered. The droids didn't move. "For God's sake! Grab the bedding! You won't have to touch her!" Four each lifted one corner of the comforter and carried the woman from the room. "Mom, stay here with the boys. They are safe here." She looked to the shower. The woman nodded.

"Take care of my baby," she called as the door shut.

"Should we tell Adam?" Maria asked following the procession down the long hall.

"He knows." Blue Boy replied. Archive must have told him. "He will return soon."

The room was the one Maria had been brought to the first night. Or was it? A terror raced through her but she stepped up next to her friend as the droid left the room. There were tables around them with instruments on them. Some looked familiar and others strange. She dug through the cabinets and found bandages and pieces of plastic to use for a splint. She bound her friend's arm and slowly, the woman was coming around. She was going to have a hell of a black eye. Her eyes flashed as she opened them and looked at Maria.

"The boys are fine." She answered the question before it could be asked. "The droids been deactivated. He had a bit of a glitch."

"A bit?" The woman struggled to sit up. "It hurts."

"I don't have anything for pain."

"I do. In my room. A bottle of whiskey. Care to join me for a swig?" Linda's eyes had something in them. She was looking behind Maria. "I'm gonna stagger that way." She nodded up. Archive was listening. Maria helped her stand. "Damn! I ain't felt this bad since my wedding night. I really tied one on that time. Sick as a dog!" The woman swayed but did not fall.

"I'll be right behind you." Linda staggered to the door. It opened and the guards moved away so she could pass. She looked back at her friend and then shot a look into the fog. Something was there and it had frightened the woman. She stepped out and the door closed.

Maria turned and looked behind her. It was the fog. It climbed the walls but she had a feeling there were no walls there. Something else. She stepped forward with her hands outstretched. There was nothing there. She stepped through the fog and gasped in horror. Many. He had said many. That was an understatement. She walked along the cylinders, feeling her heart race along with the tears that fell.

From the way the women were dressed, she estimated that it had started sometime at the end of the last century. They simply stood as if waiting. For Adam? She calculated as she walked. There were at least 500 of them. Five hundred dead women, standing in formation. Each in a big, clear test tube. Each of them bore the scars of abdomen surgery. Not just Cesarean, but full, open abdomen. Whoever had done this had not been well versed in medical procedures. The women had been hacked open.

At the back of the array were the smaller tubes that held the results. From the size of a dime, to what looked like a full term deformed fetus. Maria's hands went to her stomach. Many? These women were taken and died. Rape? Artificial insemination? She felt her stomach turn. These women had been nothing more than lab rats to Adam. What of her child?

"These experiments were failures." Blueboy noted calmly. Maria screamed and turned to find him just standing there. "They were fragile."

Some of the women had their eyes closed, but many had terrified looks on their wide-eyed faces. Had they died of fear or simply been disposed of after the experiment was over? What would happen to her? Would she be in one of these cylinders with her child in a smaller one while Adam went out to find another Omega? She could easily be replaced. The way Blue boy was looking at her told her that much. She was not his choice for this experiment. She had been Adam's choice. And at times, it felt as if he had sought her out. The way he stared at her. The way he commented on how he had no idea how pretty she was. As if he had been looking specifically for her. What was it about her? Because of her father?

"This is what he has come to do?"

"These are experiments of the past. You hold the future."

"Where is Adam?" Maria asked calmly.

"On his way. I am to take you back to your quarters."

"I am going to Linda's. I need a drink. Bring her children and mother to her. I am hungry." She walked past him and ran for the door. Something caught her eye. Bright red nail polish. She looked up at the horror-stricken face frozen for all eternity. The crucifix was still around her neck. It was just a moment in time. A chance meeting. The woman had been with her the night Adam had come. She had been alive then. Maria ran out of the room.

A guard stood waiting. She paced to and fro trying to think. She had to think! Those women had been nothing but rats in a lab for these overpowered radios! She had to put it all together. Why? Why had they done this? Why had they tried to make a man? Adam kept saying he was the first. If not Adam, then who had done that to the women? Was it Blueboy, in an attempt to make Adam? Were the droids what made him, or had Adam done that? She fought nausea, but it won. She pushed past the droid and ran for the door. He was on her, but she made it. The door that was always open. She leaned out into the night and vomited. Then she was jerked back inside.

"Where is Linda?" She asked leaning against the foggy wall. The guard pointed and then followed.

"You saw?" Linda asked as Maria entered, took the glass from her and guzzled it down.

"Bring her family here!" Maria ordered to the guard. The door shut and they were alone.

"That ain't good for the baby." Linda noted calmly.

"Not much here is!" Maria set the glass down and felt the liquor warm her body and calm her. "How long have you known?"

"About a month. I stumbled in there one day. Got lost." The woman drank from the bottle. "Would have taken the kids and run, but was hoping you weren't delusional." She gazed at her friend.

"I'm not. Keep a tight hold on Mike and that tongue of his." Maria held her glass out. "We can't have any delays or we might not make it. What day is it?"

"Sunday." Linda filled the glass. "And it's raining."

"I noticed." Maria noted as she drank slowly this time. The smell of the sweet rain was what sent her stomach flying out into the night. "He won't come until it stops."

~

"The conflict in Bosnia!" Maria called out and the news footage flashed on the wall. She had the Vietnam War going next to it. Then there was the Inchon March to the left.

"Why are you doing this?" Linda asked softly. "They will catch you!" She shot a look up at the picture of her father on the far wall.

"It helps me think." Maria stood slowly. She had a small bulge now.

"He isn't suspicious?"

"He's busy. Something happened to make some of the droids go nutso. Something about evolutionary change?" She frowned. She still had a feeling that Blue Boy had been behind that.

"Right!" Linda was balancing the food tray on her braced arm.

"Still hurt?"

"Not so much, just awkward." She sat and sighed. "How you feel?"

"Good!" Maria smiled at her friend and walked over to lift the cover. Lasagna. "Your mom is the best."

"She says you need to eat more."

"She coming to watch movies later?"

"No, and the kids don't want to either. He'll be back won't he?"

"He will be back today. That was all I was told." Maria shrugged.

"You will need time alone." Linda noted and then caught the look from her friend. Maria really didn't want any time alone with him. Now Linda was beginning to understand. Maria was a rat too, only she was in a better cage.

"I need some distraction!" Maria sat and bit into the food. It was delicious.

"Watch one of those old movies. Get you a fantasy dude." Linda laughed merrily.

"A what?"

"When I was younger, like five or six, my mom left me with this old woman while she worked. She was from England and she was really funny. She was old, like 90! Anyway, she was always talking about this fantasy dude. James Fielding." She said it was a fabulous British accent, making Maria laugh. It reminded her of her husband speaking Spanish. He was English and there was nothing more amusing than hearing Spanish with a British accent. "The most perfect man on the earth," Linda said.

"Was he?"

"According to him. He was his own best audience. Very fond of himself indeed. You must have heard of him? It's history! You had to have?" Maria shook her head in confusion. "The Genesis?" Something about that did spark a memory. "The man who went in search of God?" Then it clicked. Maria set her fork down.

"The Genesis?" Maria stared at the wall.

"You okay honey?" Linda asked.

"Yes. I need to rest." She looked to the door.

"Well, I got work to do." Linda left her.

"Archive? James Fielding!"

There he was. Adam! Maria walked to the wall, reading the news article. James Adam Fielding, 32, billionaire extraordinaire had financed the construction of the Genesis space shuttle. A self-sustaining spacecraft that was run by a super computer. Maria felt her stomach turn. It was Adam! Adam was James Fielding! She read on. The self proclaimed religious fanatic had employed the assistance of a young scientist in the design, construction and lift off of the ship. One James McMillan Sinclair. James' grandfather!

Sinclair's design of the super brain, the Archive, was monumental in the computer world, as was the shuttle. It was equipped with twenty droids to help him on his mission that would take several decades. The strange looking lightweight creatures were designed to work well in zero gravity. They were nothing but wires, microchips and a rubbery skin over their lightweight alloy bodies. Simple and efficient. James had always used that when talking to a class. His lectures were riveting.

The mission of the Genesis was what sparked controversy. Fielding was not going to find other life, or other planets; he was in search of God. He was declared insane. However, he successfully argued that he was the perfect male specimen and deserved the right to talk to the Almighty face to face. Fields was an Olympic decathlon winner as well as a devout Catholic. He had even petitioned a meeting with the Pope! Fields vowed to make God appear to the people of earth. For that, they tried to lock him up. His money bought lawyers who saw to it that he was safe on his own private island. Many speculated that he would die there. Exiled from the world. Then the craft was finished, equipped and unstoppable. It was launched, and he was never heard from again.

There were speculations that the craft was never launched. That it simply fell into the ocean. There was a hurricane in that region and investigating was impossible for a while. When rescue crews made it to the island, they found it deserted. Nothing. Only a house and a letter stating that Fielding had gone to find God. How? No one could explain. No one was there to tell. Even the natives had run from Fielding and his madness. Many proclaimed him the devil. Many claimed it was all a hoax. The rantings of a mad man with money. And there were jokes that he was still out there. Floating around in space. Looking for God.

"Oh, Adam!" Maria reached out to touch the face on the wall. It was the same face. The same curve of the nose, the same full lips. Her Adam. The door opened and Adam stepped in. His eyes flashed a dangerous blue. The door shut and he stormed towards her.

"Archive off!" he roared, grabbing her. She was thrown across the room and bounced off the opposing wall. It took a moment, but she got her bearings and to her feet. He had her then. Around the waist. He slammed her fast first down on the bed tearing at her clothes.

"Adam!" she cried out, terrified. Then she was screaming in pain. He took her roughly from behind. Slamming into her repeatedly as she screamed.

"I am the first!" He yelled, infuriated. "I am Adam! I am made in his image! I am Adam! I am the first!" Over and over he yelled as he assaulted her. She screamed and begged as he continued. It went on for what seemed like hours and could have been. He never slept and he never tired. She was fighting him as he leaned over her.

"Adam!" she screamed and he stopped.

"I found your son! I brought him here!" He yelled, thrusting hard. "He will die for this betrayal!" He yelled into her ear and then she lost it. She was screaming and flaying, trying to get away. He moved back from her. "Obedience is taught!" He took the belt from his clothing and brought it down on her back.

"Adam! Please!" she begged trying to crawl away from him.

"I am a compassionate and gracious God, slow to anger, abounding in love and faithfulness, maintaining love to thousands, and forgiving wickedness, rebellion and sin. Yet I do not leave the guilty unpunished; I punish my children and their children for the sin of the fathers to the third and fourth generation. I am a kind God, strict, firm, loving, forgiving and I have a heart." He continued to beat her. "I am the first! I am Adam! I am made in his image! I am the son of God!" His voice was level and calm as he beat her into unconsciousness.

"Wake up." Linda's voice was in the fog. Maria was afraid to look into the fog. "It's just me." There was such pain that she wished she could just die.

"Hand me a towel." Mom was there too. "You boys stay over there!" The voice was angry. "Animals!" There was a stinging that woke her right up.

"Don't move!" Linda had her hand. "We got you on your side so you don't hurt the baby." Maria opened her eyes and then it all blurred. "What happened?" tears and the pain. She shook her head and moved her hand to her stomach. "He's okay. Adam was looking at him on the wall. But your back is a bloody mess," Linda said.

"I could kill him!" Mom grumbled.

"Where is he?"

"I don't know. He just stormed out of here naked as a jaybird." Linda brushed Maria's hair back from her face. "Looks like he got a few on your face too." The cloth to her cheek was cold. "Maria, what happened?" The woman was whispering. "We ain't alone." The injured woman nodded. "They just came and told us all to come and care for you. Why did he do this?"

"I figured out who he is." Maria licked her busted lip and tasted the metal of her blood. Yes, he had struck her. He had grabbed a handful of her hair and jerked her face to his.

"Call out for your precious James now!" he ordered.

"I love you..," She gasped. "Adam!" He knew it was a lie and had hit her. He then had thrown her on her back and delivered several lashes across her breasts. Darkness took her and she woke to find him kissing her as he licked the blood from her lip. He suckled her breast hard and then mounted her.

"Obedience is taught!" he mumbled, throwing his head back to satisfy himself mumbling his mantra of being a god and the only one. The first.

"I think Sunday is out of the question for another week." With that, Maria closed her eyes.

ALISE

Artificial Life Intelligence Surrogate Experiment

"The baby!" Alise ordered.

Waldo stopped and ran back to her. There was no time. She ran. She caught the dog and called to him. He came to her. She laid the baby in the bushes near the edge of a small stream and ordered the dog to lie nearby. To guard him. She had been present many times while the dog had been trained and found it fascinating. Now she laid the sleeping boy down. Covered him with his favorite blanket, and using some rocks, she formed a wall around him high enough to keep it from touching him.

She pulled the silver space-age blanket from her pocket. Although, now no bigger than a quarter, she unfolded the silver material and laid it over the rock wall. It was king size. Big enough for all. She secured it and touched it. Instantly ice formed over it. She stepped back and scanned. There was no body heat detected. The dog would not leave the boy. He had been trained to protect. She turned and raced back to the road.

It had taken only a minute or two but she was too late. Her James lay broken on the other side of the car. Maria was screaming and Alfie was gone. She moved quickly to James. Two droids were there. She analyzed them quickly. One was by the car and one was standing over her James. She quickly saw their weakness and took advantage. The closest fell instantly after she zapped him by touching her finger to his eye. It drained her slightly. The next would be harder. It would take several seconds for her to recharge.

"Do you relent?" it asked James.

James was bleeding and unable to get up. His breathing was labored and there was blood on his handsome face. He blinked and drew in a breath. Drained, Alise could not do a scan on him. She wasn't sure how badly he was hurt. With great effort he propped himself up on his elbow and looked up at the creature. In the green glow of the droid he looked like a ghost. Maybe he was? Alejandro told wonderful ghost stories. But no, James was breathing. Ghosts did not breathe. She stood helplessly and watched as Maria was carried away.

"I told you to FUCK OFF!" James yelled, and fell back. The remaining creature pointed a finger at him. The spark came from it, but it never hit James. A small mirror was suddenly there and the flash went back into the droid, instantly shutting him down. Alise put the mirror in her pocket and gathered James in her arms. She ran back into the darkness.

His arm was not broken. His shoulder was dislocated. He would make noise if she set it now. He was waking. She breathed on him, and he fell unconscious. She then laid him next to Jimmy and using the bushes, she also covered James and froze it. She sat next to the dog and shut herself down. Thirty minutes would be long enough. Any longer, and she risked Jimmy waking. He might fall into the water, so she had to risk being scanned.

They came. But not close. The green glow stopped a good hundred yards from them. The dog ran off and the scan followed him momentarily, then moved on. Waldo made a big circle and came back. He licked Alise in the face and she woke. The glow was moving away. She checked her charges and found them sleeping soundly. She left them and ran back to the car. Alfie was just lying there as they had left him. No light. She gathered his appendages and loaded them in the back of the car.

"Are you deactivated?" she asked calmly.

"No." His eyes lit up. "I am however, in pieces." He lifted his head and looked about. "Many pieces. Half of me is there and the other half there. I think my thumb is gone though. I did a Three Stooges."

"I believe I got all of them, except the thumb. Can you steer with one arm?"

"Yes." The rest of his face lit up. "James and Jimmy?

"Safe."

"They took Maria."

"I saw. Come on." She lifted him up and carried him to the car, making faces.

"I would think that I weigh less?"

"I guess so. It's not that. You are leaking."

"Sorry."

She set him in the driver's seat. The tires were all still full of air. On the road, it would take at least two hours. Cross-country, it would take thirty minutes less, but she wasn't sure if the vehicle would make it. She looked into the darkness and decided to risk it.

"Do you see the dog?"

"Waldo?" Alfie asked scanning the darkness. "Yes!"

"Steer to him," she ordered shutting the door.

The average vehicle weighed 2,000 pounds. She looked down at her feet. If she had had an indication of this event, she would have worn her other shoes. She set her hands on the back of the car and pushed. Alfie was whistling as they left the road and traveled to where the dog sat waiting. He was in a good mood for being in pieces! Alise wondered if his internal brain had been damaged.

Alfie steered and Alise pushed. In the darkness it was difficult. Alise got them as close as she dared and hurried to uncover her wards. Jimmy was stirring. She breathed on him again and carried his cold little body to Alfie. He took the boy in his good arm and held him against his heated barrel chest. A quick scan of his blue eyes and he nodded to Alise. The boy was fine. Cold, but fine. Alise hurried back to James.

"James!" She set him up and he moaned loudly, then began cursing. "Sit still!" Alise reset his shoulder and the cursing got even louder. "Language, please!" He was fighting to get away from her.

"Maria!"

"She is gone!" The loud voice made him stop struggling. Alise rarely raised her voice. He looked at her and her eye flickered in the darkness.

"NO!" He fell against her, crying.

He was almost six months old when she first saw him. James Sr. had her sitting up in bed when he laid the boy in her arms. She had been there in the room with James Sr. for a week. He was instructing her. She was still hooked to her lifeline. The main computer. The wires ran from the back of her head to the system on the nightstand. In the mirror over the dresser she saw herself and wondered if she would frighten the child. She had no skin or hair.

"He is your son. You are to care for him and protect him." James Sr. ordered tapping the keys and watching as she held his son. "What are you to do?" She looked down at the baby and smiled.

"Care for him and protect him." She began to rock him gently. "Sir?"

"Yes, Alise?" James Sr. was still tapping into the keyboard.

"Can I love him?" The man stopped and gazed at her.

"Not as you love me," he noted.

"No, as a mother loves her child."

"Yes, Alise. That's my girl." He took the child from her. "For now, let's just get all the bugs out of you so you can love me." He carried the boy to the cradle and laid him gently in it. She watched the baby sleep as James Sr. made some adjustments, then ordered her to her knees to service him. He sat on the edge of the bed with his legs spread for her. She obeyed without question. "That's my girl., he mumbled dreamily. She was always to be his girl.

"James." She tried to stop the flickering. It was not good. "We have to get Jimmy to the Stronghold."

"Jimmy!" James sat up wincing.

"In the car. Come on now." She helped the man to his feet and into the passenger side. "James, you need rest." She breathed on him and he fell instantly asleep. She fastened his seatbelt.

"Will you fasten mine?" Alfie asked playfully.

"Why are you in such a good mood?" she asked, leaning in to strap him in.

"I was in a fight!" he replied.

"You lost!" she noted, shutting the door. She walked around, took Jimmy, fastened him into his carseat, and ordered the dog into the car.

"But it was entertaining!" the droid laughed. If it could be considered a laugh.

"You will be hard to live with now that your ego has grown," she mumbled stepping to the back of the car. "I should have worn my other shoes!"

"Forward!" Alfie called. "It's going to be a bumpy ride!" he sang out in his best Bette Davis voice.

"Go easy on the wheels. They have to last us." She called, pushing the vehicle. He didn't obey.

She ran and she cursed. She had learned to cuss from the best. James Sr. He was a prodigious curser. He did it when he was on top of her. He did it when she was on top. He did it when she was on her knees. He did it when he was angry, and when he was happy. James Sr. would cuss about the quality of wine and tea that was served to him at dinner at the club. Alise would sit, smiling softly at him. He had her accompany him often to parties and dinners. He would buy her a lovely gown, she would fix her hair and she would behave as a young, sensual mistress to make all the men jealous and follow him about without saying more than "thank you", "how nice" and "yes, James Dear".

"That's my girl!" James Sr. would laugh, hugging her to him and kissing her.

The women who did not know what she was saw her as a snob. The women who did know of her origins saw her as a party favor that their husbands longed for. The men adored her. She was built perfectly. Her measurements were 38" 22" 34", 5'11 with flowing blonde hair and bright blue eyes. Her mascara never ran, her lipstick was always the perfect non-smeared shade, she never needed to go to the powder room and she was always willing to serve. And the ongoing joke was that she could be turned off and not paid alimony.

She liked to go out with him. He always kept her close and treated her so nicely. His hand was always on her hip, holding her to him. He would go and get her drinks, he would hold the chair for her and after a few drinks, he would pull her close to kiss. He would tell her dirty jokes and proposition her. At home he would undress her and fulfill those dirty propositions. She slept in his bed. Next to him. Nestled against his barrel furry chest. She would listen to his heartbeat.

In the daytime there was a maid. Alise's main job was to care for James. She bathed him, fed him, dressed him and took him places. He was a wonderful baby and he grew into a marvelous boy. She was proud of him and she was grateful to James Sr. for giving her emotions. It made it all worth it. She followed the boy around and made sure he was safe. And like any mother, she expected respect, for her, his father and the rules. Alfie helped her but it was mostly on her to give the boy the structure he needed to become a man. And he became a wonderful man. Still, there were times he needed her.

She remembered the day she had first shocked him. He was a teen and he was angry. He called her names and screamed at her. Then her eye flickered. He stood with his mouth open, his eyes wide. It happened again, and he ran from her. That made the flickering happen more. James Sr. came running, and between the lad's screams and her babbling and flickering, he had cursed. Alfie came and led her away from the whole mess, but she sat in the bedroom with her eye flickering. It wouldn't stop. She was slamming her head into the wall when James Sr. came in.

"No! My darling girl!" He took her in his arms. "Don't do that, my darling girl!" he cooed, holding her. "James! Come here! You have upset your mother!"

James had stood in the doorway looking frightened. He was 12 and had just been told by playmates that not only did his father build fake people, he had one in his house as a sex toy! His father was a pervert! He had told them his mother, Alise, was the only woman in the house. It was then that the boys had told him that his real mother was dead. Now he was lost.

"She's not my mother!" He looked up at Alfie. Now Alfie he understood. He knew he was obviously a droid. But Alise? James saw her kiss his father. He saw her climb in his lap and laugh with him. He had even seen her mounted on her father late one night when he had been awakened by their moaning and sexual grunts. But Alise wasn't human.

"Yes, she is!" his father yelled at him angrily. "She changed your diapers, wiped your ass and your nose your whole life! She loves you! How can you do this to her?" James looked at Alise's tormented face that lay against his father's chest. The eye flickered again. "Are you so cruel?" asked James Sr.

"No." James moved to hug her. The flickering continued, but her face did not look so sad. "I'm sorry Alise." James said, but it was a long time before he called her Mum again. It was a compromise, James Sr. had told her, and she accepted it.

Time went on, the men in her family were her life. She got rid of the maid. She cleaned the house, did the laundry, the shopping and the cooking. James was old enough to care for himself. Alfie was his taxi until he could drive. She checked his homework. Typed his papers. Made his favorite meals and left his clean laundry at the foot of the bed. The eye flickered again when he went off to college. Then it was just James Sr.

"My girl!" He would call her, and she would run to him. Each day she was there for him every minute, and only for him.

Every day they had coffee and Danish. Every day he went for a long walk. Every afternoon they had tea. Every lunch was together. Dinner and a good book by the fire. He desired her less, but still wanted her next to him in bed. Twice as she lay with her head on his shoulder, his heart had stopped. Each time she had revived him before the ambulance came. He would get better, come home and life would resume. Then one day, as she was getting his lunch, he just sat down and did not move. She tried to revive him. Alfie tried. James McMillan Sinclair Jr. was gone. James came home and he took care of himself. Alfie took care of her.

At the funeral, she and Alfie sat on the front pew and stared. People filed by. Doctors, professors, dignitaries, and the famous. People he rarely saw and told openly what he hated about them. Some people looked at Alfie and Alise curiously. Alise did not move except that her eye flickered. It would flicker for years. Her love was gone. She had nothing and no one to care for. Her own existence was over. She wished to be deactivated. James had ignored her pleas. He asked Alfie to look after her. The church was filling up when the man approached them.

"Excuse me?" He was polite. Quiet and polite.

"Yes?" Alfie spoke calmly.

"These pews are reserved for family." The flickering got quicker. They were now going to remove her!

"We are sitting here." Alfie replied setting his hand on Alise's. She was shaking as if ready to explode.

"But it is for family," the man persisted.

"We are not bothering anyone." Alfie pointed out. However, if they tried to remove Alise, Alfie would be bothering them. "We are not moving." Alfie squeezed her hand firmly.

"But you must…"

"What's going on?" James was there.

"This is reserved for family," the man repeated.

"This is my uncle Alfie and my Mum," James growled, "Leave them alone."

"But sir, they are just droids!" James shoved the man.

"You ever speak to my Mum that way again and I will kill you!" He almost yelled. Alise reached up to hold his hand. "Bloody damn fool!" The man scurried away. James adjusted his coat and tie. He sat down between the two. He sat sobbing as Alise and Alfie sat shoulder to shoulder with him and held him up. He was their boy.

James became famous in his own right and asked her to be present when he was given an award. She sat staring at him. It had been years since she had gone out. He was sitting holding her hand. He had found the cure for cancer. They all wanted him, the press, the TV, the women But stayed at home, basically hiding from the world. He came to Alise.

"Mum? Will you come with me?" James sat down, he held her hand and asked. He sounded young again. "Get dolled up, put on a pretty dress and come. I need you. Mum please?" The eye flickered. Mum? "Oh, Mum, don't cry! Please!" She had looked away. "Mum, please! It's killing me to see you still so sad. I need you Mum."

"Do you?" she turned to face him.

"Oh, Mum!" He hugged her.

"I need to fix my hair," she whispered.

"That's my girl!" He kissed her cheek. His girl!

James toured. He lectured. Alise was with him. He laughed at the jokes of being a mama's boy. He would tell them yes, he was but his mother could crush theirs with her thumb. They would laugh but he knew it to be true. Alise typed his notes, woke him, made his breakfast and cared for him when he came home drunk. The next morning she and Alfie would sit quietly while he sipped black coffee and cursed. He could not curse like his father. He mumbled where his father had roared. It was still amusing.

Then came the clinic, and she went to help. She and Alfie. People were hateful and cruel. She sheltered James from most and was angered when people yelled at him. Once, she had slammed a door so hard it shattered. Alfie cleaned it with a smirk on his face. Then came the decision for James to step away so that the really ill could be helped. James paid for the clinic to stay open but he went home to rest. Then the offer from the school. Teaching. She sat next to him at the meeting with the dean.

"What do you think Mum?" The dean had looked shocked that James would ask her.

"It's your father's alma mater," she smiled. Her eye flickered as she touched his cheek. "He would be happy."

So he went to teach. For a year or so, it was enough. He would teach, do a little research, date a colleague, get drunk, have fun and she would have breakfast waiting. Many of the women he brought home gave her snide looks, as if she were no more than the hired help. She would not serve them. She was there for James and did not have to put up with them. He would mumble that he was glad she had developed an attitude so late in his life or he might not have survived his youth. Alfie would serve them as Alise sat sipping coffee and glaring. Every so often a guest, would anger her and her eye would flicker.

"Who is she?" one woman asked coldly.

"My Mum, and if you don't like it, the damn door is right there!" Alise had sat smiling at the woman.

But then he went to bring that girl to the college.

"He is all that I've read about!" James was excited. "He is huge! Mum! The man towers over me!"

She sat listening to what had happened at the Stronghold. It had been a long time since she had seen him this excited. Like a child on his way to the circus.

"Mum, he wants me to open a clinic. To treat the people and I agreed! Every other weekend I take the girl there and treat the people."

"What is the girl like?" Alise asked.

"She's pretty." he shrugged, pacing about. "Little, though. Alejandro has twelve sons and they are all as big as he is! Do you know what it's like to talk to a living legend?"

"Of course," she smiled. "I live with one."

The girl was small. And she was pretty. The first visit home was nothing special. At least not on the way there. The ride back was different. James and Maria talked non-stop. Alise saw it in his eyes. The look his father saved for her. His girl. She looked the girl over and sighed. Alise was polite, but wary. Maria was kind and gentle and she could keep up with James. She was intelligent. Young, but then Alise had been thirty years younger than James Sr. and they had been very happy.

"Mum?" James had called her, "Mum…"

"James, what is it?" She heard the pain in his voice.

"I have to take Maria home. I won't be there for dinner." He sounded like a child again.

"Shall I go along?"

"NO!"

"James?"

"Mum, I've gotten her pregnant."

"Oh, James!" She sat waiting.

"Mum, I'll be home soon." He hung up and she sat to wait. After two days she and Alfie were on their way.

At the Stronghold, they were stopped at the gate. Or at least they were told to stop. Alfie drove through and right up to the Clinic as armed men dove out of the way. He was whistling "over the river and through the woods"…Alise stepped out and was met by Alejandro and Olivia and many others. Alise straightened her clothes and stood waiting for what they had to say. Alfie climbed out of the car and walked over to stand next to her. With the car at their back, he thought they might actually have a chance. A rifle cocked and Alfie thought that at least it would be a good fight. He looked around for James.

"You need to leave," Alejandro ordered angrily.

"We will!" Alise replied. "With our son!" Olivia made a noise, and the eye flickered. Olivia took a step back. In the coming dark Alise looked very evil.

"Your son violated my daughter!" Alejandro roared.

"Not against her will!" Alise countered stepping closer. He did not step back. "I think there is fault here and it is equal. His and hers! Now what have you done with my son?"

"You need to leave!"

"You need to tell me where my son is!" The eye flickered again. Alejandro raised an eyebrow at her. "You will tell me where my son is or I will tear this place apart looking for him. You may destroy me, but I will destroy a lot more. Now just tell me!" She raised her voice.

"I will tell you to leave!" Alejandro yelled.

"Mum!" James was standing in the doorway of the clinic. Two men were keeping him from coming to her. Alejandro moved to block her view of him.

"The most dangerous place on the face to the Earth is between a woman and her child!" The flickering eye increased in speed and was almost hypnotizing.

"You cannot stay!" Alejandro roared.

"Look, you God damned ignorant son of a bitch! If you don't get out of my way, I am going to kick your ass so hard your fucking dead father will feel it! Then I am going to slap that shitty ass cocked eyebrow right off your fucking head! If I don't snatch your hairy blubber ass bald first!" Everyone stood looking shocked. "Now get the fuck out of my way!"

"Mum!" James got loose and ran to her. The men attempted to follow, but Alejandro waved them off. "Mum!"

"Hush. James." She stood waiting. The eye flickered slowly. "He is my son. He did wrong and he is here to make amends. You know it and I know it. Now, get out of my way so I can give him a piece of my mind. Or would you like to continue this conversation?" Alejandro heaved a heavy sigh and stepped aside as she barked at the other droid. "Alfie! Park the car!"

"Oh my!" Olivia crossed herself as the droid and James headed to the clinic. Alejandro looked at Alfie.

"You can park it…"

"In Paris?" the droid asked solemnly.

"Paris?" Alejandro asked, looking confused.

"Yes, by the time I get back she might have calmed down." He winked and began to whistle as he climbed in the car. Alejandro turned to his wife and laughed.

"The in-laws," he noted. Olivia huffed and walked away.

Jimmy was crying and Waldo was barking. They still had a ways to go. Alise walked to the front of the car and glared at Alfie. He smiled brightly. She had a feeling that if he had legs he would have been stepping on the brake. Damned bucket of bolts! James was stirring in the passenger seat. It was the dead of night and they were still at least 70 miles from the Stronghold. She leaned in the window and thumped the droid between the eyes. His head snapped back and forward and hit the steering wheel.

"Ow!" he yelped.

"That did not hurt, you halfwit!" She opened the door and leaned in to care for the baby. Only her face was lit. She could not risk more. Jimmy gurgled at her. He was used to her coming to him in the dark as only a soft orange face.

"Well, seeing as I am now half the man I used to be…"

"Alfie!" James yelled and Jimmy began to cry. "What happened?"

"I was in a fight!" The droid smiled.

"And he lost!" Alise plugged the baby's mouth with a bottle. The boy sucked and touched her face with his chubby little hand. She sighed. He was safe. They all were.

"The were...ten of them and one of me!" Alfie smiled at James and winked.

"The rest of him is in the back." Alise pushed the dog out of her face and Waldo jumped past her and out into the night. "Hurry back!" She called to the dog.

"In the back?" James tried to sit up and winced.

"What I could find."

"Find?" James looked confused.

"I know where my thumb is." Alfie lifted up his missing arm. Everything above the elbow was still attached. "I jabbed it one's eye and it got stuck." He made a face. "Then he ripped my arm off and hit me with it."

"Alfie!" James looked like he wanted to cry.

"I tried James. I tried but there were too many. She was still alive when they took her." The droid looked down. "I tried." James set a hand on his shoulder. "I will get her back. I swear," Alfie declared.

"Let's get you back together first." James looked to Alise. "How did we get here?"

"I drove," Alfie sniffled.

"You drove?" James looked at the end of the lights. No legs.

"He steered!" Alise snapped. "I pushed! We have to get moving. Waldo!"

"Waldo!" Jimmy called, and the dog jumped back in the car.

"Give him to me." James reached back for his son. The boy clambered over to him. "Come on, my boy."

"Watch that shoulder," Alise warned. She was looking down.

"What?" James asked.

"I ruined my shoes." He couldn't see, but knew it must be bad for her to frown.

"I'll get you some more." She smiled at him, "Doozies My Girl!" He sounded so like his father. She suddenly missed him. He would know what to do. James Sr. would curse but he would know what to do.

"You!" She slapped Alfie in the back of the head, making Jimmy laugh as the head bounced back and forth. "Quit driving through cactus or I am going to beat you with your legs!" The dog jumped in, she climbed out and in the darkness they headed for the Stronghold.

If a droid could feel pain, she felt it. She knew she was close to her end. It might be time, but at least she could get them to safety. In the darkness, she saw them coming in the distance. With Alfie glowing, she was sure they would find them. Alejandro would have patrols out to bring people into the Stronghold. Then the horses were on them. She stopped pushing and stood waiting. They had lights. There was yelling and the dogs were snarling. Waldo jumped from the car and got between her and them. He paced, snarling and snapping. The men got closer. She estimated that it was another ten miles to the mountain range.

"It's us!" James yelled from the car. Lights hit him.

"Jaime!" Miguel and Antonio came running. "Where is Mija?" Antonio asked. The lights flashed in the car.

"They took her," James began to sob.

"Oh, man! Alfie! What happened to you?"

"I got into a fight," the droid sighed. "They took her from me." He sounded like he was crying too.

"Not without a fight for sure!" Miguel flashed the light down at the man. "They took your damn legs!"

"Well, they had to have something to beat me with," the droid noted.

"Shit!" Miguel looked to his brother in law. "What in the hell were they?"

"Look in the back." Alfie sniffled again.

"What?" Antonio jumped.

"My legs are in the back." Alfie nodded his head. "And my other arm. At least I hope so."

"It is," Alise sighed.

"Tostadora Más, you look rough!" Antonio noted flashing his light over her.

"Goodness!" She stood, fixing her hair.

"Leave it!" Miguel took her hand in his. "It's not bad."

"He meant where did they take Mija!" Antonio snapped.

"I don't know." James looked to Alfie.

The droid said nothing. He had an idea. but he wasn't sure. He shook his head. He had to think. Clear the clutter from his memory banks. The strangers were familiar and then again, they were different, but it was the same and not. He couldn't process it. It was impossible! He needed time to think.

"Let's get you to the Stronghold. The door will lock soon." Antonio moved to open the door.

"We will follow you." Alise stepped before him. "They are safer in there. Alfie is leaking fluids."

"Blast!" the droid yelled, looking down. "Jimmy, I might need one of your nappies!"

"Just drive!" Alise ordered. She walked to the back of the car and began to push. There were murmurs as she ran past them.

"That is one strong droid!" Antonio noted, mounting his horse.

"She's got a nice ass!" Miguel teased.

All that was in Alise's mind was Alejandro. If she could get to him, it would all work out. She would leave them with him and he would care for them. She would then go back and find Maria. James and Jimmy were not complete without Maria. Alejandro would understand. They had an understanding. He would take care of them for her. He had promised. Then he would go and crush those creatures.

Creatures. That was what they were. They were humanoid, but not like any she had ever seen. In reality or on paper. She had helped on many projects. James Sr. had been designing a newer model at the time of his death. They were years before their time but even those were nowhere near what she had seen. These were very basic and very advanced. The construction was familiar, but they had been tweaked quite a bit. Whoever was behind this was a genius or a lunatic. The latter fit her ideas.

The large gate was open. Many armed men stood ready to shoot and defend. The car rolled through the gate and then she was directed to take it farther. To the old church. People were running, many in a hurried panic as wagons were loaded with personal belongings to be taken farther into the Stronghold. Many newcomers were being hustled along dark paths through the orchards. But he stood there waiting. Alejandro Manuel Vargas stood in the doorway of the church waiting. Alise let go and ran to him. She fell into his arms.

"Tostadora Más!" He held her.

"I tried!" she cried.

"What?" He looked into her face.

"To save them all." The lights went out and she went limp in his arms.

~

She came on and there was a buzzing. James Sr. always told her it was her headache. Too much stress. She thought for a moment that he was there with her, but she didn't hear his voice among the others. She blinked and her focus improved. The ceiling was beautiful. Angels were flying around the Baby Jesus. It was peaceful, this image of heaven. Jimmy whimpered, and she sat up, holding her hands out. He was instantly given to her and his little chubby arms went around her neck.

"Na Na!" he whimpered, as he hugged her.

"Two hundred miles in the dark, under attack and she brings him to us with a clean diaper." Olivia patted her head. "Such a wonderful woman!" Her eye flickered. She closed them and held the baby. James? Jimmy?

"How is James?" she asked.

"Fine," he called from the other side of the room.

She looked to find him, Miguel, Julio, Ernesto and Stephano putting Alfie back together. Or at least trying. He was lying on the table smiling at her. The men were trying, but she could tell they were getting frustrated. Alfie was designed to be that way. James McMillan the first had called him a walking anomaly. Years ahead of his time. She kissed the baby and handed him off to his grandmother.

"Should you not rest?" the woman asked.

"I just did." Alise looked down at her ruined shoes and sighed. She would definitely need a new pair. That was for later. For now, her family needed her.

"I just can't get...Alfie will you stop that!" She moved closer to see the droid drinking soda from a straw and sending the liquid shooting from his abdomen, to the laughter of the children nearby. For being in pieces, he was in a great mood.

"Yes, James," he laughed. James glared at him. "It tickles!" Alfie did it again and James stepped back holding a wrench and waving it at the half droid.

"What are you doing?" Alise's voice made the man jump.

"MUM!" James hugged her.

"James! What's wrong?"

"I thought you were toast!"

"No, just a bit worn." She hugged him. "Why are you so mad at Alfie?"

"He is being a brat!" With that, the droid sat up on the cart he was on and nodded to the boys. They pushed the cart around the room laughing as he sat, making sounds like a fire engine. The adults moved as the cart sped up and down the church aisle.

"They put the microwave on a cart?" her eye flickered brightly. James kissed her.

"It's good to have you back." He leaned against her. "And that was the only way to move him. Alejandro thought of it." She turned to look at Alejandro.

"It works!" Alejandro shrugged as the droid sped past them. Alfie was all for being comic relief. The boys spun him about and he squealed, making the young boys laugh.

"I can't get them back on. It looks like the socket is torn." James looked flustered holding up the wrecked leg.

"It must have hurt!" Stephano noted, watching the droid spinning.

"He wouldn't have felt it," Alise sighed. "He was too hopped up on adrenaline!" She reached out and grabbed the cart, making it stop instantly. Alfie continued to spin.

"Whoa!" He spun right off the cart.

"Idiot!" Alise growled, as the men hurried to pick him up. "Let me see what I can do. When will they close the gate?" She turned to Alejandro.

"An hour." He looked grim.

"I'll do what I can in an hour."

"Why an hour?" James sounded panicked.

"I have to leave before it closes."

"To go where?" Alfie asked quickly.

"To get Maria," she snarled

"You can't go, Mum." James stepped up next to her. "There are men that are going. We need you here."

"I said I would bring her!" Alise's eye flickered.

"Mum, I wanted to go too. But they need a doctor here and I need you. You and Alfie. We don't even know where to look. The men are going to gather information and then we will have an idea of what to do."

"She could die." Alise's eye flickered faster.

"She could be dead now. If you and I leave, many more will die. We can't. I can't. I took an oath." He looked around. "Mum, you know that this is just the beginning."

"The beginning of the end?" She asked looking to Alejandro, as if to ask if this was what he had seen in his dreams. Was this the beginning of the end of mankind?

"That I don't know my little Tostadora Más. But for now we need you here." He set a hand on his grandson's head. "He needs you." She nodded looking at the leg she held. She set the leg down and walked out into the night.

Maria. She needed to find Maria and bring her back to the Stronghold, but to do that she would have to leave. They did not want her to leave. They wanted her to stay. To help. There would be wounded. There would be many. James needed her and so did Jimmy. Jimmy. Should she leave and bring his mother back, or stay and keep him safe? James had taken an oath. But so had she. The day he was laid in her arms, she swore to look after him. And the same on the day little Jimmy was born. But she had promised to bring them all home safe! She muddled over the thoughts and images, only confusing herself.

It was now almost dawn. How long had she been down? There were fewer people now. Most had been moved back into the midst of the Stronghold or the caves. She walked about trying to figure out what she had seen and what had happened. Replaying it all and saving it for future reference. Maria. Her image kept coming to her mind. Her being taken. They weren't spacemen and they weren't what she had thought they were…things! She kicked at the dirt and spun about. Alfie. She would need Alfie.

She hurried back to find the men once again, trying to figure out how to put his legs back on. These men were hopeless and Alfie was no help. She stood assessing the problem. Well, that was easy. Alfie was the problem! She was still waking up. Things were still out of focus. She looked at the wall and found her focus. The words written in Spanish. 'One will be born of a divided nation. One who bring men to their knees. One who will unite us all.' The words swam before her and then became still. Alise stepped up moving the men as she did. Alfie was hooting at them.

"If you don't behave, I will put them on backwards," she warned, snatching the leg from James. "Then you can kick your own ass!"

ADAM

The First

"The baby?" Linda asked as Maria stood slowly. She whimpered as she tried to stand up straight. No, she would have to walk bent.

"No, he's fine. I think my ass is broken." She carefully walked to the bathroom, leaning on the wall as she walked. Each time she touched the wall, he got a reading.

Heart beat steady, breathing ragged, pulse a little high. Adam watched her and glared. He was still angry. For three days he had kept his distance. He was still too angry. Maria had betrayed him. The woman milked her and it was brought to him, but it was not the same. He needed her. This was something he did not understand. The need of a human.

This was the first time she had even moved without help. The humans were indeed very fragile. Something he had forgotten. Now he saw the baby. It was bigger and the heart was beating well. She was a strong one. And brave. Through the beating, she had protected it. At least he had not struck her in the stomach region. He had wanted to. To kill the child. He knew it would hurt her more than the beating she had taken. But it was his child. She turned, and he saw the strap marks across the breasts. He frowned. It was like a constant reminder to see her like this.

"Is it well?" Blue Boy asked from behind him.

"Yes. It is."

"Will it obey now?"

"I think so." He turned to glare. "I think it now knows."

"I would think so." Adam watched Blue Boy leave. He looked back at Maria. She sat slowly and brushed her hair. It was coming out of her head. He had pulled it pretty hard. She wasn't wearing clothing, just a light robe. It now slid off her shoulder and the bloody whelps made him feel something he was unsure of. It had bothered him to listen to her whimper and cry as she was cared for. It should not have. She was inferior to Adam. And she had betrayed him. She deserved the punishment he had delivered on her. And still, he wanted to hold her. To comfort her. But he could not go to her. He would not.

"My step daddy beat my ass one time so bad I couldn't sit for a month," Mom noted, coming to Maria with a steaming cup. "Chicken soup will cure all."

"Thank you." Maria took the cup, but could barely hold it.

"You have to keep your strength up., Mom noted, "For the baby." Maria nodded but simply held the cup. Linda took the brush and gently began to brush her hair.

"It'll be okay. Maria, it's got to get better."

Maria nodded, but still didn't move. The tears slid down her face slowly. She had been crying for a long time, almost non-stop. Adam had enough. He went to her.

"Leave," he ordered. The companions scrambled out the door, dragging the children after them. He didn't look at Maria but paced around the room. There were four guards there. He stopped to look at each one. "Leave," he ordered, and they walked out into the hall. Maria was shaking. The cup in her hand was moving rather fast then. He stepped forward and took it from her. He held it clumsily and set it on the nightstand.

The glare. Those black eyes shot through him. He frowned and stepped back from her as she held her robe shut. She acted as if he might try to rip it off her. She looked so angry! He walked around the room, trying to think of what to say. There really wasn't anything. She had been disobedient and so he had to teach her. That was his job. He looked around the room. It was clean, but there was a smell. Metal. He closed his eyes and realized it was the blood. He walked to the corner where a basket sat. The bedding was there. He kicked at the basket, then turned to find her trying to stand.

"Don't!" he ordered and she fell forward to her knees. He lifted her up and she whimpered softly.

"Don't touch me," she begged softly.

"I don't want you crawling around on the floor." He held her away from him. "Where were you going?"

"To the shower." She simply went limp in his arms.

"Why?"

"So you won't beat me." He stood holding her and trying to process it all. He lifted her into his arms and she cried out, "Don't!" He laid her on the bed and she moaned in pain. "Please! Leave me alone! I'll give you my milk and I'll carry your child, but just don't touch me anymore."

"Ever?" he asked horrified by the thought. He was getting stronger each day. It had slowed with the feeding being in a glass, but he needed her. She couldn't stop

"Go away!" She rolled on her side and hugged a pillow.

He watched her shoulders shake as she cried into the pillow. He began to pace again. Why was she doing this? He walked to the kitchen and stood thinking. Why? He thought back to his study of their entertainment. Men often hurt the women and they cried. The med did things to make amends. They brought flower, candy, gifts... he had done that and she was still denying him. He knocked all the dishes to the floor and spun around. She was fighting to sit up and turned to watch him. She looked terrified and held the pillow before her. He was trying to stop the rage building in him.

Why? Why did she do this to him? He kicked the chair and stepped up to her. She was crying harder and backing up in the bed. He fought to speak clearly.

"I forgive you." He said it slowly. Her expression went from terror to rage.

"You beat me and now you forgive me?" She threw the pillow at him. "I could kill you for this and you forgive me? Leave!" She pointed to the door. "And don't come back! Go buy a fucking cow for your damn milk!" He moved towards her and she crawled from the bed and tried to make it to the shower.

"NO!" He held her gently but firmly. "You will forgive me!" He shook her and she closed her eyes.

"Never!" She spat in his face. He dropped her into the bed and ran his hand across his face wiping the saliva from it in curious rage.

"I will never forgive you!" Maria spoke slowly and clearly.

"Then you will be replaced." He turned and walked from her. In the doorway he stopped. "I will find your son. I will find him and I will kill him!" He spoke as slowly and clearly as she had. "And when we take that one out of you, I will watch you die as the others have!" He walked on and the door shut.

Maria sat up slowly and prayed for strength. Strength to live long enough to kill him.

~

He paced. Two weeks. For two weeks, he had not laid next to her, held her, touched her or tasted her. The milk was still brought to him, but it was not the same. He wanted her. He walked to the edge and looked down at the people moving below. He did miss her. He missed her terribly. Not just the sexual relationship, but also the talks. Learning what it was like to be human. The way to laugh, to smile and to feel without the touch of his body. Feeling inside. The new discoveries about himself. And her laugh. He missed the way her hair felt in his hands as he held her head to kiss her and the way she tasted below. Taste. Something she had taught him to appreciate. The milk was good, but not as good as that. He liked to feel her and hear her. He missed her.

He stepped to the very edge and wondered. If he fell, would he survive? Was he now human enough? Would it hurt? Nothing really hurt him except the feeling in the pit of his stomach. His empty stomach. He wasn't eating now. He didn't need it to sustain life, but he enjoyed eating meals with her. Now he was lonely. Lonely for her. He had hurt her, he had frightened her, and then he had made her hate him. He leaned forward again. He was God.

Their entertainment kept him company. Archive gave him full access. He watched the stories of lost love and forgiveness. He wanted that. He wanted to go to her and beg, but Gods did not beg. She wouldn't forgive him. She couldn't. He had seen in the films that this happened and the female would kill the man. Shoot him, drive over him, poison him and even beat him. He wished she would do that to him. Beat him and make him feel better. Two weeks. He began to pace and wondered what to do to make her forgive him. He had sent candy, flowers and gifts just as the men in the entertainment. Nothing. In the movies men gave of themselves. They sacrificed for their love. What could he give of himself to make her forgive him? Then it hit him. He hurried down to her room.

The door opened and she was moving. Each time he came into the room, she ran to the shower and was soaking wet before he could do anything. This time he was ready. He moved quickly and caught her in his arms. He held her, kicking and screaming, off the ground. The children ran to Linda and her mother. He looked about and the guards were still. He was trying to form a plan when his hand found it. The bulge. It was bigger. He held her and it. The world was spinning. He had a feeling of need that was overpowering, and puzzling. He carried her from the room. Blue Boy stepped in and barked orders.

"I have something to show you." Adam carried her down. Maria was crying and kicking, but not begging. She was fighting mad and he found it stimulating. Sexually, and even entertaining. She was no match for him and yet, she fought.

The room was like all the others. Empty. Mist-lined floors and walls hid all from the eye. He set her down as the door shut. She stood waiting with her hands over the bulge. Protecting it. He walked to the wall and through the mist. She stood unsure of what to do. She was down on a lower floor. If they were on the bottom, there was an open door. Linda had told her. She could jump out and pray for a safe landing. But the door did not open. She had no choice but to follow Adam. She stepped through the mist. She saw a control panel of some sort. Adam was sitting in a chair waiting for her. She moved closer, and he reached down and touched a crystal disc like object. The wall lit up. Old movies. He touched another, and she could see the people below the ship. He took a crystal disc and held it out to her.

Slowly, she stepped closer and took it. It wasn't glass, or crystal, but something else. It was light, almost weightless, but it didn't bend. She gazed at it. Memories. It looked like an old silver dollar with a hole in the middle. She thought back to her childhood memories. It was a miniature record. She had seen the old music in the museum. The music was stored on them. Now obsolete with all the electronics. It was quite pretty, though. A clear translucent colored disc that in the light turned green and blue and red.

"What is it?" she asked softly in awe of it.

"A memory." He smiled at her. "Well, it will be." He took it from her and set it in a slot on the control panel. "What do you want?"

"What do you mean?" He shot her an amused look. She was moving closer to him.

"This is Archive." She looked up at the control panel that went up and up, into the mist. So this was what was controlling it all? It looked like an old computer. A big computer, but an old one nonetheless. Not at all impressive. But it made her hopeful.

This was manmade. This was not engineered in outer space, or from God, this was manmade! It was built by man and could therefore be destroyed by man!

"What do you want?" Adam asked breaking into her thoughts.

"I don't understand?" Maria asked as she moved even closer. He moved his seat back and pulled her gently into his lap. She let him. He felt her stiffen and then he heard the slight gasp as she settled into his lap. He smelled her hair and closed his eyes for a second. He was hopeful.

"This is a data disc. Anything you want to know, I will put on it for you."

"And?" She turned to look at him.

"And whenever you want, you can come here and look at it."

"No more free reign of Archive for me?"

"No." He traced the line of her face with his finger, pushing her hair back behind her ear. "Only with me." The bruises on her face had faded. Only a slight scar remained across her cheek and on her lip.

"So you can monitor me?" her tone was cold.

"Yes."

She sighed, and looked up at the machine. Manmade. Had there been a warranty card filed on this beast? The thought was amusing and terrifying. Someone had made this and it had been sent into the stars and returned to destroy its creator. Irony in its greatest form.

"How much will one of those little things hold?"

"As much as you want." He slid his arm around her waist.

"Everything," she spoke slowly. "I want all of it."

"All of it?"

"From the beginning to now. I want it all." She turned to look into his eyes. They spun and stopped. Almost human and then not. The eyes. They would never evolve enough. They would always be kaleidoscope. But hers were evolving. She was getting better at hiding her fear and disgust of him. She had to in order to survive.

He nodded and hit some buttons. The little disk spun and sparked. The lights floated on the mist as if shining through a crystal. He watched her face as the lights sparkled in her eyes. He felt the truth in her face. She was truly beautiful and she belonged here.

"Forgive me?" he asked softly. She stared off into nothing. The cold look on her face hurt.

"You killed my son." she mumbled as the tears flowed again.

"NO. I did not!" He hugged her tightly. "I lied." She bit down on her lip as it quivered.

"I did not find him. I looked. Maria, I searched even the remains of the dead for him. I could not find him." She began to sob. Jimmy was safe. He was in the Stronghold.

"I will keep looking." He kissed her temple. "Please forgive me? I don't know why I said that. I don't know why I hurt you."

"What are you?" she asked.

"I am Adam." She stood up and stepped away from him. "The James' made what made me." Adam explained as he sat gazing at him. "I am the Son of God. Made in his image. The King James." He spoke softly and the screen lit up with a picture of James Fielding. "I am the Alpha and you, the Omega." He reached out and set his hands on her hips, pulling her closer. "He is the completion." He bent to kiss her belly. "We are the beginning."

Maria did not know what to say. She was shaking and terrified, but she couldn't run anymore. He hugged her and she set her hands on his head. If she had a knife she could have thrust it into the back of his neck, but now she could only run her hands through his fake hair. She watched the disc spin and then it stopped. He sat up and lifted it from the console. He held it out to her. Should she take it?

"This is all that I am," he almost whispered. "I give it to you for safe keeping." It was like a shining toy. She was afraid to touch it. "Take it and forgive me? Do not hate me anymore? Let me touch you again?"

She took it and gazed down at it. All that he was? All the information she needed, and no way to access it without him. She tugged at the string on her shirt. It was just ornamental. She pulled it off and looped it through the disk, then tied it around her neck. The disk fell just above her breasts. Just below the crucifix. It seemed an act of blasphemy to have it hanging below her cross. He pulled her to him and she stood rigid in his arms. He was shaking! She set her hands on his chest and steadied herself.

She was still weak. The scars were hardened now, they had become a suit of armor against him. Her heart had also hardened. Now she was running on the treadmill daily. She was going to be ready at any moment that came open. Linda was the same. They were ready to run for their lives and the lives of their children. Maria was weak, but the weakness faded with the rage, anger and hate.

Maria knew right then that one day she would kill him. It wouldn't bother her in the least. He was not human. It would be simply like turning off the kitchen light. No, the TV.

"Let me?" he begged, holding her closer and nuzzling his face into her chest. "Please?"

"Adam…"

"I need you." He sounded so distressed that it actually made her feel better that he was suffering. More human and able to hurt. She started to step back but he held her. "Please! Forgive me! Whip me! I will let you!"

He stood and yanked at the belt, which sent her spinning away from him. Not again! She ran into the mist but he was behind her. He would not hit her again! Blindly she ran and finally hit a real wall that sent her flying back to the floor. Frantically she got to her feet and touching the wall, she ran. The mist was blinding and heavy, making it difficult to breathe. It was as if a humidifier had gone into overdrive. The air was so wet she was sure she was drowning! She looked up and stopped in horror in front of a tube.

From where she stood it looked as if it were nothing but a brain. She stepped closer to the horizontal tube and saw that it really was a brain. A human brain! She could see that it was still in the skull cavity of its owner. He was lying on his back, his hands folded across his chest looking very peaceful, save the fact that the top of his head was gone and there were wires coming out of it. For being well over a hundred and eighty-eight years old, James Fielding looked very well preserved. She followed the wires that left the tube and traveled into the mist with her eyes. What else was in there? How was this possible?

"What in the hell are you?" she asked softly, laying a hand on the glass tubing. The body opened his eyes and the fierce glare made her jump and scream, "Oh, God!" She backed up and right into Adam's arms. Maria buried her head in his chest, shaking harder than she ever had in her life.

"Yes." Adam replied simply. "It is him."

~

It was dark. Maria winced as Adam suckled hard on her breast. She was shaking and he thought it was sexual anticipation. But it was fear, fear that if he wasn't with her, she would be the next to spend eternity in a test tube.

He had hustled her out of the room and up to the roof where she had fallen to her knees, gulping in the air as someone who had almost drowned. He stood waiting.

"Now may I?" he asked calmly. She couldn't answer. Her mind was leaving her. She was going insane! She could only nod, and he knelt down to help her stand.

He guided her to the bed that was there. Candles were lit on the table where food was waiting. There were more candles around the bed. How had they done this? The roof opening was small, but then there might have been other entrances to the roof. He helped her sit and tugged at her clothes. She shook as he undressed her and eased her gently back into the bed. He undressed himself and moved to suckle. It was dark enough to hide them from prying eyes, but still light enough to see the guards standing at the edge. She would never be alone again.

His hand moved savagely between her legs and she cried out. He eased up in his pursuit of nutrition and moved to have his meal below.

The whole time she was thinking of how to kill him. How she would escape. If she hadn't been with child, she would have thrown herself off the edge, but had a feeling that was what the guards were for. Her body responded to Adam and she heard him sigh in satisfaction. He mounted her then.

He had no breath. He had had no heartbeat until she had pointed it out. He had been undeveloped, and now he was fully male. There was hair on his chest. The hair on his head was more real, and thicker. What was he? He did not sweat, relieve himself or sleep.

She tried to piece it all together in hopes that keeping her mind busy would keep it from noticing that once again, she was being raped by God knows what! He thrust harder, and she gasped, then he eased up. He wanted her full attention. He wanted all of her. He leaned down to kiss her chest and neck. He rode her hard and long with the passion of a man denied for years, and not weeks.

His hands caressed the small mound. She wanted to push him away. To keep him away from her child. To take his hands off her and the child she carried. James' child. It was then she knew that she had to get away soon. By the end of the second trimester, features could be seen in an ultrasound. She was now in her fifth month. Soon he would know, and then he would kill her and the child.

Her back ached. The scabs were being torn from her back and with each twinge of pain she knew one thing: she was human. She was human and she was alive. She knew who he was, where he had come from and what he was did not matter anymore. He was made of man, and he would die at the hand of a woman.

Maria held tightly to the bedding, fighting the urge to strike him. He thrust deeper and she cried out. In the darkness she saw his teeth as he smiled in delight that he had hurt her. Her stomach turned. He had the ego of a human. Dominance was his weapon over her.

"Take me!" he ordered sitting back from her. He set his hands on his hips. "Seduce me!" She started to shake her head but had no time. He reached out, grabbed her hair and pulled her up to him. "Damn you! Seduce me!"

They taste of him made her gag. He held her head to him and moaned loudly, throwing his own head back like some animal howling up into the night skies. She fought for breath and kicked beneath him. He finally tilted her head back and gazed down at her. He was caressing her face and touching her hair. If he was a God, then this was her hell.

She was able to move back and relax her mouth a bit. Taking the tip only in her mouth. she licked and reached up to rub. If she thought she could, she would have bitten it off! His eyes flashed blue in the night and she knew he was a demon.

"Look at me!" he ordered tilting her face up. "Look up at me!" She raised her eyes to lock on his. "Yes!" he brushed her hair back from her face, "This is how you are to always remember me!" His eyes were burning into her like lasers, but she could not tear them away. She wanted to be sure that he would remember her. Especially since one day, she would kill him! "More!" he ordered, pulling her head into him again.

It went on for a long time. She thought several times she would choke or suffocate! He was not slowing down or easing up. Her back hurt, she was in an awkward position and she was pissed. She pushed him hard and he fell back on the bed. Now she was on him. At first he reached to grab her, but she dodged his hands and quickly mounted him. He gasped loudly as she rode him. She would bring him to a point and then stop. He would reach for her and she would move off him. He would relent and she would start again. The sky was getting light as she finally let him go. Exhausted she fell into the bed. He kissed her repeatedly, but she only closed her eyes and slept.

The food was cold, but she was hungry. Wrapped in a sheet, she eased her aching body into the chair and ate while he walked about, as if he was God. Naked, he covered the entire area of the ship, strutting proudly. Maria was taking it all in. The size of it. Watching him walk, she calculated it was at least 400,000 square feet, about the size of four city blocks and about as tall. A perfect square. Maria ate and planned. The wine was bitter and burned her raw throat, but she was alive. Alive, and she was planning and calculating. She watched the sun come up for the first time in five months and felt as if she were being reborn. She ate and she planned.

Adam walked along the roof smiling. She was his again. She had done his bidding and now he was happy. He had forgiven her, she had forgiven him and she was now obedient and loving. This was all that mattered. The bright lights in the sky always amused him. Light or dark did not matter to the droids. Their sensors could only see the heat from a body. They could not see color or feel. But Adam could and now he stood, letting the heat of the coming dawn pour over him. It was good to be God.

He turned and watched Maria stand and walk about, gathering her clothing. She was holding that cloth over her. Modesty they called it. He liked that in her. He walked to her as she bent to retrieve something. Her ass was round and plump. Once more would not hurt. Once more to show her that he was kind and gentle. He lifted her up and carried her to the bed. She was trying to get away and dropping things. Talking of needing to dress to distract him. He would not fall for that again. He set her on the bed and pushed her into it face down.

"NO!" she tried to fight.

"Once more." He kissed her shoulder and entered her slowly and gently. He watched her hands clench down on the bedding. Her back moved up and down as she breathed deeply. "I won't hurt you," he whispered, moving slowly to her.

Contusions. Her back was covered with them. They were fading, but he could still see the depth of them. He kissed them. His mark on her. He let his hand travel over them as if tracing them. There was blood. He leaned in to lick it off her with his kisses. He moved down to kiss the ones on her round ass and almost lost their union. He moved back to her slowly and gently. She was panting into the bed and then he felt her sudden movement and the explosion of her.

"Tell me!" he ordered into her ear. "Tell me! But only if you mean it!" He kissed her shoulder and looked at her exhausted face. "Tell me!"

"I love you," she mumbled. "Adam, I love you,"

He smiled and pushed the hair back to kiss her cheek. Right on that dimple. He gathered her into his arms and carried her back to her room.

No one was there. They were alone. She was barely conscious. Drowsily, her head fell against his shoulder. She smelled of sweat and of him. He breathed deeply. He laid her in the bed, moved next to her and fed. She did not resist.

~

The wind picked up. Maria was sitting on top of Genesis enjoying a peanut butter and jelly sandwich, with Adam lying with his head in her lap. She was playing with his hair as she watched the gathering clouds. He opened his mouth and she playfully teased him with her sandwich. The guards were where they always were. On the edge. One about every hundred feet. She had learned to look as if she didn't notice them. But she did. How many and where they were. Adam reached up and pulled her down for a kiss.

They had been spending a lot of time up here. Alone, sort of. She was once again playful and attentive. He had the meals brought up in the good weather and they ate here. Different wonderful things that the humans ate on picnics. The blanket was spread, the basket brought up and she set it up for him. He would lie with her and let her feed him. They would play with toys, balls and Frisbees, but those flew off the edge and more than once, he had lost a droid as it dove to stop the disc. Maria would scream and he would peer over the edge and sigh. Why she got upset was a mystery. There were plenty of them. Then he would feed from her and lay her down beneath him. Sometimes they did not have sexual relations, just long conversations.

Now she spoke of her childhood. Friends, pets, brothers, and things she had never shared with him. He would listen and watch her eyes dance. Now she looked him in the eyes all the time. She would laugh when his eyes spun and he would at times make them spin at crazy speeds, just to make her laugh. Then she would kiss him. Long lingering kisses that made him want her. He would hold the child and feel the movement of it in her.

She explained about the birthing. How the child would expel itself when the time was right and that only the child would know when that time was. She told him about how her body was changing and what to expect. How it would stretch, and grow, and then shrink back after the child's arrival. How it would be the child who would feed first. That had upset Adam, but she told him that if he wanted his son strong, he must allow the baby to feed. She promised to save some milk for him. This made him smile. She would not forget him. She told him how the baby would be very fragile. Much more so than she was until the baby was a man, and that Adam must be careful. He didn't understand, but agreed to be. He would agree to anything for her.

"But I need your milk," he mumbled, nuzzling into her blouse.

"Adam!" She giggled, as he tickled her. He looked down at her beneath him, bright and smiling with her hair fanned out beneath her. Her face now a deep brown from time in the sun. Healthy. She was healthy. The scars were nothing more than raised parts of her skin. There were no more blood or scabs. In bed, he would lie behind her. He would run his hand down to her ass and cup it in his hands. She would wake and tell him to go to sleep. She needed sleep.

"I have to have it," he whispered leaning down to kiss her.

"Why?" Her curious look was attractive to him.

"I was not ready when we found you." He moved to lie next to her and propped himself up to gaze at her. "It is because of your milk I developed ahead of schedule."

"Ahead of schedule?" She frowned at him and began to play with the collar of his shirt.

"Yes, I am way ahead of schedule." He kissed her again. "We didn't expect to find you so soon."

"Me? You were looking for me?" His eyes flashed quickly and then it was gone. She knew he had let something slip that he had not wanted to.

"Of course. You complete me. I knew it the moment I laid eyes on you." He was lying. She felt her skin go cold. She smiled at him slightly.

"I love you, Adam." She sat up to kiss him. He opened her shirt and fed. Her mind was spinning. He had found her. They had been hunting her. Why? His head moved to suckle more and his hand to pull at her pants. She didn't want this. She didn't want him, but she could not deny him. She moved to assist him in undressing her and lay staring up at the sky and praying to the true God to save her, save her child and save her soul.

"What is that?" he sat up suddenly at the rumbling.

"Thunder." She took the opportunity to get her pants up. "It's going to rain." He didn't object but stood and looked about. Lightening flashed in the distance.

"How long until it comes?"

"An hour maybe?" She gathered the remains of the picnic and tossed it into the basket.

"I have a meeting." He frowned.

"Where?" She moved to hug him. He held her against him and kissed her head.

"Down there. I might have to wait." He looked at the sky again.

"How long will it take?"

"A few moments." He looked conflicted. "Men wish to ask things of me. I must say yes or no. That is all." He was leaving the ship? It must then be closer to the ground! She looked up to the darkening sky.

"You could go. It's moving that way. See how the clouds are traveling that way? Go and come right back." She kissed him tenderly. "I will be waiting in our bed for you. Promise you'll come back to me?" He looked down at her eyes and smiled.

"I promise." He kissed her. "I will go. I will come back and I will have you all night long." She smiled shyly and gathered the basket.

"I am going to take a nice long shower and be dry and ready for you." She looked down at the basket. "After I give this to Linda."

"You will be waiting?" He held her close. "For me?"

"Yes." She kissed him and he let her go.

One droid followed her. Always one. She never questioned or resisted. It was always there. She wasn't sure if it was the same one, it was but always one. The droid only left when Adam entered the room and would return immediately after. She wouldn't sleep well with the droid there. He frightened her. Now he followed. Down into the ship. She stepped off the elevator and he stepped out also, blocking the left side. The open door. She continued to her right. To Linda's.

Maria had a plan. She always had a plan. It changed from moment to moment but it was always the same. Escape! She walked to the kitchen and leaned in. Mom was at the stove. Linda and the boys were playing a card game at the table. They all looked surprised to see her. Or maybe ready. She hoped ready. Linda and she had talked. They had to be ready at a moment's notice. That moment was now. Maria's heart was racing. She had to remain calm. She had to keep her mind clear.

"Well, don't you look lively?" Mom asked. She knew that Maria was Adam's sex toy and disagreed with it. It was something she could not accept. Maria understood this, yet she felt deep shame around the woman.

"Yes, well..," Maria winked at Linda with a big smile. Not once, but three times. Linda set her cards down. "I brought the basket back. It was wonderful. There's still stuff in there. It's going to rain. I thought the kids might like it? Hate for it to go to waste. I am going to take a shower. Adam is off to a meeting down there and I need to be ready when he returns."

Linda nodded. And looked at her mother. She winked three times. The older woman was up and moving, making a fuss over the boys playing poker and gambling too much. Mike was ready. He grabbed the younger boys, and shoved them roughly towards the few toys they had. They whined about having to clean up. Mike, man of the family, put himself between the droid and his younger brothers. If this failed he was to get them out of the Genesis, no matter what.

"I'll be up to get your other dishes." Linda took the basket from Maria. Their hands touched. Maria was shaking. It was time. Linda's heart began to race.

"Don't worry. I'll bring them. I need company until he returns." Maria laughed nervously.

"Who returns?" Adam asked, grabbing her and pulling her into his arms.

"YOU!" She laughed kissing him.

"I am going to have more droids watch you." He kissed her.

"Why?" Maria's mind raced. No. No, he couldn't! It would ruin her plans! "Am I in danger? Is the baby?"

"I don't think so, but the humans are not able to relent. They argue."

"Then take all the droids but mine." She stepped closer to her guard. "I don't want you hurt! Adam, I am safe here! Archive won't let them in. But you can't go alone or without enough droids to protect you. Please!" She hurried to hug him. "Don't let them hurt you! I can't lose you!" She forced herself to sob. His arms encircled her.

"All right. I will do as you ask. Go on to your room. I will return shortly. Before the rain." He kissed her and she smiled at him sweetly fighting the urge to jump for joy and gag at the same time.

"I love you!" She hugged him telling herself to remain calm.

"And I love you." It was difficult for him to say, but he got it out. "I will return."

Maria watched them leave from the kitchen doorway. The stairs appeared and Adam and his small army of droids simply stepped down. She sighed and looked to her guard. They were the only ones in the hallway. She looked to Linda and nodded. Linda moved to the sink. The guard stood waiting, facing Maria. Then Linda poured the entire contents of a large pitcher over him. Mom hit him over the head with her skillet with a resounding 'clunk'. The guard jumped and danced. Maria got behind him and poked him several times before the little door opened. She pushed and he shut down.

"Let's go!" Maria ordered. Mike handed her the messenger bag. She had given it to him in front of Adam weeks before, stating that she didn't need it anymore. The boy had taken it to keep safe for her. Now she slung it over her neck. "Grab him!" she ordered, pointing to the droid.

Between the six of them, they were able to carry him. The guard was not very heavy. They approached the door with him and the stairs appeared. Maria was the first. They would not kill her. At least she hoped not. They ran down the stairs, hit the ground, dropped the disengaged droid and sped into the night. Past the houses and then along the street. Maria dug into her bag and found the flashlight. She shone it up at the street signs. They were close to the university. She knew where she was. She ran and they followed. They were free!

ALFIE

Artificial Life Form

"The baby?" He asked looking over at Alise. She had perked up and stood ready to spring.

"He's fine." They were working on the cabin.

James and Roberto were making it bigger with the help of Stephano and Miguel. They had added two rooms and a sun porch. Maria liked the sun. All acted as if she might return at any moment. Alfie knew she was not coming but said nothing. It had been months. He knew and he could not tell. Now he held the beam steady as the men moved the rafter into place. He yawned to tease Miguel and the man laughed. Alfie was always teasing now. He was accepted and had found his niche. Class clown.

The children adored him. He would talk to them, tell them about their history and play with them. When they came to see James, he was now the one who calmed them. He had evolved with the situation. He become a big kid joking and keeping it light, the fact that they, human, were now on the endangered species list.

James had been watching him closely. Alfie was sure he was afraid that the droid was having a meltdown. He was just opening up. Becoming how he had been in the beginning. He had to. He had to go back to go forward. To save her. To save them all. Alise knew something was up. She had tried twice to get him to tell her and he had asked her to wait. Wait until he was sure.

After four months, he was sure. He sat her down and told her. Her eye flickered the entire time. He was unsure if she could handle it but she nodded when he finished. The eye was flickering and he was tempted to smack her upside the head. It wouldn't stop the eye, but it might make her laugh. Then again, she might just knock his entire head off. She had threatened to many times. He laid out his plan and she frowned. She shook her head. They had to tell someone. He told her he would but he needed her. She nodded and agreed.

She had not had sexual relations since the death of James Sr. This felt similar to that and it bothered her but she sat still and allowed Alife to touch her. He kept apologizing until she told him to just get it done. There was a danger in this. She was not as efficient as he was. She was built two generations later. His mind was different from hers. She sat back and waited. He settled himself down and plugged into her receptor. He hated that is was located below her left breast. A joke no doubt from James Sr.

"The best way to a woman's brain is through her heart," he had always said.

Alfie hated the intrusion, but had no choice. He let it go and she accepted. Her eye flickered at an alarming speed, then slowed. She shut down and he unplugged and redressed her. He left her, calling to Waldo and walked slowly through the Stronghold, whistling and waving to people. The children ran to him. They all had to pet Waldo. Alfie moved through the small orchard to the house of Alejandro and knocked. Himself opened the door.

"We must speak," was all he said. The man allowed him to enter. They walked through the house and out to the back patio where they sat.

"What is it?" Alejandro asked politely.

"I must leave. Maria is alive and I must bring her here." Alejandro nodded.

"We all hope that she is…"

"She is." Alfie tilted his head slightly. "Do you know when I was made? When I first became?" The man looked him over and shook his head. "One hundred and sixty seven years ago." He sat back proudly. Alejandro whistled at the words. "I know. I know more than I should and I know she is alive. I know what these invaders are. At least, I think I do and to defeat them I must get close enough to be sure. I must leave the Stronghold."

"You will go alone?"

"No, Waldo will go with me." The droid somehow thought it made sense to take the dog.

"How can you be sure?"

"I saw them the night I fought them," the droid replied.

"You told us they were not anything you had ever seen before." The eyebrow went up.

"They aren't, but there was something familiar. From long ago. It took time for me to straighten..," he sat thinking…"my thoughts. I had to be sure. I will not endanger any of you, but I know that she is alive. I have information. I must go now. If not it will be too late."

"Why?" Alejandro asked.

"She was with child." Alejandro sat back suddenly. "They will know soon and will dispose of her. I must rescue her and I will. I could not stop them then, but now I remember and I know."

"Where is all this information you have?"

"Up here." Alfie tapped his head. "And now in Alise. I would not risk it being lost. James will know how to access it when the time is right. I must go. Without them knowing. You must take me out of here."

Alejandro stood and paced about. He was not satisfied. The droid could be used by the outside to gain entry and destroy them all. He was a likable little fellow. Friendly, strong and helpful. But he could not risk the safety of the people over Alfie. He frowned and stood looking at Alfie. The droid tilted his head and smiled. He looked like a child. However, Maria was his child. And she was with child and.., he sighed heavily.

"When I return I will tell you all. Until then you must trust me." Trust an android? "And I have a favor to ask."

"You do?"

"Yes, can we talk of that on the way." He stood. "Now, could we go? I don't like traveling at night."

The truth was he didn't like being alone and he was scared of the dark. The droid took water and food for the dog and walked out of one of the many secret entrances to the Stronghold. He shook Alejandro's hand and simply stepped out. Waldo trotted along side him. They kept a steady pace. When the animal faltered, he carried it. During the day they kept a slower pace. The heat was not good for the dog. He catered to the animal. It was his only companion and although Waldo did not speak, he paid attention.

It was several days before they came to where it had all began. He looked over the area. No one had been here since then. At least he thought not, and then saw signs of the lost men who lived in the wilderness. Gypsies, marauders and others. It was easy to see. The many footprints. The road was now overgrown and dust and sand almost hid it. Not even five months and it was a wasteland. He didn't know what to expect but he had to see. The dog was sniffing about. He looked and saw something sticking out of the dirt. He picked it up and smiled.

"There you are!" he laughed, and tucked his thumb into his backpack. "Come on Waldo."

They walked. First to the warehouse. The outside was rough. He found the door ajar. He had hoped this would be left untouched. They walked down to the next level and the door was secure. Hidden behind the old truck. Waldo sniffed about. The dog sneezed. It was musty and the air thick. Not very good but livable. Alfie's sensors picked up the smells of men. They had tried to get in. But he saw that they had no luck. And getting in one door to find nothing was always discouraging. The truck however, had been stripped clean. He pushed the remains aside and opened the next door. He locked it from the inside, fumbled with the switch and the lights came on. He sighed in relief. They traveled lower.

They came to the third door and he opened it. No one had been there since that night. That was something he knew to be true. Everything was how he had left it the night the terror began. He walked about, taking an inventory. Later, they might need these things, and an accurate count would be needed. Why send a human when he was already there? He walked, counted, and tried to remember things as he counted. Things that long ago had been filed away for safekeeping with a prayer that the information would not be needed. That he was wrong. He had been wrong before. Once. He hoped this was the second time.

He stepped about the little car and laughed. James had hated it. Maria had bought it for her father. It was to be a gift. A muscle car from the last century. There had been an argument. It was something that was obsolete. No one drove those. They were in museums or traded among the wealthy. James had been livid. The damn thing used gasoline! The man had been livid. They were dangerous. All cars were electric. That was why the ozone was fucked! She bought it anyway and stored it. It might be of use. He looked at the key on the wall. Why not?

It started right up. Alfie sat playing with buttons. It had an ancient CD player. He remembered those. He sat looking at it. Not this one. Another. Smaller. He remembered putting it in a control panel and programming it. Getting all the bugs out, as James and the other argued. Alfie's brother sat beside him. They both watched as the men argued. His brother did nothing. Alfie liked to keep busy. He continued working. All because one did not agree. He finished and stood next to James the first.

"We are leaving!" The words echoed on. Alfie shut off the car, put the key back, finished his inventory and locked up. He and Waldo started for the city. For the house, and for the room behind the books.

~

"Hurry!" Maria was pulling Mom after her. "Only another mile or so."

"Mile?" The woman panted. It was pouring rain and they were all soaked. As long as it rained, they were safe. At least she hoped so. They had to keep moving. Linda was carrying Billy and making faces. Her arm must have been hurting. Mike had Joey on his back.

"We have to keep moving!" Maria ordered.

"They don't move in the rain!" Mom almost yelled in desperation.

"They don't but others do! Cockroaches!" Maria made her point. The woman nodded and they ran.

In the dark, it was hard to find what she was looking for. She didn't want to risk anyone seeing them. They were women and men were about. She had seen them from on top. They wandered. Adam had told her that there were many who terrorized his subjects and they were dealt with. She didn't want to run into them. They hurried through the streets, keeping as close to the buildings as she dared. Finally, they were close enough to their destination to breath easily. Through the courtyard, up the steps and to the door. Maria turned the knob and it opened. Her hand was the key. Alfie had developed that little invention. A fingerprint-reading doorknob. They fell into the house and shut the door. She locked it and slid down to the floor.

"It's light." Linda noted breathlessly. "It didn't look like it outside."

"What?" Maria saw that the windows had all been covered. "Who...?" Just then, the dog came running.

"Shit!" Mom reached for the frying pan she had been carrying the whole way.

"Waldo!" Maria hugged the dog to her. "James!" She ran through the house. "Jimmy! Alise! James! Alfie!"

The dog was behind her the whole way.

The house was the same as they had left it except for the fact that all the windows were covered and all the lights were on. Alfie. Only she knew he was afraid of the dark. It had to be. He and Alise had Jimmy here. She ran to the nursery and found it dark. The bed was empty. She sat down and wondered who was in the house. They had taken Waldo with them. Had he just returned home instead of the Stronghold? She hurried down the stairs and to Linda. Someone was in the house.

"We ain't alone," Linda spoke softly.

"I know," Maria was still trying to catch her breath, "We need to keep moving. There is a warehouse and I have a car there. It might run…"

"It does," Alfie spoke. They all screamed and jumped. Mom hit him on the head with the skillet. He only blinked.

"Madam! Please!"

"Alfie!" Maria dove in his arms. He held her to him tightly.

"I am so glad to see you!" he stated in a strangled voice. He stood back, holding her at arm's length to look her over. "Were you followed?"

"I don't know. They don't like the rain."

"I would think not. We must go. We must get to the warehouse. We will be safe there. Come on." He moved to the back of the house.

"We running again?" Mike moaned, carrying his half asleep little brother.

"No, riding." Alfie opened the door to the garage and there sat a large trailer with sides. The inside was lined with the space blankets to absorb body heat. "Everyone in. No time to argue."

They didn't argue but clamored in. He covered them with more of the blankets and winked at them. Maria climbed out and hugged him. He held her in his arms as she cried. The others waited patiently. He set her down and smiled. Alfie, the one who was shy. He patted her head. Maria was shaking. She wanted to scream. She wanted to run and she wanted to stop and fall down and die.

"They are at the Stronghold." He spoke firmly. "Alive and well." She sobbed uncontrollably.

"My Jimmy?"

"And James." She looked up shocked.

"James?" No! He was dead!

"Alise kept her word. Except about you. Get in." He pushed her into the trailer. "Quiet now. We still have to get out of the city."

He covered them. Waldo was sniffing at the door. They were out there. Men. He opened the garage door and walked out into the rain pulling the cart after him. He shut the garage and walked on humming as the dog walked along side him growling. There were people about. They would come near and his eyes would flash blue. They knew that look and would run. Yes, he was here. Alfie knew this and accepted it. He was afraid. Of what was to come and of what the end would be. Alejandro had not been so far off. It had all come from the sky, but it had all begun on the earth.

"ALF E?" James Fielding asked looking at him. "Why that?" The dark haired man stepped back. Alfie looked at Alpha. Identical droids. Mirror images. Alfie was two years younger than his big brother, Alpha.

"He is the ninth. I. Alphabetical. The first one, ALF, Artificial Life Form, is basically the blueprint. The others all had problems in the programming. Too much information. Too much for them to handle. ALF E is number five, he has a larger processor."

"So he is not the first?" Fielding asked walking around the two droids.

"You have the second banana." James Sr. noted without looking up.

"So you get the first?" There was contempt in the voice.

"I get the experiment. You get the final draft." James Sr. corrected.

"You plan on selling these?"

"I do."

"Then they won't be the only ones."

"For now they are. Manufacturing takes time. Lots of time. I would think you didn't have that to waste?" James Sinclair finally looked up.

"I will have plenty." Fielding stepped back. "Which is better?"

"They are the same. Only mine has a few bugs that I can fix at a later date. Things to change out and update. He is ten years older. Yours is the newborn. Two year old toddler." The man bent to look over the blueprints. "This is what you had approved?"

"No, this is what I want." Fielding walked about with his head held high and his chin out.

"Fine!" Sinclair winked at Alfie. "I guess you need the best to enter the history books?"

"I do. And you will help?"

"I guess I have no choice?" Sinclair stepped around the table. "If I want to be a part of history."

"It will be history and the future. I will bring it all together. Most of it is finished. It is on my island. I will launch from there. I just need the mind. One that will sustain it all. Can you do it? I heard you had it done. Ready for the army to use and they won't pay."

"Yes, well, patriotism is hard to buy." Sinclair looked over his spectacles at the man. "Do you know the size of the hole you are going to blow in the ozone?"

"God will protect me," Fielding spoke firmly. "He is waiting for me."

"For all of us," Sinclair noted. "Judgment day is not that far off for some of us."

"I will not die!" Fielding replied. "I will return. I will bring God here to cure the sick, to make us all equal and to be among us."

"All equal. That is interesting."

"Are you prejudiced? Do you think you are better?" Indignation dripped off the man.

"No, but I am richer than most," Sinclair sighed.

"I want the first," Fielding declared.

"He has quirks. He is not as reliable." Senior noted without looking up. "He is not very personable."

"I can hire people to be personable." Fielding walked around the two droids again. "You want him?"

"Well, yes, he is the first." Sinclair took off his specs and wiped them on his vest. "He is like a child to me."

"Then he is the best and I want him!" Fielding slammed his hand down on the table.

"Take him then." Fielding smiled, thinking he had won.

"I will call him Alpha."

"Fine." Sinclair put his specs back on. "Alpha he is."

"We will be ready to depart tomorrow morning. I have everything you requested!" Sinclair nodded and the man marched out with Alpha close behind.

"Well, Alfie, I think we are going on a trip. Are you up for it?" Sinclair asked softly.

"Yes sir."

"Good."

The next day, they were on their way to the island. Big brother, Alpha, would not speak to Alfie. The fifth droid was simply dismissed by the big brother. A brother with quirks. In the first stages of reassignment, it is not unusual for a droid to take on the characteristics of his owner. Alpha became more and more like Fielding, arrogant and overly presumptuous. He expected Alfie to do everything. Sinclair had to put Alpha, in his place more than once, and Fielding did not protest. The man knew better than to upset Sinclair. He needed him more than anything now. Alfie knew this, and something else. Once Sinclair was finished, he might not live long enough to tell anyone. The way Fielding stared and talked let Alfie know that this venture meant more to him than anything, and he felt that he was above the laws of man and God. Murder would not be hard for him. Not only that....

Alfie had taken the habit of standing outside Sinclair's room as if shut down. Sinclair and he had discussed it. He told Fielding that he didn't like the droid in his room but wanted him close should he need him. The room had one door and one window. Alfie had secured that window and took his post nightly. Fielding's room was across the courtyard. Nightly, Alfie would watch the young girls going to that room. Nightly there were screams of pain and anguish. Many left limping and carrying their clothing. Many were carried out by servants or Alpha. Alfie never moved, his lights never came on, but he recorded all.

For almost a year, they lived like this. Sinclair had told him he was afraid to leave now. That he was trying to finish quickly so that they could leave. Sinclair had Alfie to ready a boat. No one was to know, but they were to leave soon. Alfie obeyed and felt a relief that was overwhelming as the time grew close. He wanted to get away from the island. His brother was no longer his brother, but his antagonizer. Alpha insisted on being told he was superior daily. Alfie obliged him and ignored him. It only made Alpha madder. He had a quirk. His emotions were not stable. Alfie stuck close to Sinclair. The day Genesis was done, they left.

Sinclair sat in the back of the small boat as Alfie steered it out into the open ocean. Water and food were tied to the floor. The water was choppy. Rough. No one should have been on the water. Sinclair sat staring back at the island. He was concerned. Alfie kept going. Putting distance between them and the island. What they had seen was frightening. Even for a droid. Sinclair said nothing until night fell.

"We have to go back."

"Sir?"

"What if…"

"No sir, he was not." Alfie set a hand on the man's shoulder. "Sir, to go back would be suicide for us."

"I know…" The man looked down at his hands. "My son should grow up and be proud. Not ashamed."

"He will be proud."

"What have I done?"

"What all men have done," Alfie sighed. "Committed crimes against man and God. One day, sir, one day we all have to answer for what we are, who we are and what we have done." Sinclair sat quiet the rest of the journey.

Later that night they saw it. The bright flash of light that streaked across the sky over them. It was a beautiful site. And horrific. It had launched. From the boat, they watched the launch in confused horror. It could not have been Fielding. No. There was no one else on the island. Everyone had fled in fear of their lives. In the night they had run. Taking only what they could carry. Fielding had complained and Sinclair had let Alfie make his breakfast that last day. Alpha was too good to do it. So it launched. How had it happened? Sinclair and Alfie knew.

~

"Shit!" Alfie cursed.

"What is it?" Maria had peeped from under the blanket.

"The door to the warehouse is open. I closed it." He set the trailer down. Waldo was sniffing about. "Stay!" he ordered to the people and the dog.

"Alfie!" Maria started to climb out.

"No, your body heat is detectable still. Stay!" He stepped into the door and waited.

Something ran across the floor. A rat? He shuddered. He hated rats! He walked on, scanning. In the dark he could detect no heat. But he also couldn't see. He fumbled with the lights and they came on. Nothing. He had taken a chance and now had to act. He pulled the cart into the building and shut the door. If anyone were below, they would be trapped. He couldn't leave the light on and the door open. He pulled the cart down to the next level. This door was damaged, but only by humans. It was still secure. He checked it twice. They had tried but were unsuccessful. It had not been penetrated. He was relieved. The junked remains of the truck had been moved. He cursed under his breath and peered about. No human. He opened the door and pulled the cart in. He shut the door and locked it. A quick scan, and he found it was as before. Musty and empty. He turned on the lights and pulled the trailer in. He ran back, shut off the lights, and raced to shut the door behind him. These lights he would leave on. More rats! He shuddered and shook. He hated them almost as much as cockroaches. Oh, and those damn green droids that had invaded them.

At the third level, the door was pristine. He sighed as he opened it and pulled them in. He shut the door. Secured it and lifted the cover off the cart. They stood and moved about. The younger children were asleep. The older boy was not and glared at him. The older woman held her skillet at the ready. Maria climbed down and sat on the floor. Alfie hurried to bring her a chair. She waved him off and looked around. It was the same as they day they left it almost six months earlier. When she had been with James. Linda sat on the chair and waited.

"Food." Alfie motioned to the boy. "Will you assist me?" The boy glared.

"Go, Mike. Alfie wouldn't hurt you." Maria fell back on the floor. "Alfie, that boy is a warrior. Show him where you hide the chocolate." That made the boy perk up and he cautiously followed the droid.

"Where are we?" Linda asked, looking about.

"Our warehouse. This is stuff we were taking to the Stronghold a little at a time." She sat up slowly. "You do know about the Stronghold?"

"Heard about it. Thought it was a myth." Mom moved out of the trailer. "Why all the silver? Aluminum foil the rage? Or does he have an Andy Warhol thing going?"

"They are blankets. Developed for space. They keep the body heat in. And you can't detect body heat outside. Those things scan for heat in the dark. They can't find what they can't see."

"How the hell do you know this?" Linda asked suspiciously.

"Because that's how most droids work. The invaders are droids. Maybe not made here on earth, but they were planned here. Or maybe their ancestors are up in the space station. Remember how all those droids got blown off into space when they started acting nutty a few years back?"

"This is more than a few years old." Alfie remarked as he and Mike returned with arms full of food.

"Donuts!" Mom reached cautiously for one.

"Coffee?" Alfie offered her the self-heating cup.

"You are a darling!" The older woman sipped the drink and sighed.

"There are blankets over there. We should cover the children." He was moving. He brought another chair and Mike got the blankets. The younger ones were awakened and fed, soon went off to sleep.

"What do you mean, more than a few years old?" Maria asked as soon as Alfie stopped moving.

"The internals are intricate. Too much for one to develop or build in a year."

"How do you know this?"

"I dissected one." Alfie smiled.

"What?" Maria blinked and gazed at him.

"I dissected one." He repeated smugly.

"Yeah, we saw that on the table and wondered." Mom finished her coffee and reached for another donut.

"Where?" Maria was looking to Alfie.

"On the dining room table. I did not have time to dispose of it."

"Alfie? How did you get it in the house?"

"I disengaged it and carried it. They do not weigh a lot."

"I know that." Maria stood and began to pace. "Won't it be missed?"

"I would think so. But no one came looking. Finders keepers." He sang.

"Where did you find it?"

"It fell off the cube, The Genesis, and I caught it. I believe he was trying for a frisbee." Maria stopped and shook her head. "You should rest."

"I want to go to the Stronghold."

"We will. But first we must talk." Alfie stood. "Rest and we will talk." He walked to the door and stood guard.

"What is he?" Mom asked picking up a blanket.

"Our savior," Linda yawned, as she climbed into the trailer with her kids and laid down to sleep.

Maria walked to him. He frowned. Alfie always looked funny when he frowned. She sat down at his feet and waited. They had a funny relationship. He was cold and sincere with her, and then he would cross his eyes and she could not help but laugh at him. And with him. He had a dry wit and was prone to pulling pranks. In the beginning, Alfie made her life a lot easier. He ran interference between her and Alise.

It wasn't that Alise hated Maria, she just ignored her. She would only speak when spoken to and Maria was afraid to speak to the droid. Even before they were married, the girl had been wary of the pair. She was polite but would not have conversations with them. Alfie helped her move her things into the room. James' bedroom. Alise had been dusting and would walk around with that flickering eye. Maria avoided her.

"She hates me," Maria mumbled one day at breakfast. James was running late and eating quickly. She was four months along and feeling fat and homesick.

"Who?" he asked reading his notes and eating.

"No one." Maria sighed.

"Of course not!" James laughed, standing to put on his jacket. "Everyone adores you!" He bent to kiss her head. "I will see you in chem." With that, he was gone. She sniffled and a napkin appeared. She took it and looked up at Alfie just sitting there.

"Don't cry. You might rust." He spoke solemnly. Then he winked. She had never seen a droid wink. He did not have eyelids. When he did it the whole eye moved and spun around. She wasn't sure if she should cry or laugh.

"Do you rust?" she asked, looking him over.

"No."

"Then why do you think I would?"

"It was a joke." He smiled then and winked. She smiled back. "Alise needs to be needed. You don't need her and now James doesn't need her. So she feels useless. The worst thing." He sat waiting. Maria sat thinking. To have no one to care for was hard. What would her mother do if no one needed her?

"Need!" Alfie ordered. Maria bit her lower lip and realized what the droid was telling her.

"Alise?" Marie called softly. The droid appeared almost instantly. She did not speak but stood gazing at the girl. Maria was trying to think of what to say or do. A tear rolled down her cheek. She wanted her mother. She was afraid of what was to come. "Am I fat?" she blubbered.

"No!" The droid hurried to her side and handed her a napkin. "You are lovely. All pregnant women are lovely!"

"I have to go to the baby doctor and James is busy. Will you take me?" The girl blew her nose and wiped her face. The droid sat next to her and patted her leg.

"Of course! Alfie…" She looked up at him. "Alfie wake up!"

"I am awake!" he snapped.

"Get the car ready. I'm going to get Maria ready and we have to go to the doctor."

"Now?" he asked, as if irritated.

"Now!"

"Okay!" He stood and moved behind her. Maria looked up and his eyes crossed, then spun around. She had to fight to not laugh. "Women!" he mumbled as he headed for the garage, whistling.

Now he just stood. Waiting. Maria reached up and flicked his knee. He giggled and kicked at her. She knew he was ticklish. She had discovered it when Jimmy was just walking. He would grab on to the droid's knee and his chubby little fingers would make Alfie dance. Now Alfie sighed and sat down next to her. She searched for what to say. He set his hand on hers and smiled.

"Tell me all of it? From the beginning?"

"I don't think I can." She sat back and he saw it.

"What is that?" He pointed to the disc around her neck.

"Oh, he gave it to me. He said it was a memory."

"May I?" he asked. She took it off and handed it to him. He looked it over slowly as if discovering a long lost treasure. The string was pulled off. "What is on it?"

"All of it," she replied. "From the beginning until the time he made it. About two weeks ago."

"He gave this to you?" Alfie gazed at her and she dropped her eyes. "What did he take from you?" She sniffled and ran her hand over her face as if to clear it.

"All of me." he nodded and then slid it into the slot below his chest. It went right in.

"Leave me?" he asked, "Do not disturb me." His eyes blinked and then the light went out. Maria touched him but he didn't move. She curled up on the floor next to him and waited. Waldo came and laid with her as she slept. For the first time in a long time, she slept peacefully.

~

"How long is he gonna be like that?" Mom asked looking at the frozen droid by the door.

"I don't know." Maria bit into the sandwich.

"And we got to wait for him?" Linda wasn't sure of him.

"Unless you can pull that cart." Maria reached for a soda and smiled at her friend. "For now we are safe, we have food and we have hope."

"Hope?" Mom sighed. "That is what we have the most of." She sat down with a sandwich and wrinkled her nose. "And food. My second husband was in the army and he used to complain about these MRE's all the time. They ain't so bad." She bit into hers and sighed. "Not as good as my cooking but we ain't gonna starve!" She looked up at the boxes piled high. "At least not for another hundred years."

"It's been like three days!" Linda mumbled.

"Sixty hours," Maria corrected. She was watching him too. What if the disc made him to be like them? She was afraid he might get a virus and go nutso.

"How long are we gonna wait?"

"Until he comes out of it."

"Mom!" Mike was calling her.

"Those kids!" Linda rose and hurried to see what her boys had found and to say no when they asked if they could get into it. The chocolate had them wired.

"You trust him?" Mom asked nodding toward Alfie.

"With my life." Maria said.

"Good," the woman sighed, "Cause you're trusting him with ours too."

"Alfie will get us to the Stronghold. To my family." Maria finished her sandwich. She had not had time to ask him about her family. Who had survived. He had said they were at the Stronghold but he had not said what condition they were in. She knew Alfie's mind. They might be dead and buried, but to him, they would be there. But he had said alive and well. He had said James! She felt her stomach turn. How to explain?

"I seen your daddy once," Mom noted casually. Maria sat waiting. "I told you my second husband was in the army? Yeah?" Maria nodded, even though she wasn't sure she had heard that part of it. "Well, he was one of the troops defeated by your pappy. The day it ended, your Daddy and his men rode through the streets to Mendoza like a grand parade. Horses, on foot and in jeeps. Him on that big black horse was a sight." The woman smiled dreamily. "He was one handsome man!"

"He still is." Maria was homesick for him. He had always kept her safe. She wanted to feel his arms around her. Not James', but her father. He would understand and forgive her for what she had done. James? She wasn't so sure. She had thought him dead. Now to find he was alive tore at her heart. She had done things that he could not forgive. Even if it was to survive, she was not sure he would understand.

"That horse was a monster."

"Muerto." Maria remembered that horse. When she was young, he was old.

"What the hell does that mean?"

"Death."

"Figures. I hear he trampled many men." The woman stared out into nothing. "My husband said later that your pappy was crazy. To sit on that horse and wait for them to kill him. Not a bullet hit him. That they were on foot and horseback and my husband's troops were in tanks and jeeps, yet they lost. He said it was a slaughter. At least he thought the slaughter would go his way. It didn't. Those men that survived? They respected and feared your pappy. Us women dreamed of him though. Then I saw your mama. Now that was one pretty woman. Classy and spicy!" Mom laughed.

"They are very happy together." Maria hoped they still were.

"They had a bunch of kids?"

"Twenty-one." Mom whistled and Maria laughed.

"Well, with a man like that I think I'd get pregnant twenty one times and enjoy it."

"Thirteen. She was only pregnant thirteen times. Eight sets of twins."

"Still!" Mom sat thinking. "Is there room for us? If not, leave me and take the boys."

"There is room." Maria reached out to touch the woman's hand. "There is room for all."

"Now my third husband. He was an ass." Maria wondered just how many times the colorful woman had been married. "It didn't last too long. He was jealous of my first two husbands. They were dead and he was still jealous. I left him for Linda's daddy. Now there was a nice man." She thought for a moment. "Sometimes a man can't live with having something that another has tasted." Maria felt her stomach turn. "And then there are those who understand."

"I think James would understand." Maria wondered if he would. "At least I can hope so." He hand went to the bulge. Would he?

"It's not Adam's, is it?" Mom asked calmly. "The baby. I think you was pregnant before."

"Why do you say that?"

"Cause I heard them talking," Mom sighed, "All those women. All of them were impregnated and all those were failures. If you was already pregnant, then they would have thought you a success." She looked over at Maria. "And I don't think you would have done what you did to live if that baby was an abomination. If it was your man's child then, you what you did was understandable."

"I hope he sees it that way," Maria mumbled.

"He will!" She looked up to see Alfie standing over her.

"Alfie!" His face lit up as she jumped up to hug him. "I thought you had gone!"

"Gone where?" he asked teasingly. "I told you to wait. You have no patience!"

"Alfie! Tell me! Are they alive? James and Jimmy?"

"Last time I saw them, Jimmy was napping and James was arguing with Alise. Everyone was well."

"How long ago?"

"Almost a month." He smiled. "They are fine. Now we have to talk. Have you eaten? Are you rested? Could you answer a few questions for me?"

"Yes!" she hugged him again.

"If you will excuse us, madam." Alfie pried Maria off of him and led her off into a quiet corner.

"What questions? What was the disc? Do you know what it is? Can you read it? Is it what I think it is?" He said nothing until they were far away and alone.

"What do you think it is?" he asked softly.

"Archive." He nodded at her answer. "And you know what it is?"

"Have you seen it?" He asked sitting next to her.

"Yes. It's manmade."

"No, it's not," he smiled.

"But it was! It looks like the old…"

"It was built by androids." She sat back watching his face. "Two of them. Me and my brother."

The silence was deadening. She waited for him to tell her he was kidding, but he didn't. He sat waiting for her reaction. Watching her clench and unclench her fists. Her breathing rate was increasing as she sat thinking and processing it all. Her face was pale and her hand went to the bulge as if to calm herself and gain comfort. She was shaking. She had heard him. She knew what he was saying and she had no reason to doubt him or not trust him, but she felt rising fear and rage.

"Would you like to strike me?" he asked calmly.

"It wouldn't do any good."

"It might make you feel better?" he sat waiting.

"Was it all on there? Everything they did to me? Everything I let him do? Everything I did?" She was shaking more now. He set his hand on hers.

"Yes."

The tears came. The sobs and the cursing. Alfie sat waiting patiently for her to regain control. He handed her a handkerchief. Slowly she was able to settle herself. When he felt she was ready to move on, Alfie moved her so she sat with his back to her. She looked over her shoulder at him curiously. He moved her shirt up and gazed at her back. They had faded. But were still visible to his eyes. He set her shirt down and patted her shoulder. They began to shake as she sobbed. He left his hand there. Comfort. It was all the comfort he could give her.

He was droid. The fifth. As he was activated, he saw his brother and then sir. The man smiled at Alfie and winked. The other droid only looked on curiously. He was just a head then. Sir was working on him. Adding to him. Taking away. One day Alfie was enraged and the next, he cried uncontrollably. Finally, the day came when Sinclair had the just right adjustment and Alfie was ready to be assembled. Emotions and reason were the hardest to establish. The body was easy. It was molded after his brother. The first.

"Second Banana," Sir called him playfully. Sir was a likeable human. ALF stood looking at him coldly, if a droid could. "You are just a bit more human then your brother. But he is older so he is expected to be moody." Alpha looked away as if disgusted in being compared to Second Banana. "We need to get you ready. We have to go on a little trip."

"Sir?" Alfie spoke cautiously.

"Yes?"

"Where are we going?"

"To help a man find his God and his destiny." Sir smiled sadly.

"I do not understand, Sir."

"Neither do I, Banana." Sir turned and looked to ALF. "What do you think?"

"It is one's duty to reach his destiny!" ALF replied coldly.

"Yes," Sir sighed, "But when you reach it and it is not what you thought, what do you do then?"

"Die," ALF replied. Banana sat thinking. He had just come to be. "What is die?" Banana asked quickly.

"What all humans do," ALF replied.

"Yes, we do." Sir nodded as he stepped up to the computer.

"Will I die?" Banana asked.

"No, you will just stop being." Sir replied, tapping keys on the computer.

"Is that not the same thing?"

"No, you see humans leave behind a marker of their life. A child, a legacy a part of history. Droids just stop."

"We have no legacy?"

"No, you are here to serve and record and act." Sir smiled as Banana looked sad. "But, you are long from not being. You will have the legacy of my children telling all that you are and such."

"But I will not have children?" The thought of little droids running about amused him.

"No. You are not equipped and that is impossible. Only animals can have children. Or Humans."

"But it can come to pass!" ALF argued. "One day. A higher being. A combination of both?"

"An abomination," Sir sighed. "It would never come to pass. God would not allow it."

"What would be God's argument?" ALF asked quickly.

"God would argue that he made us in his own image and I don't think God has a control panel in him," Sir teased. "You are here to help me succeed in all that I do." Sir patted ALF's shoulder. The droid stood still. "To keep me safe and take care of me." He turned to face Banana.

"Yes Sir!" Banana replied quickly. "Sir?"

"Yes, Banana?"

"What is God?" ALF groaned and Sir laughed.

"I am programming your mind now. From my Archive. It will take a day or two but you will understand a lot more when I am done."

"What is Archive?"

"Something like the God of computers." Sir laughed, hitting a key and then it all began. He learned it all and understood. God was the almighty. At least that was what the Bible said.

"Now what?" Maria asked softly.

"Home," Alfie replied. "We go home. As soon as it's dark, we will leave." He thought for a moment. "We will need food and water and blankets. It is very cold this time of year."

"I meant James. What do I tell him?"

"The truth. He knows you were with child."

"What?" She sat back from him.

"I told your father. He said he would have your mother have a Mass said for you and the child. I'm sure they told James. He will be pleased to have you and his child home."

"Is it his child?" Maria asked.

"I wish to scan you, but I would need your permission."

"You have it."

"Lie down." She obeyed.

The light in his eye intensified as it went from the top of her head to her feet. It took several minutes. Her heart was racing. She was stressed. His light faded. He sat calculating and analyzing. It was there. It was healthy. There was however, something else. He frowned.

"Well?" She sat up slowly.

"The baby is fine. But there is something else there. Not organic. But I do not know what it is and it is not affecting the child." She looked frightened. "If it was putting the child in danger I would remove it. However, removing it now, in this primitive environment could endanger your child. I'm afraid you will have to tell James."

"I can't." She shook her head.

"You have to. This child's life could depend on it."

"What if he hates me?"

"He is not born." It was a boy. She didn't know whether to rejoice or cry.

"James!"

"Would you like for me to tell him?"

"What?"

"I could show him." The droid's face became serious. "I am now Archive." The fear on her face saddened him. "I have absorbed it. I could show him and he would understand." She sat thinking.

"What if he doesn't?"

"Then he is not the man I raised him to be."

"How much of it?" she asked, ashamed of all that she had done, all that had been done to her and all that she had allowed. The game of enjoying it. The pain of knowing that she was only acting to save her life and her child's.

"Enough for him to understand. And accept." He made a face.

"What? You don't think he can live with it? Knowing I was a concubine to a…I don't even know what in the hell Adam was?" She covered her hand with her face.

"He is a droid. A highly advanced droid. The creation of not God, but a mad man and a droid. The ideas and dreams of two that were evil. But Adam is only a droid. A learning droid. And the more he learns and the more power he has, the more dangerous he is."

"What is he really?" Maria asked in a pleading voice.

"A droid." Alfie answered

"No, Alfie, he was different. Alise looks and feels human. Adam acts a bit odd, but human. He was…. Not." Maria fought to think on how to describe. "At first he was like you. Rubbery. As time went on, he became more real. The skin and all. He didn't breathe, sweat, fart or anything like that. He was just….there!"

"He is a droid. His mind is a chip. He has no blood in his veins."

"But he is. Like a copy of the man I saw!"

"A clone?"

"I asked him about the green ones. He said they were what he was. I asked if they were clones. He said he was the first, but I never did ask him if he was a clone."

"He might be a combination of the two." Alfie sat thinking.

"What?"

"A clone with the brain of a droid. A very unstable droid." There was an amused look on his face. "You may have saved humanity."

"How? By letting him fuck me daily and suck my tits?"

"Actually yes." Alfie gave her an amused look.

"What in the hell are you talking about?"

"You taught him to be human. To be kind and gentle. You showed him all that there was in humanity."

"Then I ran from him."

"Well, I'm sure he is angry. We must leave at first dark. We must get to the Stronghold. And this must make it." The disc was ejected from him. "If I don't make it, then Alise can decipher it." He handed it to her.

"You keep it. Having it scares me." She hugged herself. "I don't want anything to do with Archive."

"Maria, Archive is nothing but a library." Alfie explained. "That was what it started out to be and what it will always be. Just a library."

"So what do I do?" she asked.

"Help me get them ready. It is a long way and we must hurry. We can only travel at night and I would like to make it in two days."

"Two days? It's only…."

"On foot? With this contraption? If I go too fast the wheels will fall off!"

"What about the other car?" She looked to the old Mustang.

"I don't know if the tires will hold up." He sighed. Six of them, one dog and enough fuel, food and water in case it didn't work? "What the hell! I always liked the muscle cars. Sir had one when we came to the States. Before James' father was born." Alfie smiled. "He let me drive it once and I backed over the trash receptacle." He laughed. "He was not happy with me then."

~

The island was quiet. Most of the humans had left. Banana stood watch over Sir as he slept. ALF was with Fielding, as always. He was even there when the women came. Banana had asked Sir about it. The older man shook his head. A subject for a later date. They had to be careful what they said and how they said it. Fielding was not acting normal. He was agitated. The work was not moving fast enough. He had ALF build several other droids. Less alert than ALF but suitable for labor and guards. Sir was frightened of this.

"I want it," Fielding growled as Sir objected. "I want the Archive. Just copy it into the data banks! I will need it to record my findings. To show God what we are. Who we are."

"James! Don't you think God knows?" Sir had argued.

"I want it!"

"But James..."

"You will not be the only man with it!"

"I developed it!"

"I want it!" The men stood toe to toe. Banana saw that ALF stood ready to act. "Give it to me!" Sir knew too that he had no choice.

"I will have to expand Genesis' memory to hold it all."

"Do it. Do whatever it takes. I will be planning a departure for next week. Will that be long enough?"

"Yes. It will."

"Then do it."

Sir sat down to reconfigure it all. Banana watched him. He saw it all go together. And he saw the failsafe. Sir said no words aloud, but he stopped working and let Banana see. See what needed to be seen. A secret between the two. The memory was expanded and the Archive was uploaded. The day it was done, Sir packed his bags. They had been there too long. Three months too long. He wanted to go home, to see his wife, to run. He knew what was coming and it was not good. Archive went on line and they planned to leave.

But planning to leave and leaving were two different things. The door opened and James Fielding stepped in dressed as an astronaut. Sir sighed. A mad man with a fantasy that was close to being fulfilled. Tea. They would have tea and then Sir and Banana could leave. Fielding was looking over to Banana now. Banana blinked and his eye kept spinning. Sir hit him on the back of the head and it stopped.

"Sorry James. He is not what I expected. I think the first one is always the best."

"Yes, always!" Fielding laughed, turning to show ALF dressed in a suit similar to Fielding's. "He is my second in command. Together we are going to fulfill our destinies."

"Yes." Sir smiled. "Tea?"

"Come along. I will meet you on the deck in an hour. I wish to take a swim." With that, they were gone and Banana packed quickly. They loaded the boat but did not leave without permission. Fielding would just come after them. They strolled along the shore talking as the waves crashed around their feet.

"Why is it important to find God?" Banana asked.

"Because some have to see to believe," Sir replied.

"But the Bible. Is it not proof enough?"

"To some. Alpha seems to have absorbed that!" Sir looked back to the house. The first droid had taken to spouting off scriptures when antagonized. A fanatical droid. Just what the world needed!

They walked on and kept looking to the deck. An hour had passed and then some. There was noise from the shore. They walked and found ALF and two droids.

Sir stepped back quickly. He pushed Banana ahead of him and they ran to their boat. They did not wait to see. They did not wait to be sure. They ran. After a day at sea they saw it launch. Genesis was gone. They sat watching the tail of fire as it left the atmosphere. Banana asked a question that was answered and that to this day the answer shook him.

"Why did he insist on seeing God?"

"He was a very disturbed man. He wanted a legacy. Children."

"So why go into space?"

"He couldn't have children. He took steroids and they made him sterile." Sir smiled. "To want to walk with gods, you must pay a price."

Banana nodded, though he did not understand. They continued on their way and with their lives. But Banana never forgot James Fielding or his brother.

~

"How can he see?" Mom asked from the back seat. "And why don't we have the blankets?"

"He can see at night and this car engine puts off more heat than all of us together!" Maria yelled over the roar of the engine. Waldo was sitting on her lap with his head out the window.

"Aren't we taking a chance?" Linda asked.

"Yes, three days in the cart traveling only at night or three hours." To Maria it wasn't that big of a risk. It was still misting out so that cut the odds of getting caught, but Alfie wasn't taking chances. He had that car flying.

Maria knew that these vehicles had been outlawed because of the fact that the fumes had eaten away at the ozone, but they traveled so much faster than the electric cars. And they were way more fun. A Mustang. She liked the name of it. Just like the wild horses that roamed the valleys of the Stronghold and outside it. Wild and free. Fast and strong. The horse a warrior would ride. She thought of her father. How would she be able to tell him? He would see it in her face. He always could.

"So, you are now a woman?" He sat down across from her in the kitchen with his belt in his hand. She did not look up. "Could you not wait to grow up?"

"I love him," she replied simply.

"Love is not what you think." He looked to his wife. "I love your mother but there are times I should have taken this to her!" He slammed the belt down on the table.

"And you didn't because?" the girl looked up into her father's eyes. She had his fire. He sighed and looked to his wife. Why was he the one to bring order? He never could when it came to Maria.

"She would have killed me!" he chuckled, running his hand over his face. Maria was seventeen, unwed and pregnant. He had spanked her several times, but never beat her. Now he wanted to. "What am I to do?"

"Let me marry him?" she smiled slightly watching his face. He smiled too.

"Is it safe?" Mom asked.

"No. But nothing we do now is safe. All we can hope for is that we outrun them." She looked in the mirror. No green mist following them. By now they knew she was gone. He knew. What would he do to her this time? What would he do to Alfie or the people in the backseat? She hugged the dog.

The farther they got from the warehouse, the more anxious she got. What if the Stronghold was gone? What if Adam had discovered who she was? What if Adam found out about the Stronghold? What if James, Jimmy, and her family were taken? What would she do? How would she live without them?

The road curved and she prayed that the Mustang would make the curve. She had lost a brother to a fast car and a curved road. They had to make it. This was their last chance. If they had to walk, it would take days and they would be caught! The car made the curve and continued on. Alfie set his hand on hers. Comfort.

"Sir? What is it, exactly?" Alfie had asked looking into the cradle.

"Your new student!" Sir had replied, "My son!" His wife was a little woman with blonde hair and blue eyes. The baby looked more like her. He had thought the child would favor Sir. The boy farted, making a face that did resemble Sir. "This is James McMillan Sinclair II. Junior."

"I see." Alfie decided that he was happy to not be able to have any of those. They appeared to be a lot of work. And they cried and made messes!

Junior was a likeable chap. As a young man, he was more like his father than his mother. A strong man of conviction and discipline. Junior was smart, strong and talented. He married young and settled into a wonderful life with his wife. They had wanted children, but they were children themselves. Then she took ill. Soon after the diagnosis, she died. It was the first of many for Alfie. The next was Sir himself. Then his wife. Alfie was then taken by Junior to care for him. He wasn't thrilled at being left alone with the unstable young man, but he was family. Then the baby was born. Alfie liked this young one. The first and the second. The madness was easy enough to live with until Alfie saw what Junior had done…he could only shake his head at his first meeting with Alise.

Alise sat on the bed naked. In more ways than one. Her skin had not yet been applied. Alfie carried the sleeping baby in as ordered and left. He was reluctant, but could not disobey. A quick scan told him all that he needed to know. Grief had driven his master mad. There were traces of himself all over her. What was he thinking? What had he done? Why? Junior was a handsome man. He would have found another mate. But no, he could not get over the loss of his wife. And so, he created another to satisfy him and life went on. For all.

Alfie turned his attention to James. To keep him safe and sheltered from his father's problems. It was easy enough with Alise's help. She took care of Junior and

James became Alfie's priority. His favorite. Next to Jimmy. Each generation seemed to be more fun. James would ride on his shoulders with his arms extended as they 'flew' about the yard. His laugh would be carried on the wind to Alfie and his tears melted the droids circuits. Alise was jealous of them at times, but Alfie didn't care. James was his boy. With the madness came the disassociation. Junior blamed the boy for the death of his wife. But that was impossible. Alfie knew it and...well, Junior should have known it but he had forgotten. Time began to melt together for the man.

Junior loved his son. He adored the boy, but had no time for him. He would not make the time for the boy, but would for Alise. Alfie often wondered what would have happened if it had been the boy that had passed away? The first? A little tyke to always be young? There were plans of a sort in Sir's papers. Something he had stopped working on calling it an abomination and an act against God. But those plans were safely tucked away in his things. At least Alfie had thought so, until he saw Alise. Junior had found them.

They became friends. Of a sort. Two droid to assist one man. One man and a child. His main concern was the child. Hers was Junior and then the child. Alfie made sure the lad lacked for nothing. He opened up more with the young boy. Acted more human and believed more that he was more than just a droid. James told everyone he was his uncle. Young children accepted him and he enjoyed the title. Alise was more apt to pout or brood over the attention she felt should have been hers, but Junior made sure she was never lacking for his attention. As long as James was healthy nothing else mattered. At least to Alfie. And James and Jimmy both needed Maria.

It was taking longer than it should have. Maria was anxious. She kept looking back. At places, the road was blocked. Marauders had set up camps along the path, hoping to catch those trying to escape. They expected carts and bicycles, but not a 2020 super charged Mustang to come roaring up. The noise sent them running for cover. Especially when Alfie laid on the horn. Fear and surprise was a good thing. Maria held tightly to the seat and the dog while the women in the back prayed and the boys hooted along with Alfie.

"Testosterone junkie!" Maria grumbled. Alfie only smiled at her.

They drove on into the night and deeper into the wilderness. The whole time Alfie hoped that once they arrived, James would have forgiven him. And Alise. Somehow, he had a feeling that Alise was going to be the one to fear. Once she found out what he had done and what he had asked of Alejandro he would have to run from her. And she would drive over him in the car. Even if she had to push it.

ALEJANDRO

"The baby?" Miguel asked kneeling next to his father in the chapel. "You pray for her? For Maria?"

"And you." Alejandro crossed himself and sat back on the pew.

"Why me?" Miguel asked with a soft smile.

Miguel had always been the happy one. Never sad. Always up. He was religious and honest. One of the few that was not a twin. He wasn't a big man. Not short, but not as tall as Alejandro Jr. and not as broad as Joaquin. He was quiet and sweet and he loved his boys. They were the world to him. He would die for them. Not a twin, but he had two sets of his own and no wife. Crystal had died less than a year earlier leaving her husband with four sons under the age of five. He had been working round the clock to keep the Stronghold safe and his children cared for

"You look terrible. Mama says you won't come home?"

"It is not my home, Papi. I have a home." Miguel sat back in the pew.

"But no wife. And no prospects?" Alejandro's eyebrow went up.

"No. I couldn't stand to put another woman through it. More children and death looming over us?"

"So your children should suffer?"

"They do not! I am there!" Miguel was fiercely protective of his children.

"You are, but you are only half there. Look at you! You are a walking skeleton! I need you! We need you and you are half-dead already. What will happen if you die? We will have to split the boys up!" Alejandro glared at his son. Man became a boy and backed down from his father.

"It's not fair to bring a woman into my house with no prospect of marriage. To use as a maid?"

"There are many women who came for refuge."

"Many who are concerned with their own necks. Not my children." He was such a picky man! Alejandro sighed. Microondo had said it, the need was there. Alfie didn't mind being called microwave by the boys. And it was Microondo, who had had caught Miguel more than once watching them. Her. He was watching her. Watching Alise as she cared for Jimmy, working in the clinic and helping with all the other children. Of course, she was being watched. Alfie knew he was too. One false move and the men would not hesitate to destroy them. Alfie had to keep Alise under his thumb. Not to let her panic or have a famous hissy fit. He wanted her busy but even with all of that she had time on her hands and idle hands…

He was leaving and could not keep her under control. The best way was to keep her busy. Four young children and a man who was a workaholic. It seemed perfect. It would give Olivia a chance to care for her grandson. A win win situation on all parts. Except Miguel had to go along with it. Had to believe and trust. Had to understand and try to accept. It was all on Miguel. And Miguel was stubborn and religious. To most, she was an abomination. To Alfie she was Alise.

"There is one." Alejandro was looking down at his hands. His large calloused hands. "Who would die for them? Never tire of them? Love them, and you, if you let her." The words seemed unreal. "One who needs to be needed. For all our sakes."

"What are you talking about Papi?" Miguel knew when something was bothering his father.

"Do you want more children?"

"No, I have my boys." Miguel sat waiting.

"She cannot have children. Ever. And you must understand that this is pretty much a permanent situation. If you agree, she will be with you until the day you die. And with your children thereafter."

"Papi?"

"You've been watching her. She never ages." Alejandro did not look up but felt the shudder of shock from his son. Then the gasp.

"Have you lost your mind?" Miguel yelled, jumping up.

"Silenció!" Alejandro looked about the church. "Respect!"

"Respect? You talk to me of respect and you want me to lie with a robot?"

"NO!" Alejandro stood and glared at his son. "I want you to let her come take care of your home and children. I want her to work so you can rest and spend time with your boys!" The words hung on the air.

"She is not just a robot!" Miguel whispered. "She was his…TOY!" The words were spat from his lips.

"He loved her." Alejandro replied. "He loved his wife. She died. Alise is what his wife was. Tell me you haven't thought of it. To bring Crystal back just for the sake of your sons? I've seen you watching her. Wondering. It would not be accepted. Even if it were possible, but Tostadora Más can help."

"What if I can't?"

"Then you can't. You will grow old fast. Get ill and die. Maybe before me. Then what? Alejandro Jr's son said he would take one or maybe two. Antonio's wife said…"

"Okay!" Miguel sat back down. "As long as my boys can stay together."

"Try and separate them from her," Alejandro laughed. "She will be worse than your mother!"

"When?"

"Now. Your mother is dying to get her hands on the albino." They stood and walked to the clinic.

"Excuse me!" James asked looking from man to man and back at Alise. "My Mum?" He thought Miguel would crawl under the floor! "You want my Mum?" Alise stood holding Jimmy. She had hardly put the boy down. "Why?"

"Microondo." Alejandro spoke softly.

"He deserts us and then pawns you off! Incredible!" James slammed the chart he was holding down on the bed.

"He did not desert you." Alejandro noted. "He went to bring her to you."

"Impossible." James fought the sadness that haunted him. "There has been no sign of her."

Several different sets of men had gone into the city and returned with the same news. No Maria. Not in the refugee camps, not in any of the groups of people or any of the piles of decomposing bodies. She had simply vanished. Like so many women of breeding age. The term sent chills down his spine. Cheo, king of the gypsies had told them of the missing women. Women of breeding age. She was of breeding age and she had been pregnant.

"Microondo said she needed to be busy. Idle hands and a hissy fit?" Alejandro spoke slowly and softly.

"Are you planning on disengaging me?" Alise asked softly. "I can hear you. I am standing right here."

"No, not if we don't have to." Alejandro answered before James could. He locked eyes with his son-in-law. No, they would not disengage her. They would destroy her. Something even he might not be able to stop. "We need your help." Another way to put it.

"Oh, of what service can I be?"

Miguel coughed and felt his face burn red. She was a good looking woman, if only she had been real! She was just an inch or two shorter than himself and she was built just right. James glared at him. Yes, he had noticed Miguel around more. He had thought it was just curiosity.

"Miguel's wife died..," Alejandro began.

"I am so sorry!" Her face showed true concern.

"Well," Alejandro coughed. "he has four niños. All under five. He needs help. You know, a woman."

"A woman?" She stepped closer to James holding Jimmy closer. James closed his eyes waiting for her to panic and have a royal hissy fit, as Alfie called her episodes.

"To help with the house and to look after his children. I thought you could go to his home and help him?" Now he was smiling at her.

"But I take care of James! And Jimmy!" She stepped even closer.

James knew it was the right thing. Alise was getting agitated more and more easily since Alfie had left. Harder to handle, even for James. She was clingy and wouldn't let anyone near Jimmy. At times, not even him. The boy was becoming more spoiled, if that were possible. James knew he had to put his foot down, but without Alfie he wasn't sure how she would react and if the fallout would be worth it.

"But he needs you," Olivia stepped in eyeing Jimmy as a prize. "Miguel trusts no one with his boys, Miguel Jr., Ricardo, Thomas and Manuel. And they are a handful. And the house a mess! Four boys! Four!"

James sat watching it all play out and wondered what Maria would say? She would probably laugh. He smiled, thinking of her laugh. He missed her terribly. Everything had become so hard for him. To sleep, to wake, to live. And now they wanted his Mum.

"But James needs me! Don't you?" she turned to look at him. What to say?

"Mum, I do. But I won't have more children. Jimmy is all I need." He reached for the boy she was not willing to relinquish. "I always knew you would leave me." He hugged his son.

"You did? I…" The droid's eye flashed.

"Mum, you are beautiful! A young woman like you? You must have known that men would fancy you!" Alise stood a bit taller and smoothed her blouse. "I know you and Miguel talk. I hear you laughing. It's nice to hear you laugh again. And you aren't moving to the moon! Just around the corner. You'll be here to help me won't you?"

"Well, of course!" She set a hand on his shoulder. "I would never desert you as that half wit bag of bolts has!" She looked to Miguel. They had been talking. She found him charming and handsome. He was not as old as Alejandro was, but he would age. She liked older men. "How old are you?" she asked shyly.

"Old as you. Thirty-nine." Miguel answered softly.

"OLD!" Her voice rose and James groaned. Alise was vain. Her one downfall. "OLD! I am not old. I am 32!" Miguel stepped back from her.

"Mum!" James stood holding the squirming Jimmy close. "You have been thirty-two for thirty years now."

"But I am thirty-two!" She replied indignantly.

"I thought you were only thirty," Miguel sighed. Her smiled flashed instantly. "You look so pretty." He was a fast learner. Alfie had been right. "I guess I am too old for you?" Bravo!

"No, no." Alise smoothed her hair that was never out of place. "My first husband was sixty."

"Husband?" Alejandro said the word that had shocked them all.

"Mum, you weren't married to Dad." James pointed out.

"But the original was? I don't have a memory of it, but I know it happened."

"Yes Mum. They were married. But you never have been." The droid stood looking confused.

"I'm an old maid?" she asked, with a flicker of her eye.

"Oh Lord!" James sat back wanting to laugh. "Mum, go with Miguel and give it a try. Date a bit before you two decide you want to be man and wife. Care for his kids and his home."

"Like a maid?"

That was it! James winced. The one time Alise had gone totally over the top and had to be shut down was because his father had slept with the maid. Jealous was not the word. The maid was fired, his father apologized and all was well, but Alise hated maids. A whore off the street was more welcome than a maid.

"No, as my friend." Miguel stepped up and took her hand in his. "I need a friend more than a maid or a wife." Her face melted into a smile.

"Oh God!" James groaned. Why did she have to make goo-goo eyes at his brother-in-law? If they got married, she would be his sister-in-law! No, she was Mum! If her nipples could get any harder they did. He felt ill! She was actually horny! He could kick his father for making her so attuned to the male species. "Mum!" The droid tore her eyes off her intended. "Why don't you go pack some of your stuff?"

"Yes, James." She obediently went to her room.

"She has stuff?" Miguel asked cautiously.

"Well, yes. Not much. All of her clothes were in our house. But she has managed to scavenge a few things."

"Let's hope one of them isn't a wedding dress!"

Olivia noted taking the chance to snatch Jimmy up. James noticed that Miguel didn't seem to mind the idea. Alejandro shook his head and rolled his eyes. Only his son would fall in love with a battery-operated Barbie doll. What would people think if they found out he was plugging into Tostadora Más?

One down, one to find and eleven to deal with. He patted Jimmy's head. The baby. He thought not of the future but of the past.

She was tiny. Alejandro peered into the cradle and smiled. Finally, a little princess. Lucky twenty-one. Olivia was sleeping. She was too old to be having children. Everyone said so and this one was a shock. Joaquin was nine already. He scooped the baby up and she began to fuss. He plugged her mouth with his finger and she suckled slowly and faded back into peaceful slumber.

A fuzzyheaded little doll. His Bonita. He settled down in the rocker and slowly rocked her as he spoke. As he had with each son, he told her what he would do for her. They would live, love and laugh. Their lives would be full of happiness and family. She listened intently, even though she slept. He had thought he was too old to have another. He was fifty-five and ready to stop. Now he couldn't. He would have to continue on as head of the family.

He had held all of his children in his hands. All that lived and all that had not. He had held each of his sons as they died. Jose was gone, but still warm. He had cried over him. Only fourteen. So young to die a man. Trino had asked for a priest. There was none ,so his father heard his confession. Alberto never woke. But his father was there. And Francis, so gentle and sweet. He told his father he was a virgin before he went to meet God. Too shy a man to take a woman yet. Then the three babies. Ramón and Javier. Marco of illness before he was five. And Caesar. Such a waste. A fast car and a bad road. He had pulled his son from the car. No one would touch him. Yes, he was dead, but Alejandro held him.

When he thought of Maria, he thought of the fuzzyheaded baby. The littlest one. His little princess. The boys, now men, had come to see her, bringing gifts and their own children. To them she was the cutest. Their wives might not have thought so, but the men did. Maria had many fathers and uncles watching over her as she grew. For her to leave the Stronghold was unheard of. But she had an adventurous streak in her. She wanted to see the world. To live. Now he feared she was dead but he did not feel it.

With all he had. That sickening drowning feeling of helplessness as a soul left the body. Crying for joy as they rise to heaven. But not with her. He had a feeling she was alive, which frightened him more than if she were dead. Because if she were dead, at least she would not be suffering. Men had gone out and returned. They traveled at night, through the sewers to the city. There were stories. Horrible stories. Of women taken and never seen again. Into the ship.

There were bodies of men and children and older women piled high on the outskirts to deter anyone from escape. There were the hungry and the weak preyed upon by the stronger. There were some who were becoming nothing more than savages, and those who fought to survive were losing ground. The men were told not to bring anyone back. They could be spies. But they had. Each time they returned carrying half-starved children. These could not be turned away. Mothers begged. Now the men went out less. And the last few times they brought no children with them. Hope was less easy to find. For them and for Maria. Only Stephano continued to search diligently for Maria. Alejandro had not had that feeling. Not yet.

That night he had been anxious. Maria would not let the boy stay. He had wanted her to stay. James and the droids could go back, but no, she wanted to go with James and she wanted her son with them. After they left, the people had gathered to laugh and talk. A little relaxing before traveling back into the dense forest. He had a feeling. Like something was crawling up his back making the hairs stand up. A chilled, sick feeling.

He had been ready to go home, but Olivia was holding the baby of a friend and making faces and acting silly. He was about to ask her if she had lost her mind. They could not have more children and they had plenty of grandchildren and great-grandchildren. Why was the woman so silly? He was ready to tell her it was time when the horn was blown. Time stopped. Everyone froze. They all looked to Alejandro. He stood looking shocked. It was not a drill! He moved quickly to the front of the open area. He listened, and then it came. Horn after horn. All the lookouts were calling out the warning. He felt his heart jump. Maria, James and the boy should be home now. It had happened! Olivia was by his side. He looked at her in the firelight. His hand reached out to touch her face. Maris, James, Jimmy…they were lost to them.

It was a flicker of a thought. Go for them. No! He could not. He had many to care for. Men were running now for horses and supplies. Wagons were brought to bring people living outside into the Stronghold. He stood trying to not think of Maria. Stephano and Joaquin were suddenly there. He looked to them and the face of his frightened wife. The had buried eight. If they lost Maria, they would never have a grave for her. The men stood waiting. She was closest to them. Their little sister.

"GO!" He ordered and hurried to organize. "Bring her home!"

The first hours were the worst. Not knowing. People poured through the open gate. All were scanned, searched and directed on where to go. Many were shocked by the armed men at the gates. Many objected, but all wanted in, so they submitted to it. The children were the worst. Scared and small. Many had lost their families in the mad crush and were taken to the church to wait for word. There sat the old and frail. These needed beds, not blankets on the floor of the caverns. The sick were taken to the clinic and the children sat at the back, spinning in their seats whenever the door opened.

It was close. The time to shut the door. He had said five hours. It took three to make it to the city. If they could make it, they would. He waited. Directing, barking orders and greeting the hordes. Julio kept count. They still had room. Still some came. He was helping to carry a little girl and her brother to the church when the yells came. He set them down and hurried back to the door. The car rolled into the yard and Alise let the car roll to a stop. She ran to him. More like staggered. She fell into his arms, and even though he knew she was not human, his heart went out to her as her eye flickered and her mouth moved.

"Tostadora Más!" He held her.

"I tried!" she cried.

"What?" He looked into her face.

"To save them all." The lights went out and she went limp in his arms.

James was half crawling out of the car, trying to hold onto the baby. Olivia ran to him, screaming. The other just sat. The baby was fine. James was having a hard time standing. Alejandro took hold of his arm. James stood straighter and glared into the night. There were tears on his face. Alejandro knew before the words were spoken. What he had feared the most.

"They took her!" James fell into his arms, sobbing.

The man, the droid, half a droid, a dog, a baby and the car. They were all cared for. The male droid was a dripping mess. Joaquin and Miguel couldn't figure how to get him out of the car. Alejandro grabbed the metal cart used to move the communion items around the church and simply cleared it off. He looked in the car at the droid and would have laughed. Alfie was just sitting there, strapped in, smiling up at him. Alejandro shook his head and lifted Alfie out and onto the cart.

"Thanks, Mate!" Alfie patted his shoulder with his good hand, "I never really thought I would actually end up on a microwave cart!" They had all chuckled as he was wheeled into the church. Alejandro noted that the droid had crossed himself as he entered. Did droids have religion?

"Now!" He stood looking down at them all. "Where is Maria?"

He sat alone. The gates were shut. He walked. It took him a bit, but he made it. To the small cemetery at the far north end of the Stronghold. To where his sons and parent's were buried. He sat between his parents headstones and cried. Maria was gone. He knew it. He felt it. She was lost to them. She might not be dead, but she would never be the same. Of all his children, she had been the one. The gift from God. Now he wept for her and their future.

'Time heals all wounds'. It also 'makes the heart grow fonder.' All the old saying came to his mind. And fondness was all that they had for Alise. She was everything that any man could hope for. She cleaned, she cooked, she cared for and taught the children and she made Miguel smile. At night after dinner, their laughs could be heard on the night air. Hers soft and his boisterous. They ate on the back patio a lot. The fresh air was good for the children. Miguel would cook and Alise would play with the children. When the children were in bed, she and Miguel would talk long into the night.

Crystal had been a good woman. But she had not been what Miguel had wanted. She had no one and he was older. He needed to settle down. Olivia pushed and so they were married. The first set of twins came and Crystal tried but she was not capable of doing it all. The young girl who wanted a family could not handle all that came with being a mother and a wife. Miguel tried to help, and she took it as a sign of her failure, so she got pregnant again and the second two were born. Not long after, the pretty, young Crystal she took her own life. Something Miguel blamed himself for. A heavy weight to carry. That, and four little boys.

Olivia lightened up on the droid. She was grateful to Alise for bringing James and Jimmy back, but Olivia wanted Maria there too. It was hard for her to accept what she could not understand. Miguel's children were better behaved, clean and well fed. Miguel was smiling again. Something he had not done in a while. And he had a little life in his step. Something that had been missing before. Even with Crystal. Olivia had heard rumors. Rumors about Alise and Miguel. She was not happy, but Miguel was, so Alejandro looked the other way. Until he had them all to dinner at his little house.

All of the brothers, James, Jimmy and the parents and all the children. Everyone brought food and the men talked while the women prepared everything. Alise was busily helping set up, wiping noses, washing hands, drying tears, refilling sippy cups and brushing clothes clean. And not just for her four. Most of the women had avoided her, but now were in awe of her. At dinner she had her four boys seated with napkins in laps, hair combed, faces clean and using forks as she cut up their food and filled their cups as well as Miguel's and anyone else who's tea was running low. Somewhere in the mix, she heated up Alejandro's coffee, sat to eat a few bites, and even complimented the cook.

Everyone was laughing and enjoying themselves. The men were young when together. They wanted to tease the soft-spoken Miguel, but Alejandro had threatened them all. Miguel had been one that was not a twin and he liked to be alone. He was thoughtful, quiet and shy. Very much a mama's boy he wanted to please both of his parents. He was not a big man, but he was handsome and thoughtful. Crystal had needed a stronger man. One to push her. Not one to stand behind and watch her helpless downfall.

Now Miguel stood as the dessert was being passed around. Everyone was hushing children and waiting. The shy one held his hand out and Alise went to him. Now it was an urgent need to quiet everyone and listen to him. He always spoke so softly. Alise stepped up next to him and he held her to him and kissed her cheek. She was wearing her hair loose and is fell like a golden curtain as she bowed her head to listen to him whisper in her ear. She nodded and when she raised her face, it was a deep red. The eye flickered.

"I have an announcement," Miguel spoke loudly. A hush fell over them all.

"Ay Miguel, no!" Olivia started to stop him, but Alejandro held her hand. It was his decision.

"Alise and I will be living from here on as man and wife." The silence was deafening. James wished that Alfie were there so he could kick him! Miguel smiled at James. "If her son will allow it." Alise gazed at him with a deep want in her eye. She had been built to serve. And since James' father's death, she had been missing it.

"I will." James' voice was strangled. Her smile widened.

"We cannot marry in the church for the obvious reasons, but we will be common law," Miguel announced.

"Common law!" Olivia crossed herself and moaned.

"Why not?" Stephano asked. "She's hot. She got a sister?" That started more teasing and snickers. More at Stephano, as he was a self-ordained bachelor.

"If anyone cannot accept this, then say what you want and leave my house." Alejandro felt a pride in his son. One that was a long time in coming. He watched his son stand ready to fight. No one moved for a moment.

"I have an objection!" Alejandro Jr. stood and threw his napkin down. "Papi! How can you allow this?" All eyes went to Alejandro Sr. "We don't even know if she's Catholic? Why couldn't she be Hispanic?" There was a cough and then a choked laugh. Miguel fought not to laugh and Alise started to step behind him. Her eye was flickering faster. One of the children pointed and laughed, only to have little Miguel punch him.

"Don't laugh at my Mommy!" He yelled.

"No!" Alise hurried to stop him. "No fighting. We discussed this." She hugged the boy.

"He was kidding." Miguel knelt down behind her and hugged her and the boy.

"Maybe I could change my hair?" She offered looking around at everyone.

"No, I love your golden hair." Miguel kissed her cheek and she blushed.

"Why can't they have a wedding?" Louisa, Ernesto's wife, asked. "I mean, they did it way back when there weren't priests and preachers or justice of the peace."

"Papi, ain't that basically what you are? Can't you be that for them?" Ernesto asked.

Everyone looked to Alejandro. He had heard the confessions of dying men before, even his own son's. Why could he not bless the marriage? He looked to his wife and saw the answer. She would not let him. Then he saw the need in his son's eyes. A need that had not been there in a long while. A spark. Life. Alejandro nodded.

"Saturday!" Tanya, Roberto's wife, announced. "In the orchard! The flowers will be in full bloom and there will be cover and plenty of room for the people and..." Another daughter-in-law jumped in and the plans were made. Miguel was congratulated and Olivia stood and walked away.

"I think she's upset." James said as he sat next to Alejandro.

"Yes." Alejandro reached for his grandson. "I will sleep alone tonight." But it was worth it. "I have borne sons, raised them, buried them and now I marry them. I think I have come full circle." He laughed at Jimmy and the boy laughed back.

"So now you plan to die or what?"

"No, I need to hold off on that. There are things I have to do first."

"Such as?" James was curious.

"I have to marry this one, kick Microondo square in the ass and see my baby again."

"Don't forget: Save the world." James added biting in his pie.

"Been there, done that. Leave it to the young pups now," he laughed, and Jimmy laughed with him. James had a feeling there was still a lot of fight left in the old dog.

~

"Forty-six bottles of beer on the wall, forty-six bottles of beer!" Alfie was singing merrily. He had started at a thousand and even the kids had stopped. He found it amusing. Maria found it nerve racking! She wanted him to stop. Waldo was heavy and insisted on sitting on her lap so he could hang out the window. She now knew how sardines felt. And she was afraid. There seemed to be no one following them, but that was not the only danger.

Marauders. They were dangerous men with no homes or families who preyed on the wary traveler. They had blocked the road at several points, waiting for a horse-drawn carriage or people trying escape on foot. The rumbling had them scrambling and at the speed they were traveling, there was little to see with all the dust and Alfie and Waldo howling. Even the boys got into it. After the first hundred miles, there were less marauders. In the dark, it was hard to tell where they were going, but Alfie knew.

Maria took the time to think of what she would say. How she would explain and set her hands on her stomach to hold the bulge. She prayed James would understand and forgive. She prayed he would still love her. She prayed her parents and brothers would forgive her. She prayed that Jimmy would understand when he grew up. And she prayed that the baby in her was healthy. It was a long drive and a long prayer.

Midnight. Miguel wanted to be married at midnight! He had to be different. He wanted candles lit, flowers and a lovely gown for Alise. The bachelor party was scheduled for dusk. It was Friday. Alejandro walked along, whistling softly to himself. He missed Alfie. Microondo was always whistling. Alejandro now whistled happily. He had twelve sons and now ten would be married. Stephano, he would never marry. Too much of a playboy and Joaquin was not ready. But there was hope. He was seventy-five years old. This was his last battle. To see his children settled. The rest, Alejandro Jr. could handle.

There was a shower for Alise and the women gathered at Alejandro's house. He had to escape the cackling women. Alise was sitting there, looking so happy and pretty. He leaned to kiss her cheek and she blushed. Her eye flickered. His wife only rolled her eyes. She was happy to have something to take her mind off things. Things being that Jimmy was soon to be two and his mother was still missing.

It was mid-September and the evenings were getting cooler. A midnight wedding! It was going to be freezing and Alejandro needed to be nice and toasted inside. His old bones hated the cold nights. The men went into the orchard where the flasks were waiting. He headed that way and wanted to be sure there would be more for the wedding. There was singing and laughter and then there was a horn. Alejandro hurried to meet the lookout. The boy rode up on a small horse, looking very excited. All the young ones were anxiously waiting for their first fight. They all reminded him of the ones he lost. If only they knew what it would cost them.

"What?" he asked quickly with the men around him drunk and ready to fight.

"Lookout at the gate. A mustang." The boy gasped. "There is a mustang coming!"

"Well, if it young and sturdy, get a rope and get it!" Alejandro laughed at the young boy.

"No, Senor! Juan says it looks like a 2010 5.0 with turbo? He thinks anyway. He couldn't see good through the telescope. It was coming too fast!" The boy read from the piece of paper he had in his hand. "What do we do?"

It was a joke. A little joke between the two of them. They had been in a museum. One of his few times out of the Stronghold. Legal business. He had to go, and had taken Maria. She was still very scared of people. They had gone to look at the old cars. He was smiling as he walked up to the old muscle car. Memories! He circled it and Maria followed. She held onto his hand as some men came to close. He pulled her closer to him until they had moved on.

"You know Mija, I think I was conceived in the back seat of one of these," he winked at her.

"So you like this?" she asked, reaching out to touch the cold metal.

"Yes, but I really liked the 5.0 with turbo that came out in 2010. A good year!" She would remember. He had only told her once. James was next to him, listening, and trying to sober up. He leaned against his father-in-law.

"Alejandro. She bought one. For you. It's in the warehouse. It must be Alfie!" He was running for the gate.

"Are they being followed?" Alejandro asked, as he ran to the gate. Everyone joined him.

"Not closely. Some nomads farther back, but nothing green." The boy yelled over the men's cries, "They are coming in pretty fast!"

"Alfie can't brake to save his life!" James laughed hysterically.

"He has a dog in the car with him!" the boy yelled, "Riding shotgun!" There was a sinking in their hearts.

"Open the gate!" Alejandro ordered.

The men went outside the gate, with dogs to be sure, and the gate was opened. They made it to the church when the car sped through the gate and into the open area. The driver did donuts before slamming sideways into the garden. No one moved. They stood waiting. Lights were brought and shone on the car. The dog jumped out and ran to James. He knelt to hug it. The smell. A familiar smell. He stood dumbfounded as the gate was slammed shut. There was the surprised scream of a woman and children, then the driver's door opened and Alfie stepped out holding the keys in his hand.

"One bottle of beer on the wall, one bottle of beer, take it down, pass it around, and no more bottles of beer on the wall!" He smiled. The front seat was pushed forward and the women and children fell out. They looked scared. Alfie walked slowly to Alejandro. "An early Christmas." He handed him the keys. "Sorry about the parking."

"Alfie!" James hugged him tightly. "I thought I'd never see you again!"

"Pish Posh! Poppycock and whatever bullshit you can think of! I had promises to fulfill!" He turned and held out his hand as Maria climbed across the driver's seat, ran around the front of the car and vomited. "Well, it was enjoyable for the rest of us!" His words were lost in the yells. James reached her first and spun her around. Her eyes were frightened. She turned and puked again. He let her finish and held her against him.

"I am filthy!" she cried.

"No, Darling! You are beautiful!"

She was crying. Then her father was there, crying and holding her to him. They were all there, all of her brothers and nephews, climbing over each other to get to her. And they were all drunk!

"What is going on? Why are you drunk?" she laughed, being passed around from brother to brother.

"There is a wedding tomorrow!" Julio laughed, hugging her.

"Whose?" She was trying to get down and away. She did not want them touching her.

"Mine!" Miguel laughed, hugging her.

"Who in their right mind would marry you?" she teased hugging him.

"Tostadora Más!" He laughed, and Maria stepped back and the world spun. Darkness swallowed her and she fell into waiting arms.

~

She lay on her side. James had checked her over and so had Alise. She was exhausted. The crowds were kept at bay by Alejandro himself. James wiped her dirty forehead with a cool cloth and then brushed a stray hair from her face. Her eyes shot open and she sat up with fists clenched and ready to fight. Linda moved to hold her hand. Maria was breathing too fast and not seeing what was there, but the nightmares she had left behind. James moved and Linda took the cloth.

"Honey, we made it. You're home." The words were still lost in the confusion. Maria nodded and looked about. "Take it easy. The baby." Maria nodded again and felt the bulge.

"Where is Jimmy?"

"Asleep." James knelt down to look at her. She looked away. She could not bear to look into his eyes. Not yet.

"I want to see him," her voice cracked.

"Of course, Darling." He touched her cold cheek. She still would not look at him.

"We'll take you home." Alejandro scooped her up and carried her to the car. He set her in the seat and walked around to climb in. "It is mine is it not?" he winked. Maria looked off into nothing. She was different. James was looking in at her.

"Microondo says he must speak to you." Joaquin was at his shoulder.

"Let her see her son, shower and come then. Let Olivia talk to her." Alejandro spoke softly. There was something in his eyes. James nodded.

"I'll be there shortly, Darling." She nodded, but would not look at him. The car sped into the Stronghold. Away from James. He knew Alfie was there. Alfie did not give off body heat, but he had a presence. "What have they done to her?" James asked softly.

"Come with me." They walked back into the clinic that was now basically just a triage for the great battle. All that survived would be taken in deeper to the bigger, newer clinic. James sat down and waited. People were going back to the orchard to celebrate. Linda and her family were being taken to a cabin to clean up and rest. Alfie pulled up a chair and sat face to face with James. He made a face, then shrugged.

"What?" James felt his heart racing.

"This will hurt. I can show you all that has happened to her. I will explain how later. But for now, I can show you. If you want?" He sat waiting. "Only you."

"It's bad isn't it?"

"It is. But only as bad as you want it to be."

"Meaning?"

"It happened to her. Not you. How you handle this will make all the difference in the world. I can show it all to you. It will be almost instant. It will give you a headache."

"How?" James looked at Alfie.

"I will explain later."

"Why later?"

"James. You have enough to deal with just now. Do you want to see or not?" It had to be bad if it was bothering Alfie so.

"Do I?" James asked softly, looking so like the little boy he had once been.

"No, you don't. But I think you have to."

"Okay."

"Son," Alfie hadn't called him that in a long time. It only made it worse. "It will be fast and it will hurt. Take a deep breath and let it out slowly." Alfie leaned his face closer as James obeyed. "Now, look into my eyes."

The blue light was almost blinding. It was sudden. Like being shot with a laser in the eye. James felt a sharp sudden pain and then it was gone but the sick feeling overtook him and he turned and vomited. As Alfie cleaned the mess, he leaned on the desk and sobbed. It had hurt. A horrible pain in his head and his heart. It was as if Alfie had burned it all into his brain. It was fast, and surprisingly, not jumbled, but clear. He saw it all. Every moment. Everything she had suffered and done. He also saw how in her sleep she had called for him.

"James," her soft pleading as she slept. She had never forgotten him. The one she had thought dead. Always asking for Jimmy. Adam would come to her at night and push her hair back. "Adam, please! Leave me alone!" She would beg. He would not. Afterwards, she would cry and call out for James.

"James," Alfie was sitting down again. This time he had a small trash can that he set before him.

Always looking out for him. He remember being sick as a child and Alfie holding his head so he didn't drown in the toilet. Then there was the first time he got drunk on very cheap wine. The droid had taken care of him, and then scolded. If he was to get falling down drunk, he should at least steal the good stuff. Dry toast, tea and a lot of aspirin. But James didn't think there was anything to take away this illness or pain. He had his eyes closed.

"She is afraid you won't understand or forgive her."

"Forgive her? For what?"

"For doing what she had to do to survive. I think she would have fought to the death if not for the child."

"Is it mine?"

"Yes. And no. There is something there with the child. Something implanted. You need to pull yourself together. She is going to need you. And your son. It is a boy."

"And Maria?"

"You saw her. She has some healing to do. You must be patient. You have to, or I will turn you over my knee!" James had to smile at him. He had done that before and it was an experience he did not doubt the droid would do. Or that James would want to happen again. "Give her time. Let her come to you."

"What kind of monster would do this?" James asked as the droid reached out with a handkerchief and wiped the tears away.

"The worst kind. The manmade kind."

OLIVIA

"The baby?" She asked stepping into the bedroom.

"Sleeping." Maria was leaning against the door watching Jimmy. Afraid to touch him. As if to do so would make her wake and find him not there. "He's grown so much!" She brushed away the tears.

"It's been a while. They change everyday." Olivia hugged her daughter. "Just as you have. I prayed each day that you would come home."

"Are you alright?" Maria asked, stepping into the hall to see her mother clearly. She was flushed and out of breath. Even she had changed. Mommy never changed.

"I ran all the way!" The woman laughed, hugging her daughter again. "We thought you were dead!" She began to cry. Maria wished she were dead, rather than have to face all that she had fought to get back to. "You smell!"

"I've been in the car with Waldo in my lap, the windows open and Alfie driving. I think I pissed myself!"

"Into the shower. A hot shower!" Her mother ordered.

"Where is Papi?" Maria looked about.

"Outside pacing! Go!" The woman pushed and Maria went.

The bathroom was new. Roomy and warm. She turned on the hot water and undressed slowly, letting the room steam up before she climbed in. She didn't want to see what she looked like. The hot water poured over her and she closed her eyes. They were talking. About her, no doubt. There was the strong harsh tone and then silence. She moved deeper into the shower. Into the corner and faced out. She closed her eyes and tried to relax. She always felt safe under the water. It was where he could not touch her. After a few moments to get control, she washed herself and her hair. There were fluffy towels waiting. She wrapped herself in one, draped one over her shoulders and used it to dry her hair.

"Come sit." Her mothered offered the chair before the vanity. Maria sat and gazed into the mirror. At least this way she didn't have to really look at her mother. "I used to comb your hair like this. Remember?" Olivia was nervous and that was scaring Maria. Her mother was never nervous.

"Mommy?"

"Did you know that you are the reason your father and I are still married?" What a question! "We were this close to divorce." The older women held out her hand to show a small distance. "Then you came along." There was more to this story just by the way the woman was talking. "You saved us. Our marriage, our family and my sanity. You have always been a blessing." The woman gently kept combing out the hair. Maria sat.

"Do you know why there is nine years between you and Joaquin?" That was out of nowhere. But yes, it was a bit strange. There were no more than three between the other siblings. Maria shook her head. "Well, only three people know why." The older woman smiled slightly. "That are living. And now you will know. But it is something that cannot leave your lips." Maria nodded.

"You know that my parents died when I was young. Leaving only me and my sister?" Again, Maria nodded. Now her mother was avoiding her eyes. "My sister, Anita was older then me by two years. She was very pretty back then. We went to live with an aunt in Mendoza. We were new and the boys flocked to her. She had many boyfriends. I was shy and did not. But I made friends easily and I had a few boys who liked me. One was your father and the other was a boy named Frederico. Now, Frederico was the brother of my sister's best friend. Her name was Rebecca. And I did not like her. She was mean."

"Rebecca liked your father. So did my sister." Olivia smiled and picked up the brush. She continued to comb Maria's hair. Very gently. "But your father was older and he was a busy man. He was an only child and his parents very wealthy, in Mendoza anyway. Rebecca thought that since she was the prettiest and from the nice family. Your father thought otherwise. He liked me." There was a soft blush on her mother's cheeks. "This made Rebecca mad and she did and said things that made my sister mad at me. And others."

"Like?" Maria couldn't help but get drawn into the story.

"That I was loose, a hussy and that I was a flirt." Olivia frowned. "I did flirt a little. I was just fifteen. Young and foolish. And your father was very handsome. It was harmless. I thought so anyway. But Rebecca then got her brother to start talking to me. Frederico decided that he was what I needed. I did not agree. We were friends, but no more. He tried, but I would not be more. I knew that I would never have a chance with Alejandro, but a young, poor girl, who is not as pretty as her sister or the rich girl. Can dream. I liked your father. He was so handsome and fun. All the time smiling, laughing and whistling. We all knew that one day there would be wonderful things said about him. He was brave and sincere about his love of family and country. Even a girl like me thought so."

"But you are beautiful Mommy!" Maria almost yelled.

"Shhh! You'll wake the baby!" Olivia smoothed her daughter's hair.

"But you are! You are the most beautiful woman I know!"

"I am Mommy!" Olivia laughed. "When your father joined the army it shocked everyone. When he showed up here in uniform and said he had a twenty-four hour pass and wanted to get married, everyone froze. He came right up to me in the diner and got on one knee! I was fifteen! Almost sixteen! My aunt signed the papers and we were married two days later."

"Just like that?" It was so romantic and wonderful.

"My aunt was old. He promised to send money to take care of me, so I was basically sold to him." Olivia sighed. "I thought I loved him though."

"You didn't know?"

"I wasn't sure. I didn't know what love was!" she laughed. "I learned. Nineteen sons later!" Maria looked confused. She had twenty sons. "We moved back here when he retired from the army. To settle down. His folks were gone and their house was just there, so we came back. All of us!" The memories were happy, yet sad. "We had friends here and I had my sister. She had married Louis and they had a nice little home. Rebecca had married a wealthy man and she fancied herself the queen bee of Mendoza."

"We got here and I was too busy to deal with her or Anita. I had children and a family and your father wanted to move in here. The rebellion was brewing and... It came. We buried our sons, and his parents and my aunt. Here in the Stronghold." She looked sad. "Your father was busy with all the details and all the people coming to him for help and advice. Rebecca's husband was the mayor and he didn't like that he was no longer the one people went to. Two people who were so jealous! And unhappy. No children. She didn't want to ruin her figure," Olivia looked down at her own body, "Then there was Frederico." She frowned.

"He had run from the fighting. He was a coward. He came back when it was over. He was a worthless person. His father had left him some land on the outskirts and he and his friends were out there partying and causing trouble when they could. He was getting old and not liking it and he hated your father." Olivia began to braid the long hair that had lost its shine. Gone, like the shine that was not in her daughter's eyes.

"One night, when your father was away, I went to my sister's. We talked and had a nice time. She told me lots of things. About how she was not happy in her marriage and lonely. She too had no children. I guess I was just overly blessed." She laughed at the thought. "It was getting late, so I headed home. Just across town and then down the road. But my tire went flat and there I was just outside of town when Frederico pulled up. He asked to let him give me a ride but I didn't like the way he was acting. He was drunk. So, I walked home. Roberto was home from school then. Just back from the university and I knew he could go and get my car. So I walked. It was only a mile or so." There was the look again.

"He hit me." She said it slowly. "I had never been hit like that. Like a man would hit another man. He threw me in his car and drove me to his place and...he raped me." She set her hand on her daughter's shoulder. Maria set her hand on it. "It went on for a long time. I couldn't get away. He kept me there for several days until Alejandro came and got me."

"Papi was mad?" That was a dumb question.

"Papi went crazy. They had all left. Gone into the desert. Left me to die. Your father burned the place to the ground and went after them. The police got involved and Rebecca tried to stop it all, acting like she was our friend, but your father was in jail for a bit. Frederico ran. Coward!" She spat the words. "My sister came to help take care of me and your brothers. She would come every day. Then she and her husband came and stayed. Then Rebecca would come. When your father was released, he was busy again with this place. He was feeling that everything that happened was his fault. He wanted to make it up to me." She looked around. "To build me a kingdom."

"Did you ever see how he is with Joaquin? So close to him? Like he is giving into him more? Everyone thinks it is because he is the baby of the boys!" Maria sat waiting. "It is because he is not Alejandro's son. He is Frederico's." Maria watched her mother's face. "Joaquin, me and your father know. And now you."

"Mommy!" Maria turned to look up at her mother.

"I was a bad mother to him. I could not stand to look at him! I ignored him! Your father took up the slack and watched over him more. I could not hold him! My own son!" She was shaking. "I laid in bed and cried after he was born. Rebecca came around and she knew when she saw him. He looked so like Frederico. She wanted to be there for her nephew and she was. And his father."

"Papi? With her?" Maria felt rage and pain for her mother.

"A man has needs. Any man. And your father had needs."

"He and that woman?" Maria couldn't believe what she was hearing. Her father had been unfaithful? No!

"Yes. She was there, he had needs and I denied him. For years. So when Joaquin started kindergarten she and he began to sleep together. I knew. I saw it in his eyes when they were near. The desire of a man. And she would gaze at him across the room, not caring who saw. Her husband and your father were working on building the Stronghold for the community, and there she was." There was a bitterness in her mother's voice. "I knew. He knew I knew and she knew I knew and she began to rub it in my face. Always wanting to see her Joaquin! Always hugging him and telling him how he looked just like his father! The whole while she knew what he had done to me, but she had people convinced that I had an affair and Frederico had left me."

"No one believed her?"

"Oh, they did. I could handle anything but the pain on the faces of my sons as they listened to this. How her brother had been run out by my lies!" Olivia was looking down now. She sat on the bed and Maria moved to sit next to her. "He was an animal. He wanted me and if I would not be his, he would make it so no man would want me." Maria gazed at her mother in confusion. "When Joaquin took his first communion I watched him walk down that aisle and I prayed to God, to the Virgin Mary and to any saint I could think of to give me strength to forgive Frederico and to forgive Joaquin. It was not Joaquin's fault but I had treated him as if it were. I hated my own son for the sins of his father. And I learned how to hate Rebecca."

"I would have too."

"She was a desperate woman. At the communion party, my sister and Rebecca fought. They were yelling and Rebecca was calling me names and my sister was actually trying to defend me, but it was all there. The boy who looked like Frederico and was closer to Rebecca than me! Then I yelled. I told her never to come near my son or my husband again! I told her never again! And she laughed at me. She said I had already lost." Olivia sighed. "So I slapped her."

"Good for you!"

"I went to the house to pack. I was not staying. Me or my sons. The ones who were young enough were going with me and the others who were grown could stay or follow, but I would not stay in Mendoza. Your father came and brought me here. He took me to the house he had built. Built with his hands for me! He set me down and he begged for forgiveness! And I begged him!" She was a simple woman, wearing a simple button down blouse.

"He brought me here and told me that I would never have to leave the Stronghold if I did not want to. That he would make this our own world. That I would never have to face those people again. He and I made love for the first time in a long time. A very long time. Just as we had when we were first married." She unbuttoned her shirt slowly. "That night he looked at me for the first time since the night it happened, and he saw me. Not this."

The blouse fell back and Maria fought not to scream. The healed cut marks covered her mother's chest. Across each breast and down her soft stomach. Horrid jagged scars that crisscrossed and covered most of her stomach. Olivia did not look up, but stood and turned to show the healed whipped marks on her back. Then Olivia sat down and pulled her shirt on. She said nothing, but reached out to hold her daughter's shaking hand. There were tears as they fell into each other's arms. Olivia rocked her daughter in her arms. They cried for a long time.

"No matter what was done to you, he suffers with you. I have not spent one night away from your father since then. I am afraid to. He brought me back. Made me whole and human again. That night, angels brought you to us to save us. Don't push James away. Let him help you heal." Olivia made her baby sit up and looked into her eyes. "You have a son and another on the way. You can't run and hide. You have to face this. Your father and I will be there for you." Maria nodded. "Take time to heal, but don't hurt as you heal. It takes time. A lot of time. And a lot of love. To go on and forgive."

"I don't understand." Maria wiped her face on the towel.

"My sister died a slow painful death. I only saw her a couple of times after that. I would not leave and she would not come. She was still Rebecca's friend. She wanted the popular life." Olivia laughed. "Drink, cigarettes and fun. Anita had lung cancer. Rebecca's husband stole money and killed himself rather than go to jail. Then Rebecca was in a car crash and her face was scarred terribly. She died alone in an empty house. No one found her for almost a month. By then, her cats had eaten most of her." Maria shivered.

"And Frederico?" It was the one she knew would be the worst.

"Joaquin shot him." Olivia spoke softly. "He was the man that took you." Maria felt her stomach turn. A memory she had suppressed for years.

The men rode up and Olivia stood pushing her behind them. The guard and her. The men were dirty and in jeeps. Maria had been ten and curious. Frederico had been in the first jeep with another man driving. He climbed out and walked over to them. Olivia told her to run. Maria had clung to her mother. The man grabbed her mother and kissed her roughly. Olivia fought and the guard moved to help. He was shot. Maria screamed. Olivia and she ran. The man grabbed Maria by the hair and jerked her back. He struck Olivia and dragged Maria to the jeep, hitting her in the head as he did. He was laughing. She remembered that sick laugh. It had haunted her dreams for a long time. Somewhere along the way, he knocked her out. The next thing Maria saw was his face in hers and he was tearing at her clothes. She was crying, he was laughing, and then he was gone. Her mother was there. She remembered that. And Joaquin kneeling over the man. She never saw the gun.

"Papi?" Joaquin had spoken softly to the man who lay gurgling as he choked on his own blood. Her father was there then holding Joaquin as the young man was sick. Joaquin was nineteen then. Just recently a man. They had left without burying any of the fallen, Maria on her father's horse sitting before him wrapped in his shirt. Joaquin rode with his mother behind him. They had never spoken of it.

"Did Joaquin know?" Maria asked softly.

"Yes. When we moved into the Stronghold, he was told. He forgave me." She smiled slightly. "He accepted my love of him. He is my son after all."

"But not Papi's?"

"Oh, Mija, he is more like your father than the rest. Osmosis is what I think you scientists call it." She chuckled lightly. "He is the one who will save us all!"

"Mommy, this child is James'."

"I know."

"I just don't know after what they did if he will be okay."

"He is a baby. You will love him or you would not have fought so hard to come home. To James."

"I thought James was dead. The baby was all I had left of him." Maria looked up with tear-filled eyes.

"He thought you were dead too. All he had was Jimmy."

"Has he had other women? Here?" Olivia laughed loudly.

"As if they could get within a mile of him with Alise there! She scared any woman off! Her and her blinking eye!" They both laughed. "My daughter-in-law the droid!"

"Sounds like a good title for a soap opera!" Maria teased.

"She is good for Miguel and the children. He loves her so. He is happy now and so I have to accept it. Plus now she won't be making cow eyes at my husband." They laughed again. "I never did like her or trust her." Olivia looked ashamed. "But that night...She brought them here. The baby dry and fed. James hurt but alive and Microondo in pieces. Do you know how they got here?" Maria shook her head. "She pushed them in your little car. The whole way. All by herself and the only thing she said when she got here was she had tried. Tried? She pushed them. When she came to she was going back for you."

"Me?"

"She was going to put Alfie together and go for you. James had to force her to stay here. And the only complaint she had? She had ruined her new shoes. She is one tough little droid. And I trust all of my children and grandchildren with her. You must be strong. For your brother. He loves her."

"I will, Mommy."

"Mija, let me see?"

Maria looked down and then let the towel slide away. The few remaining bruises were slight but there had been some tearing of the skin. Scars. Small and nothing compared to her mother's, but then she had been the prize to Adam. The bite on her shoulder had not healed well. He had taken skin off there. A lot of it. Olivia leaned forward and kissed the shoulder. Maria was stiff. Afraid to move. Afraid to live.

"Do not let him win. Do not lose yourself. You have to come back to us. Mentally. Don't do as I did and hide for years. Your children need you and James needs you. All he thought of was you. He tried to go after you the first night. We couldn't let him. He only stayed because of Jimmy. And then when Alfie went, he felt like less of a man for not finding you." Olivia sighed. "You must get past it all. It will take a lot, but you can do it. You are my daughter. I know you can forgive and live with the memories. I did."

"I'm afraid," Maria mumbled.

"And so am I," Olivia spoke softly. "Your father keeps me sane. If I get scared, I run to him. He holds me and all of it goes away."

"I can't go to James! What if he finds out?"

"He will find out. You will tell him. As I told my husband. He will cry, and you will cry, and then you will each find a way to deal with it and go on."

"What if he can't forgive me?"

"Then you will forgive him." There was a knock at the door. Maria quickly covered herself. James stepped in carrying a dress, some shoes and some lingerie. Olivia stood and held her daughter's hand, giving it a good squeeze. "I have to go to the shower. Once you get dressed you come too." She kissed her daughter's hand and left them.

Maria had pulled the towel over her shoulders and held it tightly against her. James set the clothes on the bed. He just stood. Maria could not look at him. He knelt down slowly and moved to lay his head in her lap. She sat rigid as he cried. She waited and slowly he sat back to gaze at her. It was when their eyes met that she saw that he knew. Alfie! She began to shake. He sat on the bed next to her and she was trembling! He lifted the covers off the bed and wrapped her in them. She sat, still not moving.

"I'll let you get dressed." James mumbled after some time. He kissed her temple and left the room. Maria pushed all the covers and towels off and ran for the shower. She turned on the hot water and stood crying. Only here was she safe.

~

Shoes! Everyone had gotten Alise shoes! She sat in the chair in the middle of the room trying them on. Little Thomas and Manuel were toddling around in women's shoes. Alise helped them try on different ones. The women were teasing that Miguel would get mad at his boys wearing ladies shoes. The twin boys smiled and climbed all over Alise. As Maria slowly stepped into the room, the women raced to her. Alise stood and ran to hug her. She stood rigid. She knew Alise. She loved Alise, but like Alfie, Alise was one of them.

"I knew it! I knew it!" the droid squealed, "I just knew it!"

"Knew what?" Maria couldn't help but laugh.

"That you would come when you found out I was getting married!" Alise stepped back beaming. Now her eye was flickering. "I knew you would know."

"Know what?"

"That James needed you!" As if Maria had been on vacation or something! It was unbelievable! "His heart was calling to you! Giving you strength because he is drained!"

How terrible! Maria had been so worried about what they would think of her that she hadn't even looked about her. The situation here was different. It wasn't just her family but many new faces. Many scared new faces. Just as Alejandro had predicted, people had flocked to what they had laughed about. But the Stronghold had held. Now she looked about. The faces of her family were smiling, but concerned. They were tired. Working twice as hard to keep them all alive. Taking care of her husband and son. Worrying about her. She looked to her mother and saw the pain and fear. Were they afraid she might lose her mind? Well, it wasn't that far fetched. She had come close. Dying had seemed a lot easier then living at times.

"Come sit." A chair appeared for her.

"I think I want to see James," Maria fumbled with her words, "And Jimmy."

"The microwave is with him." Her sister-in-law, Caryn, pushed her to the chair. "And James is getting drunk. I think he needs to. And you need to relax. Not think." Alejandro Jr.'s wife, Elisabeth, patted her should. Maria sat and took the glass of punch offered. Later. They always had later. They had forever.

It all gave together in a mindless blur for Maria. Gifts, women and young girls. Alise put her boys down for the night and was there in the middle of the games laughing and smiling. She was happy. A happy droid. Before, it would not have been weird, but now it was. There were many things that were weird. Maria sat sipping her punch and thinking of weird. She had twenty brothers. Eight had died, seven before she was born. She was the only daughter. The only daughter of a great man who was probably the last living warrior. The last great leader.

The world was coming to an end. It was. Not just a rumor or a fairy tale. The world had come to its end by what they had built. They had made droids to make their lives easier, and now androids made by man were taking over. Taking over and ending it all. Her father had been right. Do it yourself. If a machine does it, then it is not as good. He was a man who was adamant about how things should be done. Not how to do them easily. Most people did things easily. The easy way. Let the machines do it. Now they were lost. Civilization was lost. All because people took the easy way.

There was suffering here in the Stronghold. But not the kind of suffering she knew was on the outside. Not what Linda and Mom had told her about. People begging for food. Children starving and men being blown to bits or selling their souls to the devil himself to stay ahead. Civilization. Was it like this all over the world or just here? Would anyone know? Her father would. She would have to talk to her father. To tell him. To let him know what she knew. She knew she was going to have to tell them. Yes, Alfie had it all in his head. But it wasn't as good. She had to tell. And she had to start with James. He had to be the first.

Olivia watched her baby's face. She smiled at the right moments. She blushed and looked away when talked to. She was alive. She was home. She was pregnant and now she knew the secret. A secret that might help her deal with what had happened. Then again, it might not. Olivia set her glass down and walked out onto the patio. It was late and the weather was holding. Almost October. It wasn't cold, only crisp. She hugged herself and walked slowly to the chapel. The chapel where all her sons and her daughter had been married.

Three hundred years before it was a mission. A mission and a vineyard. Priests who made wine. How perfect. The chapel was huge and the outlying buildings wonderful little homes. They were used by people who had come here to relax and reflect:. the Spaniards, the Indians and then the government. When Alejandro had first decided to build the Stronghold, their army life was over. The world was changing. And they had to change with it to survive. For the sake of their children and grandchildren. They had to go back. He had told her. Explained it and believed it. She loved him, so she had agreed.

She had followed him across the ocean five times. Taking her children each time. Sometimes she had to leave some. College or their lives kept them in the states, but she had gone. He was her husband and she loved him. She had learned how to live in different countries. To shop, to care for her children and to make a home for him. They had fled in the middle of a war. They had stayed in the middle of another. There was always a war and always a need for a man like Alejandro. But the home they knew was changing. He had told her it was another civil war. A war he would not fight in, but would fight. Nonetheless, she didn't understand until it had come to their door. To their home.

To everyone he was a hero. To her, he was her beloved fool! Then the call came. Men were running. Running to get guns to join or running to hide. To be dragged into the conflict. He stood with his thirteen sons. She held the youngest back. Nine went with him. Each kissing her cheek as they left the home. She stood, pregnant and afraid. He kissed her gently and patted the baby, then her ass. She hit his arm laughing as she wiped away the tears. To him it was just a little fight. To her it was a nightmare. For some reason she knew Trino and Alberto would not be coming back. It was as if it were written on their handsome faces. Jose and Francis. Twins. So close that they thought as one. And died together. Ricardo was born the next evening. Her victory baby.

It was told in history that she had gone into labor upon learning of the deaths of her four sons. The truth was she was two weeks overdue. If not, she might have gone with them. Alejandro mounted that horse and sat looking down at her. She was frightened. He saw that, but had no choice. This was their home. They had to make a stand. The boys were with him. Her sons. She held one in her arms and tucked the younger ones behind her.

"I'll be home for dinner," he winked, and they left.

That day was hot. No rain for days and the dust was swirling about. They could see the troops coming for miles across the desert. They were coming for him. If he were in the lead, all would follow. The army knew this. So did she. She stood on the roof of the church rectory with the father and the nuns. She had to be kept safe. If he resisted, they might come for her or the boys. From there she saw him. Sitting in the road. Laughing and talking to the men that had come with him. Here it was a bottleneck surrounded by rocks and trees. A perfect place to wait. And they waited. She had rubbed her hands raw waiting.

Then it was there. The jeep, the general, and her Alejandro. Now over forty, but still tall and handsome. He sat on the horse at the bottleneck and spoke loudly for all to hear. He would fight. He would lead, but not for anything but a United States of America. Civil war was not a war he or his family would participate in. If the enemy advanced, then Alejandro and his men would defend. The guns were raised, the dust blowing and the shots rang out. There was a rush of everything. Blinding dust, smoke and deafening screams, yet and there he sat. He pointed his rifle, touched his heels firmly to the stallion's flanks and fired. The enemy general fell and the war began.

Dinner. She set the table and slowly they came to sit. One by one, hugging her, kissing her cheek and wiping the tears, blood and sweat from their faces. Four chairs were empty. They said a prayer, ate dinner and waited for what was to come. Alejandro had an idea. He had a vision, even though he would not tell anyone except her that he had visions. He was sure of one thing: they would be safe in the Stronghold with the ghosts and the mission. It was a blessed place. A place that he had seen standing for another two hundred years with his children's children there. His Shangri-La. Their future.

"What is it?" Alejandro asked. She smiled to herself. How did he always know? Even when they were going through the toughest of times, he was always there for her. He slept next to her nightly. After the attack on her, he would not touch her unless invited. And she didn't invite. Not for almost eight years. But he was there.

"Remembering," she hugged herself. He stepped behind her and hugged her to him.

"Forget," he teased kissing her neck.

"Easy for you to say," she mumbled. He held her tighter.

"No, it's not." She knew it wasn't. He had not been raped, but he had suffered as she had. Daily. Not just the rape and the mutilation, but the guilt and pregnancy that neither of them wanted. A pregnancy that because of their faith they had to see through. Not a choice for all, but it had been a good one. Joaquin was a wonderful boy. "Mija?" She couldn't say it. She only nodded. He hugged her tighter. "We will get through this."

"But will they?" She wiped her face on the sleeve of his shirt.

"Oh, I think so. He is over there just waiting for a chance to talk to her."

"And you? You drunk yet?"

"Have been for some time." He kissed her neck again. "You watch her and I will watch him. They will be fine. Time. They need it."

"Do they have time? Do we?"

"What does that mean?"

"It's getting closer," she whispered, turning to gaze up at him.

"It is, but we are safe. Here is where we stay. She is here and now it is over. The entrances are closed as of tonight and no more in or out. If any go out then they do not come back."

"Sickness will come?"

"Maybe. We will be fine." He leaned down and kissed her. "How long until you are a great-grandma again?" Amelia. Alejandro Jr.'s middle daughter was more than ready.

"Tonight. Maybe tomorrow. She is like me," Olivia smiled. Twins. On the first time.

"They are all like you." He held her against his chest. She listened to his heart beating strong and loud. "We will be here for a long time to come. The Vargas' will be around for a long time."

"Just hold me?" she asked softly.

"Always." He looked up to see Maria making her way to the chapel. She looked lost and frightened. This was something he could not fix. This was bigger than all of them. "You go to her and I will bring him." He kissed his wife's forehead and was gone into the night. Olivia felt alone and scared. Not only for her youngest, but for herself. She was sure Alejandro was right, but there was that bit of doubt that made her wonder. Doubt and fear. Would dying be easier than fighting to live?

Maria wasn't kneeling. She was just sitting. The old priest stepped out from the rectory, but Olivia waved him off. This was for her. She walked to the pew. It was so quiet here in the arms of the church. She genuflected and sat next to her youngest. Maria was just sitting. The tears were falling slowly down her face. Her eyes were fixed on the huge, wooden crucifix over the altar. The figure on the cross looking up with pain-filled eyes as blood ran down his face. His kind face.

"For God so loved the world that he gave his one and only Son, that whoever believes in him shall not perish but have eternal life." Maria quoted the Bible verse as a small child would. "How ironic." She almost laughed.

"What is, Mija?" Olivia set her hand on her daughters. The girl shook her head. No, she could not tell her mother. Her mother was a devout Catholic. Something like this was too far out there. She would never understand or accept it. "What is ironic?"

"He knew when born that he was just put on the earth to suffer and die. To die for us." She shook her head. "To save us. And look what we have done. Humans."

Olivia fought to find comforting words.

"God is a forgiving god…"

"No!" Maria jumped up and moved away from her mother. "Don't say that!" The panicked look on Maria's face was enough for her mother to wait before she moved to jump in God's defense.

"But it is true."

"God and I have some things that just aren't what I expected." Maria almost laughed. No, none of it was what she expected. Her husband was alive, her son safe and still…

"What you expected?" That was all Olivia would hold her tongue for. "God gave you life! A husband! A child! And another!"

"Oh, Mommy!" Maria wailed. "Not this God!" She turned and hugged herself. The words of the prophecy stared at her. Etched in the walls of the old church. To be seen by all and thought on. Hope. God had given them hope in the way of words. Was it enough? For Maria it was. "Not ever this God."

"There is only one God!" Olivia stood and announced with conviction. "One God that we worship! That evil thing is not!" So the stories had reached the Stronghold. "Is he the one that did this to you?" Maria would not look back at her mother but nodded. "Then the one and only, the mighty God, our God, the true God, will strike him down and all that follow him. He will burn in hell!"

"Step down from the pulpit," Alejandro ordered as he and James walked to the women. He set a hand on Maria's shoulder. She wiped her face and looked over her shoulder at her father. His hand traveled up to caress her cheek. She sniffled, but didn't pull away. "Come along. They have a lot to talk about." Alejandro patted her head and took his wife's hand. Olivia stopped to genuflect and followed slowly.

"Come sit?" James stood waiting. Now Maria did look at him. He was thin, pale and tired looking. Older. He had aged. But his eyes were soft. "Please?"

With a long deep breath, she walked over and sat down on the pew. He genuflected and sat next to her. They both sat gazing up at the crucifix for a bit. How to start? What to say? What to ask? What to do? She tried to clear away the fear and find the facts. The nightmares and the night terrors. That would help. A lot would help. A lot of alcohol. She needed tequila. Suddenly she remembered Linda.

"My friend and her children?"

"They are in the older store house. It was big enough. Only has four beds, but the children are fed and sleeping. I believe her mother is at the bachelor party, getting toasted," he smiled softly. There was that awkward silence he had not wanted between them. "Would you like to go back to the house? To Jimmy?" They could wait to talk. He wasn't really up to listening to what he already knew.

"Alfie showed you?" she asked softly.

"Yes."

"What do you know of the creature?" She was holding her hands tightly. She couldn't even speak his name.

"He is from somewhere other than here. He is not human but has evolved into a humanoid. He declares himself a god. Adam. The first. Other than that, we know nothing. No answers to questions. Royalty, dignitaries, common and the wealthy are all treated equally. Without any concern. As if we were nothing but…."

"Ants." She flexed her hands now. "What did Alfie show you?"

"Only what had happened to you." He reached out to set his hand on hers and she stiffened. "That was enough for me." His stomach had still not recovered.

"I will not ask you to be with me if it disgusts you…I would understand if…" She looked over at him, surprise but not the rage she saw.

"Expect what? That I would not want my wife and child?" His face was a deep red. "You were taken, in the night with a good fight from Alfie, and you were raped. Now I should just walk away and leave you?"

"You are not going to be held to the marriage vows. I would understand," she stammered.

"I love you!" He spoke through gritted teeth. "I love you more than my own life! I faced your family! I faced your mother! Alone! How can you dare say these things to me? TO ME?" she sat listening. Her heart was racing in relief and hope.

"There you are!" That voice! James rolled his eyes as Maria's flashed. Fiona!

"Damn!" James sighed, and stood to meet the very gorgeous woman who hurried to them.

Fiona Malloy was a young doctor who was more than a little infatuated with James. She had the movie star glamour. Tall, curvy, blonde and blue eyes. Gracious, elegant and perfect. They had dated as residents, but she had dumped him for fame and fortune which, ironically, he found and she did not. Only the semester before she had gotten on staff at the teaching hospital where James did most of his research. For a while there, Fiona was at him daily, but once she got the message, especially from Alise, that he was happily married she had faded into the woodwork. Now that the world was coming to an end, the cockroaches were coming out of their holes.

"It's true!" She flashed her capped teeth smile at Maria! "You've returned from the dead!" Maria clenched her teeth. The looks. James and her. Just as her mother had said. Or was it? "He had been mooning over you all these months! It's wonderful to see you home. Safe." The eyes traveled over her. Those scheming blue eyes. "My little Jimmy must be so happy!" Her little Jimmy?

"My son is asleep. He will see me in the morning." Maria clenched her fists and glared.

"He is a doll! Just a little man. We've had so much fun with him, haven't we James?" the woman reached out to set her hand on James' arm. She smiled at Maria.

When she had first come to the hospital there had been a luncheon. She had mooned and practically draped herself on James. Maria had simply stepped aside. James had been polite, but was attentive to Maria and that just made Fiona try harder. She was always stopping by, or needing a bit of time, or having a problem that only James could solve. At times, it was hard on Maria. She would see him smiling at Fiona and think back to when she and James had been sneaking around. Was he? No, he swore he was not. Alise had told her that the woman was poison. No other details, but if Alise didn't like her, then she was. Now Fiona was holding onto his arm.

"Fiona, will you excuse us?" James peeled her hand off.

"Have some catching up to do?" That cold little smile. "Some explaining?"

"My wife does not have to explain anything to me." James stepped over to set his arm around Maria. She stiffened but didn't pull away.

"James, it's been five months. Everyone is talking how she's been holed up with some nomads! You really don't think that you can just come back and everything is peachy?" The woman stepped closer, eyeing Maria. The little girl that she had sent crying from his office more than once. Little innuendos that tore at the girl's heart.

"This is my home," Maria spoke firmly. "My family. My son and husband." She stepped forward to gaze at the woman. "One word from me and you will find your peachy ass hiking for the nearest bunch of nomads." James turned his head away to keep from laughing. For Maria to be so cold was unbelievable. "And I was not with nomads. I was in that damn ship." The look. "The rumors are true. And I escaped to return to my family."

"Well, I guess you do have some talking to do," Fiona was trying to regain her grace. It wasn't happening. "I'll leave you two alone."

"Fiona?" Maria called and the woman turned to look at her.

"Stay away from my son and my husband."

"Or what? You not going to sick Alise on me? She's too busy with her wedding!" The woman just didn't know when to stop.

"I will toss your ass off the mountain myself," Maria warned. Then smiled. The other woman backed away, and then hurried out of the church. Maria turned to face the crucifix and crossed herself. "Forgive me," she mumbled sitting down. James sat next to her. There was that deadening silence.

"She showed up about a month out. Bought her passage out of the city and then got lost. They found her wandering out there in stilettos and brought her in and...."

"You two?" Maria didn't look at him.

"The world is ending, but it ain't that bad!" He laughed coldly. "She helps out in the clinic. Works under Alise. Does not like it but is terrified of my Mum."

"She's been with my son?"

"No, he hates her and is too dirty for her. She is after your brother, Stephano," James chuckled. "Now she has Stephano on the run. He hates her. Runs every time she comes around like a hunted rabbit."

"What do we do?" Maria asked softly.

"She'll leave us alone. Mum will have her scrubbing bedpans if..."

"Not about her!" Maria actually laughed a little. "About us?"

"What about us?" He leaned down so that she had to look up and into his eyes. "You are still my wife?"

"Yes."

"Did you miss me?" He asked foolishly.

"Yes!" She gripped his hand in hers. "I thought you were dead!" She was shaking.

"I knew you weren't." He squeezed her hand and brought it to his lips to kiss. "Too damn tough for such a little thing. I saw you fighting them." He looked down at the ring she wore. How was it she had never taken it off?

"I saw you die," she whispered. "At least I thought I did."

"What you saw was a very pissed off Mum." He smiled and they sat silent for a few moments. "Tomorrow Alfie will show your father what he has in his head. And what happened to you." She began to shake harder. "Only him." She nodded knowing that it had to be.

"James..." She was cold. She was terrified. She was shaking. "Hold me?" He didn't hesitate. His arms around her were strong. Strong enough for both of them.

"Anything you want." He kissed her head and closed his eyes.

"I have to tell you. I have to tell Papi and Alfie but I have to tell you first." He held her tighter even though he wanted to hold his hands over his ears. "I just need you to listen." She buried her head into his chest and waited.

He didn't want to hear it. He didn't want to remember what had been slammed into his mind. To have someone else's memory put in your head was not only confusing to your memories but the emotions too! He was angry, scared and more. He was downright terrified! It was as if it had happened to him. And then it wasn't. To see her held down like an animal and raped repeatedly had made him wish he were dead. The beating she had taken had terrified him. Now he was jumpy. He couldn't do it here. There was too much rage in him. He gathered her in his arms and carried her up to the very front. Underneath the figure of their dying Jesus. Here he would be calmer. With another who had suffered. He sat down with her in his lap.

"Tell me," he ordered.

"Since the night I last saw you, almost everyday I was raped by something. I was pregnant. I was going to tell you once I was a bit farther along but I didn't get a chance. Only me and Mommy and Alfie knew. And well, Alise, but she knows all…

"So now they heal each other?" Olivia asked from the alcove where she and Alejandro stood watching.

"Yes." He hugged her to him.

"Now we go on living?" She could be hopeful.

"No, now we get ready to fight." He kissed her cheek. "You really didn't think this was going to be easy did you?" There was that gleam in his eye. A wildness of his youth.

"You are an old man," she warned.

"That I am. But I am your old man." He pulled her out the door. "Leave them to talk. I want a drink and a little time with you. Alone."

"It will happen soon?" She asked following him as a young girl would her lover.

"I don't think so. Years maybe. We have time to get ready." He put his arm around her and drew her into the warmth of him. "To get them ready." Olivia looked back at the chapel they were leaving. "Like us, they need time."

"Time and more," she mumbled.

"Then we will give it." He ordered, giving her a look. It said let it go for now. "Wait for her to come to you." She wondered if Maria would ever be able to. There was a look in her eyes. A look of unspeakable terror that she did not want to share. Olivia was afraid that she might one day have to hear it. Alejandro also was afraid. But he knew he would have to hear it.

JIMMY

"The baby?" Jimmy asked, patting the mound of her stomach with his chubby little hands.

"The baby. Your brother." Maria leaned down to kiss his cheek. He turned his face from hers. She thought he was rejecting her, but it was simply that the older boys did that when their mother's kissed them. He made a face and then hugged her.

"Mama!" he sighed dreamily. She held him fighting the tears. He had remembered her.

He woke to find her in bed with him. She was familiar to him, even after five months. She still smelled of Mama. His father was lying on the other side of him with his arm draped over him and holding her hand. Jimmy rubbed his eyes and looked about. The sun was out but there was no noise. Usually there was noise. People waiting to see the doctor or children playing. Alise in the kitchen with all his cousins running about. He was cold, his diaper wet and heavy. The tousled hair and blue eyes were all Sinclair. A carbon copy of James.

"Hello?" Alfie stood at the foot of the bed awaiting his acknowledgement.

"Alfie!" The boy was scrambling from under the limbs and covers to dive at the droid.

"Good morning, sir!" The droid's blue face glowed.

"Daddy! Alfie!" The dog came in barking then. "Waldo!" Maria sat up, as the dog jumped on her and licked her face. She turned to escape and got a quick peck from James. She sat looking shocked.

"Morning, Darling." He climbed from the bed and took his son. "We have duties." He announced and guided the boy to the bathroom. Maria sat up looking out the window. She felt his presence, but said nothing. It was not an intrusion. Alfie never was.

"All went well?" he asked.

"You showed him?"

"I made a decision. It had to be. I did it for very selfish reasons." She now looked at him. "I love you all. If you can believe that. You are my family. I don't want to lose that." Alfie crossed his eyes, winked and smiled. "I would not be functional if I did."

It was colder in the morning. She shivered and climbed from the bed to make for her own bathroom. Her head hurt. She had cried many tears. They both had. It was a nightmare. A nightmare she had to relive. Only this time he was with her. It hurt that she was afraid of him. That his touch made her skin crawl. She came out of the bathroom to have Jimmy run to hug her. His hands on the mound of her belly.

"The baby?" He put his nose to it as if to smell it.

"The baby. Your brother."

"Want cereal," he ordered, and ran for the kitchen.

"Just like all the men in my family. Food first," she laughed softly.

"It's good to hear you laugh." James reached to kiss her and she moved off to find some clean clothes. Not yet. She just couldn't yet. Maybe never. Olivia had been raped once and it took her eight years. Could James wait that long? If not, there was always Fiona. She shook her head at the thought. "What?" He laughed watching her.

"Evil thoughts," she mumbled.

"Darling, come sit with me." He sat on the bed and patted the place next to him. She stared at him. Had anyone else been in that bed with him? How could she be jealous? She shook her head again. "Why not?" James asked patting the bed again.

"I was just thinking." She moved to sit a bit from him.

"About?"

"I don't know," she lied. He smiled at her. "What?"

"You are the first woman to sit on my bed." She sat staring at him. "I made this bed!" he laughed. She looked down at the homemade mattress and felt the comfort of it.

"You made it?" She ran her hand over the thick ticking.

"Plucked so many damn chickens, geese and turkeys that I swore off fowl for a bit!" He fell back onto the mattress. "All the time thinking of me and you on it. That was all I thought of!" he laughed. "It took me four months! I just got it finished! What do you think?"

James McMillan Sinclair III, who had discovered the cure for cancer, was excited about plucking chickens for a mattress for his wife. She laughed at him as he rolled to and fro on it. He grabbed her and pulled her to him. She was stiff but trying. He kissed her cheek and then her nose. She stared at him, embarrassed at her fear of him. Of anyone. He fell back and gazed at the ceiling. She curled up next to him and sighed. His heart was beating. Slow and steady. She didn't have to tell it to. It did it on its own.

"Alfie is the microwave, Alise the toaster oven. What do we call that son of a bitch?" he asked half-heartedly.

"Son of a bitch sounds good." She mumbled. "He isn't real. Not human."

"I know. Alfie and I had a rundown on that after I put you to bed." She remembered him tucking her in with the baby and leaving her. Later he was there. On the other side of Jimmy with his arm over her. It was comforting. Not intrusive. "A clone with cyborg abilities. And then there is the regeneration. We discussed the effect of the mother's milk." At the words, she fidgeted. "What?"

"They ache," she mumbled.

"Are they dry now?" He moved to examine her and she pulled away. "Sorry, darling." He said. "Cold or hot towels will help with that. Give them a rest before the next one gets here." His hand went to her stomach and it felt good. She felt lost. She knew Jimmy had to have been weaned almost immediately. "

With everything going on he and his sippy cup were inseparable." James continued. Maria felt as if something had been stolen from her.

"Don't worry darling, the next will be here soon." His fingers traveled over her face. He had so many questions he wanted to ask, but was afraid she would answer them.

"Adam said my milk helped him develop ahead of schedule. A cyborg can do that?" She was now into the mood to find out exactly what Adam was so that they could kill him. Could he be killed? He wasn't alive. Was he?

"We're going to review some things this morning," James said. "I'm meeting your father and brothers. Alfie and I. And Alise. If I can get that smile off her face!" He shook his head. "My Mum is marrying your brother. Is that not weird? Now is he my step-dad?" Maria didn't smile.

"How did all that come about?"

"I don't know. He liked her, he was alone with four little ones and..," James sighed heavily, "Alfie had a hand in that. I think he knew that if she didn't find something to do she would short circuit. It's not so bad. I mean, Miguel seems very happy with her and the boys adore her."

"This meeting? Who all will be there again?" She rolled on her side and curled into a ball around a soft pillow.

"Me, your father, all of your brothers, Alfie, Alise, Fiona..."

"Fiona?" Now she sat up.

"Well, she is a micro-robotic specialist," he defended the woman. "Cyborgenetics is pretty much what she does. And that is what Adam is."

"No," Maria shook her head. "There is more to him than just a replaced artificial limb."

The field was still young. Only a few were experts in it. And Fiona was one. The replacement of amputated limbs with flesh covered alloy steel prosthesis was a miracle in itself. The regenerative flesh-like material was organic and lifelike, but not. It was grown in a Petri dish. It was manufactured. Skin tone, texture and elasticity were ordered.

"It is like he was altered. Like a droid that had evolved. And he evolved quickly." She shuddered at the memories.

"Meaning?" James sat up slowly. That look. The lost look. The one that made him think of her in a long hallway looking for answers and was afraid to open the door to the question.

"It was like child to adult in five months. And insanity that was there the whole time." She looked over to be sure they were alone. "James, he is not human. He is an animal. And we are nothing to him. Nothing."

"Darling, you are safe here with me." His arms around her were comforting.

"Not me. He won't kill me. He thinks he needs me," she was crying. "But you? Jimmy? Everyone?"

"No worries. You are home. All we have to do is breathe." He kissed the top of her head. "Let's get breakfast and meet with your father. Let's just get this over with." He stood and pulled her to her feet. She looked down. "What? What is it?"

"I don't have any clothes."

"And you can't wear mine," he laughed. "They would swallow you whole! Well, your bottom half anyway. He suddenly dropped to his knees and held her firmly in his hands. As if measuring. "I am going to have to examine you." She had a slight look of panic. "It's either me or Fiona. For now we are all there is in the way of medical personnel. Aside from two retired nurses, a dentist and a podiatrist. Oh, and about four or five EMTs and ten or so firemen. All men."

"I guess it's you," she frowned.

"Darling, I examined you when you were pregnant with Jimmy!" He kissed her stomach.

"I know." She reached out cautiously and touched his fine soft hair. It felt so real! So wonderful. He leaned into her touch. Wanting it and more. More she could not give. At least not now. A thought hit her. "Alfie and Alise should be there. Something is different. I don't know what, but you might miss something." Something? He gazed up at her.

"I missed you." He kissed her stomach again then stood to kiss her lips, making her jump. How was it so easy for him to do this? As if she had just gone on a short holiday? "Grab a shirt of mine. I'll trot over to Amelia's and see if I can get a pair of jeans out of her. She'll be happy to get rid of them."

"I'm not a great aunt yet?" Maria calculated in her head.

"No, she's overdue but not in any danger. Just uncomfortable." His hands lighted on her shoulders. He was being careful of where to touch her. He was trying too hard. It was making her uncomfortable. He noticed it and stepped back from her. "I'll go find a shirt. I don't have too many, but you can wear any that you like." He kissed her forehead and was gone.

Maria wandered around the room. It had been just a little two-room cabin when they moved in. Now it had three extra rooms and what looked like a small exam room in the back. The kitchen had been set out and opened up more. She stood in the doorway and watched as Jimmy sat tossing cereal loops to Alfie and Waldo. The two were catching them in their mouths. He looked up at her and smiled.

"Look, Mommy!" he waved and smiled brightly. Her hands were on the mound and she felt as if it were moving. But no, it was too early. She had time. Time to make up for all she lost.

"I want some," she noted, hurrying to sit with her son.

"I'll get you some coffee." Alfie patted her shoulder as she sat down. He 'winked' at her and a thought hit her.

"Alfie?"

"Yes?"

"His eyes? They did not evolve. Why?" The droid stood still and she suspected he was reviewing the Archive.

"I have a suspicion." Alfie was moving again. He set the cup of coffee before her. "Not very scientific but more religious." He had a very soft smile. "Or maybe animated?"

"What are you talking about?" She hated it when he talked in circles.

"I think the eyes are the cameras of the soul."

"What?"

"Maria, he was manufactured. Not born. He has no soul." She sat looking more confused. A soul wasn't real. "He was what you wanted."

"So I created him?" There was panic in her voice.

"No…" Alfie tried to calm her, but couldn't.

"I didn't. I did not want any of that!"

"Maria!" The raised voice made Jimmy jump. He pouted and climbed into his mother's lap.

"Mommy!"

"I'm sorry, Chap." Alfie patted the boy's head.

"He was the basic human. Like just a skeleton. Without a real design. His electro chip mind basically took any suggestion you had and expanded on it. He is James Fielding. A clone, but he can only be what he knows. James does not talk now, does not breath, does not…see. He is, but isn't."

"What did they do to him?" She was hugging her son. Alfie sat thinking on how to explain.

"Let's wait until your father is here, it's hard to explain and once will be enough." Moreover, he had to think of how to explain it. "You should eat and get changed. What's your fancy?"

"Eggs." She moved her son on her lap and picked up the cup of coffee. She sipped it and sighed. "Bacon."

"Toast?" He was already at the stove.

"Yes." She looked about. The kitchen was set up as the one at home. Alise. Maria hugged her son to her and got herself together mentally. Waldo came and laid his head in her lap. She set her coffee down and petted him as Jimmy let him lick the spoon. Home.

~

The room was filled with the men in her family. She held her son on her lap. A shield against the angry glares from her brothers. He was also there to keep them from losing their senses and heading out to the city in search of Adam. Linda and Mom were there also. To be questioned and give their input, but they had instead started serving coffee and whatever they could find to the men. When Fiona sat next to James, he promptly moved over to sit with Maria, and Alise sat in the vacant spot. Fiona gazed at Maria with a cold, calculated desire. It was all so evident. The woman wanted what Maria had. Her husband, her child, her position and the love of a family.

It began with Alfie trying to explain. When that didn't go over, he turned to face the wall and his eyes projected the images there. Like a big TV screen, they all saw it. All they would be up against. The cube. The droids. The women in test tubes. The many jars of unborn. The many that had failed. Maria shielded Jimmy from the sight by kissing him and making him laugh. More was seen. The Archive and Adam. Alfie kept most of Maria from being projected. There were gasps and there was cursing. Then there was the history.

James Fielding. His image was on the wall and Maria shuddered. James set his arm around her and held her. Jimmy was crawling over the two. Alfie explained who Fielding was and what blip he had left on world history. Or attempted to. The news clippings, the news reports and everything. Then Alfie stood with his eyes spinning to a stop. The projection stopped too. The men stood watching and debating. What if it was all fiction? What if the droid had gotten it wrong? What if….? Alfie turned to face them.

"Questions?" he asked.

"What is he?" Julio asked. "Man or machine?"

"Both." Alfie looked to Maria. "He is a cognitive mixture. A robotic humanoid skeleton with a very advanced micro organic covering. His mind is basically a series of computer chips that take in information and relay it through or to the Archive. Five to be exact. The reason his eyes are not more human is because the human eye cannot focus or hold anywhere near as much as his electronic ones can. They zoom, cut to and take it all in. Different spectrums and speeds. Something no human can do. The droids have to do that to be able to record for the Archive."

"And the Archive is?" Joaquin asked moving to sit next to his sister. He settled on the floor before her and leaned back against her legs.

"The Archive is just that. An archive. It was developed to hold all the information in the world. Similar to the internet, only for a more private use. As if it were the memories of man. It was to be part of the mainframe for the United States government, but other options took precedence, so it just continued on."

"It's a big library?" Miguel asked.

"The biggest." Alfie explained. "It's comparable to the contents of every library in the world."

"Comparable how?" Roberto asked.

"Comparable as in it is as big as, and holds all the information from everywhere, whether TV, radio, written, spoken and in development." Alfie stood waiting. "Everything. Everything we need to defeat him is here!" He pointed to his head. "In Archive."

"So you absorbed this?" Fiona asked cautiously.

"Yes. A long time ago. When I was first."

"First what?" Manuel asked, now moving closer to Maria himself.

"This." The droid held out his hands to show everyone. "Became? My creator also created Archive. James McMillan Sinclair Sr." The silence was heavy. James didn't say anything. "He was one of many scientists developing such programs for the military. Back in that day, there was a need for the instant use of information. The Cold War and all."

"Cold War?" Thomas looked confused. "How long ago are we talking?"

"Last half of the twentieth century." Alfie stood smiling. "I am officially one hundred and fifty-eight years old."

"Wait!" Alejandro Jr. moved to look at Alfie. "You? You've been working that long?"

"Yes. I hold my age well."

"You are saying all of this happened over a hundred years ago?"

"Well, it began then. The launch of the Genesis was a little over one hundred and fifty-five years ago."

"Was there a launch?" Fiona asked, drawing all the attention to her. Something she liked. "I heard about this. The crazy, rich, religious fanatic who supposedly launched himself into space in search of God. They say it was all faked. That he just lived out his days on that island."

"No, there was a launch. I saw it." Alfie shrugged. "Me and Sir. We told no one. Until now."

"Why not?" Alejandro asked quickly.

"They were acquaintances, and I suppose Sir just assumed Fielding would be better off out in space. He couldn't hurt anyone out there. At least we didn't think so."

"But he has." Julio set his hand on Jimmy's head as he sat on his mother's lap. He just couldn't bring himself to touch her yet.

"No, he hasn't. He is dead. What has done this is not human. It was only created by a human."

"So it can be destroyed?" Ernesto inquired.

"Yes, we have everything we need. The plans, the diagrams and the specs and the advantage."

"What advantage?" Alejandro asked quickly.

"When The Genesis reentered the Earth's atmosphere it shut everything down. A total blackout," everyone sat waiting for the punch line. "No satellites, no computers, no information..."

"He cut his own lines of communication." James spoke slowly as he realized what Alfie was implying.

"Exactly!" Alfie laughed. "Adam and Archive are one in mind. They know all because they had it all at their fingertips. Everything a person does is somehow uploaded into a databank somewhere. Access that database and know all. Archive had the ability to access everything. But now..." Alfie looked around the room. The men sat thinking on what he was implying.

"He doesn't know what we are doing. Or anyone that is not in his reach!" Alejandro Jr. smiled. He liked where this was going.

"And we are out of his reach here. In the Stronghold where nothing electronic works, we are safe." Stephano thought out loud.

"For now." Alfie began to pace.

"Forever." Joaquin countered.

"No. From the droids? Yes. From men? No." Alfie looked sad.

"Men?" Fiona asked.

"Men will follow Adam." Alejandro spoke up. "Desperate men. And men can get into the Stronghold."

"To do it will take planning. Even then we cannot be sure we will succeed." Alfie stood rocking on his heels.

"We, Microondo?" Stephano asked with a grin.

"He hurt my family. I will see him dead, destroyed or shot back out into space if I have to kick his ass there myself." The room erupted in giggles. "We just have to dissect all the information."

"They are fearless," Ricardo noted, "And people fear them."

"Get a fire truck. They are terrified of water." Mom noted, filling Alejandro's coffee cup. "All of them."

"What kind of senseless garbage is that?" Fiona held her cup out and the woman bypassed her to fill Julio's.

"They are afraid of water. Even him." She nodded to the wall where Adam's image had been projected. "Maria was forever diving into the shower to keep him off her." Mom could have kicked herself. The men all growled and Fiona actually smiled at her. Info for this one to use. Mom would get her.

"We all did." Linda was passing around a tray of sandwiches. "I got knocked out and all of us were in the shower until we got help." She shot Maria a side-glance. "The only reason we got away was because it was raining. Otherwise they would have been right behind us."

"Do they melt?" Antonio asked quickly.

"No," Alfie smiled, "They are water and environment proof. From dissecting one, I discovered that they are a very simple design. Their skin is organic. Not as advanced as Adam's is. It is almost indestructible. It does not puncture easily, but will burn, slowly. It was quite impressive."

"Glad you approve," Manuel replied angrily.

"If it is indestructible, how did you dissect one?" James asked catching the hint.

"I peeled its skin back," Alfie smiled. "It is applied in layers that conform to the shape of the exoskeleton. Then seals itself. Very simple. Very ingenious. Very human."

He waited for it to sink in. "Difficult to get through, but not impossible. Nothing is impossible."

"And once this 'skin' is peeled back?" Alejandro Jr. asked.

"They are defenseless. All of their strengths are in the skin itself. The exoskeleton can be bent or broken easily. Getting to it is the problem. They will fight."

"They can be turned off," Maria noted. "On the back of the neck. The left side. A sharp push and the little door pops up and just push. It shuts them down." Linda nodded.

"And does this Adam have a little secret door?" Fiona asked with a cold smile. The room went silent.

"You are a bitch!" Mom noted pushing her daughter out of the way to stand in front of Fiona. "I don't know who you are but I will tell you one thing. All of you!" The woman stood facing them. "I've been married five times. I buried three husbands and divorced two. I have been beaten, kicked, whipped, hungry and cold. I ain't no little daisy like this bitch here, but I have nothing on the courage of what that girl there went through to protect her child." Mom pointed to Maria. "He beat her! He raped her! He..." The older woman was fighting for control. Maria looked down. She hadn't wanted it all out there.

"Mom." Linda moved closer to her mother.

"No!" Mom stepped even closer to Fiona. "That thing is the devil!" The tough old woman was shaking now. "But if I thought he would have harmed my Linda or my grandkids I would have kissed his ass and called him God to protect them!" She spun to look around the room. "She had no choice! They held her down!" The tears spilled and the woman turned to her daughter. Maria sat shaking. She hugged Jimmy closer. "I would have!"

"It's okay, Mom," Linda hugged her mother, "We made it out. All of us."

Maria felt Jimmy wiggling. She couldn't move. James lifted her and the baby into his arms and held them. Fiona was looking down. She had been put in her place, once again.

"Why water?" Ricardo asked trying to break the heaviness that hung over them.

"Oh, that's simple," Alfie sighed, stepping closer to set a hand on Maria's shoulder. "James Fielding drowned. The Archive is somehow connected to him now and Adam is experiencing his persona of sorts. I would suspect their aversion to liquid would be a residual memory that is basically a fluke. Like Alise's flicker."

"A quirk?" Miguel asked quickly.

"Exactly. He is dead. They know he is dead."

"But I saw him," Maria shuddered, hugging her now squirming son close. Alise stepped up and took the boy.

"You did. You saw him." Alfie stepped back to look around the room. "You saw his remains. His preserved remains. His body is still going, but he is dead. His essence is now in Archive, but so are his terrors and fears. Especially the last moments of his life. They are exceptionally heightened now. In fact, that is all he experiences." Alfie seemed happy that they were now understanding him.

"You mean all that is in that man's head now is drowning?" Julio was trying to get a grasp on what was being said. He was more a realist. This was all way over his head. "And his drowning is projected into this archive and the droids feel it?"

"I'm afraid so." Alfie replied.

"How is that possible?" Antonio asked.

"The human mind is run on electrical waves. There is electricity going through his brain. He is not thinking. It is just the residual self."

"A hundred and thirty years after the fact?" James asked, holding his shaking wife closer. "Is that possible?"

"Mummies? An airtight containment that is climate controlled? I haven't gotten that far yet."

"His eyes opened." Maria was staring off into nothing.

"Reflex." Alfie noted. He reached out and took Jimmy. The boy was holding his hands out to him. He hugged the boy, making a soft growling noise before setting him up on his shoulders. "Dead bodies are known to sit up during autopsies. The body is a brilliant work of art. More complicated than anyone knows. The human mind is even more so." He spun slowly as the boy laughed. "The body sometimes doesn't know when to stop. And it has a very strong will. Hence the ideas of ghosts."

"So he's a ghost?" Mom asked, looking more in control.

"Not exactly." Alfie was talking and making motor sounds that had Jimmy giggling above. "He is there in spirit and I would say in body, but he is dead. I think he is just a buffer between the Archive and Adam. Nothing else."

"So he drowned?" Julio asked, thinking to himself that was one of the worst ways to die.

"Yes." Alfie spun again, making Jimmy squeal in delight.

"You're sure?" James was now picking up on the feeling that the droid was not being very forthcoming.

"I am. I was there."

The words floated on the air with the laughter of the child. The room full of men all waited. Alfie sighed. Time to remember.

James Fielding lay on his back with his milky blue eyes staring up at the heavens. Alpha stood over him with two of the droids that had been built to hasten the departure. A simple, ironic twist of fate. The one who was searching for God had found him. Just not the way he had wanted. Sir looked down at Fielding and then at Alpha. The droid was not moving. There was no need to. Fielding had been dead for a bit. An hour, maybe less, but he was dead. Too far to revive. But reanimate?

Fielding's body swayed as the tide came in. Sand slid across the palm of his hand. He did look very peaceful, staring up at the heavens. Had he found God? Was he facing him just at that moment? Alfie and Sir had not thought that the man would go so far. Had he? Had it been Fielding or had it been Alpha? Another desperate soul, of sorts. Alpha had been brainwashed into believing what Fielding was preaching. A God who would grant wishes. Alpha had a wish. Alpha wanted to be human. The Pinocchio complex.

"Go!" Sir pushed Alfie and they hurried to the boat. No words were said. As they headed out to sea, they could see Fielding being carried into the ship. That was the end. Or so they thought. Then the launch. "That damn devil!" Sir cursed. "James has altered Alpha."

"Is that bad, Sir?" Alfie asked.

"I did the same to you," the older man smiled at his companion. "Made you my protector. You are to keep me safe at all costs."

"I thought that was protocol?" Alfie asked simply.

"You would, " Sir sighed. "I think James took it a bit farther with Alpha."

"Meaning?"

"Meaning I think he wanted immortality at all costs." Sir was staring out into the water.

"But he drowned," Alfie pointed out.

"Yes, he did," Sir mumbled.

"He killed himself?" Alfie asked, almost sounding shocked. To travel into space might take longer than a human life could sustain. One that was preserved though, could..

"To commit suicide is a mortal sin." Alfie spun again, making the boy squeal. "To die is not. Especially if you are then on life support."

"Damned monster!" Alejandro growled.

"It makes you wonder, though." Julio looked out the window.

"What?" Manuel asked in disgust.

"What they found out there." Now they all understood. It was man made. It was from earth, but it had come back altered. What had it brought back with it?

"That is easy!" Alfie was spinning faster now. Jimmy was laughing. Alejandro stood and snatched his grandson off the droid and stood waiting. "What?"

"What is easy?" he asked quickly.

"What they found." The droid tilted his head a bit to the side thinking of the sadomasochistic bastard that had done this for his own inglorious delusions.

"Which is?" Alejandro's voice rose.

"Hell."

~

"You pretty!" Jimmy laughed, hugging his mother's neck as she carried him to their seats. He planted a kiss on her cheek. She smiled and sat down in a chair to wait.

"She is beautiful," James corrected, sitting next to her and leaning in for a kiss of his own with a playful pleading in his eyes. His tie. She balanced the boy on her lap and fixed his tie. His eyes were locked on her face. She was still shaking. The meeting had gone on for hours and the questions were intense. Her brothers and her father did not want to know details about what had happened, but there were some questions that only she could answer. James had been very proud of her. She was a rock. He had taken a shower and puked for an hour. "The most beautiful."

"I'm getting fat," she whispered, leaning in to inspect his collar. Fiona was sitting three rows back looking ravishing. James turned to follow her gaze.

"She's nothing." He kissed Maria's lips softly. She fought not to pull back. "There was never a doubt in my mind that you were alive." His soft eyes covered her face. A slight scar on her cheek. His finger traced it lightly. "You are too damn tough to let a world invasion stop you." She blushed at his joke, and he kissed her again. This time with more feeling. She moved back slightly shaken. "There was and is or will be no one for me but you. And if and when you do die, you had better be waiting at those pearly gates for me."

"Purly?" Jimmy looked up at his father.

"Very pearly." He kissed his son's head. "Watch Mummy. I have to give the bride away."

Jimmy nodded and sat waving to everyone. The family welcoming committee. It was all so pretty. Maria was taking it all in and smiling. They had taken a long nap. Maria was exhausted from reliving it all. James had tucked her into the new featherbed with Jimmy and let her sleep. She woke several times in terrified confusion, only to find James sitting next to the bed reading or just sitting. Jimmy would snuggle closer and the warmth of his little body kept her from screaming.

James tried to hold her and she would beg to be left alone. She called out to Adam. Making his heart stop. But not wanting Adam, wanting him to leave her alone. The pleading in her voice tore at his soul. He held her and she would pull away and fall into the bed to hold Jimmy. To sleep and not rest was very exhausting. Slowly she slipped into a troubled fitful sleep. She was worn out more when she finally woke than when she had climbed into the bed. However, she was happy with Jimmy there.

"Time. She just needs time." Olivia had told him. He understood, but he just couldn't leave her alone.

Jimmy was the anchor for both. Maria clung to him and he to her. James was the median that they both clung to. Between having a few patients drop in and the coming nuptials, he had done his best to let her alone. She wandered about. Through the house and then at the clinic. Fiona ignored her and that was fine. James ignored Fiona. But then he had been doing that for a long time. Amelia had given him several pieces of clothing that Maria had been able to fit. The little rose-colored dress looked lovely on her. She walked about slowly with one hand on her bulge. Jimmy was trotting around with her. He had grown so much in five months that he found her sometimes just staring at him.

"What should we do about his birthday?" she asked as he peered into the microscope.

"Celebrate it!" James laughed, "Two is a very big deal. I hope to have him housebroken by then." He had taken on the single parent hat with gusto.

"Potty trained," Maria laughed with him. They had discussed it before. Well, she had discussed it and he had grunted as he read through a medical journal. He had been a good father before. Just busy. Now he made time for them. She liked this side of him.

"Whatever!" He looked up smiling. He smiled more now. Why? Maria looked away from his smile.

"How many women are expecting?"

"Fifteen. So far." James looked into the machine again. "Only about five are from here. The others came that way." She looked up quickly. "No, not from him. Their men died to get them out of the city or paid dearly." He looked up. "It was quite wild for a bit after it all happened. I was very busy for a long time."

"I'm glad." She was messing with some instruments.

"You are?"

"Well, then it was easy for you to go on." Her face began to burn. She wanted to hear him say it. To mean it.

"It was not easy." He stood and walked to her. She backed up and tripped almost falling. He caught her in his arms and set her on an exam table. "Not one moment." His eyes were intense. "Not for one moment did I ever stop thinking of you." He watched her struggle to swallow. All of this was hard on her. "I wish I could just take it all from you." His hand pushed her hair back and guided her face up so her eyes could gaze into his. "But if I did, you would not be you."

"And who am I?" she asked softly. She was so unsure. All the time she was a prisoner, she had wanted to come home. Now that she was here, she found she was still in prison. One of her own making.

"My wife." He kissed her forehead and stepped back. "His mother." Jimmy looked up smiling.

"Mommy!" She fought not to cry.

"My world." He moved to kiss her cautiously. She sat stiff. His lips touched hers tenderly and briefly. "I almost died without you. I would have died if I had thought you gone. No matter what, you are what keeps me going through this and what we have to face together." His eyes. They held hers intently. She had to look away, giving him the opportunity to kiss her cheek and neck finally making her giggle. Something he missed. Her soft little girly giggle. The same one that made him feel dirty for bedding a child. "Let's go watch Mum marry your brother."

She did not object to him holding her hand as they walked. Jimmy was holding her other hand. The perfect family. A fantasy. A fantasy that was shattered as they got closer to the celebration. It was dark. Almost midnight, but with the torches and candles she could see the faces clearly. The curiosity, the fear and worst of all, the pity. Even though it was her family, it was still hard to walk among them. Many reached out to pat her shoulder or hand, and she would flinch and move closer to James. She wanted to turn and run.

"You look lovely, Darling." He kissed her again and she took her eyes off of Fiona and fixed them on him. "I get a dance." He winked at her and started back to where the men were waiting.

It was not a church wedding, but it was a very pretty setting. Lots of candles and flowers. It was chilly though. Almost cold. Everyone was bundled up for the wait. Jimmy moved in against her and she felt hands on her, making her jump. Joaquin set the warm shawl over her shoulders and around them. He patted her lightly and then stopped to kiss her cheek. She was shaking. Joaquin held her lightly, then lifted the boy onto her lap. Her new security blanket. Jimmy hugged her tightly, feeling her uncertainty.

"Mommy?"

"Yes, Darling?" she gazed down at her little angel.

"I love you!" The fear melted away. His little hands hugged her and she relaxed.

"Nice night for a sacrilegious event!" Alfie noted, sitting next to her. "Candles, midnight, what about sacrifices?"

"Alfie!" Maria chuckled.

"You're right. I think you've sacrificed enough." He patted Jimmy on the back. "I might one day like to marry."

"You would?" She looked at him. He had on a silly bow tie and a top hat. Only Alfie.

"Sure, if they can adapt the equipment." He 'winked' and his eyes spun.

"You are bad!" She laughed and caught a glimpse of Fiona watching her.

"That one is bad!" he chuckled. "They found her out there half dead. For days she was trying to run this place until she saw James and then became the damsel in distress!" He smiled. "Alise gave her hell and she has been pretty much biding her time. Well, time's up. You are back and she is mad. You look terribly sultry when you pout. She looks evil. I love the whole soap opera of the human life."

"And the one you create?"

"Me?"

"You! Papi told me how you asked him to have Miguel and Alise fixed up."

"Oh, that," he waved his hand, as if shooing flies. "She needed someone or I would have had to shut her down. She was so into caring for James and feeling the guilt of not bringing you back that she was due to overload. I needed to find you and I needed time. A little distraction. I didn't think he would fall in love with the toaster oven."

"And the microwave?" she asked, watching him sit expressionless. "Well?"

"I think I have to get my family in order before I answer that." He smiled slightly. Not just the family here.

"Hoy?" Olivia teased as she sat down next to Alfie. Jimmy tumbled from Maria, over Alfie, to his grandmother. A chill went through Maria. Had she been replaced?"

"Everyone stand!" Alejandro ordered from the front, "Please!" Her father looked very handsome in his suit.

Miguel and all of his eleven brothers stood waiting. Their wives on the other side of the makeshift altar. And then the children. There was a soft tune from the violinist. All turned to look, and as if a vision from some far off fantasy novel of days gone past, Alise stood waiting with James. He looked so handsome! Maria felt her heart flutter. It was like the first time she had seen him. A man she knew nothing about but was insanely in love with. A young girl crush of epic proportions.

They came down the aisle with the boys. All four dressed in suits and beaming at their father and their new mother. People were smiling at them and at her. Alise seemed to float. The dress was perfect. The hair, make up and veil were perfect and Maria was sure, borrowed. The bouquet of orchids set it all off. Nowhere on earth was there a more beautiful bride. Or one so perfect. Alise was perfect. But then, she was not human. A chill went through Maria's spine. Was this the future of mankind? She felt short of breath and Alfie's hand on her elbow helping her sit. She sat and prayed for forgiveness, the ability to forgive but to not forget.

It had occurred to her during the meeting that to forget was to accept. She could not accept. Not what was done to her and not that she was now responsible for more women going through what she had gone through. Yes, she knew he would do it again and some poor soul would be held down and raped repeatedly. And if she wasn't lucky enough to be pregnant to begin with? In the very first stages of a pregnancy? Then she would find herself in a test tube. Maria was guilty of passing the fate on to someone else. A guilt she would live with. Her hands were on her stomach. For her child she had done it. There was guilt, but not regret.

"All of you here!" Alejandro called for attention. Miguel stood holding Alise's hand in his. The brothers sat with their wives and children. James stood waiting. "Who gives this woman?" James looked over at Alfie. The droid nodded at him with a beaming blue face.

"My Uncle Alfie and I," James announced loudly. He lifted the veil and kissed his Mum's cheek, then returned to sit with Maria. She was shaking, he suspected from the cold. He wrapped the shawl around her and gathered her close to him. In a surprise gesture, she accepted laying her head on his shoulder.

"To all this may seem strange..." Her father spoke firmly, "But love is strange. And I believe in God, man and love. The love of God the almighty, my wife, my children, my grandchildren and my friends. My extended family." He looked out into the faces. "My son has chosen to spend his life with this woman." He looked Alise up and down very slowly. "And what a woman!" Everyone laughed. "She is for him, she loves him, she loves his children and she is loved by us. Together they will live here in the Stronghold until the day our Father in Heaven calls them home and we all accept it." There was the warning. No one said a word. Alejandro stood waiting. Miguel took the hint.

"Alise, I ask you to be my wife. I want you to share my life and my children. You are a sweet, funny, beautiful, wonderful woman." Alise's eye began to flicker. Miguel reached out to caress her cheek. "I love you. And I will love you and be faithful to you from now until I leave this earth. And I will wait at Heaven's gate for you." The flickering got faster. "Because I believe that God knows you have a soul and would not make me suffer eternity without you by my side. Will you be my wife?"

"Yes." the droid smiled brightly as her face began to glow. "And Miguel, I will be the best wife and mother to you and to my boys." She looked down at the children who stood off to the side. "I will protect, obey and stand by you for all that is to come. I will love you and care for you, your children, your grandchildren and all after until my time to join you. Until the end of time." There was a whisper among the guests. "This is nowhere near the end, my love." She reached out to touch his face. "This is the beginning. For all of us." Alejandro stood taller and silence spread. "A beginning of happiness and life."

"Good save." Maria heard Alfie mumble. His hand reached out to hold hers.

Maria looked at him. He was identical to Blue Boy, yet he wasn't. Alfie had a nice face. A pleasant smile and a very nice shy disposition. She had never seen him angry, never seen him hurt anyone or anything and never seen him with an annoyed look on his face. His face was always lit up. And when he smiled, it was really lit. As it was now. Jimmy climbed in his lap and pulled the droids metallic arms around him. He hugged her boy and leaned his lips down to touch the top of the little blonde head. A kiss. How could two identical beings be so different? Alfie looked over at her troubled face and pouted.

"I'm fine," she smiled a bit and sighed. She had no choice. She had to be.

"I now introduce my son, Miguel Castro Vargas and his bride, Alise!" The cheer and applause went up as Miguel kissed Alise. The boys ran to hug them and then they were swarmed. James was one of the first to kiss his Mum and shake Miguel's hand. The rush of people made Maria jump. Alfie set Jimmy in her lap to calm her and stood to block any intrusions. James was there instantly.

"Darling?" He pulled her into his arms, "You're freezing!" He hugged her and Jimmy. She let him. "I believe you owe me a dance?" She smiled and gazed into his eyes. There, behind the smile, she saw the pain. Did it pain him to hold her? Was it obligation that held him to her? Did he love her? Really? Could he love her after all of this? After what had been done to her? She was unsure, but had to put it all aside for now.

There was food, music, dancing and laughter. Maria danced with her husband, her father and her brothers. She held Jimmy in her arms and danced about with him. If only it was really this way. She sat holding her son as he slept, a soft little breath on her neck and the wonderful smell of him under her face. Alfie came and took the boy home to his bed. She knew it was a sign for her and James to have some time alone. Something she was not up to. Not now anyway. He was busy toasting his Mum for the tenth time.

She stood and walked along the trees of the orchard. It was getting chilly now. A hard winter was coming. She could feel it in her bones. The number of people in the Stronghold was times ten the usual. Was there enough to sustain them for all? Had her father prepared enough? She pondered this question as she walked along under the shade of the trees. Here and there, moonlight dripped through and made the branches and shadows dance. She passed by one of the armed guards. He bowed his head to her and stepped back into the shadows.

They were always there. She knew it. Since she was a child, they had always been there. Just inside the very darkest of shadows. You could not see them, smell them, hear them or even feel them but they were there. They lived on the very edges of the Stronghold. Very primitive. Very loyal to her father. Now it had become a cause. Before, it had just been the predictions of an old war hero. Now it was a reality, and that old war hero had hundreds depending on him and his plan. He also had a daughter who was now very confused.

She had no loyalties to Adam. She wasn't about to go back to him, but she had to remember him. She had to use what she knew to defeat him and to do that she had to do to relive a nightmare that she would rather just not. It was hard at times to go on. Now and then. There had been times when she had been on top of the cube and thought of just diving off. Ending it all. However, suicide was a sin and she knew that Jimmy was alive. James no, but Jimmy. Alise had made a promise and she had lived up to it. Now she was married to Miguel. Alise was now her sister in law! What was it all coming to?

The trees ended and the vineyards began. Maria leaned against a tree and gazed out into the night. She was tired. Bone tired, but afraid to sleep. There was a song about sleeping when you were dead. She wondered if that was true. Would she rest when she died or would her mind just go on spinning as James Fielding's had? She closed her eyes to the memory of him lying there looking up at her. In that glass tube, he had looked dead. Somewhere there was a nun who had died years ago and she still laid in state. Barely touched, held in time, yet well preserved by the grace of God.

"There but for the grace of God, go I." Maria mumbled softly, hugging herself. "Father in Heaven, help me?"

"Help you what?" James asked, making her jump. He stepped out of the darkness as she spun around. She held to the tree to keep from falling over. "Forgive me?"

"Forgive you?"

"For not coming for you?" He moved closer and she backed into the tree. Clinging to it to keep herself from falling over.

"You couldn't have. You were hurt. I know that. I saw you fall." She dug her fingers into the rough bark of the tree. "I thought you were dead."

"I did too." His teeth were bright in the darkness. "You are shivering!" He took off his coat and slid it over her shoulders. It was warm and comforting. It smelled of him. A thought flashed. Adam had no scent. No musk. James had a strong musk that was not unpleasant. It was welcome. She hugged the jacket to herself and stood waiting for what was to come next. "Alise had other ideas."

"I wish I could have been that brave."

"You were. You lived." He moved his arm to lean against the tree with his body inches from her.

"I have a question."

"Ask." His hand moved slowly to push the hair from her face.

"If I could never lie with you as a wife again, would you stay with me out of obligation?"

"Of course." A quick answer that she had not expected. "I am obligated because I love you." His fingers traced the lines of her face. "I love you. I don't have to have sexual relations with you for that." She took in a slow breath. "It would be an added bonus to the package, however!" He laughed making her more comfortable.

"I'm sorry."

"For what? Coming back to me?" He moved to kiss her temple. "I have prayed for this for months. I love you more now than then. I will wait, and if it never happens then so be it. I have you."

"Do you?" The question was almost inaudible.

"What is it?"

"I can't get him out of my head. My dreams. Every moment I have to myself, I see him. On me, in me, his face, his eyes and…" she felt her heart begin to race.

"Well, I may have to just make love to you all night long." James kissed her head again making her jump. "Just so you can remember me." He was smiling.

"It's not funny."

"I wasn't kidding." James moved to kiss her and she stepped away. "What happened has happened. There is no changing it. No going back." He wanted to hit the tree. "But we must go on."

"Can we? Knowing what you know?" She turned to gaze at him.

"That I love you? Sure. I can. Can you?"

There was that tone. The one he used when she said something he considered stupid. Immature. Like when she had accused him of flirting with Fiona. That had been their first fight.

Married almost two years and she had seen the looks from the woman. Once, she had gone to his office, Fiona had been coming out, straightening her clothes and making everyone whisper. Maria had stormed out of the office. She been packing to return to the Stronghold with Jimmy when James had come home. He had promptly plucked the baby off the floor, handed him to Alise, and pushed them from the room. He shut the bedroom door and turned to face her.

"What the bloody hell are you doing?" he asked, leaning back against the door.

"Going home." She was zipping the bag shut.

"This is your home," he remarked calmly.

"I thought it was." She was moving to the bathroom now. The floral dress swirling about her legs. A very grown up dress on a very young body. "I don't think so now."

"Why? What did Fiona say?"

"Nothing. She didn't have to." He knew she didn't. The snickers from the people in the office when he stepped out wiping lipstick off his face and his secretary telling him his wife had just left. The administrators were going to have his ass. First the prodigy and now the new professor?

"Fiona is a bit of a drama queen. She likes to create it. And you are helping her by acting like a spoiled brat!" That tone.

"I am not a spoiled brat!" She turned and threw the bottle of shampoo at him. He ducked and it exploded on the door. She had better aim with the conditioner. The full plastic bottle slammed into his shoulder and he was now covered with it.

"Very mature, Maria! You want to run home? Go! But my son stays here!" The brush was next and before he could duck, the body lotion. Later he would give thanks for the containers being plastic! He charged and she was moving for more objects to throw.

"You bastard! You will not take my son!" She was swinging.

He had never fought with her. They had playfully wrestled during sex or lovemaking and he knew in his mind that just by size and weight, he could easily overpower her. Or so he thought. He was not prepared for the little assassin that turned and swung at him. The blow struck him just on the tip of his nose. The tears came instantly and then she was hitting and kicking him. He had no other option than to grab her and fall with her to the floor. She was fighting and he was trying to see! He closed his eyes and pinned her beneath him. He was able to get a hold of both of those little fists and hold them in one of his hands while with the other, he felt his nose for blood and fractures. Slowly, he was able to see again. Able to see her. He smiled and she fought harder.

She was beneath him seething. A little wildcat! He smiled at her and moved his body between her legs, which promptly got a good heel to the back of his calf, and a wonderful Charlie horse! She got a hand free, scratched the dickens out of his neck, and got a yank of his hair. He yelled and she almost got away but her held her and glared at her. That had hurt. She was grim faced and ready. Alejandro had taught her to fight like a man. A very mean man.

James flipped her over onto the floor face down and had his body on hers. She beat at the floor and reached back to scratch but he had her pinned. Kicking and pin wheeling was wearing on her. She was panting and sweating. It smelled so good. She had a delicious musk. He ducked as she threw her head back, trying to hit his face. He would tweak her ticklish sides to keep her going. The anger was something he had never seen and was enjoying it. She was cussing. The filthiest threats were coming from her pretty little mouth. He wondered if she were possessed by a sailor! His excitement was not unnoticed. He thrust against that little round ass and she fought harder. She did have a temper.

"We can do this all day," he noted calmly thrusting again. "Either or?" His hands were on her shoulders, pushing her down. "Which will it be?" He laid on her, pinning her there, her face lost beneath the silky curtain of sweet smelling hair. "Fight or fuck?" His hands pushed the dress up and he was on his knees now, leaning over her and pulling at her underwear.

"I will kill you!" she screamed. His hand moved over her soft ass and found its destination. It was hot and wet.

"Go for it," he offered, unfastening his pants and pushing them down. "It might be worth it!" His hand was around her waist and he simply jerked her up to meet him. She screamed with anger fueled passion and he groaned just as loudly as the joining sent them into a swirl of emotions.

He had often wondered what Alise and Alfie had thought of that afternoon. He missed a lab. They lay on the floor, tangled in clothing and bedding he had jerked off the mattress as she rode him. Stripped down to the bare waist with that dress hanging off her and hiked up over her hips, he had laid beneath her, moaning and begging. She was a damn good student! They wrestled and he had her beneath him again, laughing as he kissed her breasts and suckled. Jimmy would have a bottle of expressed milk. Just this once, she had been all his.

The next day he had gone to the office whistling to find Fiona waiting with everyone watching. He smiled brightly. He did not open his office door but stood by his secretary's desk as the blonde clung to his arm and explained her latest dilemma. Would he help her? She desperately needed him. He stood smiling and watching the people in the room moving to hear better what he would say.

"Oh, Fiona, I can't. I missed a lab yesterday and I am in a bit of tiff with the administrators."

"Missed a lab? How?" She tried to not look eager. She knew he had rushed out of there the day before. She had seen the look on that little wife's face and the tears.

"Well, I spent it having sinfully wonderful make-up sex with my wife. We went at it all day and night and well…" he rubbed the back of his head smiling and tugged at his collar, showing the red claw marks. "I'll take a smack on the bum from the admins over that. But it was certainly worth it. So sorry about your problem. dear." He stepped past her into his office and shut the door smiling. Fiona still hadn't learned, but she would get the point.

"It's cold out here." James noted. "And dark. Let's go home. Unless you want…I can stay elsewhere." She looked up at him. No anger. Just concern. She shook her head. He set his arm around her and they walked back to the house. Past the ongoing celebration and to their bed.

He changed. Brushed his teeth, washed his face and stepped out into the bedroom to find her in his bed curled up half asleep and looking very uncertain. She was wearing one of his t-shirts. He wished he had thought to get her some lingerie. Even in the Stronghold, there were ways. If you had what someone wanted you simply traded. And everyone needed a doctor. She was looking across the hall at Jimmy's sleeping form. James walked across the hall to scoop up his son. The boy didn't even flinch. Worn out to the bone. He set him into his wife's waiting arms and climbed in to hold them both. Maria smiled at him. He made a face.

"What?" he asked softly, reaching to touch her cheek.

"Nothing," she relaxed into the pillow.

"Did you think I was going to attack you?" he asked calmly.

"You were thinking of it." she smiled.

"Got that right! Bloody damn right!" He kissed her forehead and then his son's. "Hay mas tiempo de vida." There is more time than life.

~

Jimmy sat playing on the floor with specimen cups. He was getting really good at stacking them. James said it might come in handy in college with all the beer cans. Maria had laughed slightly. She really hadn't laughed too much about anything except Jimmy. Now she was staring up at the ceiling with her body exposed as her husband and Alise stood between her legs and inspected her very private region. It was the first time they had to do the exam. Amelia had given birth to two seven-pound boys right after the wedding. Then there was more headaches with a virus that went around making, every child puke and suffer from diarrhea.

"Well?" she asked nervously.

"It appears to be a chip." Jimmy was straining to get a better look at the sonogram. "Metal. Small. I mean small. It's just implanted itself into the placenta. It's not doing anything." He moved to inspect her again. His gloved well-lubricated fingers moving in to feel about. She hissed and tensed up. "I'm so sorry, Darling." The fetal rate increased. Nothing worked in the Stronghold. Nothing electronic at least. But Alfie was more than electronic. He was a self contained monitoring system when projecting onto a wall.

"It's not a threat. Not yet. It hasn't moved closer to the fetus." Alfie refused to step past her waist. A perfect gentleman, he stood at her side facing her head. Now he examined the projection. "May I?" he asked politely, patting Maria's hand. She winced and nodded. His eyes lit up and he scanned her body quickly. "There is no reaction except when you come close to it. The baby reacts."

"So can we remove it?" Alise asked calmly.

"I wouldn't," Alfie sighed. "It will expel itself once the child is born."

"I hope." James removed his hand and moved Maria's legs from the stirrups. Alfie helped her sit up. The door was locked. This was only for them to know.

"And if it doesn't?" she asked, pulling the gown down for modesty's sake.

"We'll remove it." James tossed the gloves into the biohazard bag. "I have a few swabs I want to test, but the baby seems to be fine." He kissed her nose and stood.

"What if it's a tracking device?" She looked to her son. What if she had led them here?

"It is not emitting anything," Alfie assured her, with a kind pat to her shoulder. At that, Jimmy squealed loudly in delight. "Unlike others I know!" The droid dropped to his knees to play with the boy.

"Get dressed. We have a party to host." James kissed her cheek. She nodded and reached for the maternity pants she had shed. "Someone is turning two!" He scooped his son up and kissed the boy, making him laugh.

"I'm getting as big as a house!" she mumbled as he handed his son off to Alfie.

"You are lovely." James smiled, checking the swabs to be tested.

He was nice. So very nice. Too nice. It had been two weeks since her return and he had not touched her in a sexual manner. He kissed her cheek, her temple and her lips lightly, but with no passion. He held her hand, hugged her and guided her with a hand on her elbow through all the touchy moments. When panic was close to setting in or the crowds became too much or more often, when the pity of other people weighed on her. He was fulfilling his marriage obligations to her. He was the loving, caring, supportive husband. He just was not James.

A small gathering. That was what is was supposed to be, but everyone wanted to see Maria. To be near her and to hint about where she had been and what had happened. The party had been moved to her parent's house. The less people in her house the better. She was not ready to share her private life with them. Alfie, Linda, Mom and the boys were usually the only visitors to come in. Her brothers stopped by but never came in. They would stand on the patio to talk or just say hi and go on their way.

Linda and her boys had found a wonderful man to spend time with. Hal had been a truck driver. His truck had simply stopped on the highway and he had followed the masses. He had been one of the volunteers who had gone into the city looking for Maria. He had not found her, but had discovered that he had lost his wife and son in the invasion. Together Linda and Hal were moving toward building a life in the Stronghold. Mom and the blacksmith, Rocko, had been seen laughing together. Two tough old birds. Everyone seemed to be going on with their lives. Everyone but Maria.

It was hard to go back to the way it had been. She was not the same. And it was hard to go forward. She wasn't sure who she was. Jimmy was all she was sure of. She was his mother and he knew this. At the party he ran about laughing with Alfie watching over him. Maria helped serve the food, greet the guests, open the gifts, blow out the candles and serve the cake, but she was still on the outside. James was by her side. A light touch here or there and then he was off again to solve some problem or help someone. He was more at home with her family than she was. It was something that frightened her. What if she could never get past it?

"He had a long day." Her father sat next to her. She held her son in her arms. His face was covered with chocolate and a sleepy smile.

"He did," she kissed the chocolate cheek.

"How are you, Mija?"

"Fine, Papi." She leaned her head on his shoulder. He set his arm around her and squeezed.

"You will always be my baby." He kissed her head and held her.

Always? She sighed and leaned on him heavily. Would she? Did he see? What had he thought? Had she done the right thing in his eyes? For her it had been the decision for her child. For her children. Jimmy was heavy in her arms and everything was blurry, then he was light. Gone! She sat up reaching for him. For his warmth and found another. James was lifting her into his arms. She blinked and looked about to find her son in Alfie's arms. James was carrying her as if she weighed nothing at all. They were heading home.

"I have you, Darling." James whispered holding her close. She only nodded and laid her head on his shoulder.

"Such a lovely family," someone said, and James chuckled.

"A growing one!" he laughed as he followed Alfie.

Jimmy was in the bed with a clean diaper and face. He still had on that filthy shirt, but he was sleeping soundly. James set Maria the bed and pulled off her sneakers. He folded her into the bed with a kiss to her cheek and then went to shower. He was humming. The sound of the water invaded her sleep. She couldn't sleep. There was a feeling. She sat up looking about the dark room. It was always dark there. He was always watching. She was safe in only one place. She climbed from the bed and undressed as she walked to the shower.

James had his back to her. He was whistling now. A good mood. Had he been with someone? Like her father? Waiting for her to get over whatever it was she was supposed to? He had his body lathered up and was scrubbing his face. It was long past the five o'clock shadow. He hadn't shaved that morning. He rarely did on weekends. At least back home. He always teased that he liked to make her squirm with his whiskers on her inner thighs. And he would. She suddenly missed him.

"Shit!" he jumped as she touched his shoulder and he hit his head on the showerhead. She stepped back from him as he rinsed the soap off his face. "What in the bloody hell are you trying to do? Are you trying to give me a fucking heart attack?"

"I'm sorry," she stammered reaching for a towel. He stood, looking very angry.

"Get over here!" He grabbed her arm and pulled her into the water spray, kissing her roughly. Suddenly, her body came alive, as did his and he had her pinned against the wall instantly. She closed her eyes to him and winced. "Look at me!" He ordered, kissing her again. "Damn you! Look at me!" Her eyes opened and he was there. "Don't you ever close your eyes to me! When I make love to you I want you to see only me!" He thrust and she didn't close her eyes. She gasped and held onto him.

"James!" Her body was convulsing beneath his.

"Alfie!" James called over the running water.

"Sir?" the voice came from outside the room.

"Put my son in his bed." He thrust again and Maria nodded.

"Very good, sir." Alfie whistled softly as he lifted Jimmy up.

"Scared." The sleepy boy mumbled, hugging Alfie.

"Nothing to be scared of, old man." The droid whispered, patting the boy's back. He carried the boy from the room before he got a lesson in sex education.

"Want Mommy to sleep with me," the boy argued sleepily.

"No, she has to sleep with Daddy," Alfie informed the boy as he tucked him in.

"Scardy cat Daddy," the boy pouted as he drifted off to sleep. Alfie nodded, listening to the moaning and carryings on from the other room. At least they were out of the shower.

"Something like that," the droid replied shutting the bedroom door.

~

"Hello, Love!" Maria jumped at the voice. She was still jumpy. "Sorry." She held onto the counter and held released breath. He moved closer and set his hand on her shoulder. "I am sorry."

"It's okay." She gulped and turned to smile at Robin. The man stepped back looking ashamed. He was a very good-looking man. English. He and James spent time talking about their home. Every so often, Robin would just 'pop' in for a chat. 'Pop' was a good word for it.

Rockin' Robin Whittier had been a rock star. He had been on stage in the middle of a concert when Adam had arrived. He had been so stoned that he thought it was all part of his show. His manager and band mates dragged him off the stage. They had hidden beneath the stadium for days, then escaped the city through the sewers. He had gone cold turkey in the wilderness. He, three of his band mates and their families, a couple of roadies and their manager had made it to the Stronghold. The blonde-haired man had been a bit hard to handle at first. He was a star and felt he should be treated as such. Alejandro had other thoughts.

There were only three rules to living in the Stronghold. All were equal. All worked. And all respected each other. If a person could not live by these rules, then he or she were asked to leave. It was not law, it was a way of life, and the people who followed Alejandro and his sons lived by the three rules. There was the militia who were there to enforce the rules and the word of the King. He lived by the rules, his children and grandchildren lived by them, and he expected everyone to do so.

Robin had been hurting bad when he was brought in. thin, sickly and hugging his guitar. James tended to him and then the others. Robin wanted room service. He was promptly moved from the clinic to a cabin on the southern border to work in the garden there. At first, he refused, saying he was too ill. When better, he refused because he was a star. However, a quick talk with Stephano about how a star is nothing but a fading light that could easily disappear in the night, and suddenly Robin was in the garden yanking weeds. He was not pampered. If he wanted to eat, he had to work. So Rockin' Robin the rock star became a gardener.

He was funny. The women flocked to him when he came to gatherings. He brought his guitar and would play and sing. His old band mates would join in and there were impromptu concerts. However, it was at Jimmy's birthday party that he had noticed Maria. James had been busy dealing with some children who had runny noses. She was sitting there holding her son and laughing with him. She was very pretty, and her laugh was soft and light, like an angel that had settled there from Heaven just for Robin to stare at. She looked up, saw him staring, and looked away bashfully. A shy one? Something rare in the Stronghold. He had moved closer to talk to her.

"Hi Robin!" Jimmy had waved, breaking the ice.

"Hello there, mate!" Robin knelt down to shake the hand of the little boy as he climbed from his mother's lap. "Who is this lovely woman?" His eyes covered her quickly.

"Mommy!" Jimmy turned to hug her leg and she lifted him back onto her lap.

"So it's true?" Robin moved to sit next to them.

"What?" Maria asked softly.

"The dead do rise?" He was teasing but she frowned slightly.

"I wasn't dead."

"Really?" Robin winked at Jimmy. "I'm glad. I heard a lot about you."

"From?" Her pretty eyes narrowed coldly.

"Your husband. He's a mate of mine and you are all he talked about after a drink or two or three. A little loose on the lips about love and all when he's had a few under his belt. And he is in love with you." She smiled shyly. "And I can see why. You are prettier than he could have ever described."

"How did he describe me?" She was curious. Robin smiled at her.

"He said you were the most beautiful woman he had ever laid eyes on. Small, with long black hair, soft dark skin that tasted salty and sweet at the same time. That your eyes were as black as the night and shined brighter than any star in the heavens. That angels were jealous of your beauty." Maria's face burned red. "He said his worst fear had been that he had let you down. That he prayed nightly for you to return and forgive him."

"Forgive him?" She let her wiggling son out of her lap and looked over to see Alfie following him.

"For not rescuing you. For not going back." Robin shrugged. "I asked him why he hadn't."

"And?" she was wringing her hands.

"He said he had taken an oath. First, do no harm. He was a doctor and there were many who needed him. It tore him apart that he had put that oath before you." She stared off into nothing. What would have happened if he had come for her? She knew. He would have died. "You alright?" Robin had set his hand over hers. She jumped and started to stand. A pain struck her and she winced and sat down hard. "Hey! James, mate!"

"No! Don't call him. I'm fine." She winced again and held the bulge. Robin sat back.

"You're pregnant?" He sounded more than a little shocked. So he hadn't really been paying too much attention to the rumors. By the looks the passing women were giving him she had a feeling he did little talking with them. Men were more apt to talk reason over gossip.

"No, I had a large lunch," she smiled at him devilishly, making him laugh. "Yes. I am." She rubbed her hand over the bulge.

"You came all the way back to him pregnant?" Robin sounded amazed.

"It is his child," she noted with a cold tone.

"Oh, to be sure…" He reached out tentatively to touch the bulge. "I'm sorry." He pulled his hand back quickly. "May I?" His eyes moved up to her eyes. She nodded slightly. His hand settled over hers. It was warm and strong. The baby kicked and he smiled widely. "Wow!"

"Do you have children?" she asked. There was a look in his eyes. A far off lost look.

"No." He sat back, still staring at the bulge. "Not that I know of." He seemed sad. "One, she said she was and I was bound to do the paternity dance with her in court once I got back to England. I guess I don't have to worry about that now." He did seem to be worried. "I'll never know."

"She might have made it," Maria noted gently.

"Oh, I hope, but I won't ever make it back." He looked up at the mountain walls behind them. "I am here for the long haul. There are weeds and I am the man to pull them." He looked lost.

"There is nothing wrong with that. You feed us and we are grateful."

"Jimmy hates broccoli and he is not grateful," Robin chuckled, thinking of the little boy's face when Robin had brought some to the clinic for James.

"Well, I love it." Maria sat forward and held his hand. "Thank you." From that moment it was different for him.

Robin usually stayed in the mountain range but was now coming in more often. Each time he would stop to see James, and if Maria was not with him, then he would go to the house and there she would be. Her, the droid, and the boy. And the dog. Waldo hated Robin and growled at him more than once. Maria always apologized, but the dog had made his point clear. He did not like the man. Alfie had been less forward and just stated that he thought the man had too much time on his hands. Magically, there was more work and he was moved deeper into the mountains. Now he only came every other week or so. This day was the 'or so'.

"Are you okay?" he asked, pulling a chair out from the table for her to sit.

"I'm fine." She waved off the chair and handed him a cup of coffee. Carrying hers, she waddled to the rocker by the fire. Jimmy was curled up on the floor with the dog. The droid was not in the room. "You just startled me." She settled down and pulled a pink blanket she was crocheting onto her lap.

"Pretty." He nodded to her work. "For the baby?"

"Yes. Only not mine. I have some for him. This one is for my niece. She is having one soon. A girl."

"So you are sure it's a boy?" He pulled a chair close and sat watching her hands move.

"Yes." Maria smiled softly. "A healthy boy."

"Is this the last for you two or will you be trying for a girl?"

"I don't know. I think my niece broke the family curse," Maria laughed. "All boys! All the grandchildren were boys until now. I think this little one will be the next princess."

"That's right. You are the only girl," Robin laughed with her. "The Princess. Was it hard to live up to?"

"What? Being beautiful and charming? Smart and babied? No, quite easy, actually." She blushed. It looked good on her. Her deep coloring seemed to glow. "I adore my brothers."

"They adore you." Robin sat back. There was something in the way he said it.

"What does that mean?" She barely looked up from her work.

"I'm being moved again. Farther away." He was watching her face for a reaction. There was none. Now he saw it was true. She was just being polite. He had hoped for more but she hadn't given him any signs. Just polite conversation and a cup of coffee now and again. "Farther from you." Now she looked up.

"Me?" There was surprise in her voice.

"I asked around about you." He looked into his cup. "I thought...Well, I thought maybe..." He sighed and looked at her.

She was very pretty. No, gorgeous. She was just sitting there with her hair about her shoulders and a shawl across her arms. The firelight shining off those dark eyes.

"Thought what?" Her eyes were searching his.

"That you and James were on the outs because of..." He nodded to her belly. "It not being his."

"What?" Her voice rose and the dog growled.

"I mean..." He took a deep breath and decided to spit it out. "Everyone says that the child isn't his. That he took you back because he had to. Because of who you are. Alejandro's daughter and all. I thought it was true and that if it were...Well, I thought..."

"Go on!" she ordered, setting the blanket aside.

"I wished it were true. I wanted it to be." He licked his lips. "I would take you and the child as my own."

"As your own?" Maria picked up her cup of coffee from the little table next to her and sipped it slowly. She was thinking and he was hoping.

"This child is James' child. I was pregnant when I was taken. It is probably the only reason I was allowed to live." She set the cup down again. "James is my husband and I love him. He loves me."

"I know." Robin looked into his cup again. "I can see it when you look at him, but I also see the doubt in his eyes when he's watching you." That got her attention.

"What do you mean?" Maria's voice rose again.

"You laid with another. I know everyone said you had to, but you were with him. Not once either. A mate knows. He's not feeling as if he's a man. Not man enough. He didn't save you and he didn't go after you."

"He took an oath!" Maria defended him, even though deep in her heart she felt as if it were true.

"Damn his oath!" Robin stood suddenly and Waldo stood snarling.

"Waldo!" Maria ordered, and the dog laid down with his head on Jimmy's leg. "He is a man of honor."

"No. If it were me I would have moved heaven and earth to find you. Dead or alive." Robin set the cup down before he threw it. "I have to leave. They want me gone today. It will be a while before I can come see you again. If you need me though, just get word to me and I will come." He turned to leave.

"Robin." Maria stood slowly. He turned to face her. "There is no reason for you to come. If you wish to speak to James you can see him at the clinic."

"Maria!" The man looked panicked.

"I am a married woman. A happily married woman. I don't think it is appropriate for you to come here when my husband is not here. Not anymore."

"Are you? Are you truly happy?" There was a crispness to his voice.

"Yes!" She spoke quickly, hoping she sounded convincing. He stood studying her. Her face was still and her eyes glistening. He stepped closer.

"There are those who say different."

"Who?" she knew before he said it.

"The doctor. He and her were cozy before. You coming back put a bit of a dent in their intentions."

"No, I don't think so," Maria shook her head.

"Are you trying to convince me or yourself?" He reached out to grasp her chin and force her face up. His eyes were now searching hers. "She is in love with him and he is attracted to her. His vows to you are all that keep him in your bed. But only at night. They are lovers. Is that how you want to live? Is that your version of happiness?" A tear slid from her eye. He brushed it away and then leaned in to kiss her softly.

"Please leave," she asked, stepping back. "I don't want you here."

"Maria..."

"She asked you to leave." Alfie was behind him. "Should I assist you?" Robin turned to face the droid. The blue face was a dark hue. Maria settled back in the rocker.

"Please show him out, Alfie." She began to crochet again.

"Maria!" Robin stepped towards her and a hand fell on his shoulder. He expected it to be anything but human.

"I think it is time you left, mate." James was there. Robin looked to Maria. She was looking down. Then he looked to James. Alfie was back behind him.

"Right." Robin turned back to Maria. "I meant what I said. If you need me." He stepped past his friend and left. Alfie followed. James walked over to his wife. He sat in the vacated chair.

"How much of that did you hear?" she asked softly.

"Enough." He stretched his long legs out before him and crossed them at the ankles as he leaned back in the chair, waiting. If they were going to fight, he was going to be comfortable.

"How much of it is true?" The tears were flowing but she would not look up.

"I love you. You love me. That's about it."

"Are you and Fiona lovers. Again?" Maria was really moving her hands quickly now.

"Again, is it?" His amused tone only made her crochet faster. "My darling, you were still in nappies the last time I bedded that bitch." The tone changed to a dangerous growl that made even Waldo whimper. Maria still would not look up at him. "Alfie?"

"James?" The droid had that amused tone to his voice. The one he used when James got himself in too deep.

"Take my son to his room. His mother and I need to have a word." The droid was already moving. He lifted the sleeping boy up and started from the room. "And the dog."

"Waldo." The dog followed.

James stood and stretched. It had been a hell of a day and he had come home early hoping for a bit of love making before dinner. Not to find a man vying for the affections of his wife or for her to believe his lies. He moved to her and she was really moving that needle. He was sure she was calculating where to stab him with it. He knelt down and set a hand over hers. She was shaking. He took the blanket from her and laid his head in her lap his other hand settled on his son in her stomach.

"What shall we name him?" he asked softly.

"You know," Her voice was choked, "The first for your father." Her hand lighted on his head and she ran her fingers through is soft fine hair. "The second for mine."

"Oh, that's right." He sighed thoughtfully. "And if it's a girl?"

"You know it's a boy."

"Well, the next one might be a girl." His hand massaged the bulge and he got a kick for his touch.

"Next one? You want more?" She sounded shocked.

"I planned on trying to beat your folks," he teased.

"No!" She shook her head. "No way will I have twenty one children!"

"What about an even dozen?"

"No!" Now she laughed.

"Lucky seven?" He offered, sitting up to smile up at her.

"Maybe." She touched his face and he leaned into the hand. "If they all look like you."

"Me?" He cried, "No, they must look like you! I want all my children to look like you! Beautiful."

"I don't think you are so bad looking." The tears were still sliding down her face.

"Don't cry, Love. Please. I swear on Jimmy's soul that I have no feelings for anyone but you. I love you. I did however hope that a movie star or two would have come here but they happen to be Republicans." Maria hit his shoulder with her hand, laughing at him. "I have been with no other woman but you since the first time I laid in your bed with you. No one. Just you." He stood slowly and held his hand out to her. "Come help me make some dinner. I am hungry and I want to spend time with you." She took his hand and let him lead her to the kitchen.

"How was your day?" she asked picking up Robin's cup and hers.

"Bad. We lost someone today." He sighed heavily. "A child." She stopped walking and waited. "Little Rita Sims. It was chicken pox. I thought I had immunized them all, but that one got past me." The guilt. He had tried to keep his records straight but with all the incoming people, he had missed one. One adorable little girl with red curls. "Mum is checking all the other children. We have to stay on top of this or it could get away from us."

"It's not your fault." Maria continued on to the kitchen. "How many children do you actually see? Most are well and don't need you."

"All need me." He opened the refrigerator to take out the milk and eggs. "Omelet?" She nodded, and sat down at the table. "I just didn't pay enough attention to the children." He took out the vegetables and handed them to his wife to cut. "She was only ten."

"Now what?" Maria took the knife offered.

"I work until all are immunized. I might have to have Alfie go to the warehouse. There is some vaccine there."

"Do we need it? Now?" The thought of anyone going there frightened her.

"No. Not yet. I think we can make do." He reached for the skillet. She knew he was thinking that he should be the one to go. And not just for the vaccine. Robin had hit a nerve. His oath or his family?

"James?"

"Yes?" He was still thinking.

"Do you think this is your child?" She cut the vegetables.

"Yes."

"The DNA says so?" She didn't look up. He didn't turn from the stove. The butter sizzled in the pan.

"Yes." She knew.

He hadn't really doubted her, but he had the amniotic fluid tested. For everything and anything and for DNA. Alfie had given him a stern look when he requested the test, but had given him the answer. It was his child. It was human and it was healthy. Maria was another matter. The initial tests were good, but then there was something else. Her heart. There was a lot of strain on her and her heart. The beating had taken her to the edge of death and she had only survived by sheer will to give her child life. To heal had taken a lot from her. She was anemic, slightly diabetic and her blood pressure was high. Stress was a big factor. The rumors, the accusations and the pregnancy. He had vowed not to stress her out and now she was asking questions that were stressful.

"Then Fiona knows too?" That question was not what he expected.

"I hadn't told her." He turned to gaze at her.

"Tell her. Let her know. Then maybe she will keep her mouth shut or I will shut it for her." She continued to cut the vegetables. She was smiling.

"I will let her know tomorrow. If I see her." He turned his attention back to the stove. "Mum and Fiona will be very busy for the next few days. Chasing kids with needles." He reached for the eggs and a bowl. "Mum will love it." He was smiling, knowing how much Fiona hated children.

"I hope one bites her," Maria muttered.

"They wouldn't. They love Mum!"

"I wasn't talking about Alise!" Maria growled. James knew.

~

"Mommy kitty?" Jimmy asked, standing on tiptoe to kiss his mother's stomach.

"Yes, Darling." She smiled and patted his head. He was dressed as a dog. She held his ribbon leash as they walked along the little settlement for his treats. Halloween was the one holiday that was still very special for the children. Homemade candies and treats were handed out and there was a little haunted house. Ghosts ran wild on this night. James sidestepped two ninjas and almost tripped over a little princess mumbling.

"Devils!" He muttered, reaching for her hand. She handed him the ribbon leash and he frowned. He wasn't going to come along but the thought of her being knocked over by a bunch of thuggish children had him trudging along in the dark.

"They are ninjas!" Maria teased, holding tight to the little cookies she and Alfie had made and wrapped in paper and tied with ribbon.

"I guess. Beggars!" He snarled at a little boy who ran past.

"For someone who loves children, you are a grump on their holidays."

"I just think that they should be home in bed, not out begging."

"It's not begging."

"They go from door to door knocking and holding out a bag for food. What do you call it?"

"Grump!" Maria teased, holding tighter to the ribbon. She looked wonderful dressed as a kitten. Her hair was long and the little ears poked from her curls. Alise had painted her nose pink and little black whiskers on her rosy cheeks. It was chilly, but she only wore jeans and a long sleeved sweater. And white knit gloves. He had noticed that she had tacked one of his long black socks to her ass for a tail. It was amusing, but he liked being grumpy.

"Careful!" he yelled as two preteens ran between them, almost making Maria lose the cookies. "This holiday should be outlawed as well as the one tomorrow!"

El Día de los Muertos was one holiday James would have liked to skip. The Day of the Dead! The walk to the cemetery was long and too rough for Maria. Alejandro had arranged for a carriage to take them but she had nixed that. A hayride was a better idea. Then all the children could ride. He had agreed and now James was having to ride with all the younger children in the main area climbing over him. Mostly, he was trying to keep them from climbing on Maria. She loved the ride but he was worried. It was a hard, bumpy ride. Too bumpy for her. But she wasn't listening to him.

Since her return, she had changed. No longer the little girl, she had grown into a woman. A fiercely independent woman. She didn't ask. She did. Fiona had learned to duck her rather than face off against her. Maria throwing a Petrie dish at the woman had sent her running. Alfie, Alise and James had all stood stunned by her actions. Maria had only shrugged and smiled. James had been troubled by it. Was she acting irrationally? Why had she done that?

"The bitch was staring at you like a love sick dog. Thought I would just get her attention and let her know I was alive and standing right here!" James nodded, unsure what to think, but Alise had laughed. Alfie only shook his head. Maria had grown up and become very territorial. Especially when it came to her husband and her children.

"You didn't have to throw that at her. You might have hit her!"

"I was only trying to get her attention. Think I succeeded?" she asked sweetly, tilting her head to look up at him. She was so sultry!

"I think so." Now he was walking through an orchard, holding tight to her ribbon leash. He felt utterly foolish but very excited. He wanted to take her home and make her purr! She handed out more cookies to several children. Jimmy tugged at his leash as he headed for the next cabin. It was Linda's and she was waiting with candied apples.

"Look at you!" she laughed as Jimmy ran to her for a treat. "A cat, a dog and...?" She stood gazing at James.

"A grump!" Maria laughed, taking one of the delights. "These are for the boys." She handed the woman three large candy bars. James was about to object! He had those hidden for his very sick young patients! She shot him a look and he sighed. Before, she never would have even thought of doing such a thing, but then before, she would have just gone to the corner store.

Times were very different now. There was no corner store. There was the trading post that Roberto's wife, Tanya and her daughter Sylvia, ran. All that was available in the Stronghold was there for trade. There was no real money anymore and if you were in need then you were given the necessities, but the extras had to be traded for. And James knew for a fact that there were no chocolate bars there. He had checked. His own stash was running low. He thought he had them well hidden. He was wrong.

"You are big!" Linda reached out to touch the mound. "You look so healthy now!" Maria smiled, holding her hand over a spot to feel a kick. "Wow! He's a busy little guy!" James smiled now. Yes, the baby was very active. A good sign of a healthy baby.

"I feel like a house!" Maria laughed.

"You look very nice," Hal noted from the doorway. He was a gentle, quiet man. Older than Linda, but accepting of her boys. Mike included. The boy had been hard to handle. Alejandro had to have a long talk with him and it seemed to settle the boy down. "Excuse me, I need to check on the boys." He stepped past them and hurried down the path.

"He's afraid Mike will get into more trouble," Linda sighed, "He worries so about that boy."

"Has it been very bad?" Maria asked. They had all been through so much, but Mike still had a rage in him that was hard to let go.

"Fights. Mostly about you."

"Me?" Maria squeaked. James rolled his eyes. He hadn't wanted her to hear these rumors.

"Oh, you know kids. They hear folks talking and expand on it. They say things that aren't so and he feels the need to correct them with a punch to the nose."

"I had no idea he was being protective of me." Maria was now worried.

"No, not so much." Linda made a face. "He just thinks they should shut up. Like if we don't talk about Adam he will just go away." A child's point of view. "He has to deal with it."

"I guess we all do." Maria stepped back into James and his arm went around her. His strength kept her going.

"Come on now. Your mother will be so mad at me if I don't get you over there." He reached down to lift his now very sticky son into his arms. "Night!"

They walked along and Maria thought about the situation. She really hadn't talked to anyone about what had happened. Not even James. He knew. He saw. He had understood. But she had never told him. It was all bottled up inside her. She fought not to think about it. And he fought to keep the memories at bay. But that wasn't helping them or her. And it definitely wasn't helping those close to her. Especially the ones who had escaped with her. It was something she had never thought about. Each had their own hell. Mike had seen his father stand against the invading army and had seen him fall.

"Nosy little kitten," James whispered in her ear.

"What?" She had been lost in thought.

"Found my chocolate, did you?" He had a smile on his face. He was trying to draw her back to the present.

"Oh, I did that by accident. I was looking for a gun." He stopped dead.

"What?"

"I had a bad dream and I was looking for something to protect me." She shrugged, looking embarrassed. "Not that it would have done any good. I think he's indestructible."

"You thought I had a gun in the house with Jimmy crawling about?" He wasn't sure how to take that.

"I hoped you did." She stepped over a root that was sticking up from the ground. "I put a knife under my pillow and it helped."

"Did it?" He could not help but sound sarcastic.

"It was in the beginning. I was scared."

"Why didn't you just come to me?"

"You were in bed with me." She turned to look at him. "I dreamed he came to kill you. I needed something to protect you." Now she sounded like a child. He stepped closer and hugged her.

"You don't have to protect me. I am here to protect you." He kissed her head.

"I know that now," she laughed lightly. "I told you. It was in the beginning."

The beginning? The middle? The end? Which was it now? She hurried along to her parent's house so they would not talk. She needed to talk to someone who understood. And she needed to do it alone. Joaquin waved to them as he handed out candy to some children. Her father was there with oranges and her mother with a bunch of popcorn balls. Maria felt a sense of relieved homecoming when they were waiting for her. A time when she was a child coming home from school always sprang to mind.

"Look at you!" Joaquin laughed, circling her. "You look a little feral."

"She's tame enough," James teased, holding up the ribbon lead.

"This one is the wild one!" Olivia reached for Jimmy. He was candy covered. James moaned feeling the chunk of candy stuck in his hair. "Go to the kitchen and get water!" His mother-in-law ordered. James hurried in with Alejandro and Joaquin laughing. Maria took the chance.

"Mama, can you watch them and Joaquin, can you walk with me?"

"Where?" Her brother asked, nodding to the cookies she held.

"Just come!" She handed him a bag of cookies and gave the rest to her father. "Tell James I will be right back and that I am with Joaquin." She pulled her brother along.

"What am I being dragged into?" he asked through a mouthful of cookies. "These are good."

"I need to talk to someone and I need to do it now and James would argue." She hurried along. He held back.

"He ain't gonna try and kick my ass is he?"

"No!" Maria tugged harder. "He might just bust mine."

"Oh, okay." Her brother was all for the adventure then. "Where are we going?"

"I need to talk to Mike."

"Mike who?"

"Linda's boy. The oldest." Maria knew most of the teens at the haunted house. They always hung out there. Once you got to an age, you thought you were too old for Halloween, you went there to see everyone.

"Who? The little boxer? He's a pistol!"

"Glad you approve!" She frowned back at him, making him laugh. She looked like a pouty cat.

"Well, the kid is tough. I mean tough! He is just a little powerhouse. Papi wants to bust his ass! I want to place bets on it!"

"Do you have to be so brutal?"

"It's just in fun!" Her brother laughed. "Fight club! Come on! It's old school!"

"It's barbaric!"

"After what the world is coming to? Barbaric is how we live!" He grabbed her hand to pull her back. "What you want with the kid?"

"I just need to talk to him." She pulled her hand free and walked on with her arms wrapped around herself.

"Hey, you sit there by the church and I'll go get him. If you go, they'll call him Mama's boy." Joaquin pushed her to the bench and hurried on to the haunted house.

It was quiet there in the garden. Jesus had gone to the garden to think the night before he was taken. She sighed, wondering what he had thought about all of this. He had given mankind a chance and they had flushed it. All His suffering was wasted on them. Just then, two little girls ran past laughing. Well, not wasted. The children were the prizes. He had said, "let the little children come to me". She prayed He was there to greet her children should they all end up dying, fighting against the one who claimed to be God. The false god.

The thought of Adam invading the Stronghold terrified her. There were passages through the caverns. Each of the Vargas children and grandchildren knew what to do and where to go should it all come to pass. They knew where to wait and meet up. It was a plan that was instilled in them from birth. They were taught to be survivors. They could shoot, they could survive in the desert for days if they had to, and they were taught to fight. They were taught from the day they were born that there was God, Jesus, the Holy Spirit and the Church. Nothing else mattered as long as these were the top of the list in necessities.

Even when she had been alone. Well, not exactly alone. Her hand went to her stomach. She and the child had never really been alone. Not in the darkness or in her despair. She knew this then and now. It was He she had prayed to and he had kept his word. Jimmy was safe, and the added bonus was that James was alive as well. All she had suffered was nothing compared to what His Son had gone through for mankind. She felt foolish for being afraid. She had Him holding her the whole time. It was more than a slight comfort. It was strength to go on.

"What do you want?" Mike asked coldly, which got him a good smack on the back of his head from Joaquin.

"Joaquin!" Maria scolded.

"Watch how you talk to my little sister!" the man warned angrily. "I'm gonna go light a candle." He was now eating candy. Her brother was just a big kid.

"Sit?" Maria offered. The boy looked her over in the moonlight, then sat down as far as he could from her.

"What do you want to talk to me about?"

"I need to ask you something." She rubbed her hands on her thighs.

"Ask." The coldness in his heart radiated from him.

"When you saw your father…When he stood against them…" she breathed in deeply, "They did the same to James. Alise stopped them before they could kill him, but I thought he was dead." She looked down into the darkness and fought for composure. "I felt my faith sliding away." She looked over at the boy. A boy who was a man. A hate filled man. "You are the only one I know who saw it too. I just wanted to know…I guess…" she took in another breath and spat it out. "Did you want to die too?"

"Why do you ask?" the boy asked softly.

"It is a mortal sin to kill yourself. I didn't want to live. It is the same thing. I thought at the time that God, the real God was punishing me for not having enough faith."

"And now?"

"I see that it was a blessing. My husband and son are safe. I knew Jimmy would be. Alise had promised, but James…" she shuddered, "I was afraid." The night was still. The sounds of children laughing in the distance was almost lost in the heaviness of the past. The boy sat thinking.

"I don't." His eyes glistened and a single tear slipped down his cheek. He quickly wiped it away. "My dad was gonna take us camping. In a park. Not out here." He looked around at the orchard. "We was gonna fish."

"We fish here too," she smiled thinking back to her youth.

"Yeah, well, I just…." He sighed heavily. "I was mad at him."

"Why?"

"They came. He went to fight them and I was mad that he was leaving us. I didn't want him to go. I was scared." The tears started again. This time they came faster and he did not wipe them away. "I didn't know what was going on. I thought whatever it was would make us miss the trip, so I went after him. Snuck out. Mom was busy trying to keep Grandma from spazzing. They were all just standing there. A bunch of the men."

"Where?" Maria asked gently.

"At the end of the cul de sac. All our dads. Even Mr. Cuper. He was kind of wimpy. But they were all standing there, and that thing asked if they relented. My dad yelled 'no' and then he was gone. There was just a bright flash and he was gone. I didn't know. I was running for him and Mr. Cuper shoved me into his house. He was crying and praying and…" the boy stopped talking to stare into the night. "My dad died." The boy looked over at her. "You think he suffered? That he was scared?"

"I know he was scared." Maria felt the cool breeze on her tear streaked cheeks. "But he was brave." She remembered James standing alone, cursing the invaders. She reached out to hug the boy and he fell into her arms crying. She cried with him and knew there was still a little boy in that body. Slowly, the crying subsided and he lay with his head in her shoulder.

"I want to be brave," Maria sniffled. "I don't think I am."

"I think you are." The boy sat back. "All that stuff happened but you got us out. I didn't think you could. I wanted to believe that this place existed but…"

"It does," she smiled using James black sock to wipe away the tears.

"Why did you want to ask me?" Mike sat wiping his face with the sleeve of his shirt.

"I just never really thought to ask anyone about it. Anyone that was there."

"It's not a good memory. I just want to forget it." He wiped his sleeve under his nose.

"We can't forget." Maria took his hand in hers. "If we forget, then no one will remember." She shook as she breathed. "No one will ever know that your father stood against them. That we lived through it and escaped and if we don't remind people, then they might forget that there really is a God. The God and that Adam is just… just…"

"An asshole?" the boy offered.

"Yes. An asshole!" She laughed a little and he smiled. "If we forget, then we disrespect the dead."

"You think there is really a Heaven?" the boy asked quickly.

"I know there is," Maria smiled.

"Then I know my dad is there." The boy sighed. "Probably fishing." They both laughed.

"Don't fight it Mike. Remember it. Let the others know. I wasn't there. I don't know." Maria patted his head. "It will make you a better man."

"Is my Mom going to hell?"

"What? Why would you say something like that?"

"Well, she's in his bed." He looked angry again. "They ain't married. Like the robot and that guy."

"Oh!" Maria now saw the anger source. His father had been replaced in a way. "No. There are reasons. Adult reasons. I'm sure they have them and this is a very different time. I mean, we are on the edge of extinction."

"Yeah, I guess. Is it like when you were sleeping with Adam?" Maria felt her heart skip a beat. "I know you didn't want to, but you did anyway."

"No, I don't think it's the same. Mike, I was a prisoner. Your mother likes Hal and he likes her. He's nice to you kids, isn't he?" The boy sat staring into the night. His eyes glistened again. "He lost his wife and son. I think he is lonely for boys and he wants to take care of your mom."

"I guess," The boy blinked and wiped his eyes.

"He's just being a good friend. I mean if he didn't, you would all be staying in a very small cabin. You have your own room and…"

"I know, I should be thankful." He was looking down again.

"But?"

"But I miss my dad." The sniffle got her.

"When we were in that ship I missed my dad too," she smiled softly.

"Not your husband?"

"Well, him too. But I thought he was dead. I wanted my father to come and rescue me."

"But he didn't." The boy was having a hard time dealing with a lot of this.

"No, but he couldn't find me. I just had to keep fighting. I had to make him proud of me."

"I want my dad to be proud of me too." There was hopelessness in the voice.

"Then make him proud. Do him honor by being the kind of man he would have wanted."

"I will," Mike sighed, collecting himself.

"Good." Maria felt better. Maybe she had gotten through to him.

"I'm going to kill Adam." The boy made the statement calmly as if to say it made it so. "One day. I will kill that son of a bitch and make my dad real proud."

~

"For the baby?" Jimmy asked, setting another cookie on the little table.

"Yes, one for baby." Maria bent to kiss his head. "El pan de muerto." She touched one of the little breads.

"Ew!" James groaned as he walked by to get coffee. "Day of the Dead bread!"

"James!"

"It's disgusting. Last night with all the little demon beggars and now a party in the cemetery." He winked at her and Jimmy pouted making sure the bread sat on the little altar table correctly.

"You are being so bad!" she moved to sit with him. "Why do you hate Halloween?"

"Daddy bad!" Jimmy hurried to sit in his chair. Waldo moaned, yawning big. "Waldo says so!"

"Well, it's unanimous!" Maria dunked her toast in her coffee making him frown. "Why do you hate Halloween?"

"I just do and the Day of the Dead is just as bad!" He was in a mood.

"Watch it or you are going to be in trouble, mister."

"Then I guess I will have to stay home and miss the party as punishment?"

"Nice try." Alfie noted, setting plates of food on the table.

"I could have cooked." Maria pointed out, eating her eggs.

"Rest," Alfie said, setting a bowl of cereal before the waiting boy. "The party tonight will be long and you need to rest."

"Everyone is trying to get me to rest," she mumbled irritably.

"Who?" James knew that tone.

"Fiona decided to tell me that sex this far into a pregnancy was not good for the baby. Too risky." Maria's voice rose an octave in exaggerated concern. "She also said you look like you haven't been getting enough sleep."

"I haven't." He leaned over to kiss her. "And I hope I won't be for a while." He had a devilish smile.

"Do I have to eat this?" Jimmy asked, looking at the vitamin that was set next to his glass.

"Yes," Maria replied.

"Do I have to eat the nanny?" James mumbled, taking a sip of coffee. "I miss the morning paper," he pouted.

"You don't have to." Maria laughed. James loved the taste of cabrito as long as he wasn't reminded of what it was!

"I just have one too many beers and the next think I know me and nanny are too close for comfort."

"At least it's not menudo," Alfie noted. Something Maria had been craving.

"Oh!" James set his coffee down and pushed his plate away.

"I'm the one that's pregnant," she laughed. He had been having the worst time with it all. Cravings for ice cream and pickles had him absolutely on the edge of sanity. Olivia had made ice cream but it wasn't Cherry Garcia. He was hopeless.

"And the gas you have after eating it is proof enough!"

"Love you too," she blushed.

"Yes, well, I do love you. All of you, expect the menudo farts." He wrinkled his nose at the memory of the evening before. "Stick with the goat."

"Yes, James." He leaned over to kiss her cheek.

"I don't want to have to hold my breath tonight. I'd like to go for a while," she giggled against his kiss. "And not be mad at you for wandering off!" He gave her a look.

"I told you I went to the church. With Joaquin. He lit a candle."

"And you talked to a boy?" She winced. Joaquin could not keep a secret to save his life!

"We just talked. He's having a hard time. Like me."

"Well, he better straighten up his act or your father will do it for him." He was up for an argument. Another like the night before that ended with him using that ribbon leash to tie her to the bed and ravish her. A little adventurous and carefree, but he had been gentle. Well, as gentle as he could be under the circumstances.

"Hello?" Julio stepped into the kitchen, smiling. He kissed his sister's head, Jimmy's and patted James' shoulder.

"Hungry?" James pushed his plate over and Julio sat down and dug in.

"What are you doing here?" Maria asked, knowing it was not good.

"Microondo and I have some things to go over." He looked over at Jimmy and shrugged. "I have some questions on the specs and…" Alfie set a cup of coffee down in front of him with a bang. Not in front of Jimmy. Julio bit into his toast and shrugged.

"You done, son?" James asked standing. "I need some help shaving." He scratched at the scruff furiously, making his son giggle and his wife blush. The idea of playing with shaving cream had the little boy shoveling food in faster. Then his bowl was empty and he was skipping after James. "We'll be back in a bit." Alfie stood waiting.

"I already shaved." Maria smiled at him sweetly.

"I thought you might like to avoid this?" The droid asked politely.

"You thought wrong. Please, go on." Alfie frowned.

Well, if a droid could frown, what he did would have been considered a frown. The hues of blue changed with his mood. Maria wasn't sure if she liked the melancholy or the embarrassed.

"If James is a grump tomorrow, I will blame you," he warned.

"No blame needed." she smiled at him again.

"What question?" he turned his attention to Julio.

"The water?" Julio had his mouth full of eggs. "What is the process for dispensing it?"

"Hey!" Maria had a thought, "They fear water but it was all over the place. The mist, the showers and…" She stopped talking to look at Alfie.

"The exterior of the ship needs to be cooled. Water is run between the interior walls and the exterior. Circulating cool water and keeping the integrity of the ship. No water and it explodes."

"So get rid of the water!" Maria ordered.

"Much easier said than done. The ship absorbs the water from our atmosphere. The morning dew, the rains and even the standing waters. Lakes, ponds and such. It's a continuous process."

"But without the moisture, the ship is just a chunk of rock?"

"It's not even rock," Alfie mumbled.

"The inner hull is basically an old space shuttle. The Genesis itself. Somewhere along the way, it picked up the outer hull. That is what is foreign to earth." Julio spoke between bites. "They shot everything they had at it and not a dent in the damn thing."

"They?" Maria had missed that.

"The Army. Navy. Air Force. Marines. Hell, even some 'right wing we hate the US' group. Nada."

"Has there been any contact with anyone else?" she asked slowly, "Is Adam the only one?"

"As far as we can tell? Yes. The open seas are still viable. Many took to the water once the black out hit."

"Other places are rebuilding. No electronics, but they are thriving. Even Russia is better off than the US. And Great Britain? The prime minister was in a panic. That old bird they have, the Queen? She was on a hunting trip and led the troops herself. Martial law and jolly all that. Parliament is lost, but she is back in power. Her great grandma is busting her girdle with pride."

"So why is Adam here?" Maria looked to the one person who would know. Alfie.

"I think it's like a homing pigeon," the droid shrugged. "He thought he found God and came home to show everyone. Rub their nose in it."

"He was from here?" Maria looked surprised.

"No, he was English, but the island is just of the southern tip of the New Reconfigured United States. That was where it was launched from."

"And we are the lucky hosts for the asshole," Maria frowned.

"Once he entered our atmosphere the entire world shut down. The rest got to rebuild and start over. Primitive, but a chance. We are still under his thumb, of sorts.

"Meaning?"

"Most who could escape have gone over to the other side." Maria frowned at her brother. She hated when he talked in circles. They always did that when they were trying to protect her. To speak around her as if she couldn't hear and make decisions. "They became Democrats. Immigrated to the New Reconfigured United States and left the Republic of the Americas. The mountains stopped Adam and the great Lakes. Others can't make it, don't want to or are too afraid. You figure, once Canada took her share and the Puerto Ricans and the Cubans left, it was about a forth of the size of the United States. Easy to rule. The mountains north made it impossible for them to take, lots of mountain people are there. But the southern states are Adam's. He's looking."

"For what?"

"No clue, but once he finds it, everyone hopes he will leave."

"But if he does, it will happen again," Alfie pointed out.

"What will? Maria asked afraid of the answer.

"The disruption," Alfie shrugged. Maria watched his face. He didn't think Adam had any intention of ever leaving the earth. He was a God. He thought he was the God. He wanted to rule it. This much she was sure of.

"What if what he is looking for is impossible to find?" she asked softly.

"Like?" Julio got up for coffee.

"God?" She gazed out the window.

"Not impossible," Julio sighed, "God is the 'all being'. He is everywhere."

"But if you tried to make God into an object and he isn't..."

"Then you're fucked," her brother laughed.

"Fucked!" Jimmy laughed as he ran back into the room.

"Excuse me?" James' voice was deep and menacing. Jimmy ran to Maria.

"You don't say that dear." She shot her brother a look. "That's not nice."

"Wooee said it!" the boy pouted at his uncle.

"I did, I meant it and now I am going to run. Meet you later Microondo." He kissed his sister and made it out the door before she could scold him.

"So we have to go visit the dead?" James was pulling on his jacket and holding Jimmy's. The boy already had on his hat and gloves.

"I guess." Maria stood and stretched her aching back.

"We have to stop at the clinic. I need my bag restocked." He was holding the leather satchel. He had come to carry with him always.

"Why?"

"Someone is always sick at these things. A child is always dragged over to me by his worried mother. I figured I'd just kill two birds with one stone."

"Meaning?" she cocked a questioning eyebrow at him.

"Spend time with the family and attend to the ill."

"You seem to be getting along so well with them." She picked up her coat.

"You sound a bit jealous." He was teasing, but then the look on her face was a hurtful one. He was getting his son into the coat. "Darling, your family adores you."

"They used to. Now I am the one they pity."

"Envy." He stood and drew her into a hug, "They envy you."

"What is there to envy?" She was feeling fat and useless.

"Your beauty, your strength plus you have me!" He laughed and she had to laugh with him.

"I'm fat," she mumbled.

"You are pregnant." He kissed her. "Have you heard the rumors?" Quick change of subject.

"Which ones?" There were so many floating around. "Not the one about Fiona and you?" She shot him a look. He had to grin. She was jealous still. It was flattering to him.

"Not funny." He smiled and hugged her to him. "And old."

"She at the clinic?"

"Yep, I go to the party and she holds down the fort. Not happy, but I care? Not."

"I just don't want to spend the day with her following you and me sitting." Maria mumbled.

"You don't just have to sit. Why do you when she is around?"

"I hold onto the chair so I don't slap her."

"Oh!" He had been wondering.

"So?"

"What?" He pulled his hat on.

"The rumor?"

"Your father wants to rename the Stronghold."

"Does he?" She thought that was strange. It had always been the Stronghold.

"Yes, he wants to name it Esperanza. Is she someone special?"

"James, you speak Spanish!" Maria laughed.

"And?" He looked confused.

"What does Esperanza mean?" She pulled on her hat and stepped past him into the cool morning air. He had to think. It was there. On the tip of his tongue. It came to him suddenly.

"Oh!" he smiled. Hope. "Why Hope?"

"El que vive con esperanza, muere alegre." She quoted her father's favorite phrase. 'He who lives with hope dies happy'. James thought it did fit. Hope was mostly what they had anymore. Hope and love.

~

"You gonna eat that or just spread it over your thighs?" Stephano asked, sitting next to his sister and eyeing her piece of pie covered in whipped cream.

"Will it hold my pantyhose up if I do?" Maria asked slyly.

"Do you wear those? Can we find them in your size?" He leaned back to gaze at her backside. She flipped a glop of whipped cream at him. He wiped it off his shirt and popped it in his mouth.

"Creep!"

"Hey, I don't waste food."

"Neither do I."

"Obviously!" he ducked her playful fist.

"Why are you picking on me?" she asked, turning her attention back to her pie.

"It's Thanksgiving! We always pick on you!" He nodded to her brothers who were busy annoying Miguel.

"Not this year. I guess everyone expects that I'm too fragile."

"No, you're too fat!"

"I hope you get married soon," she growled, "To a very fat, short woman."

"I ain't getting married," he laughed, looking around at all the prospects their mother had invited. Only he and Joaquin were still single. Olivia was bound to have them all married and settled before she died. Stephano planned on Olivia being around for a very long time. Joaquin might settle on a pretty little sweet thing, but Stephano had other plans and they did not include a wife and kids. There were enough grandkids running around anyway. The idea of him being a bachelor drove his mother nuts. Joaquin was the baby. She could be picky with him. One was giving him the eye so he had decided to hide behind the big pregnant baby sister.

"Have you told Mama that?"

"Oh yeah. She hit me. Said I needed a good woman."

"What did you say to that?"

"Told her for the night was okay but not for much more than that." He winked at her. She smiled. He was fifteen years old when she had been born. At thirty five, he looked and acted much younger. His hair and eyes were dark. Not a grey hair in that head. Or a wrinkle. He was the hunter, the tracker and the one his father turned to when there was a situation. Stephano could be quiet in his kill.

"You are bad!"

"I know. That's what they like about me."

"Who is they?"

"The women." He leaned back in his chair. Even here, he was armed. A gun and a knife were on his belt. He was good with either one. She looked over at her son sleeping in Alfie's arms. Her brother looked over at him too. "It happens. I will take him." He noted calmly. She stopped eating to look at him.

"Why?"

"The others have children of their own. Me and the Microwave have it planned. We will get him out. Him and the other." There was a silence. Maria felt her stomach turn. She stopped eating. "Maria, he will come."

"I know." She looked to James as he laughed across the room. Adam would come for her and the child he believed to be his. James would stand and James would fall.

"He took an oath. An oath he lives by. He will be needed to help. The boys will be safe with us." Her brother put his hand over hers and she began to shake. "Come on." He took her hand and pulled her after him.

They walked from the house and out into the cold air. It was cold. Too cold still for the snow. Stephano set his coat over her shoulders and pulled her after him. They walked quickly. She stumbled, he caught her, and half carried her to the church. It was warm inside. He shut the door and turned to face her. His hand cupped her chin. She looked so young. She was, to him. She would always be a little girl. He had wanted to kill James the day he brought her back with child. He argued not to let them marry. He knew James would ruin her. But she was strong. Strong-willed and strong. Now she was shaking.

"Let it go," he spoke softly. She fought not to, but the screams came and the tears.

All she had locked up in her flowed from within. She screamed, yelled, and cried. He held her and let her beat on his chest with her fists until she collapsed against him and sobbed. He held her to him and prayed that God would give him strength. The strength to leave her behind when the time came. He had made many trips to the city looking for her. He had walked knee deep in dead bodies searching for her. To know she was dead was better than not knowing anything at all. There were days he did not sleep wondering about her. He felt her there, just outside his reach but couldn't fine-tune his feelings. He hadn't found her. He had brought many back with him. Mostly children and women. Some men, but mostly the children. One little girl he carried the entire way. She had reminded him of his Maria.

"We better get back." She sat up slowly wiping the tears from her face.

"That pie calling you?" he teased. She sobbed a little more and then he bundled her up and led her back to the gathering.

"Thank you," she spoke softly as they got back to the house.

"No problem." He held the door for her and patted her head as she stepped past him into the house.

ALEJANDRO
&
ALPHONSO

"The baby." Maria groaned as she sat up. It was cold! Too cold to get out of bed. The hardwood floor was freezing. She looked across the hall. Jimmy's little blonde head was barely visible beneath his burrow of heavy blankets. James was snuggled down deep in the bed. He moved, reaching for her. She eyed the toilet and frowned. It was cold! Why did it have to be so cold? And why did she have to be pregnant and big as a house in the dead of winter? She set her foot down and even with the thick socks, it was cold. It was something she hated. Her back was aching. Maybe she could wait? No, she had to pee!

"Alfie?" she whispered softly. James mumbled but didn't wake. She sat waiting. Alfie appeared almost instantly in a hue of soft blue. It was very comforting to be half-awake and see him moving down to hall to check on Jimmy, and at times her. She would wake from a nightmare to his soothing blue face. Most times James was out with the sick and alone in bed, she would wake terrified. Alfie was just there and it was enough for her to return to sleep.

"Yes?" he waited patiently.

"It's cold." she whimpered.

"Is it?" She hated that he had no temperature control and a dry wit. "Would you like me to rush Spring?"

"Alfie! I have to pee! OW!" He had that smirk that made her want to scream!

"Are you in pain?"

"I am uncomfortable, the size of a hippo and frozen! My back is killing me and I need to pee! Please! Alfie!" she fought not to cry. All week long she had been hormonal.

"One moment, madam." He bowed very formally and stoked the fire, making the embers roar to life, then walked to the bathroom and touched the floor and toilet with his finger. Maria mumbled as the water in the bowl began to boil. He didn't have to heat it that much! They weren't going to cook eggs! She sat shivering. He returned and scooped her up and carried her to the steamy hot bathroom. "Should I test the temperature?" he asked, setting her down.

"Goon!" She pushed him out of the room and shut the door.

"Hmm! How rude!" He stood waiting for her return.

"Alfie?" He smiled as she called through the door.

"Yes? Would you like a moist towlette?"

"No, I need my husband and his mum." She grumbled, opening the door and stepping out holding onto the doorframe with one hand on her back. She was bent forward.

"Excuse me?" He gave her that always hilarious confused look and he glowed a bright, almost white blue.

"My water just broke." His eyes spun wildly and his body lit up illuminating the whole room.

"What?" he screeched. Maria was happy that she, in the midst of some of the most horrible pain known to man, had shocked the calm droid.

"What the bloody hell?" James sat up, mumbling and shading his eyes.

"James! Be a good lad and get up! We have a baby on the way!"

"Whose?" James asked yawning, stretching and scratching. He was calculating in his head who was close to dropping a little bundle of joy. Why did it always have to be in the middle of the night?

"Yours!" The moment was more than comical. James looked at Maria holding the doorframe and then back in the bed as if to say that she should be there.

"Mine? It's time?" He stood and danced around on the cold floor. He couldn't sleep in socks and suffered every morning as he searched for his pants. "Now? It's early!"

"Tell him!" she groaned, struggling to get to the rocking chair.

"Now? Damn the floor is cold!" He was practically yelling in his excitement.

"Well, in a bit!" Maria moaned, sitting back in the cold wooden rocker. Waldo was whimpering and getting in the way. James tripped over him and ended up sitting on the cold floor. He crawled over to Maria and laid his head against the bulge that was now contracting.

"What time is it?" James ordered, standing up and planting a kiss on Maria's lips. He seemed to be in better control and excited.

"A little after three in the morning," Alfie noted calmly as his eyes spun.

"Figures!" James was hopping around trying to get his pants on.

"What?" Maria groaned.

"Our child would be born on Christmas Day!" He was scratching his head again. "I knew it!" He almost yelled. All through Midnight Mass she had been shifting and fidgeting. He had asked her, but she complained of gas and he had rolled his eyes, knowing she had eaten a lot of that horrid menudo. "Alfie, run and get Mum. See if Miguel will sit with Jimmy. And then go and get Olivia. She said she would kill me if I didn't call her. Hurry!"

"Daddy!" Jimmy was calling now. "I got to pee!" the boy yelled.

"Come on then!" James was pulling on his boots.

"It's cold!" the boy wailed.

"God help me!" James hurried to scoop the boy up and deposit him in the warm bathroom.

"It's hot!" he wailed.

"Give me a break, son! Mummy is hurt. We have to get to the clinic."

"Mummy!" The boy shot past James and dove right onto Maria in the midst of a contraction.

"Hold on, Mijo!" she moaned through gritted teeth.

"Mummy!" The boy began to cry harder.

"Hold it, son!" James held the boy as his wife panted through the pain. "How close?"

"Close enough." She reached out for her son. He clung to her sobbing. "I'm okay darling. Just hold onto me!"

"Maria!" Alise was now rushing into the room. She looked about, summed up the situation, and then moved. "Miguel, take Jimmy to our house. Bundle him in a blanket!" Her husband gave the boy enough time to kiss his mother before snatching him from her arms.

"Everything will be alright, Maria." Miguel kissed her head, "Alise will take care of you." He was out of the room without looking back. Alise was more than capable. She was completely dressed. Not a hair out of place.

"Sorry to wake you," Maria huffed.

"Oh, we weren't asleep. We were…"

"Oh for God's sake! I don't want to know, Mum!" James was still trying to get his pants on.

"We were wrapping gifts!" Alise glared at her son, "Not what you think! Dirty minded little man!"

"Sorry, Mum!" James kissed her cheek.

"We had a lot of sex after church!" James moaned and Maria laughed, and then she moaned.

"You are early." Alise helped her out of the wet gown and into her warm robe and boots.

"I know. Tell him that." Alise draped a blanket over her.

"He won't listen," the droid grinned. "Come on. We have to get to the hospital." Maria bent in pain.

"I don't think I can walk!" she groaned, fighting the urge to just lie down on the floor.

"You don't have to." Alejandro was there and simply scooped her up. "James!" Her husband stumbled after them and out to the front of the house where the horse-drawn sleigh sat waiting with Olivia holding the reins. James pulled on his shirt and jacket.

"I'm surprised you didn't drive the Mustang!" James teased, settling in next to his wife.

"It doesn't have good traction!" Alejandro laughed.

"Everyone in?" Olivia called, and before they could answer, the buggy was off.

"Merry Christmas!" Alejandro shouted watching the snowflakes swirl about.

"I would think so!" Olivia laughed.

It was all a mad rush. Through the orchards and to the hospital. People were coming out as the sleigh bells and hoof beats woke them. Many children ran out looking for Santa Claus. Everyone waved and called greetings and best wishes. Olivia drove like a woman on a mission. Alejandro was cursing under his breath about women drivers as they stopped before the doors. Alfie was there, holding it open for them. Maria was carried in, and set on the table by her father, he gave her a kiss and left the room. Fiona pushed her way in.

"Already?" she asked breathlessly.

"James! Get her out of here!" Maria screamed through gritted teeth. She was on the table, feet in stirrups, belly exposed, pouring sweat and Alfie, the sonogram, was humming away. Alise gazed at the image projected on the wall. Fiona stepped into the room as if it were a stage and she the star. She looked ravishing and ready for a curtain call.

"What do we have?" the woman ignored Maria and leaned over James' shoulder to peer at the image. Alfie and James had been staring at it.

"Impossible!" James declared softly.

"Oh James! My poor darling!" Fiona set her hand on his shoulder and Maria watched his head drop.

"No! It can't be! It wasn't there the last time!" He shook his head in despair.

"What is it?" Olivia asked, as Maria puffed away. Alfie moved to hold Maria's hand. Alise stood looking too. Her eye flickered.

"A shadow," James muttered softly.

"A what?" Olivia looked at the screen and wished for someone to focus it for her.

"Another child." Alfie spoke softly for James, who could not. "It's not alive." Maria was shaking her head. "There is no heartbeat." Alfie tried to explain but she shook her head and huffed.

"We need to get this over with." Fiona still had her hand on James' shoulder. "How far is she dilated?"

"Get her out of here!" Maria almost screamed.

"Not far enough," James mumbled after a quick check, "Not near enough."

"Then we have to do a C section. We have to try and save her." Fiona was looking about. "The baby is a lost cause. One is gone and the other is in distress." She pointed to the fetal monitor. "If we are to save Maria we must take them." Maria was shaking her head. "Maria! Don't be so selfish! You might one day have more children.

You really didn't want this one anyway, now did you?" Maria looked to her husband who was staring at the projection. He reached out to touch it.

"James!" she screamed reaching out for his hand. He took it and stood waiting. She huffed and she puffed.

"Darling…"

"Get that whore out of here and let's have our baby!"

"Now see here..," Fiona started. Olivia was ready to pounce when the door flew open. Maria saw the crowded waiting area and Linda and Mom stepped in.

"Get that bitch out of here!" Maria screamed again through gritted teeth. Linda didn't blink but shoved Fiona out the door and slammed it. "Thank you!"

"Well, I'd say you don't look so bad but I'd be lying!" Linda laughed, "Figured we was there at the start so we ought to see it to the end." Linda grabbed a cloth to blot the sweat from her face. "Let's move it along, Doc."

"Maria, you will have to deliver them both." James wasn't sure she understood.

"Do it!" Alise was checking her.

"She's dilated and fast." James stood unsure.

"But she wasn't…" he looked dumbfounded.

"Alfie!" Maria was grumbling under her breath.

"Yes?" He stood at her side facing her. The projection was lost and James seemed more confused.

"You are gonna have to go south of the Mason Dixon Line!"

"Excuse me?" There was panic in the droid's voice.

"Get down there and deliver them! James is no help!"

"Dr. Malloy…"

"You bring her in here and I will dismantle you myself!" The droid looked at her face, then down at the other end and shuddered violently.

"James?" James turned and the droid slapped him. The blow sent James back to the floor. "Snap out of it!" He ordered and held onto Maria's hand. "I'm a Yankee!"

"Alfie, she doesn't understand..," James looked confused.

"She understands! Now do what needs to be done! I do not go south of the Mason Dixon!" James picked himself up rubbing his face. He settled back in the seat between Maria's legs with a red handprint on his cheek.

"Hold on, Darling. Don't push just yet. I need to get gloved up."

"Do it fast!" Maria screamed, straining against the pain.

"Hold on!" James snapped.

"Easy for you to say!" she hissed.

James took a breath and fought to stay calm. There were two. A shadow that had just appeared. Impossible. It must have been there the entire time. It had to be. Twins ran in her family. It was possible. Wasn't it? Now what? Only one heartbeat meant only one thing. One lived and one did not. He steadied himself and checked his wife. He would now deliver his sons. One dead and one alive. He said a quick prayer and felt a firm hand on his shoulder. It was warm. Alise was always warm.

"I'm right here," she whispered and he nodded, blinking away the tears.

"Darling, I need for you to get ready to push."

"Ready!" Maria snapped, making Olivia and Mom laugh. Linda only smiled and mopped Maria's brow.

The head, the shoulder, he rotated the small body, and when it was head down, he nodded. They all yelled the order and Maria pushed. The boy slid right out into his hand. A quick swipe of the mouth and a rub with a towel and he was squawking. A boy. Yes, it was a boy. Ten toes, ten fingers, two arms, two legs and a little penis. James handed him off to Alise and turned back to the grim job of delivering the second. Sometimes twins can hide. Their hearts beating so closely that it was seen as one. He looked at the monitor and saw nothing. No heartbeat. The head was there. He rotated and found that this infant was different. Rubbery and too soft. Almost like there were no bones in him. The little body slid into James hands and he saw that the baby was very premature.

"Impossible," he mumbled, looking at the other who was now being held by Olivia, screaming, and shaking that angry little fist. He was full term. How could one be and the other not?

"James?" Maria was trying to sit up and see. "James!"

"Let her see," Mom ordered, "It's easier to let go once you've seen." He looked at the woman. Experience talking? He wrapped the baby in a blanket, cleaned out the mouth and rubbed the still body. The coloring was even off. Not blue grey or pale, but a chalky brown. The skin had two patches of roughness. One on the side of his face, over his nose and below his eye. It just lay across his little cheek and the other on his shoulder. James looked at the little unfinished face and his heart ached.

"James." Olivia had handed the baby off to Mom and now took this one. "Dios Mio!" she cried, "Little angel."

"Mama?" Maria was lying back now sobbing. "Mama? My baby!" Linda was holding her.

Olivia carried the child to her. Maria took him and looked at him. He was James'. The chin, the nose, and the big soft lips. The hair was dark, but she knew it would get lighter. Jimmy's had been dark and was now almost white at times. He was so little and helpless. The little eyes were closed and the eyelids almost translucent. She held him to her chest and the tears fell on him. He just wasn't ready. Her mind was spinning. But the other was. The hands. She looked and saw that he had no nails. Adam. Adam in the beginning.

"Sweet Jesus!" Maria prayed, "Please! Have mercy on him? It's not his fault!" The tears fell as she prayed. "Jesus! Please!"

"Mija!" Olivia moved closer to her daughter. "It happens."

"No!" Maria shook her head. "No! You have to breathe! To live you must breathe!" She covered his mouth with hers and breathed gently. "Your heart must beat. To live. To be, you must have a heartbeat." She breathed again and the little chest moved and dropped. "You have to breathe." She did it again and the hand moved slightly. "You are my son! You are a Sinclair! You are the grandchild of Alejandro Manuel Vargas! You will live!" James was looking down as Alise moved him. She cut the cords and removed the placenta.

The young mother's words and pleadings tore at all of them. She was breathing life into him, but he wasn't responding. Alise patted her leg. It was heartbreaking even for her to hear the woman pleading for the dead child to live. How could they live with this? They had been through so much already. For them to go on and this little angel who never saw the world to not be. It was unfair. He had suffered in his mother as she fought for their freedom and life. Now she begged him to live.

"I can't hear your heart beat. You aren't real unless it beats." She breathed again and the little fist closed.

"Sweet Jesus! Mother Mary of God!" Mom began to pray. James looked up and watched as the little fist shook.

"Cry and fill your lungs," Maria ordered, breathing into him again. James was by her side then. The mouth opened and the most horrible gurgled cry came out. James used a bulb to clear his mouth. "You must feed." Maria moved her gown and the little lips moved to the breast. He suckled and his fingers moved slowly.

"Impossible," James looked horrified, "He was dead." He turned to look to Alfie.

"Is he alive now?" The droid was looking over the child. A quick scan and he looked thoroughly confused. He turned and scanned the other and then Maria. His blue eyes lit up with each scan. He scanned them again and then moved to scan the placenta afterbirth. It was gone. The chip was gone!

"Well?" James asked quickly.

"Congratulations, James." Alfie looked about. "You have twins."

~

"Now you need to sleep!" Maria was burping the baby. A nice loud belch. He smiled slightly as she kissed his nose. His brother lay on the bed looking about and moving his hands.

"As if they would!" James laughed, coming in with Jimmy. "The two are working round the clock at depriving me of sleep. Waaa! Waaaa!"

"Now, James, they are just babies!"

"Demons!" He teased, leaning down to kiss Alejandro Manuel Vargas Sinclair's face. The seven-week-old baby called Alex cooed. "This one for sure. He shit on me!"

"He's an innocent little baby!" She smiled at the little boy. Blonde curls, blue eyes and dimples. She laid little Alphonso Jesus Sinclair, called Jesse, next to his brother. He lay staring and his kaleidoscope eyes spun as they focused. Two peas in a pod. The boys were identical save the dark discoloration over Jesse's check and nose. And the eyes. The kaleidoscope eyes that had haunted her now made her laugh. He was learning to focus and made the most hilarious faces as he did. They were a deep blue. Just like James'. They were unnerving at first, but slowly they had become more human. "My baby!"

"Mine!" James reached for Jesse and held him close, kissing his stomach. The baby kicked and James winced. "Ow! He is a strong little bugger! But light as a feather!" He held the rubbery baby up with one hand.

"James!" Maria snatched her offspring from him.

"Well, he is!"

"That's because he's an angel from heaven!" She kissed his face, making him gurgle.

It had been easy to hide them. They had been premature and it was cold. The family had simply relocated to the house and stayed locked up. People came and when they did, James simply put eye patches on Jesse and explained that his eyes were not ready for light. No one argued. They held him, kissed him and accepted him. And Alex. James' shoulders hurt from all the pounding on the back and the patio smelled of cigar smoke. Fiona was forbidden entry and Linda and Mom sworn to secrecy. Olivia and Alejandro seemed not to notice any difference as they spoiled the boys.

The little rubbery body slowly began to conform. Maria fed him and he seemed to thrive. With almost two months of constant delicate care, he was almost caught up to his brother. He was delicate looking and small. His skin was almost translucent still and even though he had nails, hair and his bones had developed, he was still rubbery. His hair was a soft golden with big curls, but it felt unreal. Like a wig. Like Adam's. Maria kept rubbing it. Hoping to soften it up. Side by side, they were identical, save the patches of discolored skin. Only Jesse seemed to weigh less. As if his bones were hollow.

In the seven weeks since their birth, they had been through a battery of tests. Alfie had done most of it and the results were shocking. They were twins. The DNA said their parents were James and Maria. The mysterious chip had simply disappeared. There was no signal or anything. It was gone and Jesse was there. Maria had her ideas but listened as Alfie explained. James held the boy and she Alex. Sitting side by side, they were identical. They seemed to be drawn to each other and cried when separated.

"He's a clone?" Maria asked softly.

"Yes, and no." Alfie reached to take the baby. "He is, but he is a genetically altered one. He is what they wanted, but could not achieve. He is human." Alfie kissed the boy and sat smiling. "He is a miracle."

"He is human?" James was not sure.

"Very. He was a bit on the slow development side. Most of Maria was taken up with Alex and little Jesse just waited his turn. If he had been inserted at the time of conception of Alex they would have been equals. He was a day or so later and had to wait."

"But?" Maria reached to straighten his bib.

"He is going to be stronger, faster, smarter and he will live a considerable amount longer than most humans. He is a super human."

"He is Adams' son." James reached for the boy with a heavy heart.

"No James, he is yours." Jesse cooed to James. "He was just implanted by Adam. The DNA does not lie. You are his biological father. It is as if a sperm was added to the egg and it was put in the uterus. He is of you and of Maria. There is no other DNA." Alfie sat waiting. "Don't you see? Adam has no DNA. He was cloned off of Fielding. He cannot pass on what he does not have."

"He is mine?" James held the baby up to gaze at.

"He looks just like you. They both do." Maria was shaking. Alex grumbled. She moved her blouse to feed him and she heard Jesse smacking his lips. Jimmy had done that. She shook her head. So had Adam. The baby suckled as she rocked him. "I'm sorry, Maria."

"For what?" She wiped away a tear.

"That they will look like this goon." She looked up and he winked. "You two basically got one child the old fashioned way and one through artificial insemination of sorts."

"Of sorts." Maria looked down at her son. He closed his eyes and smiled. She handed him off to Alfie and took Jesse. He suckled hard and his little hand lay on her breast so gently, as light as the lighting of a butterfly.

"What do we do?" James asked, "It's obvious. The eyes, the skin."

"It is a birthmark and his eyes are improving. With each day he becomes more like you." He looked to James. "The eye is a quirk."

"A fluke?" Maria caught the hint. Alise? All came from the same source. Created by a Sinclair.

"Not exactly," Alfie smiled, "An oddity? Heredity?"

"What do we do?"

"Live with it. It's entertaining." Alfie chuckled.

"You know what I mean. Adam will come for him."

"Maybe, and then again, maybe not." Alfie smiled at the confused looks. "He is not perfect. The patches. Your skin tone." He looked at Maria.

"He's beautiful!" She hugged him and kissed his head.

"To us. In a lab he would be a failure." She shot him a horrified look. The women in the tubes and the fetuses that had been cut from their bodies. "He is Alphonso Jesus. He does not favor Adam and is nothing like him. Alphonso Jesus is human. The more human little Jesse becomes, the more of a disappointment he will be to Adam. Adam wants a God. And he may never know of the child."

"He knows." Maria sighed. "He knows."

"Well, it doesn't matter." James moved closer to kiss the little fuzzy head. "He is mine. DNA or science be damned. God gave me a son. And I am very happy with him." Maria felt a fear rise in her mind.

"For God so loved the world that he gave his one and only Son, that whoever believes in him shall not perish but have eternal life." Maria quoted the Bible verse. "How ironic." She almost laughed.

"What?" James sat back.

"He did this." She looked down at the child in her arms. They gazed at her, waiting. "Not Adam," Maria smiled. "God. He sent this one to save us all." She gazed at her husband and realized what she was implying. "God doesn't like anyone to mess with his creations." Adam would pay. One day. He would pay. And it would be at the hands of Alphonso Jesus Sinclair.

"The prophecy?" James asked looking to Alfie. "One will be born of a divided nation. One who bring men to their knees. One who will unite us all."

"Words on a wall James. How they are interpreted, depends on how they read. Not what is read into them." Maria sensed the fear of the prophecy in the droid. It was too much.

James had left her. He needed to walk and to think. The boys were identical and not. They were his and they weren't. Confusion was hard for him to deal with. He was a scientist. He had to have facts, not what was there in the crib. Those were impossibilities. His sons? One or both? A clone? A child? He kicked at the frozen ground hurting his foot. He limped on through the woods. What was he to do? How could he go on as Maria did, acting as if nothing were wrong?

"It is hard." The voice made him jump. James turned to find Alejandro walking to him.

"What is?" James asked hoping it was not no evident on his face.

"To take a child as your own that is not." Alejandro smiled at him. James searched his eyes. He did know. "Walk with me?"

The two men walked. Alejandro talked and James listened. Every so often James would stop and stare at the man in disbelief. Then hurry to catch up to Alejandro's long strides. The story was horrifying. Almost as bad as what had happened to Maria! Olivia raped? James felt an now very familiar rage taking over his body. He had always been a practical, calm man. Now he was ready to explode and kill all that hurt his family.

"So Joaquin in not your son?" James asked slowly.

"Not by blood." Alejandro stooped to pick up a stick. He used it to knock some pecans free of their perch and cracked them in his hands. "But, he is my son."

"I don't know that I am as big a man as you." James mumbled. Alejandro looked him up and down.

"You're a bit short, and slight, but I think you have the heart of a giant."

"You know what I mean!" James was not in the mood for joking.

"You know what I mean." Alejandro looked down at the cracked nuts in his hand.

"Do I?" James almost growled.

"What if I told you that we should kill it?" Alejandro flicked the shells out of his hand. He put the meat of the nut in his mouth and chewed. "It is decided. Kill it. Maria will be told it was the crib death. Bury him and go on." James clenched his fists tightly.

"Try and I will take that stick from you and beat you to death!" The words were cold and calculated. "I will not allow you to kill him."

"Him?" Alejandro raised an eyebrow. "It!"

James lunged at the man. They connected and fell into the snow swinging. James was on top, hitting the man he respected. The man he loved as a father. His hero. The father of his wife. All of that was lost in the fact that the man wanted to kill his son. Alejandro blocked each blow and James was pulled off by the guards. Stephano and Julio were both smiling at him. James jerked free.

"Any of you bloody bastards go near my son and I will kill you!" James yelled loudly and then listened to the words echo on as Alejandro was helped to his feet.

"Good to know." The man winked at him.

"A test?" James almost screamed. "You did this to me as a test?"

"No," Alejandro dusted the snow off himself. "I did it to prove to you that he is your son. Blood or not." James stood letting it sink in as the men walked away. Stephano looked over his shoulder and grinned.

"Bloody bastards!" James yelled after them before turning back to the clinic. He had to help Maria get his sons home before it got any colder.

"My big boy!" James was now lying on the bed holding the baby up over him. Alphonso hiccupped and spittle dripped from his mouth and onto James' face. "EW!" James gagged and he moved the baby dangerously.

"James! Careful!" Maria ordered dislodging Alex from his lunch. The boy sputtered and cried.

"Save some for the old man!" he laughed.

"James! You are downright childish!"

"You are so right!" He sat up, carried the baby to his room, set him in the crib, and returned to take Alex. Alfie was waiting in the hallway. Jimmy followed the droid and James shut the door. "And I am starved!"

"James!" Maria moved to get off the bed but he dove on and held her in it with him. "No!"

"It's been seven weeks." He kissed her neck, making her squirm. "As your doctor, I can say that it is safe for you to participate in sexual relations." He kissed her. "And I haven't shaved in three days!" The stubble tickled.

"James!" she laughed at his antics.

"Now, lie still," he ordered, leaning down to suckle the soft breast. The warm milk shot into his mouth and he sighed. She moaned and threw her head back. "Time for me to taste the product," he ordered, moving his kisses down her body. "I've been patient and shared long enough!"

The fire was dying. Maria moved back into James' arms. Her little ass rubbing him. He moaned and pulled her closer to kiss her cheek. It was a bitter cold day. She smelled stew and her stomach rumbled. What a day. A very happy Valentine's. Their anniversary. Four years, and not only had they changed but so had the world. They had survived and would go on. For now, they were safe in the Stronghold and as long as Adam did not know about it, they would remain so. Jimmy's voice carried through the door. He was singing a lullaby off key. Maria winced. Terribly off key. James giggled.

"Boy can't sing to save his life!"

"He's a baby," she defended her eldest. The little man loved to sing to his brothers. And their eyes lit up when he spoke to them. Jesse's spun at amazing speeds. "He loves his brothers."

"He does." There was a calmness to his voice.

"James?" Maria sat up and gazed back at her husband. "What if?"

"What if what?" He knew, but is was something they had to discuss.

"What if he comes for him? What if we have to leave? Is he a beacon? If the people reject him?" There was concern on her face.

"No, he is not transmitting. We scanned him every which way and there is nothing. Blood, flesh and bone. My blood flesh and bone. He is my son!" There was determination in his voice. Determination to believe.

"But if..?"

"I have already got that covered." He pulled her back into the bed. Her ass rubbed him again and he moaned. "Keep that up and we'll be going at it again." He kissed her shoulder.

"What do you mean?"

"Want a demonstration?" He thrust against her and she rolled onto her back to glare at him. He sighed and flopped onto his back. "If it comes to that, Alfie will take him." Stephano had been true to his word.

"What?" She sat up quickly, not sure if she liked the idea.

"Listen." He put his hand over her mouth to stop the threats and accusation. "We don't know what is beyond the Stronghold. Can we survive? Me, you, Jimmy, Alex and Jesse? Will they starve? It's not just you and me. Alfie and Stephano will take

Jesse and he will keep him safe until we can get to them." She looked unsure. "If it comes to that."

"He's just a baby," she mumbled behind his hand.

"So was Jesus and look what he did. You said it yourself. Alphonso has a bigger job than any of us. God has a plan and we have to have faith in Him. God has taken very good care of us so far."

"So Alfie will save him?"

"Your crazy brother has a plan. He and Alfie will ensure the safety of our children. That is all there is to it."

James was right. Through it all, she had prayed. Nightly, daily and always the same. Keep Jimmy safe. And Jimmy was safe. He had been the whole time. She was home. Safe in James' arms. The boys were healthy. She had a great life and it was because of her faith in God and his generosity. James had never been a religious man, but now he had faith enough to carry them all. She was suddenly ashamed for not having as much as he. The boys were in His hands. That should be enough for her. She rolled on her side and let James hold her. Jimmy was laughing and the babies cooing. It was enough.

~

Alfie sat in the rocker holding Alphonso Jesus in his arms. The baby was lying on his back, wildly kicking his legs and waving his little arms, moving as if trying to take flight. The droid did a quick scan and the baby cooed at the blue lights that showered him. The kaleidoscope eye spun wildly. Alfie held a finger up and the eye stopped and focused. Alphonso grabbed the finger and pulled it to his mouth. He was still kicking wildly. He was a very active, healthy baby. Jimmy stood on tiptoe and kissed the baby's cheek, then went on to play with his toys.

"You are a miracle," Alfie marveled, The eye spun and stopped on the droid's face. "You have a lot of growing to do. It's a big job to save the world." Such a big job for such a little person. Alejandro gurgled loudly, as if to remind the droid that he was still in the crib. "But you have a lot of help. And love." Alfie lifted the baby up and carried him to the crib. He laid the boys side by side. "I am here."

ALPHA

"The baby?" Not the child. Not it. But 'the baby'. Adam stood at the edge, looking down at the people running below. He thought they looked like ants. He could squash them all.

"No. Nor her." Blue Boy stood waiting. Adam did not move. In fact, he had not moved since the sun had come out. He had simply stood at the edge, head bowed and hands clasped behind his back.

"It is the child I want." The words were cold. "What about the others? The other woman? Her mother? The children? Any sign of them?" He wanted them also. Dead. Crushed beneath his heels. He had a feeling. Something was amiss. She had been gone for some time. Simply disappeared. No sign of her, but now on this day, he had a feeling. Something that was just there and he could not reach it.

"Gone."

"She is somewhere. They all are." He rocked on his heels. If he fell, would he be damaged? What if he jumped? He wasn't himself. Since she had fled, he felt himself fading. It wasn't just the lack of milk. There was an emptiness that had devoured him. It was her voice, the feel of her, the smell and even the taste. The way she fought not to come to him. The way she avoided his touch. The soft sigh as he fed, arching her back and moaning. Her firm stomach moving as she tried to stop the excitement of having him there holding her. He focused back on the people below. "Why are they all running about?"

"It is a holiday. A religious holiday."

"What day is it?"

"Christmas." Adam looked up and smiled. He then knew what it was. The feeling.

"Perfect!" he laughed, "Just perfect!"

"What?"

"My son! He has been born!"

"What do you want to do now?" Alpha asked evenly.

"Start over." Adam felt a new strength in him. A need. Not just for her.

"She was the only one. The prophecy..."

"Damn the prophecy!" Adam spun and walked away. "Find me another to feed from!"

"As you wish!" Alpha followed him down into the bowels of the ship.

They parted company at Archive. Adam sat down and glared. Betrayal. He had been fooled and betrayed. The mixture of hate, anger and regret spun in his mind.

The want and need of his loins was confusing to him. He wanted to find her, to kill her, to bed her, to hold her, to feed from her and to cry to her. He wanted to crawl into that bed and find her warm soft body waiting for him. He needed her. He was dying and knew it, as well as Archive and Alpha. Another would sustain him for only a short time. He needed her!

"Archive! The contents of Maria's bag! The pictures!"

They flashed across the screen. Her face, the child's and that man! Other people including her father. He gazed at the large man. Her eyes. He had given her his eyes. And his spirit. Their child would have this spirit. He knew this. He walked around the room and the pictures spread out. He stopped at one of her and the child. She was smiling. A smile he had not seen since the beating. She would smile. But not this way. Not at him. He reached up and let his fingers move along the mist. His heart ached for her.

He stepped up and took in each picture. She was laughing. He could still hear her laugh. The one he loved to hear. That and when he stopped moving, he could hear her soft gasp as he brought her to him. He closed his eyes and imagined her breath on his chest as she fought to sit up. Satisfaction. He opened his eyes and looked at the photo of the man and child. All the kingdom and they were not there. It was all checked. No, they were not there. They lived. In hiding or out in the open. They lived. The last of the dead were catalogued, and they were not among them. None of her family. A distant relation or such, but none close to her. But they were somewhere. Hiding from him. He gazed up at James' image and sighed deeply.

She would have gone to him. She loved him. She still called out for him in her sleep and in the deep thrust of Adam's sexual dominance. It was he she wanted. He and the child. She had gone to them. She had left him for them. She would not return to him until they were taken care of. Until he had them. Once this happened, she would return to him. To his bed, to his arms with her breast to his lips. He thrust his fingers savagely into the eyes of the image. The mist swirled, then reformed to display James' smiling face.

"Hello, brother."

Watch for
Legacy:
A trilogy of James
The continuing journey
&
Revelations:
A trilogy of James
The conclusion

Made in the USA
Charleston, SC
10 August 2011